A WAY OF KNOWING

A WAY OF KNOWING

a novel by
Nolan Porterfield

Originally published by Harper's Magazine Press (Harper and Row).

Copyright © 1971, 2000 by Nolan Porterfield

ISBN: 978-1-5040-3286-5

Distributed in 2016 by Open Road Distribution
180 Maiden Lane
New York, NY 10038
www.openroadmedia.com

For Don Cotten and Grover Lewis

GRADY-CUM-LADY, T-ELLY-GO-PRADY. On July 6, 1946, Grady Owens Haker was thirty-eight years old. He sat on his guitarcase beside the highway leading out of Lamar, Texas, reading Bertrand Russell's *A History of Western Philosophy* and sipping from a quart jar of vanilla extract he had bought at a Piggly-Wiggly store in Lubbock, passing through. He had bought one jar and stolen another. Now the first was nearly gone. The air was still and hot and his back hurt, and he frowned over a passage in the book about the delineation of the universe involving the dodecahedron and Plato and the soul's compound of indivisible-unchangeable and divisible-changeable as the third and intermediate source.

Grady looked up, thinking—Schema of substance permanence of the real in time, lordy, lordy if that old sonofabitch ain't burning in hell there idn't no use in having one, as he gazed around slowly, back toward the cluttered junky edge of Lamar in the motionless yellow-white sun- 1 light glaring over a cotton gin, boarded-up seed-and-feed store, cemetery far away, high gray water tower inscribed "SRs. 1942-'43" in spattered red letters, one-pump gas stations, Dixie Burger Drive-Inn, a tractor repair shop, all sprawled and bunched on trashy dirt plots along the highway, small unpainted houses scattered behind, backed on fields of dull green cotton thin and wilting in the rising heat of midday. "Happy birthday," Grady said aloud, popping his suspenders. —Blow out the candles, children. If A is bigger than B and littler than C, A is big and little. Red, yeller, green: stop, wait, go. She cried and waved her wooden leg. Well, you've kind of got to hand it to old Bertie Russell, childern. Anybody that don't like Socrates can't be all bad. Anybody that can see what a shitheel old Plato was. Just a big-time fascist, is all he is. Dishonest and sophistical in argument, bygod Bertie m'boy. And a big-time fascist. Yessir the rulers of the city m'dear Adeimantus are charged to tell lies for the good of the state in matters of war and politics. For the good of the state, childern. Oh she cried and waved her wooden leg. Heh.

He saw a route sign down the road, and he got up and limped toward it, put his guitarcase down against it, and sat down and leaned back as much as he could against the signpost. Doing that seemed to relieve some of the strain. He was sore and worn out, but leaning back seemed to settle it down within him, and he sat for a long while with his head against the high shoulder, firm and easy yet free when he needed it, like a horse's locked knee.

Nothing moved on the hot level land. Across the fields along the horizon he could see field hands hoeing cotton, 2 tiny dark sticks of people spread through the haze, but

they were so far away that they seemed motionless, suspended. He scanned the highway back and forth, drowsily: tattered billboard on the other side, old six-sheet
peeled and curling "Gable's Back! And Garson's Got
Him!" clear heat waving up, shimmering on the horizon
before him as if through fire, black floating blotches on
the bleached asphalt where chugholes had been patched
and the edges crumbling off into the sparse gray gravel
along the right-of-way, the cotton gin once more and
from inside it somewhere occasional hollow clangs of
somebody pounding pipe and beyond that the low dull
glare of the town, yellow stucco shacks, old dumpy
bungalows, parched grass, dirt streets leading off the
pavement, sandy ruts and mounded ditch banks grown
up in weeds, big electric sign in front of the Church of
Jesus Christ of the Pentecost, down a shifting lane across
the way the black metal arch of the cemetery and the
tops of tombstones scattered through the thin stand of
Chinese elms, nothing moving, and over it all drifted the
strains of Bob Wills and the Texas Playboys doing "Take
Me Back to Tulsa" from the jukebox of a deserted truckstop. *Take me back to Tulsa I'm too young to marrrrry.* . . .

—Bygod, Grady thought. —Ever town on these damn
plains smells like a old greasy cold french fry, I'm a
sonofabitch if it don't. He drank some of the vanilla and
huddled down on the guitarcase, rocking gently, tapping
his head in easy rhythm against the post. "Vixi duellis
nuper idoneus et militavi non sine gloria," he said, drawing ligatures in the dust with a dead twig. —I believe I
like "puellis" better. *I have lived of late in a manner
suitable to the girls.* . . .

He snapped the twig and leaned back again on the
signpost.   3

—Ah wretched men, he recited, what grief is this ye suffer? Shrouded in night
   in heat, bygod
shrouded are your heads and your faces and your knees
   yes, and your twisted backs
   and kindled bygod is the voice of wailing, and everybody's cheeks is wet with tears and the fuckin walls and the fair mainbeams of the roof are sprinkled with blood, and the goddam porch is full, and full is the courtyard, filled with ghosts that speed backwards beneath the gloom, and the sun has done gone and perished out of heaven, and a evil mist has overspread the world. Grady chuckled. —Shitfire. It was a woman drove me to drink, and the dastardly scoundrel that I am, I never even wrote to thank her.

He held the vanilla bottle up to the sunlight. It was almost empty. He looked back at the town and then off toward the cemetery. —I wonder if they buried the old fart out there, he thought. —I wonder if anybody would let them. I suppose so. He belonged here. That's more than they'll say for you.

A whirlwind turned slowly in the still heat out across the field toward the cemetery. Grady thought about walking out to see if he could find the Jedge's grave, but the vanilla and the heat worked against him. He took the bottle and raised it before him in salute. —Hey, there's a slug up on p-eye, you happy old bastard, he said, grinning sadly, and took a heavy swig. The vanilla extract made his nose water, and he sniffed it back, shifting his weight on the guitarcase slowly, feeling the alcohol and heavy sweetness inside him and the heat of the land.

4   —Wasn't no sign it would go on forever. Just because

he always had work and whiskey for you whenever you showed up. Lordy what a paper we used to put out in those days.

Sometimes twenty-four pages. Just me and that old man. Work seven days and nights at a stretch
work around the clock and
he'd bootleg it in
Jim Beam bygod, by the case
for me
from god knows where
Jim Beam. Long as I could hold a makeup rule and feed that goddam old fourpage Babcock, but now it's a chain, Jedge.

Like some five-and-dime. They're running the old *Messenger* like a business
not like no newspaper, it's all big-time now Jedge, a bunch of big-time fascists printing her on a webfed Duplex and running straight matter just to keep the ads apart   got no use for us

He rubbed his eyes and spat. —Well, you and me I guess we wasn't much better.

He said aloud: "It's the place ruined us, Jedge," staring out across the fields. Then he dropped his head and chuckled, long arms on his knees, hands dangling loose between them. —Hoooooeeeeeeee (to himself) she cried and waved. Jumped up there on that box and yelled "Ca'dbo'd, ca'dbo'd, five cents a sheet." Cried and waved her wooden leg. Well, I don't care. Always was a shitheel town, and that'll bring you down ever time. How the Old Jedge stood it all these years. I never could. Now and then. Just on the short haul, childern, but the quantum of substance in nature is neither diminished nor increased 5

by appearance in time and calling the cat a canary won't make a feline warble. How'd it ever ruin you. How'd it bring you down, Grady. Well, let's see: how *did* it
good and bad I guess
bad   shitfire: first time I ever blew through. Remember even then, thinking what a shitheel town it is. Pup of a kid, how'd I know anything back then. Nineteen-and-twenty-three. Or -four, maybe. Well, I don't want to think about it no more, that's a long ways ago. Too much under the bridge. Yessir childern the man said. What. He said, yessir all change of appearances . . . the time in which all change of appearances has to be thought remains and does not change, and I'm a sonofabitch if it ain't the clock that turns and this old face yes is always
time changes. Its ownself. Heh.
woa, Grady
It ain't no time. Time, no. Just is. Her. Changes everything. Everthang. And nothing. City Limits Lamar Pop. 1,149 according to this here handy dandy sign with shotgun holes in it and Fuck scribbled on the pole put up by the Texas Highway Department. Why hell's bells there must of been more than that even back in the Depression. Well anyway friends and yessir-you-better-believe-it, old Grady Haker come along and done his part   ever two or three years
to raise the number
that cowboy's wife that was keeping house for the Jedge one year. And Letha. Old Jojo the dogfaced girl. That one, that cooked over at the City Café, what was her name? I ought to have went and looked up old Jojo. If she's still around. Wonder what census that is. Nineteen-and-forty, must be. War hasn't done much for this
6   town.

—Yessir, old times. Just a kid. Know. I said then Lamar was a shitheel town, and ever time I been back it's just that much worse. Only fucking place in the world where you can stand in mud up to your armpits and the sand'll blow in your face. Heh. That old typo. I don't guess I'll ever forget. Yessir. Piss 'steada Pass. Yeah, that was the time. Wonder how that type case got scrambled. Maybe I done it on purpose. Must of been . . . the first time he run me off, I guess
or first time I just decided it was better to ramble. Adios, Jedge.
well, Grady you think too much. That's a disease.
He took the second jar of vanilla from the guitarcase, singing aloud, "I got tears in my ears from laying on my back in my bed cryyyying over yewwwww." He drank from the jar and settled himself against the post to doze, but comfort did not come; flies buzzed around him and it was hard for him to breathe in the heat, and images and words persisted in forming within him, against his will, flushed up from some part of him he could not control. A sense of places he'd been, drifting out of twilight-shadowed time; not names of places, or pictures of them, but their presence, gray and distant yet continuous with him, therefore inseparable, immediate; people he'd known, whose faces he could not see but who touched him, the feel and odor and anguish of something now-and-gone that gave him rapture he could not bear until finally he came up with it away from the fitful numbness of his half-sleep and began to play with it, dreamily, grinning to himself. —Yessir, bygod, first time I was ever through this little ole town . . . days of the oil stampede at Vernon and Breck and Burk, old times wild and wide open when a man's word was his bond, false-front stores and mud 7

streets and those old guys in them crazy old hats, flat brims and peaked crowns like Mountie hats and what they used to call Carlsbad crowns, them crazy mad bastards running around everywhere wheeling and dealing, wildcatters and roughnecks, cardsharks, lease-shufflers and paperhangers and promoters of varied stripe like the Old Jedge and a jillion con artists running blacksmith shops with a shirttail full of type and watering whiskey and putting sawdust in T-Model transmissions, and some real men in those days, one or two railroad dicks I knew in San Antone and that Ranger that somebody finally killed down in Palo Pinto County, but the cops are all fascists these days. Hoooeeee, she cried. Ca'dbo'd, ca'dbo'd, five cents. Lamar wasn't nothing but a mean little old shacktown, real outpost of the frawn-tier, and many a man died of defective vision in those days

because he didn't see the other guy draw, yessir childern, it was a slow time in Lamar when the weekly rag did not report a dozen instances of robbery, embezzlement, rape, arson, vagrancy, and similar misdeeds, not to mention at least a killing or two

a rate of demise which according to the Old Jedge reflected great credit upon the community. Because, said he, there is so goddamned many people here that needs killing

especially scissorbills

mescans

tramp printers

and merchants that don't advertise

—Well, in those days a man got his whiskey from the drugstore, and there was more drugstores than churches praise lord

8   more churches than

christians, and not a single paved street in the whole town, a situation rectified finally I believe by the presence of Judge Matthew Arnold Piroute (he giggled and then began to laugh audibly), who figured how to get the hardtop down at no expense to the taxpayers

and behold the plan was put in operation as the pistols roared and the coroner came and departed, the recently deceased was stacked in rows of sturdy coffins, the aforesaid to be planted in the streets and filled over with the sandy loam of the Texas caprock plain, thus

contributing something toward civic improvement in their eternal repose a moment of glory which regrettably I have just been deprived of sharing. Your card ain't no good in this shop, the man said. We got an open shop now, no goddam union, and it ain't open to tramps. I never heard of nobody called Judge. That's what he said. "Get off, get off, you railroad bum" and he slammed that boxcar door. Slammed that old printshop

Grady opened his guitarcase and took out a sack of Bugler and a cigarette roller. He made a tuck in the cloth on top of the roller, placed a cigarette paper in the tuck, scattered tobacco on the paper, drew a lever across the top, and took from the other end a thin but perfectly formed cigarette, which he licked thoroughly and then lit with a large kitchen match cracked into flame with the tip of his thumbnail. —Well, pure mathematics consists of tautologies and right along the main stem here cows used to munch the dogweeds hence the reason waddies call them doggies, just as Co-cola swiggers are called cokeys and so forth. Maybe that's cocaine. The beer drinkers were guzzlers, childern, the wine drinkers were blottos and

the whiskey drinkers we called gentlemen. The gentle- 9

men far outnumbered all others at the time, but Lamar has sunk low on the social scale since then . . . there are no more colonels, massahs, jedges, and so forth. Only in transit do we have a true, honest, and noble man of the bar

a refined gentleman of the old school of mint juleps and the hammock strung beneath the magnolias, yours truly, Cunnell Grady O. Haker, Esq. "Grady, Grady," he said aloud, shaking his head. —Let your mind roll on.

He leaned over and picked up another small stick and began to trace the letters M, T, E in Caslon Old Style Bold in the dirt. —Pick that cotton theah, you pickanninies, tote that bale (waving the stick grandly) . . . and brang me another mint jew-lip out heah on the vee-randa. He swigged the vanilla extract. —But alas, Ion, the magnolias. In the farmed-out land of my blood's country, we had bowdark and live oak but

none exist on the plains

for when the live oaks seen how it was in Lamar they decamped, leaving the vast llano estacado to the jackrabbits and prairie dogs

red ants

coyotes

blow flies,

and blow hards

the souls of the people is as level as the land they inhabit, and Lamar would have died and turned to dust but for the reflected glory, and no little of the profit, of greater places and larger men, reviving the town so that it is today a true and authentic zombie, happy and sordid in its gloomy trance, a state of hellish grace known only to those of us who pass its outskirts and lift its skirts. But

10   of course none dare stand before a mirror

the shock of what they'd see

From the café jukebox came *I'm walkin the floor over you, I can't sleep a wink it is trewwwww* . . .

—Thank god the lady zombies is better constructed or maybe

arrived here from better lands than these plains. Yes, childern, I recall a beauteous redhead, circa 1932

aroused me to a frenzy, that flaming beauty with bedroom eyes. Hell of it, they was crossed, and I got in the wrong bedroom. Had to dive out a window, bygod. Discretion in choice of directions and escape hatches is a must. Yes, all said and done, I've probably hustled more poon in Lamar than any other single place all these years . . . in that respect it can be said I suppose that Lamar is a fucking good town. All there is to do. Heh. Well, I have enjoyed the hospitality of its citizens many happy hours in bygone times and I have lingered amongst its *Messengers* for days

whereas I stayed only fourteen hours in Lubbock, the metropole of auction-barn chili and vanilla extract, its cold-eyed sacrificial heifers, its dumb and deluded Technocrats known as the Red-White-and-Blue Raiders. I abhor Lubbock. It savors of the nouveau riche and all bourgeoisie bastardizations, whereas Lamar is poor and proud of it and the railroad track merely proves that the Blueweed Special passes now and then, twice a week if memory serves. Ah, but the fault dear Brutus lies not in the stars.

He spat and raised the bottle of vanilla before him. —To Lamar . . . skoal. To the Jedge, to them all: another nail in your coffin, another coffin in your street, another street in your city

He picked up the book again and began to read. While   11

he was reading *a very different doctrine, to the effect that there is nothing worthy to be called "knowledge" to be derived from the senses,* a car appeared from the direction of the town. It traveled the short distance for a very long time and he was aware of it without looking up. Finally it hovered before him, not ever seeming to stop completely. The man driving it gunned the motor several times and let the sound fall away, fenders and hood flaps rattling and smoke spreading out from under it, out around Grady, while the driver worked the choke and throttle knobs to keep the motor running. At last he raised himself to peer over through the window at Grady, and said, "Which way you headed?"

"Howdy," Grady said. A '35 Ford. Maybe '36. So battered and dented he couldn't be sure. The paint was mottled blue and brown and gray in ragged patches where it had chipped into the primer, a weird camouflage of chance, it seemed to Grady, and he gazed dreamily at the wild formless patterns.

"I'm only going out this road a piece," the man said. "I turn off on the dirt road towards 'Lysium a couple of miles out, but I'll take you that far, if you're headed towards Big Springs."

"Well, actually I thought I might just go to the City of Dis," Grady said.

"I don't believe I know that," the man said. "Is it one of them little towns on down off the caprock?"

Grady laughed. "Yeah," he said. "It's on the road to Fort Worth."

"Well, I live on out in the country here," the man said. "But you're welcome to go far's I can take you."

"What's the name of that place?" Grady said.

"'Lysium. Only it's just a wide spot in the road. Gin,

store, filling station. Couple houses. Church. I farm on out past there, down towards the Double U Ranch."

"Bygod," Grady said, "I believe if I had my druthers I'd druther go to 'Lysium. Reckon there's any work out that way?"

"What can you do?"

"Oh, name it . . ."

"Ever swing a gooseneck?"

"Used to, some."

"Get in."

He stood up and put the book and the vanilla bottle in his guitarcase. The car door was held shut by a piece of baling wire, which they had to twist loose and then re-wind when Grady had gotten in. The seat had no up-holstery and its springs were broken, so that when he sat down in the wads of cotton padding, he could hardly see over the dashboard. The driver sat on a breadboard atop the springs, but it gave him very little elevation, and he drove peering through the spokes of the steering wheel. Grady thought of Great Exercises in Futility: Antigone, the Lincoln Battalion, Sir Thomas More. Grady Owens Haker, headed toward Elysium. He rode away in the old gray car, holding his guitarcase between his knees and chanting silently the faded words of a gone time come tapping through the rattles and spires of dust that spread from the scorched pavement flashing away in his wake: the litany of his misshapen youth, the high, country voice of his mean sweet sad old daddy chanting *Grady-cum-lady, t-elly-go-prady; tee-legged, tie-legged, bow-legged, hump-back Grady* . . .

A IS BIG AND LITTLE. For a long time the car was little more than a mirage, existent only as the source of the swirling ridge of dust that rose and funneled behind it far away across the land. Elliott looked up toward it from time to time. The car did not seem to change its place, yet the churning dust cloud gave it motion. He went on along the rows of early cotton, hacking at a tangle of goatheads, then lifting the hoe and carrying it along like a boat pole, dipping, pushing, slowing to clip a blueweed, scrape away little shoots of beargrass, bank fresh dirt against the frail plants that were wilting in the morning heat. Gnats harried him in the hot stupor rising from the sour, powdery ground, and his throat ached through parched striations down into the hollowness of his chest. He stopped and leaned on the hoe, watching the car, and reached back on his hip for the war-surplus canteen. The water was already warm and flat, but it washed away the thick dry strands in his mouth and cleared his head. The car had traveled the far horizon and turned toward him, getting closer, and although he still could not define its shape or color, he knew it was his father.

He turned again to the cotton row and in the shadow foreshortened against him caught himself posing—striding heroically along with the hoe handle at port arms, jaw set firm, legs tensed—and even he understood reduction into absurdity. Grinning morosely, he played with it. By standing at a certain angle to hide the blade and length of the hoe and exaggerate the low-slung canteen, he was able to project a fair reproduction of the familiar black vision that had spread before him on other bright hot days, along the North African coast and into Sicily and Salerno and on up the peninsula. To Valmontone. Colli Lazaili. In l'inglese, the Alban Hills. Capeesh? Then Bagnoli. Finally to old Bagnoli, he thought, leaning on the hoe, and what a place that was. Lieutenant Susy said Mussolini had it built for a fair. And wouldn't you know, the Army would make a nutward out of it. Old Lieutenant Susy. Ell-Tee Susy. Some lady. Her and the Major. Bagnoli. That stupid dang big white sign red and black letters, I'll never forget that sign. The Major. And his Scotch. But after that it was all over for me.

When he came home, his father had said, "What are you now, what's that?" pointing to his sleeve, and he said, "Three stripes, that's a buck sergeant," thinking about it, remembering very strangely what the Indians who killed Custer had said: the soldier with the three stripes on his sleeve fought bravest of all, and was last to die. He thought about the Army and how much he had hated it, and he realized now that he hadn't really hated it, just certain parts of it and the war. He had liked the three

15

stripes. The uniform had given him something he had never had, a time and a place, an identity. But not the fighting and dying and slogging around.

Only recently had he come to realize, at some indeterminate point in the last few months, that he could think about all that again, call it back out of the whiteness, dwell on it longer and longer before the blinding circle came again. He always stopped before that happened, but at odd moments, without plan or design, he picked at it cautiously, pushing further and further, testing it, probing, pulling back, searching again in the soft umbra of another mask, a new evasion. None of it bothered him much now. Not even Rich. But that was close to the center, and so he thought only of the good times. With Rich on leave in Chicago, getting picked up by some society girls who thought they were Marines. Rich kidding him about his drawl. Rich doing his impressions. Roosevelt hates war, Rich said. "I hate-wauh. Myah dougg Fala hates-wauh. Myah wafe Eleanouah hates-wauh. Show 'em youah teeth, Eleanouah." He could do Lionel Barrymore, too. And Churchill. "Ef the Britisssh Empih sshould laast foah a thousand yehs, men will shtill saay this! was theih-fines-towah." Rich playing the trumpet for a crowd of dirty little kids in the streets of Casablanca. Arguing history with Rich, the origins of Rome— That was too close. A nerve in his arm jumped, and he met it with a gesture of defiance: glaring quickly up at the sun, squinting to catch its hard white ray in a milky film across his eye, closing down on it slowly until it went away. He turned back to his game with the hoe, shifting slightly so that the tool's blade became the butt of an M-1 in his shadow. It was very good. Only his baseball cap gave it away. There was no way he could make it resemble in outline the dome and flanges of an infantry helmet. But set at the proper tilt, it almost formed the crushed cap of a fifty-mission fighter pilot, especially with the canteen half hidden to resemble in silhouette a holstered .45 automatic, and he liked that image better anyway. Finally he gave it up and went on down the furrow, hacking with the hoe.

At the edge of his vision he watched the car, still far away and blurred by the heat waves. He's sure taking his time, Elliott thought. He's getting to be a regular windshield farmer. But he knew that when the crops were good his father was always in the field; it was only in the bad years that he found excuses to go to town or sat around Box's store over at Elysium, playing dominoes with the loafers and drinking NeHi Cream Colas.

The car crossed the cattleguard and came bumping on along the road toward the house and disappeared behind it. The house itself was obscured from Elliott's sight by a clump of mesquite trees. Gaunt and flimsy, it had settled, sunwarped, on the bare prairie, its roof uneven and its walls leaning and bulging until it had finally lost all definiteness and fused with the plain itself. Once, just after they moved back from Fort Worth, his father had painted it, but the old boards, dry and naked so many years, soaked up most of the paint and the sand scratched the rest away, and now the house was almost as gray as he remembered it when it was his grandparents' and he sat on the big rock that made a front porch and ate sugar and butter on hot biscuits his grandmother gave him when she came out to water her moss buckets and the lilac bush.

Memory, like a dying star, flared up in him and perished, an instant's reverie of that childtime in Fort 17

Worth: snug, wet-haunted winters, greenwood springs covered to the sky in leafy clusters, vines, blooms, the rambling white house with high galleries and a grassy yard in back where he ran with a huge black dog and lay in awe of summernight skies. He dropped the hoe and trudged across several rows to have a clearer view of the car as it stopped at the house, but instead of pulling in beside the porch where they usually parked, his father drove on around to the cow lot, the trail of dust piling up and drifting over the car as it stopped, hidden once again from Elliott's view by the clustered outbuildings.

He went back to the hoe. When he looked up again, the car was at the turnrow gate, and he saw a small, limping figure get out and open the gate and drag it back while his father drove through. Then his father had to get out and help close the gate, because he always kept the top wire stretched tight so there would be absolutely no sag in the gate and it was almost more than one man could do to get it closed. Elliott muttered, "That damn gate," thinking how he always mashed a finger or got splinters in his arms trying to hold the gate up and squeeze the wire loop down on top of the endpole. Fences can all fall down, he thought, but he's got to have that gate so tight you can play a tune on it. As the car came down the turnrow, he could see only the top of someone's head beside his father, and at first he thought it was a child, maybe one of his cousins, but then he remembered the broken-down seat, and when they got out as he approached them he saw that it was a man, small and thin, with a high shoulder that bent him down. He carried a black guitarcase almost bigger than himself, cradling it in his long arms.

18   "Knocking 'em out, are you?" his father called.

Elliott, drythroated, grunted.

"Well, I brought you some help," his father said. "This old boy says he knows how to swing a misery stick. I told him we had the weeds, if he had the urge."

"We're not going to get anywhere spot-hoeing this stuff," Elliott said. "We ought to have a bunch of Mexicans in here."

His father pushed his hat back and squinted down the row. "Well, a frog ought to have wings, too," he said. "I can't see putting no more money into this crop till it rains." He looked at the cloudless sky. "Reckon I ought to say *unless* it rains."

"If the drouth don't get it, the careless weeds and goatheads will," Elliott said.

"Lordy," the man said. "Careless ain't a weed, it's a tree."

"I believe you've cut a few," Elliott said. He looked at the guitarcase. "Your hoe got strings on it?"

Elliott's father said, "I figured he could use mine. I got to go over to Ode's awhile this afternoon and help him move a brooder house."

"Where'd you leave it?"

"I believe it's down yonder where we was ending out yesterday evening. I looked at the house and around the barn. I must of left it down yonder where we was coming out."

"Mister, if you'll go down there to where you see those short rows coming out. Ought to be a hoe just the other side there."

"Grady," the man said.

"What?"

"'Mister' always kind of sets a little too heavy. My daddy named me Grady. I'm Peewee to some, and Six-   19 point to others, and one old man I thought a lot of called me Pissant, and now and then I've been addressed by appellations it wouldn't do to mention in the presence of your wife, mother, or sweetheart, god bless 'em. It's your money, you just take a choice."

"Okay," he said. "Grady."

"It don't show a lot of imagination," Grady said, "but I reckon it'll do." He moved off to look for the hoe, still lugging the guitarcase. Elliott watched him limping away on the short leg, splaying it out as he walked, and he wondered how long he would last in the soft, shifting furrows. Grady wore hightop black shoes, laced to the top, like the old-fashioned brogans Elliott's grandfather had called "dress shoes" and had always worn to county reunions and to church. Grady's shoes were almost white with dust. "You think he intends to carry that guitar with him all day?" Elliott said to his father.

"Might be. He put it in his lap when I picked him up, and he kept her there all the way out. I ain't seen him put it down yet."

Elliott pulled a file from under a tall cotton stalk on the turnrow and knelt to scrape his hoe, straddling it with the blade up on his knees. "You ought to be careful about picking up guys," he said, resting back on his heels.

"I know," his father said. "But I been out on the road a few times my own self, and he didn't look like he could do no harm to nobody, not the way he was toting that guitar. An old boy with a music instrument is usually a pretty good old boy."

"You just keep believing that till one of them cuts your throat."

20 "Well, get what work you can out of him. You ought

not to push him too hard with that game leg . . . not that I'm scared either one of you will bust a gasket."

Grady came back with the hoe, and Elliott handed him the file. "You bring out any fresh water?" he said to his father.

"Dang," his father said, looking at the canteen on Elliott's hip. "Anybody that has to carry their water tied on him like a spare gas tank." He squinted at the sun. "Ought to be dinner in a hour or so. You-all can last till then." He went to the car and brought back a frayed straw hat with part of the crown missing and handed it to Grady. "Least it'll keep the sun off your face," he said. He glanced at Elliott. "Not like some I know, wearing a danged silly beanie hat that wouldn't make shade for a suck-egg dog, and carrying his water jug around with him . . . and you both better roll them shirtsleeves down or you'll have a worser case of sunburn than you ever thought about."

Elliott said, "I've already got a tan. All over. Might even take my shirt off, after while."

His father spat, shaking his head. "I don't know, son," he said absently, as if to himself. "For a kid that's already been off to war and almost grown. I don't know what it'll be when I'm too old to handle this place my ownself. Have to hire me a hand, I guess. Too bad I'm not more like old Joe Teed; he's raised him enough boys to do the work. Now he can just set back and farm through the windshield of that old Dodge pickup he's got. I guess I ought to of raised me another boy or two. One for smart, and one for getting the work done."

"Before you go over to Uncle Ode's," Elliott said, "you better drive down through the orchard and see if you 21 can't get Old Phoebe Lou back in the pasture. I saw her slip that corner gate a while ago."

"That danged old nag," his father said. "Too old and lame to work, and too onery to die. Only thing she knows is getting her belly full, and she'll open ever gate on the place and tear down ever fence to do it."

Elliott thought about the old sorrel mare, old even when he was a boy, and lamed then, too, from an accident in the field years before. He was the only one ever allowed to ride her, but not ever with a saddle, because that had caused her to be lame, when someone looped a cotton sack over the saddle horn and the dragging sack spooked her and she ran until her left foreleg tangled in the sack and was wrenched at the knee. Her back was so big and broad that when he was a boy he could lie down on her and she would plod all over the pasture, favoring the knee, with him jostling flat on her back and gazing up lazily at the clouds spinning and shifting overhead. She became so gentle that he could climb all over her, as if she were some huge stuffed toy; he mounted her by pulling her head down with the mane and then climbing up her neck. Sometimes he was Ken Maynard or Bob Steele galloping off to save the rancher's daughter, but Old Phoeb always walked, in her gentle, gimpy way, and when she was tired she would stop and wait for him to get off, if it took half a day. His father and his uncle sometimes talked about getting rid of her, but his grandfather claimed that she had once saved him from a mad bull in the feed lot by opening the gate and lunging at the bull, and he kept her all through the dry years when there was pasture enough for only one team of work stock and cows with calves, letting her graze in the sparse sudan and feeding her maize that was sometimes worth more than cotton on the market, feeding her and cursing her gently almost every day of his life.

"Looks like there's a bank making up back in the north," Elliott said, as his father walked off toward the car. "Maybe it'll rain."

"Yeah, and maybe I'll rustle my feathers and crow sunup, but you don't hold your breath about it. Them thunderheads got to make up a lot earlier in the day to do anything this time of year." He drove off, circling the field slowly to peer down the rows of wrinkled cotton stalks. At the clump of scraggly apple and cherry trees they called an orchard, he stopped and flushed the huge old horse and penned her back in the pasture and then drove on.

COLOR BETWEEN THE LINES. Elliott watched his father until he had disappeared on the horizon; then he said, "Well, if you're ready, let's make a round or two. I'm carrying three rows through here where it's thin, but maybe you ought to just take two for a while, till you get used to it."

Grady carried his guitarcase across the turnrow and locked it to a fence post with a length of sash chain. "Maybe one's enough," he said, chuckling. "Ever row I hoe is a hard one." But when they started, he picked up three rows beside Elliott and began a steady pace, working back and forth across the center row in an easy stride that kept him always moving, lifting and bobbing on the short leg as if it were a lever that worked his arms. Elliott sauntered along, cursing the dirt in his boots and hacking erratically at a weed here and there, pausing to sip from the canteen. When Grady saw him falling behind, he began to break his own stride and dropped back until they were even again.

24

"You're pretty gung-ho, aren't you?" Elliott said.

"Oh, I don't know. I suppose I am. What does that mean, anyway?"

"Means eager, jumping through yourself. You know. A company boy. It's something we said in the Army."

"You did, huh?"

"Yeah. It's from a movie. Randolph Scott or somebody. All those G.I.'s running off to do-or-die, shouting 'gung-ho.' "

"Why'd they do that?"

"I don't know. They just did. It was a commando outfit or something. Bunch of glory hunters. Always yelling 'gung-ho.' "

"What's it mean?"

"I just told you. . . ."

"No. I mean in the picture show."

"Heck, I don't know. It's Chinese or something. They just said it, that's all."

"Where'd you serve?"

"What?"

"In the Army. Where were you?"

Elliott took a long breath. "Italy. North Africa and Italy, mostly. That Randolph Scott movie, I saw that in Casablanca one time when I was on leave, they had this big fancy hotel there all set up where the Red Cross showed movies for G.I.'s and they always showed these war movies. I just remember old Randolph Scott, every time they'd start to move out or something, he'd yell 'guuuuunnnng-hooo.' . . ."

"You get in much of the fighting?"

"Some," he said. "I was with the 36th Division at Cassino."

"That goddam big-time fascist Mark Clark," Grady 25

said. "They ought to have hung him when a tater vine would of done the trick."

"What?" Elliott said. "General Clark? Why?"

"You ought to know. You was there."

"I didn't have much to do with generals. We heard rumors about some of the snafus. All I know is, it was a pretty bad time. Everywhere."

"You'd probably strangle on a gnat and gulp down a camel. 'Pretty bad time.' Hell, Mark Clark butchered a bunch of stupid country boys that didn't know any better, just to get his name in the paper, and they gave the son-ofabitch a medal for it, the big-time fascists. Bygod, the U.S. Congress is going to investigate him, then maybe you'll understand. . . ."

"All I know is, it was just as rough at Salerno or Anzio."

"Lordy, lordy, was you in all that, too?"

"More or less." He'd begun to like telling about it, and yet he knew that afterward he would wish he hadn't. But what the hell, he thought. It's just a crummy tramp. He won't know the difference. You don't have to lie about it. It all depends on the way you tell it. "We were just in reserve at Anzio," he said. "Funny, though. That's where, ah . . ."

"Yeah?"

"Where I got hit. During the breakout from the beachhead. After Cassino and all those other places, when things were finally looking up . . ."

"Where'd they get you?" Grady said. He stopped to pull a tangle of goatheads. "I said, where was you hit?"

Elliott fell behind, hacking vigorously as if he'd encountered a thick growth of weeds. Suddenly he felt very cold. He wished that he had some story already made up, something brave and adventurous with a beginning and an end that made sense. He'd planned to do that, to have a story ready, but somehow no story had ever come to him, and he knew now that he wouldn't be able to tell it anyway. He couldn't do that to Rich, and it wouldn't mean anything without the light and Bagnoli and the Major and a lot of other things. He couldn't tell about the light.

Grady mumbled apologetically. "I wasn't thinking, damn my soul. I been told time after time, they might not want to talk about it, still I blunder in—"

"No, that's all right," Elliott said. "It wasn't anything much, really. Shell shock mostly. What they call battle fatigue." He repeated the phrase slowly to himself. "I just got tired. Don't pay to be gung-ho." He grinned blankly, straightening up, and suddenly it was there before he could stop it, the circle of light rising up in him dim and distant through black webs, a white ball thinned and hazy at the edges and hard fiery orange and white again clear and sharp then pale green icy and a purple bruise and sometimes the sun again and Rich before it

—Holy-comoly, Rich said. —T. Texas, you really stupid you know that? They were the sons of Mars, suckled by a lioness. Not a she-wolf

—Where the fuck is that advance party, the captain said. —We got the map coordinates . . . Valmontone . . . fucking hills haven't been secured, I'll bet a fucking nickel

—Remus kicked the wall down see, Rich said, and old Romulus outs with the old equalizer, as Damon Runyon used to say, and gives it to him as follows: bang, bang

"Grim-visaged war hath smoothed his wrinkled front," 27

Grady said, moving on down the row without looking back. "How sharper than a serpent's tooth it is. Lug the guts."

—Sergeant, have the men spread out

Sergeant have the men. Skirmish line. He could see them, black stumps against the circle of light. They were moving. But they did not move. Then they were gone. Line of skirmishers. The light, and Rich before it

—What does he think this is, Rich said. —Skirmish line, for chrissake. The Germans are already hauling-ass through Rome by now. City of Seven Hills. Remus. Gone.

—All it says on this fucking map is Colli Lazaili, someone said. —That mean Velletri? Where the hell is Second Corps? T. Texas. Lug the guts.

—It wasn't a she-wolf, for chrissake, it was a lioness. You're talking to a college man, remember that T. Tex. Christ you're dumb. T. Texas Randall, Boy Corporal.

"But I made sergeant before I got out," Elliott said. "I made buck sergeant. Three stripes."

"That so?" Grady said absently, still not looking back at him.

The black came and they were all gone. But not the light. The light was always there.

—That's a triage for certain. I can look at that one and tell you he won't make it. Put him over there.

—C'mon check him out doc. I can't find anything. . . .

—Why man, that's brain tissue.

The light came through a bottle. A motor turned in the silence. *Ka-whin, ka-whin, ka-whin.*

—But. Sir . . . it ain't his.

Faces looked at him from the darkness. Grady's face. He was safe in the darkness. It was like a room in a high house. Like Fort Worth. It had been safe there, before they came back to Elysium. He cried softly.

"You feeling all right?" Grady said. "Maybe you had too much sun."

The sun smelled like wet cut grass. Then it smelled sour and hot like vomit. And Rich before it

—Easy, Tex.

—Pulse?

—Eighty on the button.

—Well, hell, get a pressure before we triage him off

—One-twenty over eighty. Textbook normal.

—Shit, take it again. That's a dead man. But if you're going to screw around with him, at least see if you can get some of it cleaned away

They were lifting him up. The light rose and swung. It was a long time, with the sun, the circle of light, and there was another place. Then he could see them spread out across the field again. They were naked. Just their helmets. Line of skirmishers. They went away in the light, and he began to cry again.

—It's all right son, a face in the light said.

—Down to Ward C.

—Basal metabolism, someone said.

—Sodium amytal.

—Take the blocks, son. See the colors. Put these colors like this. Can you do that. Can't you even set them up. In the lines, like this.

"Maybe you ought to just set down over there," Grady said. "And have you a swig of water. Too much sun, maybe."

"Yeah," he said. "Too much sun. Don't pay to be gung-ho."

29

—Cmon, T. Tex. Relax, Rich said. —What is it guy? Lemme tell you about Rome, see, how it's going to be. Hey, you bucking for another stripe? Gung-ho? We got plenty a time. The Old Man doesn't know what he's talking about. He's out of his mind

The Old Man is out of his mind. The circle of light came up, flashing and rolling. This time he could hear it. The noise made him sick, and he cried out. His stomach was hot and twisting and he couldn't breathe. He saw himself, and the circle of light and Rich before it

—Fucking goddam nebawoofers! They were yelling.

—Mortar rounds! Mortar rounds! Take cover. Take cover!

Nothing but the light the sun the men yelling and running but not running the noise the cramp in his stomach the circle of light spreading and Rich before it like a flock of geese across the sun

Their faces in the sun. —Godamighty it's Tex. Jesis what a mess. Easy, Tex. Easy. Oh them fucking nebawoofers. Medic! Medic!

—Get a poncho over that body. What's left of it. You want all these men standing around gawking

—Right in the fucking head, and all over Tex

He watched the light. The noises were far away. It was easy. It was easy if he didn't think about Rich. If he didn't think about Rich. Old Rich was crazy.

—Are you going, Rich? Errol Flynn

—No, I'm not goingrich. Holy-comoly, T. Tex. "A Arrul Flen picture show." You got to be kidding. Nobody talks like that. Not even from Texas. You and Judy Canova and Lum and Abner and Bob Burns and T. Texas Tyler and all those other hillbillies.

30   Are you going, Rich. Are you going. The circle of light

was cool and white and he watched it for a long time. They were dragging him. Then it stopped, and he lay there watching the light. Why couldn't he talk like everybody else. Once he wanted to be a radio announcer, until that time at the fair in Lubbock when a man made a record of him talking, him and Uncle Ode, and after they heard the record Uncle Ode got mad and swore it was a trick to make them sound like a couple of country hicks. He lay there watching the light.

—Bad?

—Sir, I can't find a scratch on him. Where's that fucking medic?

—But my god all that blood and

—I can't find nothing, unless maybe he's got something broke inside.

—Do something about his eyes. Can't you close 'em.

—Hey Tex. Can you hear me. Can you see me Tex

—Okay, quit fucking around, couple a you men get him back to battalion aid.

—Gimme a weed.

—Here comes old Band-Aid Boley, doin the Anzio amble. Oh them fucking screaming no-good sonsabitching goddam nebawoofers

—Always a hour late and a dollar short ain't you Boley

—Where the hell is Richards?

—They were both up here together, sir, last I seen.

—Yeah, that's him, first round landed right on top of 'em.

—You ain't got a match neither? How you fixed for spit. Maybe you'd like me to stick my finger up your ass so you can get some suction.

—You. Take some men and get that body covered and get it down

—Anybody that would smoke Chesterfields would eat shit. Ain't nobody got a Lucky?

—Get Regiment. Tell 'em the fucking krauts are counterattacking. Tell 'em they got those fucking rocket mortars on us and we better damn well get some fire support on those positions in the Velletri sector . . . and ask 'em just where the fucking hell is Second Corps anyway, what's all this shit about a breakthrough from the beachhead and linking up when their advance party can't even read the fucking map

"Hey, you going to make it?" Grady said. "You don't look too good."

It was smooth and dark, and through the window around the light he could see the scattered figures white and frozen across the stone courts and the low buildings with stairways along the walls.

—Hello soldier, said another face from the light. Would you like to talk to me. Your girl won't mind. Do you have a girl. Back home. Well, maybe I'll just sit here with you for a while, how will that be. My name is Susanne. Luba. What's your name. I'll talk, and you can talk to me if you want to, how will that be. Maybe you'd like for me to read to you, would you like that.

—Try scopolamine. Quarter cc. Half?

—electrotherapy, I suppose

—No but

—pupillary response

—convinced it isn't

—do you think

—Nothing

—ECT then at oh-eight-hundred, Lieutenant Luba. See that it's scheduled. Have them start with eighty into point one. If that doesn't make him shake, go as high as

She took him along the buildings. Arches and rolling walls and square columns and white porches stretching away to the pine trees. A maze of trellises and gardens that came through the light, and the figures scattered across in the shadows. Many rows and ridges of design on the buildings and the cold white signs with black and red stenciled letters: 225TH STATION HOSPITAL, 3D CONVALESCENT, 45TH GEN HOSP NEUROPSYCHIATRIC U.S. ARMY MED CENTER BAGNOLI, arrows pointing in all directions.

—Mussolini built it for a fair, she said. —The gardens are lovely, aren't they. And we have all sorts of swimming pools over there. But I understand they're going to take down the statues soon. Would you like to go swimming sometime. The statues don't have any clothes, do they. Except those silly helmets. I suppose they are Fascist statues; that's why they are taking them down.

When they took him along the hall and lowered him and put things on each side of his head, the light came all over and then it stopped. There was the oily burning taste in his mouth, and his head hurt. His arms and legs felt wet and rippled and tired, as if they had been cramping and then stopped. When the circle of light came back, it was smaller and he could see things through it.

—Now, let's see. Try. Look at me son. Can you hear me?

—more alert this time, doesn't he?

—But you've got to say something son. Can you hear me?

The light was there, and it went away. He tried to speak and the light came again and then it went away. —Can you hear me?

—Nossir, he said softly, and he began to cry again.

After that the light got small again, and he did not cry. 33

—Today let's draw things, shall we, she said. —Draw a picture for the Major. Here's some paper for me and some for you, and all sorts of colored pencils. Why that's very good. You're doing a house, aren't you. And a tree, with a lake beside it. Is that a lake. Now let's color the picture. Do you know what color this is. And this. That's it. Watch the lines. Color between the lines. He made the light go down on the paper, and he held the stick against it, on the edges. —That's it, she said. —Very good. Maybe tomorrow we'll make things. I know where there's some clay, and we'll get it and make things, would you like that.

"Yes," he said.

"Reckon you ought to know," Grady said. "But, man, you give me a real scare, there for a minute. You sure you gonna make it?"

"Just the heat," he said, standing up shakily. "I'm good as new." He unsnapped the canteen and took a drink.

"Sure? Maybe you ought to just go on out to the end and set there awhile, find you some shade by a fence pole or something. . . ."

"I'm okay," he said, picking up his hoe and moving on down the row. To show that he was steadier now, he stroked briskly with the hoe, swinging it back and forth across him without changing hands or slowing his pace.

"Easy enough to overdo it, hot day like this," Grady said. "Kind of forgot how to pace it, myself. Been a long time since I swung a gooseneck." He worked deliberately to stay a little behind Elliott, holding back, but it was harder that way. Stopping and starting and fumbling along tired him more than a brisk, even stride. "Yessir, I guess I haven't hoed any cotton, except for a little pickup money along, since about nineteen-and-thirty-five or so.

Occasion when I contributed some three months of my time and effort to the agricultural enrichment of the State of Alabama, that exalted and excrementitious cradle of the Confederacy, backwash of civilization, base and demented outpost of progress, heart of darkness. . . ."

"Huh?"

"Ninety days on the county farm gang," Grady said. When he saw Elliott stop and look back at him abruptly, he said, "You're dealing with a hardened criminal, y' know."

Finally Elliott grinned uneasily. "What'd you do?" he asked, trying too hard to be casual.

"Which stretch? That time in Sing Sing? Leavenworth? Or the big one, twenty-to-life on the Rock. . . ."

"Aw, come on."

"Well, when the stars fell on Alabama, it was purely a case of being in the wrong place at the wrong time, with a slight and merely temporary deficit in my profit-and-loss statement. My pleas, however, fell upon deaf ears. The authorities decreed open air and an abundance of exercise, to be performed with the aforementioned cotton hoe . . . which they generously placed in my trembling and eager hands, having first secured approval by breaking two ribs and my nose with the handle, or a reasonable facsimile thereof, of the aforementioned instrument."

"You really, ah . . . served time . . . in all those places?"

"Son," Grady said, "but that I am forbid to tell the secrets of my prison house, I could unwind you a tale whose lightest word would harrow up your very soul and freeze yore young blood solid, a story of hideous intolerable knavery to make thy eyes start out of their spheres like two stars blasted acrost the firmament. Or, forsooth," he said gently, "to cite a source closer my own size, I   35 have long been studying how to compare this prison where I live unto the world."

Elliott worked on silently for a while. Then he said hesitantly, "Listen, now, if you're in trouble with the law or something—"

Grady laughed. "I'm not wanted for nothing, far as I know. By anybody. Nossir, I'm about as unwanted as a man can get, these days." He turned, shaking his head and chuckling.

They were working in long rows now, contour rows that warped around almost the full length of the quarter section, following a wide arc that swung toward the fence line of the ranch. When they reached the far turn-row, Elliott squinted at the sun. "Well, let's work another through, and then go to dinner. One more through will put us closer to the house."

"I believe if it's okay with you, I'll just set down here on the end and catch my breath awhile," Grady said. "I've come a long ways since morning."

"Suit yourself," Elliott said. "But a man's got to eat if he's going to work. I guess Dad threw in meals with your wages."

"I don't believe we talked about it," Grady said. "What are your wages?"

"Whatever's the going rate. Fifty cents an hour, I suppose. That's standard. And meals. That's not standard, but . . . a man's got to eat."

"Your wages is slave labor," Grady said, chuckling, "and one a these days the proletariat is going to raise up and cast off their chains. Gonna strike down this here outmoded and decadent system of parasites that thrives on the exploitation of the masses—"

36   "What you talking about?"

"Why . . . the old class struggle, childern. Bourgeoisie exploitation of labor, means of production and exchange . . . destruction of the State . . . workers of the world arise. Hell, I don't know. But it sounded pretty good, didn't it?"

"Listen, mister," Elliott said uneasily, "what it sounded like to me was some kind of commy or nazi or something. I heard a lot of that kind of talk during the war. A lot of us went off overseas and got shot at, and a bunch of them got their heads blown off, on account of a bunch of nazis and thugs talking wild stuff like that. All I got to say is, if you don't like what we pay you, you can go someplace else."

Grady laughed. "Come to think of it, I guess it does sound kind of like some of them goosesteppers. Just change the words a little and keep the same tune. All a bunch of big-time fascists." He shrugged. "It was mostly a joke. But, son, I don't believe you'd know the point if somebody was to tell you."

"Listen, it didn't sound like any joke to me—"

"You-all own this piece of land?"

"Well, Dad does. Him and the bank. I sort of work for him, on shares."

"What did you and him make off of it last year?"

"I don't know what that's got to do with it. Anyway, I wasn't even here last year, mister. I was off fighting a war—"

"Well, waving your flag won't do it. That still don't mean fifty cents a hour for hard labor is a decent wage," Grady said carefully. "But it don't mean that I'm a nazi, either, or even a red." He was chuckling again. "I've been called lots of things, but I believe that's the first time I've been called a nazi."

"You can call it nazi or commy or whatever you want to. Just sounds to me like you don't want to do an honest day's work for an honest day's wage."

"Maybe you tell me what an honest day's wage is," Grady said casually, but when Elliott tried to answer, he cut in swiftly: "Listen, scissorbill, I've worked for a lot less than fifty cents a hour. Harder work than you've ever done, and glad to get it. That ought to warm the cockles of your smartass reactionary heart." He walked across the turnrow and sliced away a row of thistles growing on the fence line. "I still like to know how much your old man makes off a crop on this place."

"Not near enough, I'll tell you that," Elliott said. "He was doing okay until the Depression, him and my grandad. They almost had the place paid for. But even with the war, prices up and all, he just barely gets the bank paid off what he borrows to make a crop every year. Pays the crop loan, and interest on the note, and maybe if he's lucky, in a real good year, he can pay something on the principal. But that doesn't leave much to live on. You can look at this place and see all the luxuries we got, how we're just rolling in wealth."

"I've seen it," Grady said dryly. "That's my joke. But all that *still* don't make fifty cents a decent wage, and long as you can't see why not, you're right where you belong, dragging your stupid butt through the dirt and swatting weeds for the princely sum, by the price you yourself just set, of fifty lousy cents an hour. Maybe even less, depending on what the bank maybe has in mind."

Elliott glanced up at him, then looked away, thinking about it. He chewed his lower lip and snorted softly to himself. The novelty of Grady's point of view intrigued him, although he still half suspected some subtle and possibly treacherous twist of reasoning. "It's a gamble, all right," he said. "But for somebody who's got everything all figured out so neat, you don't seem to be doing so well. . . ."

"You mean, if I'm so smart, why ain't I rich?" Grady said. He turned away, shaking his head slowly.

"That's right," Elliott insisted.

"How old are you, boy?"

"What's that got to do with it? Darn near old enough to vote, if it makes any difference."

Grady heaved wearily. "I guess it don't really have anything to do with nothing. But for a mere callow youth, you've come a long way in a short while. Looks to me like you'd have learned a little something, just from looking at the scenery going by."

"You sure talk a lot not to say anything. What's that got to do with making money?"

"Look, son, I don't want to argue economics with you. I imagine when it's all said and done, we've got pretty much the same ideas. A man's worth whatever he can command. Right now, I seem to be commanding about fifty cents a hour. That is, unless you just fired me—"

Elliott frowned, staring out across the field. Grady said, "Yeah, I guess it's time to move on already. You done figured I'd murder you in your sleep or rape your womenfolk or maybe embezzle the family fortune, and now I've convinced you I'm a bolshevik, or a mad nazi. . . ." He turned and shouldered the hoe.

Elliott watched him for a moment. Then he said, "No . . . wait." He fidgeted with his hoe, scraping the blade against his boot. "It's not my place to fire you. Dad took you on."

"No law against a man quitting is there?"

"No. But you're a long way from nowhere. It's twenty miles back to town."

"I suppose there's some other cotton patches along the way. . . ."

"Yeah, but they're just paying fifty cents, too." Elliott grinned. "And no meals."

Grady laughed and put the hoe down.

"Come on," Elliott said. "Let's work this through and go in."

"No," Grady said, "thank you just the same, but I believe I'll just set down here on the end and rest awhile. It's been a long time since the cock crowed."

"Suit yourself. You're welcome to come in."

"You go ahead. I rarely eat up in the heat of the day. Gluttony is one sin I stand innocent of, for it is by such vice that the devil has great might in man, when he makes a god of his belly, a sack full of dung. . . ."

Elliott went on, off across the field toward the house, pecking here and there at one row but walking faster than he had all morning. For a long time he could hear Grady muttering and laughing to himself, and when he got to the pasture fence and put down his hoe to crawl through the barbed wire, he looked back and saw him standing at the faraway fence post where he'd chained the guitarcase. He was drinking from a huge jar that he held cupped in both hands as though he were sounding through it, calling away to the gathering thunderclouds on the edge of the northern sky.

IF I KNEW HOW BAD YOU TREAT ME.

"Hear you got you a helper," his mother said.

Elliott dried on a faded towel that was worn smooth in the center. He took the porcelain basin to the back door and emptied it across the yard in a high arc, aiming the water toward a cluster of chickens strutting and pecking at the hard bare ground. He looked down at the gray bubbly scum in the basin, the residue of Lava soap and gypsum water, and he opened the screen door wider and threw the pan at the chickens. They scattered in a peal of beating wings and frenzied cackles, the basin left to bounce and spin and finally settle beside the storm cellar on a pile of caliche rocks, its porcelain pinging and rattling away in tiny chips.

"Now what did you want to go and do that for?" his mother said. "That was a perfectly good washpan, and you went and threw it out."

He stared through the screen door, past the yard, fixed

absently on nothing in the motionless bright heat that bleached the land and sky. It was cool inside the house, and he could feel a faintly tingling line around his face and arms where he had washed, where the skin was cool and free of dust and the tension gone. "Mama," he said finally, "we need a bunch of hands. Not just one hunchback bum he finds by the road."

"Well, he does what he thinks best."

"There's no use hoeing it at all if we don't do it right. You can't spot-hoe a quarter section—"

"Honey, there's times when you've just got to do what you can, like the little boy says, and that's what your daddy's doing." She stood at the old yellow stove, stirring, her back to him. The kerosene from the stove made a close, heavy stench through the house.

"Well, after this he can do it without me." He went to the big round kitchen table and sat down, rubbing his face with open palms, massaging his eyes and temples with the tips of his fingers. "Grandad dang sure wouldn't of ever worked a crop this way."

"No, I don't suppose he would. But things aren't like they used to be."

"Mama, things never were like they used to be."

"Well. Maybe next year it'll rain."

Elliott shoved his chair sharply back from the table. "This has got to be the best next-year country in the whole world," he said. "That's what Grandad always said: 'It'll next-year us to death.'"

"We ain't having much for dinner," she said. "I aimed to fix a chicken, but your daddy said he wasn't going to be here, and I haven't been feeling too good this morning. So I just fried that ham we had left and opened up
42   some black-eye peas. Them's them good black-eye peas

we canned two years ago." She paused, remembering, then sighed heavily and turned back to her work. "Law, that was the summer your grandaddy died, and on top of everthing else I had to see to, there was all that garden to put up. But your grandaddy sure did enjoy the peas and beans and okra that summer, before he got so bad. Oh, we just had all kinds of stuff that year, the best garden I guess we've ever had. . . ."

"From the looks of that orchard, it may been the last one. Somebody sure has let it go down since I left. Grape arbor's almost covered up in sand, and least half those fruit trees won't ever bear again."

"Oh, there was just so much to do," she said. "You'll never know. With your grandaddy sick and all, and your daddy working hisself half to death just trying to keep the place going. The crops wasn't much the last few years, but just seemed there was always something to be done, we never could get caught up. Oh, 'course we've had plenty to eat, from butchering and what I could raise in my garden. Though lord knows I'm not able to enjoy it, can't hardly eat a thing with these new teeth—my store-boughten teeth, as the little boy says. I swear, my gums are still sore, and I can't stand the things in my head for long at a time. The doctor, really the dentist I should say, Dr. Johnson you know, the one that pulled your fang, that squeezed-up molar, remember, when you was just a little feller? Well, he was the one done my teeth and he said I oughtn't to have any trouble, seeing how my mouth was well formed and the old teeth wasn't much trouble. He *said* they wasn't, but lord I thought I'd die. He pulled 'em eight at a time . . ."

"I bet that hurt," he said absently.

". . . and the last time I went, I just bled and bled. 43

They had to keep me there overnight. Your daddy was pulling cotton, you know, weighing for the hands and hauling to the gin and all, and he couldn't come to drive me and I was too weak to drive home, so they went and kept me overnight and I bled all that blessed night long. Dr. Johnson, they had to call him about two in the morning to come down and give me something to stop the bleeding, only it didn't stop—"

"When I came by the well on the way in," he said, "it looked like the overhead tank was leaking. I suppose there's something wrong with that new windmill."

"I never have liked that thing," his mother said. "Little ol' flimsy tin thing. Your grandaddy built the big old wood tower, you know, out of timbers they had to haul up the caprock by mule team. That was the year before you was born, before we moved off to Fort Worth. There wasn't hardly a road in this whole country back then; they had to come up through the ranch some way, around by Post City, as I remember. But the old windmill finally rotted down. It outlasted your grandaddy just about a month. Poor old feller, he's so much better off. I tell you it was hard on me; but I won't complain. I was with him night and day there at the last, waiting on him, and he got so bad those last months . . ."

Elliott hoped she would not go through it all again. Although she talked about it constantly, it was hard for him to feel that his grandfather was really gone. He had not been there for the old man's dying, or for the funeral, and so it often seemed to him that his grandfather was only away visiting neighbors or in town, that he would return at any time. It was when Elliott sat down to eat at the heavy round table in the kitchen that his grandfather's absence was most real and permanent. Through the years, although they had not been conscious of it, the family had evolved a seating pattern around the table, his mother and father always across the table from each other, he at his father's side, his grandmother and grandfather together near the high, massive old buffet, in later years the old man there alone. When company came, the pattern was sometimes interrupted briefly (—*you set there, Mr. Lightner, and you, Miles, just take a chair there anywhere, make yourself at home*), but his grandfather always sat in the same place and opened every meal with grace, beginning, "Ouah Fathah," in his soft, sepulchral voice, "bless this food to the nou'ishment of ouah bodies and ouah bodies to thy su'vice." He thought of his grandfather at church, singing *Amazing grace how sweet the sound I once was lost but now am found* in a small clear voice that was never like an old man; and the same old man listening to the Chuck Wagon Gang on the radio in summernoons when he came out of the field to the cool house for fried pork chops and okra and sweet iced tea. There was a record, too, that the old man and the boy played endlessly on a windup Victrola, a wailing, scratchy country song about a man who was always sad. Elliott couldn't remember the words.

"Why didn't the man come in?" his mother said.

"What?" He was gazing absently through the globe of the kerosene lamp surrounded in the center of the table by the turrets of jelly jars, hot pepper sauce, a crusted catsup bottle, the broken cup that held toothpicks.

"The hand. Didn't you ask him in for dinner?"

"I tried to get him to come in, but he said he wanted to just rest awhile, maybe make another round or two."

"A body can't work out in that sun without some sort of nourishment," she said. "I'll fix him up some stuff for   45

you to take back. I've got some biscuits left from breakfast, and I can fix some of them with that ham and maybe
put in a fried pie. When you get ready to go back, you
tell me, and I'll make him up some tea, too; it ought to
stay cold till you get out there if you wrap the jar in a
wet gunny sack. Law, I wish we had some Kool-Aid, I
told your daddy to get some in town but he forgot it.
Here, you want some more cornbread?"

"No, I've had enough," he said. "I don't know if the
guy'll want anything or not. You're probably going to a
lot of trouble for nothing."

"Law, you don't eat enough to keep a bird alive," she
fussed, clearing away his dishes. "I ought to have fixed
you some of the Kraft Dinner, you always like that, but
I thought maybe I ought to save that for Sunday." She
put the dishes into a large galvanized dishpan and
poured steaming water over them from the teakettle.
"That fellow seem kind of strange to you, did he?"

"He's strange, all right."

"What? . . . You think, sort of crazy? Or what?"

"Oh, he just talks kind of funny at times. Tells a lot of
wild tales; you don't know what to believe. Reminds me
of Old Man Merrill when he gets wound up."

She laughed. "I remember Bascom Merrill come to the
house one time, that was back when times was hard, him
and Maudy lived up on the Cranks' place then, he come
down one time when your daddy and your grandaddy
was building the chickenhouse, and he told them a windy
story about how he could just look at where a board
ought to go and then saw it off without no rule and it
would fit ever time. Said it was some kind of power he
got once from a tent preacher. So your grandaddy handed
46 him the saw and says to him, 'Okay, Bask, I'll just let

you saw them ceiling joists for me,' and I'm a fool if Bascom Merrill didn't do it, ever single one, and your grandaddy like to had a fit. But your daddy said Bascom Merrill was just so liquored up, that's how he done it. Said he was too drunk to read the rule anyway, and he sure couldn't read it sober. Why, I don't suppose Bascom Merrill ever learned to write his own name. But after that your grandaddy wouldn't hardly let him on the place. But then the chickenhouse fell down, and they got to be friends again."

After he had eaten, Elliott went into the shedroom behind the kitchen and spread an old quilt over the chenille spread on the bed and lay down. He liked the shedroom. He had always slept there as a boy and he liked the way the roof came down low over the bed. It had been like being in a cave, or in the tower of a castle, or in a ship's cabin. It was never his room, exactly, as some boys have a room where they can put up pennants and keep secret treasures, because the house wasn't big enough. He'd always had to share it with the cream separator and a cupboard that was too big to fit in the kitchen, and they all took their baths there in a round laundry tub. Still, he liked the room; it had always been his in a way he couldn't quite understand.

"Take your boots off," his mother called. "There's enough sand gets in this house, without you tracking it all over my clean spread."

He was very drowsy, and it was good to settle himself there in the coolness, with a faint breeze sucking the yellowed gauzy curtain against the window screen, but he could not sleep. He lay there for a long while, easy and drifting, thinking without concentration, a soft flash of small images that floated across his mind. He thought 47

of people he used to know and of the war and of how
Rich had died. It seemed easy to think about now. He remembered Fort Worth, vaguely, the wide vacant streets
of the 1930's and the river, Aunt Edith and Norm. Coming back, in the square black cars of that time, the sand
blowing, his grandfather. Going away again, and the war.
He thought of the Major and the Major's daughter and
San Francisco and Chicago and how great it was to be
there, and he remembered how he and Rich had been
picked up on Michigan Avenue by two girls in a '38
Cadillac who thought they were Marines. Then before
the war when he and Bobby hunted rabbits on the turnrow over by the Double U, when he rode an old yellow
bus to school at Elysium, the good times in the fall when
it rained and the bus couldn't make its route over the
gummy roads. He read then, and listened to the radio
with his grandfather or played the Victrola. Sometimes
there was real music, when Less Pirtle and T. F. Carroll
and Old Man Teed and his boys got together, sometimes his Uncle Ode and his father played with them . . .
but that was in the summer, when they all went to somebody's house at night with the guitars and mandolins and
a fiddle and sometimes a banjo; they started with old
stomps and breakdowns, "Corinne-Corinna" and "Rubber
Dolly" and "Boil Them Cabbage Down," while the wom-
en cranked freezers of mushy ice cream on the back
porch and the kids played hide-and-go-seek in weedy
patches just beyond the yellow lamps of the house, a hot
rushing excitement of running and falling and throbbing
under wagons and behind sheds where, growing older,
he'd first felt girlflesh, forever mystic, while "Under the
48   Double Eagle" rose dimly from the distant house and a

faraway voice said —ninetynine hunnerd here I come ready or not. After the ice cream was gone and the kids went to sleep, they played waltzes and country ballads, Leroy Teed singing "Great Speckled Bird" and "Wildwood Flower." If Elliott's grandfather was there, they played the one he liked, about the man who was always sad, how did it go? There was a part of it, something about leaving Texas . . . then he remembered: *I'm going back to Colorado, place that I started from; if I knowed how bad you treat me, Texas, I never would have come.* He thought of how hard those years had been and how trapped he felt coming back, remembering the night one of the boys from town came home with him after church and how his grandfather was sitting in the living room in his dirty long underwear listening to the radio hillbillies and a shouting preacher selling the *Sing and Be Happy Songbook* with the Big Gospel Surprise Package, including a Miracle Picture of Jesus

you jist hold this wondraful pitcher of the Lord before a strong light, my frins, then look at the sky and you'll see Him there, praise Jesis, plus 150 Questions and Ainsers from the Bible: is it a sin to go to a fortune teller? should you own a dog? what about taxation? when can men and women come together? what does the number five mean? can you drink out of a paper cup? these and many-many more my frins when you send your love offering to me, care of this station, XELO Clint Texas

and his mother and father arguing in the kitchen, and how the city boy had asked where the bathroom was, and there wasn't any, and how they had slept together in the shedroom, the city boy putting on striped pajamas, the first he'd ever seen, and he'd slept in his baggy shorts. He   49 stopped going to church not long after that, and he'd never gotten to know the boy very well. It was all a long time ago. Maybe it never happened.

"Honey, you'd better get up now. You'd better be getting back to the field."

He got up and went in the kitchen carrying his boots.

"Here," his mother said. "Set down and drink yourself a glass of tea while I finish fixing up this stuff for the hand. Better eat some of this peach cobbler, too, while it's still warm." She set a large bowl before him.

"Dad say when he'd be back?"

"Oh, sometime this evenin, I suppose. I imagine it'll be late . . . but you ought to get on back to the field anyway. You've rested enough, and it's cooler now. Some clouds building up back in yonder." She leaned across the sink to peer through the window. "If it would only rain . . ."

"Yeah, if a frog had wings. He wouldn't bump his butt."

"Listen, now," she said. "That's not a nice way to talk."

"You think he'll be home in time to milk? I'd just as soon not have to hoe all day and then do the chores, too. I might even want to use the car. It's Saturday, y'know."

"Well, I imagine he'll get back as soon as he can. Him and Ode was going to move one of the chickenhouses, and I think maybe he was going to help Ode with some fence."

"How come we always have to do everything for Uncle Ode? How come he can't ever help us any? Those boys of his are getting big enough to do a little work around the place. . . ."

"I know it," she said. "But your daddy always has done for Ode, and it's got to where it's sort of second nature

50

with him, as the little boy says. Seems like he tries to do for everybody. It's just one thing after another. I tried to get him to sell the place and let's move to town after your grandaddy died, but he wouldn't hear of it."

"I told him a long time ago to get out," Elliott said, pulling on his boots. "I told him how it would be. But he's just like every dirt farmer I ever knew. Stubborn. Ignorant, maybe."

"Now, don't say things like that about your daddy. He's a good man, a real good man. If you're ever half as good as he is, it'll be a miracle."

"I know," he said coldly.

"He works hard . . . works *hard*, your daddy does. Always has, and never complains, you'll never hear a word out of him. And I don't want you saying nothing about him, you hear?"

"I guess I just don't understand," he said. "I can't help it if . . . if I don't like this place." He was filling his canteen, a dipper at a time, from the drinking bucket on the cupboard shelf.

"No, you don't like the farm," she said in a level tone. "You're by that the way I am. I tell myself I'm used to it, but I'm not. Living out here away from everybody and everything. I tell you, I thought I'd go crazy when your grandpa was sick. Guess I would have if it hadn't of been for the work. I was so sick myself I couldn't hardly stand up, and there was your grandpa, so withered and feeble, poor old fellow, and no one but me to take care of him. The rest of them just left me to do it all. None of the family ever come to see him, unless they wanted something."

She paused for a long while, and then went on, in the same tired voice, as if she'd never stopped. " 'Course your daddy was here and he helped some, but he was working 51

the crop night and day, so I done it all, really. Taken care
of your grandpa all day, stayed right by his bed, you
know, feeding and cleaning after him, then I'd spend the
night cleaning the house and washing. Why, I'd go for
days without hardly a nap. It was hard. Law, it was awful hard. It's a shame to say it, but I was relieved when
the poor old man died."

"I know it was bad, Mama. I wish I'd been here to
help."

"But, honey, the hard part was that nobody cared what
I done," she said, and began to cry softly. "No matter
how much I worked and slaved, they never cared. They
never helped me none, but I didn't mind about that, I was
glad they stayed out of my way. But they never cared
what I done or tried to help me even a little, or give me no
encouragement. Your uncle Ode, the only time he'd ever
come, he'd just bring all them kids and I'd have them to
wait on, too, along with trying to tend to your grandaddy. Ode and Bess would go on about how busy they
was at home and how they'd help if they ever got caught
up, only they never did. But they had time to come and
let me wait on them, and then go and say mean things
about how I didn't take good care of your grandpa, how
I'd let him go hungry, said I'd yell at him, things like
that. Can you imagine? Here I was killing myself and
they wasn't doing a single thing, but still they'd tell lies
about me. Why, he never knew none of us there at the
end, or even who he was. And I wouldn't let him go hungry. Poor fellow, he thought he was hungry all the time
but he'd never eat. I tried for a while to give him something when he'd cry out—you know he'd cry, make little
whimpering noises all the time, till I thought I'd go mad
—I'd try to feed him when he'd cry, had to handfeed him,

poor thing couldn't hold a spoon, but he wouldn't eat, so finally I just fed him when we ate. And they'd go and say I was trying to starve him." She left the food she was preparing and sat down at the table.

"Now, Mama, don't cry. It's all done now, it's all over with," he said.

"I know. I know it is," she said. "But I can't forget how they done me. Why, Bess, that sweet old aunt of yours which everybody thought butter wouldn't melt in her mouth, why, she was telling everybody the only reason I taken care of him was to get his money. As though he had any. She was just mad because she knowed they wouldn't get whatever little bit was left. And there wasn't any. All he had was this place, a hundred and sixty acres of poor dirt and a shack and two old barns, and he'd done made out his will and give that to your daddy before he got sick. Why, I wouldn't of gone through what I went through for fifty times this piece of dirt. But still they'd go and say things like that. That's what made it so bad."

He finished the glass of tea and without speaking got up and went into the living room. She seemed not to notice, sitting slumped in the chair, looking at the floor, and she kept talking as though he were still in the room with her.

"Yes, they've said terrible things about me. I know I've done wrong, I've always said it, I just had it in me to do wrong, but lord I never deserved all the evil things they've done to me." She began to weep again.

"Mama," Elliott said, clearing his throat, "stop talking about it. You know it won't change anything. And it's not your fault."

"Oh, you don't know, you just don't know . . . how hard it was."

He got up and walked to the door and stood there look-ing at her. Finally he said, "Mama, listen to me. Listen. I know. I know about it. But it's like all our troubles and being apart and . . . it's all gone and past, it's all over. You've got to forget about it."

"Well," she said, drying her eyes, sniffing, "I guess you're right."

"It's past now. You can't keep hurting yourself, keep making it worse—"

"It's just . . . the things they said."

"How many times have you told me, 'Don't mind what people say, or even what they think'? How many times? All my life, Mama. And you know what these people are. Hell, I don't even know if they're really people. They eat and sleep and fornicate . . . but heck, pigs do that. They just live from day to day, crop to crop, from baby to baby. They live in dirt and die in it, get their whole liv-ing from the land . . . but they call it dirt, and there's no hope in that. Nor nothing else." He straightened up. "They're dumb, Mama, and they're proud of it."

"That sounds like you've been to too many picture shows, or something you got out of a book," she said. "It's not true. There's lots of good folks here."

"Sure, they're good. Whatever the hell that means. But they're also stupid and shallow, and you've got no busi-ness letting them bother you. Especially a bunch of shirt-tail relatives. Why, Mama, you've been places and seen things and known things . . . things they can't compre-hend, can't even imagine. You remember the way it was in Fort Worth."

"We should of never left," she said vacantly. "You lose things in time." She looked up at him. "But you can't talk about people that way. They're our people, your own relatives, folks you grew up with."

"I know," he said quietly. "I know." He took a deep breath and then turned and walked back into the living room and sat down.

She was quiet, and then she said, "You know, Elliott, you're a snob. You always was biggity, awful high and mighty, and now you're just a plain snob." She spoke in even, measured tones, as though she were discussing the weather, and he knew she was still sitting in the same position, staring at the floor. "You never cared about nobody, or even what they thought. You always put yourself above everybody else, even your own people. You don't even know what happened, you wasn't even here, but you come home from the Army and tell me to forget it, it's just the people. But that's me and your daddy, too. And your grandaddy. You ought to find you some more snobs, because you don't belong here. Why don't you stay with the ones that give you all them big ideas?"

"No," he said. "I don't belong there either. And I'm not about to go on fighting with you, like it was before I went away, nobody making sense and nobody right. Now I want you to shut up about it."

She continued as if she hadn't heard him. "I always said the only good thing I ever done was to have you. But I don't know. You never was anything but a toy to me. To a man it's different; he wants a child to carry on his name, to be something that goes on when he dies. But to a woman, a baby's just something to play with . . . that's what you was to me."

"Well, that's nice to know," he said. He looked at the cracked linoleum on the floor, worn in ridges where the floor was uneven, and he felt the hot breezes rising against the old house. The yellowed curtains flapped and stuck to the screens, and he thought of San Francisco and the high buildings of stone and steel and how Russian Hill looked in the rain, when you ran along the streets and went to a hotdog stand named the Hunk-a-Dory, sea smells mixed in the scorched air of roasting coffee from under the west end of Bay Bridge, wine and yeast and fish and gardenias, the heavier, sweet fragrance of eucalyptus, the crowds of pretty girls in Union Square. He remembered the old house when it was his grandparents', when he and his mother came from Fort Worth to visit during the summers, and then when his grandmother died they had come back to stay, and his father began to farm the place again when his grandfather got sick. His father hadn't really wanted to come back; he had been gone a long time and had found a good job in the Katy railroad shops, but the Depression was coming, and it was the "home place" and he came back to it without thinking he should or could do anything else: it was the home place and he came back.

Elliott remembered working in the hot, barren fields when he was a boy, and walking barefoot in chicken dung and fighting boys who thought he was a sissy because he once wore a cap to school. He thought of sandstorms in the spring, when yellow-brown dust filled the sky and shut away the sun, other days of howling earth when the land rose before the wind to stifle him—stifle them, his mother and father: days when his mother in the strength of her youth and knowing had raged against it, with the then-sense of time and futility had sat weeping silently as she did now. *If I knowed how bad you treat me, Texas, I never would have come.* He thought then of

56

all the people who'd never hoed cotton or walked through chicken dung in their bare feet, boys who could always wear caps to school and lived in big, safe houses with rugs on the floor and wide lawns, people who lived free in cities or by mountains or great foaming seas, and he got up and walked across the room without hurrying and went out the front door, closing the screen behind him carefully, not letting it slam. He walked around the house and out past the cellar toward the field. He was stooping to squeeze between the wires of the pasture fence when his mother called from the back door.

"Wait, honey," she shouted, holding up the paper sack. "You forgot the man's dinner." She came out to meet him. "There's a jar of tea in it, too," she said, handing him the sack. "We didn't have much ice. You better go by the well and wrap some towsack around it and wet it good."

He took the bag without looking at her and started back toward the fence. When he was going through it, still not looking back, she said suddenly, "Oh, honey, you never got to eat your peach cobbler. . . ." She began to cry again.

Finally, when he was further away, he turned and called out to her quietly. "Okay, Mama," he said. "I'll have it for supper." When he got to the well, he looked back again. She was still standing there, small and frail against the old house. Then she turned and went inside.

CROSS MY FATHER'S GROUND TO ANY HOUSE OR TOWN. Grady turned over and sat up. "Sweet remembrance of the just," he said. "Lordy if the sleep of a laboring man ain't truly honeysuckle and sweetmeats. Honeysuckle, sweetmeats, and hog dew."

"What?" Elliott handed him the paper sack. "Mama sent you out some dinner."

"You never heard that?" Grady said. "I thought everybody knew that old saying." He sat in the shade of his guitarcase where it was locked to the fence post and took out the ham and biscuits. "Well, I don't reckon a guy can call it pure-dee exploitation," he said, grinning, "when the bourgeois capitalist boss feeds a man, on top of paying him wages. Or does this come out of my fifty cents a hour?"

"You better drink that tea," Elliott said, "before the ice melts."

Grady gestured at Elliott's canteen. "What's that you've got on your hip there? I might have me a swoozle of that."

"It's just rainwater. I sort of get the cottonmouth between rounds."

"*Water!*" Grady shook his head. "Bygod, I believe you're telling the truth. Well, Grady, it's your own damn fault," he muttered.

"What?"

"I swore to myself," he said grandly, "a fair and baleful oath that I'd never set foot again on these godforsaken bone-dry local prohibition plains. . . . It's all a mad and devious plot between the preachers and the bootleggers. Why, there's so many bootleggers in Lubbock, Texas, they have to wear badges to keep from hustling each other, and between them and the Baptists a poor honest man can go choke in his own spit. Got to prime your peter to piss, the Old Jedge used to say." He looked off across the field. "And the Old Jedge knew, didn't you, Jedge." Then he laughed, still gazing out over the flat land. "Yessir, Jedge, if you ain't boiling in hell, they might just as well sell the place." He sipped from the jar of tea, swallowed some, then spat in mock disgust.

"There's some well water in a crock down yonder by that big thistle," Elliott said. "Or you're welcome to some of mine."

"Never touch it myself," Grady said. "I've seen what the stuff does to the inside of pipes. Hear some people even take a bath in it. But let me tell you, son, I have also heard it said that thick wine, on the other hand, is like unto the virtuous worthies, you know that? And yet— why should you and me strive to be gods and immortals? Yea, three bottles and you can verily understand the Great Tao. A gallon, bygod, and you'll get yourself in accord with all nature."

"What's the Great Toe?" Elliott said.

Grady roared, almost choking on a mouthful of biscuit and ham. When he had stopped laughing and could talk again, he said, "Ah, them that know don't tell." He grinned at Elliott. "And them that tell don't know."

Elliott ignored him. He filed their hoes and they set off, heavy and lagging now in the late still heat of afternoon. From time to time they could hear the low distant whine of a tractor, too far away to be seen, its clatter sounding and echoing across the empty plain. Whirlwinds rustled here and there in the fields, rising against shimmering heat waves. The sky was dark in the north and west, and puffs of dirty white appeared along the edges of blackness. After an hour Elliott saw the sand rising, a roiling brown hedge on the horizon. "Well," he said disgustedly, "it looks like we're going to get a little dirt in our office."

"Pretty late in the year for dusters, idn't it?" Grady said. "Looks to me like there's a bank of thunderstorms behind it."

"Anybody that tries to forecast the weather in West Texas is either a fool or a newcomer." Elliott leaned on his hoe, watching the clouds.

"You've heard that old saying, too, have you?" Grady said. He laughed. "Reckon which one I am?" A gust of wind whipped at his hat, and he started moving again. "I can't speak for newcomers, but nobody but a fool would stand here in the middle of a cottonpatch and scratch his crotch while half of Oklahoma and New Mexico come howling down the Panhandle on top of him—"

Before they could work out to the end of their rows, 60 the wind had begun to scatter trails of dust down the furrow. At the turnrow the blinding front of sand hit in full force, and even then big raindrops were falling, clearing the air before a hard, fresh breeze, spattering in the dry dust, and settling it and making smudges on their dirty faces. Grady limped over to the guitarcase and began trying to open the lock on the chain, and the rain roared down over them. "Go on!" Grady yelled. "No use in you getting wet, too."

"It's okay," Elliott said. "I haven't had a chance to get rained on in a long time, myself. Might like it."

Grady gathered up his guitarcase and Elliott carried the hoes. They slogged down the turnrow, slipping and cursing happily and spitting water that dripped off their noses. The rain settled into a steady downpour, and the land that had been powdery and faded now turned deep and brilliant under the bruised sky.

At the house they huddled beneath an extended eave over the back porch. Elliott scraped his mudcaked boots on a horseshoe set in cement beside the door, and Grady took out a small metal rectangle that looked to Elliott like a miniature hoe blade and used it to clean the mud from his hightop black shoes.

"You-all get in this house," Elliott's mother scolded from the kitchen. "You're going to catch your death. . . ."

Grady kept his distance, occupying himself with a careful, elaborate cleaning of his shoes that amounted almost to a ceremony. Elliott opened the screen door and stood inside. His mother said, "Just like a bunch of brooder chicks. Not got the sense to come in out of the rain."

Grady grinned at her, wiping his shoes carefully on a cloth sack she had spread on the porch. "There's no quicker way to purgatory than tracking up a lady's floors," 61 he said, picking up the guitarcase. "My old daddy used to say, a man that soils the work of woman is a serpent in the temple."

"Well, it'll dry," she said. "I'd lots rather clean up mud than sand, lord knows I've shoveled enough grit out of this old house. You-all get in yonder in the other room and find some dry clothes."

"Just a heavy dew, ma'am," Grady said. "I don't want to put you out."

"No bother. I don't know what we've got that'll fit you—" She would have said the same thing to any stranger, but now she saw that it would not do. "What I mean is, both my men is big fellas . . ."

Grady nodded to her, easy. "Yes, ma'am."

". . . but anything dry is better than them squashy things. You go on in yonder and he'll find you something."

Elliott rummaged around in a box in the closet and found a pair of nearly new overalls that had been bought for his grandfather just before his last illness. They were almost Grady's size, and by taking up the straps as far as they would go and rolling a cuff on the legs, he made them fit comfortably. Elliott gave him dry socks and one of his father's gray workshirts. "Lordy, lordy. You wouldn't know me from a pure-dee old scissorbill," Grady said wryly, with satisfaction.

Elliott changed into fresh Levi's and one of his old Army shirts, and they went into the kitchen. His mother poured them steaming coffee, and they sat at the big round table, sipping. Then she remembered the peach cobbler and dipped out a bowlful for each of them. The rain beat down. They could hear it sloshing off the roof and through the gutters into the charcoal filterbox and then dropping a long, hollow way into the cistern.

"All a man would need to get into heaven," Grady said, "would be to hold out a taste of this cobbler to old Saint Peter, and then offer him the rest to let you in."

"Why, thank you," she said, fussing over the table. "I don't get many compliments around here, I'll tell you that. The men on this place don't care a thing, just set theirselves down and go at it. Long as it's hot and they don't have to fix it. Sop gravy and say nothing, as the little boy says." She was at the sink, and she watched the rain through the window. "Law," she said to Elliott, "I guess your daddy'll be proud of this. He'd just about give up on this crop."

"He'd better get on home, or he won't be able to make it in," Elliott said. "Water's already up across the road down there by the pasture."

"Oh, I imagine he'll just stay all night with Ode and Bess. You know how him and Ode are when they get together. Probably slopping around out in the field by now, like two kids, to see how much it's rained." She turned back to the table. "They've sure suffered with the drouth this year," she said tiredly.

"This'll help, if it keeps up," Elliott said. "But some of the crop's pretty far gone. That young cotton over by the ranch sure was suffering these last few days, up in the heat of the day."

"One thing," she said. "You'll have plenty of weeds to cut. This'll make 'em grow wild."

"Ah, the great weeds grow thus apace," Grady recited.

"If I have my way about it," Elliott said, "we'll get a bunch of Mexicans in there and get it over with and quit messing around."

"Well," Grady said lightly, "I was looking for a job 63

when I found this one. Yea, I am like unto a weed its ownself, flung from the rock, to sail the ocean's foam where'er the surge may sweep. . . ."

"Nobody ain't going nowhere till the roads clear up," Elliott's mother said. "We might as well get around and fix you a place to sleep before it gets dark. We've got that old bedstead down in the cellar, I reckon that's as good a place as any."

She put on her bonnet and a ragged sweater and a pair of Elliott's old field boots, and they sloshed out to the cellar, carrying a broom and a can of kerosene for the lamp. The rain had eased to a slow drizzle. The cellar walls and floor were cemented, but the smell there was like old wet dirt, heavy and soured. To Elliott the cellar had always been a safe place. In his childhood it was where they went when the sand blew. He could hear his grandfather saying, Looks like a cloud back in yonder to the north. Can't never tell what's back of that sand. Other times, he was forbidden to play there, but he often hid in the dark cellar and pretended it was his secret lair, crouched for hours beside an old chest of drawers in the weak icy light that sifted down from the cracks in the sloping door.

Elliott's mother lit the lamp and it made blurry shadows behind the massive quilt box and stacks of trunks and in the rows of canned vegetables and fruits in Mason jars and jelly glasses on high shelves across one wall. "Here," she said, "one of you take this broom and sweep up some of this dust off the floor." Grady put his guitarcase down in a corner and took the broom before Elliott managed to stir. "I swear," she went on, "looks like that sand's practically ground into the cement. But I guess

64

we can make it fit to live in for a time. You, Elliott. Get me some fresh bedding out of that quilt box. I usually always get the cellar cleaned so's we'll have it ready case a cloud comes up, but we didn't have nothing this past spring but dusters, and I've just been feeling so bad lately, my rheumatism and all, I never got around to it. . . ."

Elliott fumbled in the quilt box and took out sheets and a pillow and quilt and handed them to her. In addition to bedding, the quilt box held books that belonged to his mother, old novels and books of verse she'd acquired when they lived in Fort Worth, many small boxes of various shapes tied with ribbons and strips of cloth, pictures no one could identify, discarded dishes, endless bundles of paper, a jumbled, fragmentary history of the family. Elliott found bits of schoolwork he'd done, and some of his childish drawings that his mother had put away carefully in binders. He found a picture of a girl he'd once loved, and an old scrapbook with most of the pages blank or torn out, and he found the book about Custer that the Major had given him and the ribbons and decorations he'd brought home from the war and thought he'd thrown away, the campaign ribbons for North Africa and the Peninsular Campaign, the unit citation for Cassino, the Purple Heart and the Combat Infantryman's Badge, a Fifth Army shoulder patch and his sergeant's chevrons. He remembered how the Purple Heart had impressed them most of all, and he laughed sadly to himself, because it hadn't even been his blood or his wound. Beside the quilt box there was a fruitbasket full of old phonograph records, and he lifted them out hurriedly one at a time, looking for the one his grandfather had liked. 65

Many of them were by Jimmie Rodgers or the Carter Family, blue yodels and country hymns, and some of the titles he remembered only vaguely: "Tuck Away My Lonesome Blues" and "T for Texas" and "Away Out on the Mountain" and "Little Darling Pal of Mine" and "That Heavenly City." Then he saw the one he was looking for; he recognized the yellow label with the bird on it. "Man of Constant Sorrow" was the title, and he began to remember now just how it went . . . *I'm a man of constant sorrow, I've seen trouble all my days since I said goodbye to Colorado, where I was born and partly raised,* and there was another verse that began, *Your mother says I'm a stranger—* But the record was cracked, and he put it gently back into the fruitbasket and put the others on top. He closed the quilt box and went over and sat down on the cellar steps beside Grady's guitarcase.

Grady finished sweeping and perched on a trunk at the foot of the bed. The top of the trunk was higher than his waist, but he got on it by backing up to it and putting the heels of his hands on the edge, behind him, and levering himself up.

"There," Elliott's mother said, puffing up the pillow and swatting the quilt to see if there was dust in it. "Them old bedsprings is kind of rusty, but that ought to make you a pretty good bed."

"It's fine," Grady said. "And thank you, ma'am."

"Well, we'll get out and leave you be," she said, picking up the broom and kerosene can. "I'll put this lantern up here on this shelf. But that's one of my good lamps, you be careful and don't turn it up too high and smoke my chimney."

Elliott moved over on the steps to let her pass. "Honey," she said, "you better go on and milk pretty soon. I don't imagine your daddy'll be home." Elliott said nothing, and she stood at the top looking down at him for a moment. Then she went away.

Grady eased himself over on the bed and stretched out. "All I need now is about three fingers of good Scotch whiskey. Or even bad Scotch whiskey."

Elliott thought of how the Major had always managed to find a supply of Scotch wherever they went. He looked up. "Yeah," he said. "You're only about two hundred miles from the nearest liquor store. Legal beer in the next county. Place called County Line. Even that's at least sixty miles. Hard liquor's a lot further. One hundred and ninety-four miles and four tenths, my grandad used to say, from Elysium to the front door of Pinkie's Package Store in Big Spring. That's the nearest one."

"Your grandaddy sounds like a man to know."

"He was," Elliott said.

"Oh, for a beaker of . . . the true, the blushful Hippocrene," Grady said, "that I might drink my joyful fill and leave unseen these . . . these goddamned desiccated calcinated dry fevered fucking abominable plains. Here it is my birthday, and a man can't even celebrate. What in hell's name is it about these flat-land farmers that makes 'em vote dry, can you tell me that?"

"You know the saying. 'Vote it dry and drink it neat.'"

"Full of them one-liners, ain't you? Well, it's a bunch of ironjacketed hardshell hypocritical sonsabitches. Bigtime fascists. Oh she cried and waved her wooden leg: hang them Baptists while a tater vine'll do the trick."

"Has its advantages," Elliott said. He was chipping at the cement step with the broken blade of his pocket 67 knife. "No age limit, for one thing. Kid can buy a beer as soon as he's big enough to carry fifty cents and find a bootlegger."

"That's right. You know any bootleggers?"

"Heck, in town all you got to do is go down to the flats and ask around. They'll run over each other getting to you."

"Free enterprise system," Grady said. "But that's in town. There's twenty miles of muddy road between us and them. What about your friends and neighbors?"

"No moonshining around here that I know of. Used to be an old guy over at 'Lysium, but I don't know if he's still around."

"You sure you haven't got a little soothin syrup of some kind stashed away on the premises?"

Elliott grinned and went back to chipping at the step.

"Hell's bells," Grady said. "Hand me that guitarcase over there. You do take a drink, don't you. A *drank*, as my old daddy used to say."

"Heck, in the Army I tried a little of everything from bay rum to rubbing alcohol," Elliott said lightly but a little too hastily to be entirely convincing. He stood up and reached for the guitarcase.

"Well, what I'm offering is sure not Seagram's or Johnnie Walker Black Label."

"Hey," Elliott said, lugging the guitarcase. "What's in here? Feels like about a ton of pig-iron." Half dragging it, he backed across to the bed and Grady helped him lift it up.

"This here is Colonel Grady O. Haker's Jot 'Em Down Store," Grady muttered, unsnapping the catches. "Traveling medicine show, haberdashery, saloon, and lending liberry."

"Son of a gun," Elliott said, peering over to look. "There's everything but a guitar."

"Matter of fact, my clear and melodious lute lies gathering dust beneath the bower of a sweet young thing, a bright flower of Walsenburg, Colorado, who in the summer of nineteen-and-forty-three— Well, the gory details I leave entirely to your imagination, trusting that like all country boys you have a filthy and diseased mind. . . ." From beneath a wad of soiled clothes in the guitarcase he withdrew the bottle of vanilla extract.

The guitarcase held several nondescript boxes and objects that Elliott could not identify in the dim lamplight. Most of what he could see was books, and he reached out gingerly to turn them and look at the titles. In addition to *A History of Western Philosophy,* he found *The Story of My Life,* by Clarence Darrow; *How to Write Advertising That Sells; The I.W.W. Song Book; The Flying Yorkshireman and Other Stories,* by Eric Knight; *The Pocket Bible* (Abridged); *The Story of Frederic W. Goudy; Discourses of Epictetus; God's Little Acre* in paperback ("He screws Darlin' Jill on page 76, I believe," Grady said dryly); Volume III of an elegantly cheap edition of Scott's *Waverley Novels; Babe Gordon,* by Mae West; Bright's *Anglo-Saxon Reader;* Tony Wons' *Scrapbook* for 1944-45; *The Cloister and the Hearth; They Shoot Horses, Don't They?* and *I Should Have Stayed Home,* by Horace McCoy; *Six Shakespearean Plays;* a beautifully bound copy of *Typophile Chap Book VII,* with an elaborate title page that read: "Roman Numerals, Typographic Leaves, and Pointing Hands: Some Notes on Their Origin, History, and Contemporary Use. Paul McPharlin. 1942. With 40 figures in the text designed by the author, and C. R. Capon, Warren Chappell, W. A.   69

Dwiggins, Robert Foster, Clarence Hornung, Oscar Ogg, Hal Zamboni. Southwork-Anthoensen Press. One of 495 copies"; also a battered *Thesaurus*, ragged copies of the *Reader's Digest, Graphic Arts, Editor & Publisher,* and *Plasticman Comics;* several dried oranges; three dozen Ramses prophylactics; a whiskey bottle with a wooden Masonic emblem inside it; a blackened skillet; a .41 Army Colt Pistol, Model 1898 ("old thumb-buster I got off an old boy that used to run with Clyde Barrow," Grady said); and several strangely marked metal rules, four or five Hohner Marine Band Harmonicas, a cigarette-making machine, plastic cigarette cases with oval holes cut out of them, four ignition points, unmarked medicine bottles, half a dozen ball bearings, a miniature bale of cotton, a can opener, three shot glasses, and a handful of the oddly shaped little steel plates like the one Elliott had seen Grady cleaning his shoes with.

"Makeup rules," Grady said.

"I thought it might be some new kind of guitar pick. What's a makeup rule?"

"Printer's gadget. Use it to build ads, make up straight-matter, clean your fingernails, open beer, most anything that needs prying, scraping, screwing, or splitting."

"You a printer?"

"Mostly. Let's see how it goes: 'Jour printer by trade, do some in patent medicines, tragedy-actor, take a turn at phrenology and mesmerism when there's a chance, teach singing-geography school now and then, sling a lecture sometimes, most anything that's handy, long as it ain't work.' That's from *Huck Finn,* the Duke talking, and I believe I got it about right."

"I've only read *Tom Sawyer.* What's a jour printer?"

"Hell if I know. Sounds good though, don't it. You

ought to read *Huckleberry Finn* sometime. It's a lot better than *Tom Sawyer*. Tom Sawyer is a prissy little shit."

"I guess there's a lot of things I ought to read. Maybe I'll have a chance to catch up on these, if it's okay with you."

"Three-day loan, and two-bits for ever day a book is late." Then he grinned. "Sure. You're welcome to 'em."

"Where'd you ever get all these books, anyway?"

"Oh, one place and another," Grady said. "Helped print some of 'em. I pick up books here and there, read 'em, throw 'em away or give 'em to somebody or just lose 'em. Read all the time, like a madman, don't understand half of what I read and don't believe the other half. Maybe it's a habit I got from my old daddy...."

"He read a lot, did he?"

"My daddy? No, not much." He chuckled. "I don't suppose he could read his own name the day he died."

"You know," Elliott said, "sometimes I feel like if I could just read enough books and find out enough things, I could get everything straightened out. There's so much I don't know, haven't even heard about...."

Grady chuckled and took a swig of vanilla. "Pabst Blue Ribbon has got old Milton beat a mile," he said, "when it comes to figuring out the ways of the Almighty. Here, you just need to sip a little of this soothin syrup."

Elliott took the bottle and held it absently on his knee, staring off into space. "But I don't ever do anything," he said. "I just mess around, and time goes on, and I don't even know where to start."

Grady said, "Place to start is wherever we can lay hand on more goodly beverage. Don't your daddy ever take a nip? Maybe he's got a bottle hid someplace."

Elliott shook his head. The idea of his father being a   71 secret drinker amused him. "Cream soda or Kool-Aid is about as wild as he ever gets," he said.

"Jesus Christ and General Jackson," Grady said. "I've fallen into the hands of the Dubya-Cee-Tee-Yew. Seized in the clutches of the Missionary Society. Surrounded by ever bluenose and dry in nine states . . ."

"He doesn't have anything against it, much. He just doesn't keep any around the place."

"Well, take a snort of that and hand it back. It ain't much, but it looks like that's all we got."

Elliott gulped a mouthful of the vanilla. It was sweet and oily going down, and it lay heavy in his stomach. But he could feel the rubbery warmth spreading out, easing the cramp in his bowels and the tightness across his chest. "If your dad couldn't read, how'd that get you started?"

Grady waved him away. "Oh my god, it's a long story. Action and reaction of time in opposition. Simultaneity and succession of appearances. Those, as the only relations in time . . ." Elliott frowned.

"Here," Grady said, thumbing through the book he had been reading that morning. "How about this? 'If appearance really appears, it is not nothing and is therefore part of reality; but perhaps some will say, Appearance does not really appear, but it appears to appear. This will not help, for we shall ask again, Does it really appear to appear or only *apparently* appear to appear. . . .'" Elliott took another swig of vanilla and continued to stare at him anxiously.

"Well?"

"That's interesting. . . ."

72 "Logos!" Grady yelled, snapping the book shut with a

sharp whack. "In the beginning, there was The Word."
He squinted at Elliott. "You know what all that I just
read means?"

"Well . . . I'd have to look at it. . . ."

"O-yes, certainly," Grady said, dropping the book back
inside his guitarcase. He rolled a cigarette through the
machine and lit it. "Used to sing me a song, had a line in
it . . . 'Daddy, let your mind roll on.' Yessir, she cried and
waved her wooden leg: Daddy, let your mind roll on.
What about that bootlegger you used to know at Elysium?"

Elliott heard his mother calling. He went up the steps
and raised the cellar door, holding it up with his shoulder,
and he could see her on the back porch, with a tin pail in
one hand and her egg bucket in the other. "Honey, you
better go on now and milk," she said sternly. "It's going
to be dark before long, and I've got to go gather up the
eggs."

"Hey, Mama," he said. "I think me and the hand are
going to go over to 'Lysium. To the store. He's gonna
need some gloves and stuff—"

"Why, honey, you've got to milk," she said. "Besides,
that's four miles through the mud. You-all don't want to
go slogging through all that, and besides, I'm going to fix
some supper after while."

"We'll take the tractor," he said. "We can eat when
we get back."

"Your daddy won't like it." But she saw that he was
determined. "Anyway, go on and milk first."

He stood there a minute, looking at her, then pushed
the door wide open, slamming it over and down on its
cradle. He stalked out toward her and took the pail and   73

went back to the cellar. "Come on," he called down to Grady. "And bring that stuff with you. Put it in your shirt."

They went around the smokehouse to the side away from the house and urinated, and then Elliott jogged on ahead toward the cow lot, picking his way carefully around, trying to find the places where the scrubgrass had grown together in a tight mat over the pasture but still sloshing in the low places and in the web of trails where the cows had churned off the grass and kneaded the ground into gray powder that was now dissolved into ooze and scattered with soggy manure chips and shreds of feed stalks and chaff. Grady followed along, limping, blowing a mournful note now and then on a wheezy harmonica.

Three cows were bunched around the feed lot, nosing through the fence and bellowing occasionally. Two of them had calves in the pen. But the cows were mostly interested in the feed trough. One of them, an old tawny jersey, skittered aside and went flopping off into the pasture when Elliott came up. He drove the other two into the lot with their calves. The calves rushed to suck.

"Yea, lo," Grady called out. "They loosed their sweating steads from the yoke and tethered them with thongs and brought kine and goodly herds and provided theirselves with some lipsmacking honey-hearted wine and corn and gathered much wood. . . ."

"What's that?"

"Nothing. It's just ranting. Knew an old boy once that could go on all day like that."

"Sounds like one of those preachers on the radio," Elliott said, watching the calves suck. It was the brindle heifer's first calf and she did not have a lot of milk. The calf was greedy and kept jabbing its nose into the cow's bag to make her give. The cow flinched and threatened with her hind leg.

"Well, you might say he was a preacher," Grady said, sipping from the vanilla jar. "He ran a country newspaper. Most guys that run newspapers think they operate under some kind of divine inspiration." He climbed up the lot fence, one slab at a time, and perched on the top plank, braced against a corner pole. "And maybe they do."

Elliott put a rope around the calf's neck and dragged it away and tied it to the fence. The brindle heifer stood at the feed trough, munching cottonseed. "I'll be through in a hurry," Elliott said, squatting on his heels beside the cow. "Just open her up a little and let the calves have the rest."

"I'd help you," Grady said, "but I'm afraid I'm a bit out of practice at that kind of thing."

"Jes hand me a little more of that jar."

Grady took a drink and gave it to him. "Kill it."

Killing it required several swallows. Then Elliott flipped the bottle over a stack of maize bundles beyond the feed lot. "Nother dead soljer," he said. "All a soljers dead." He stared quietly toward the place where the bottle had landed. Then he laughed, a big happy laugh, for the first time in many days, and he began to hurry again, faster now, untying the calf, roping off the other one, tugging frantically at the second cow's teats. The cow pivoted around on her forefeet and he followed her in an awkward crouch, cursing absently. One of her teats was cracked, and she kept flicking a rear leg at Elliott whenever he pulled too hard at it. With the pail less than half full, he gave up and turned the calf back to her, then went under the shed, hurrying, and began spreading more cottonseed in the feed trough.

After the rain the clouds had hung low over the land, and now far above there was the black of coming night and along the distant horizon lay a thin icy white band of sky that spread cold shadows from the west. In the lightless gloom under the shed, Elliott worked feverishly, feeling the alcohol numb and fire him at the same time, washed in a dream sense of his own frenzy drawn against the hard silent surface around him, out there, the gray air, fixed points of silver and black, the animals rolling cuds dully munching quietly, Grady rocking gently on the rail fence.

"Here," Elliott said, handing him the milk pail. "Take this on to the house. I'm gonna see if I can get the tractor started. Just give it to Mama, or put it on the back porch. She'll find it."

The tractor was behind the barn, parked beside a cluster of kerosene drums along the pasture fence. Elliott set the hand clutch and opened the throttle and began to heave at the heavy flywheel, pulling it through a quarter turn. The compression threw it back and he heard the thick, sucking slush of the cylinders. After six or seven attempts, he stood back and leaned against the bullwheel to catch his breath.

Grady reappeared. He had a slip of paper, on which Elliott's mother had written

> 5 lb potatoes
> light Bread
> s. pork (lb or so)
> canned toms.
> Koolade—get some of each

"She said to tell you, just charge it," Grady said.

"I don't think anybody's going anywhere to charge anything," Elliott said. "Somebody forgot to put the can back on the smokestack." He pointed to the upright exhaust pipe above the motor. "We always keep a tin can over it when she's not running. Or supposed to. Somebody forgot. Probably me. Anyway, it rained in her, and she's drowned out. Damn these old Poppin Johnnies . . . I wouldn't give two cents for every John Deere ever made." He was secretly proud of the tractor, the first his father had ever owned, and he was more disappointed than angry that it wouldn't start. He climbed up on the toolbar to check the throttle again, and saw Old Phoebe nosing up to the fence in the falling light.

"Grady, there's a rope halter over there on the fence behind that coal-oil barrel. Can you reach it?"

"Godamighty," Grady said, "that's a plow horse."

"Well, you're not Gene Autry. You want some beer or not?"

Old Phoebe bowed her head obediently when Elliott went to her with the halter. He swung up on her gently, and when he was settled, she moved forward very slowly. "Climb up on the lot fence," he said to Grady, "and I'll ride her over there. She ought to be able to carry double, no bigger than you are."

"Smooth as a spring buggy runnin in damp sand," Grady said. "O flow, good wines, and wimmen, deign to smile. . . ."

Now it was dark. They rode down through the pasture, past the orchard, and across a patch of maize toward the road. The bar ditch was wide and deep and running slow with foamy dark water; they got off and led the horse carefully across, then remounted and went on up the muddy road in the starless night.

DEAL. The shack was brown and wet-black. A blurred window held the faint, jaundiced glow of a kerosene lamp. "What you want," said a dark figure in the door.

"Is Sed here?" Elliott said. "Mister Sed?" The figure disappeared, closing the door, and finally they heard the heavy, masculine voice.

"Hey, hey. Somebody looking for ole Sed?" Then he was at the door.

"Mister Sed," Elliott said grandly. "Mist*ah* Sed."

"Hey, yes sir, heavy on that 'mistah.' Now, what you-all need?"

"We thought you might have some suds around," Elliott said. "Or maybe a little lightning."

"Do I know you boys?" Sedberry said.

"You know me," Elliott said. "Elliott Randall. This is Grady."

78   "Mistah Randall's boy," Sedberry said. "You changed

some since I recall. Let's see. You was the one in the armed force, I believe. When you get out?"

"Quite a while now. In the spring."

"I don't believe I've seen you all this time."

"No. I stick pretty close to home."

"And you-all is looking for some old juice. Heh. Well, you-all just step in and we'll look a bit."

The room they entered was tiny and dark, seeped through with a heavy sweetness of copper and urine. Sedberry took the lamp and went into the back room, leaving the door open, and they could hear his voice and that of the woman, quarreling quietly, through the thin shadows from the door. Grady squinted intently at something on the wall, a page torn from a magazine and held with straightpins at the top corners. The page was yellowed and curled. "Why Young People Go Wrong," he read softly. "Sheik Fathers and Flapper Mothers." He saw the neck of a guitar protruding from beneath a bed in the corner, and he went over to look at it.

"What you-all rather have?" Sedberry said from the back room. "You-all rather have beer or whiskey?"

"Whatever you've got," Elliott said. "Hardest thing you got, I guess."

"This here is Mister Sed's first-class world's-fair deluxe soothing juice. Heh." He held up a fruit jar in the door, and the light behind it centered in the cloudy brown liquid. "This here fix you up everything that ails you."

"Looks like homebrew to me," Grady said.

"It almost is. Almost nearly. It's some I hain't capped up yet, don't have no great fizz to it, but sholey do the trick, if you only looking for something to sip."

"You mean it hasn't cooked off yet?"

"This here my special recipe, don't need no cooking off. 79

You go on, take you a taste." He handed the jar to Grady.

"Smells sort of like apple cider," Elliott said.

"Godamighty, it ain't," Grady said hoarsely. "Tastes more like six miles of barbed wire. I've drunk horsepiss and coal-oil that wudn't that bad."

"Green as a gourd," Elliott said, coughing. "This all you got, Mister Sed?"

"Matter of fact, it is," he said. "Been working on a new batch, gonna have this capped up maybe two or three days."

"You mean this stuff isn't even a week old?" Elliott said.

"No, but it got the punch. And I sell her cheap."

"How much?"

"I sell you that jar there for one dollar. Done cheap at twice the price."

"Let's have another swig or two to get in the bargaining mood," Grady said. He pulled the guitar from under the bed. "You play this thing?"

"Yessir, I bangs on it some."

"Come on," Elliott said. "Let's go find something to cut this stuff with—"

"Hang on there, far-darting Achilles. I want to hear him play. What do you play, Sed?"

"Oh, not much." He took the instrument, making hollow bumping sounds in the exchange. "What you want to hear? 'Silver Dew on the Blue Grass'? I can do that one pretty good. Maybe something like 'Pistol-Packing Mama.' I heard that old boy on the radio, he sure enough—"

"You know any of those old blues songs, like Lemon Jefferson does?"

"Who?"

"Blind Lemon Jefferson."

"Nossir, I don't believe I know the name."

"Or Leadbelly or Scrapper Blackwell, like 'Ain't You Glad'?"

"That the one they call 'Blood Done Sign My Name'?" He sat down on the bed and crossed his legs, carefully adjusting the guitar in his lap, shifting his arms and settling it against him, then sighting down the neck for a chord he could not possibly see there in the airless shadows. He struck the strings carefully, slowly, and began a shuffling, throbbing rhythm that broke and descended at intervals into heavy aching runs that seemed deeper and greater than the battered rosewood box could bear. Then he settled into a tinny, mechanical strum and began to sing

in my hand, in my hand, yes the blood done sign my name

in my hand, in my hand, yes
the blood done sign my name
ohhh   blood   done   sign   myyy   name

He looked up at Grady. "That the one you talking about?"

"Yes. Something like that."

"Well, it ain't no blues. That's a church song. I don't know what you want to hear that old stuff for."

"That ol' box sounds pretty good," Grady said.

"You want to peck on it awhile? Here, go ahead."

"No," Grady said. "I'm a southpaw. The wires is upside down. How'd you like to sell it?"

"Well. How'd you like to buy it?"

Grady turned to Elliott. "What'd I earn today?"

"Oh, let's see. Four and a half, maybe five hours . . . call it two dollars and a half."

"Give you two and a half for it," Grady said.

"Nossir, I couldn't hardly do that."

"And let you rub the hump for good luck."

Sedberry laughed nervously. "Nossir, I'd have to have about five dollars."

"Looky here," Grady said. "It's all beat up, the bridge is split, neck's probably warped, and I'd have to restring it before I could hit a note. On top of that, today is my birthday. Yessir, I come into this old world thirty-eight years ago today." He grinned. "All that, looks like you could cut your price some."

"Four dollars and six-bits."

"Four and a quarter."

Sedberry laughed apologetically. "Nawsir," he drawled, shaking his head slowly.

"Split the difference. Four-fifty."

"Naww, can't . . ."

"Come on. Last time. Four and a half."

"Add on a dime, and you got you a deal."

Grady looked at Elliott. "Am I good for another day's work?"

"You're good for it."

"Pay the man. And *you* can rub my hump for luck. Way we're getting taken by this man, you'll need it." Sedberry laughed.

"Come on," Elliott said to Grady. He was losing the light edge of the vanilla and liquor they'd drunk. "Let's go on down to the store before it closes and get some Orange Crush or grapefruit juice or something to kill this with."

"Don't you think we ought to talk him out of another
jar, just in case of snakebite?"

"Tell you what," Sedberry said. "You-all are pretty good boys. I'll let you have the jitter box and two jars of my juice all for six dollars and, hmmm, forty-seven cents."

"What's the odd cents for?" Elliott said.

"Heh. Well, a man's got to figure his overhead close. I'm just figuring the overhead close for you-all. I swear, I lose money on ever deal, but the turnover keeps me going."

They left the horse tied to a spindly thicket of lilac in Sedberry's yard and went off down the road toward the two lights that glared in domes of silver mist above a clump of buildings.

They passed a church and the cemetery, and Elliott thought of his grandfather buried there, and he'd never once gone to see the grave. Beyond the church were the ruins of the building where he'd attended school, now abandoned and decaying in the high summer weeds, and they passed small dark houses scattered at intervals along the road, then into the light across the silvery ginyard bright beneath the floodlamp from a high pole beside the weight office. They went into the darkness behind the gin and found the door to the seedhouse open and put the guitar and liquor there, each taking a big burning gulp from one of the jars before they hid them in a corner and covered them with cottonseed.

Across the road they could see several men up on the high porch of the store, scattered about on benches and upended soft-drink cases in the dim shadows of a single bare yellow bulb that dangled down from the wooden awning above an ancient gas pump. As Elliott and Grady picked their way across the muddy ruts in the road, a small boy dashed from behind the pump, kicked the pop   83 case from under one of the men, and ran the length of the porch into the darkness, screaming a mortal joy. "You little son of a bitch," the man said, getting up and throwing the carton after the fleeing boy. One of the men said, "Them pop cases is kind of hard on the old nuts when you fall thataway, ain't they, Dud?" The men laughed. Dud said, "If Box don't do something with that little shit, I'm gonna stop trading here."

"Hey, that'll put the fear of the Lord in 'em," a man said. "Box couldn't keep his doors open if it wudn't for all them Dr. Peppers and peanut rounders you eat."

Elliott nodded to the men on the porch. He knew most of them: Old Man Brewster, Less Pirtle, Chinless Bill Story, Tom Lightner, Leroy Teed, several others who were familiar but whose names he could not recall. There were two younger fellows he didn't know, or didn't recognize, the one called Dud and a thickset kid who wore sideburns and a Navy dungaree shirt. His face seemed faintly familiar and when Elliott passed him he saw the word "Teed" stenciled on the dungaree shirt and knew he must be one of Leroy's brothers, but there were so many of them he couldn't remember a name to go with the face.

"Yawl get much rain down yore way, Elliott?" Old Man Brewster said.

"Little over an inch," he said, observing the ritual. "You?"

"Gauge is broke," the old man said, spitting beside the bench he sat on, "but I'd say three-quarters to a inch."

"Seemed like it was pretty general, wasn't it?"

Old Man Brewster nodded, and another of the men said, "I was talking to Burney Elkins, lives up yonder by Three-Mile, said it come a gully washer out that way, clear on into Lamar. Says they was water running in town dang near up over the hubcaps."

"Dad went over to Uncle Ode's before the cloud came up," Elliott said. "He hadn't come in when we left the house, so I guess they got it over there, too." He could feel the liquor deadening along the sides of his face, flushed and easy all at once, and he went on talking with the men as he rarely could, about crops and machinery and the weather, until his glow began to fade and he thought again about Grady and the cache of liquor and remembered why they had come to the store. "Well, we got to get some things and get on home," he said.

There were no customers in the store. A plump girl of about sixteen sat on a bent kitchen stool behind the counter, reading *Screen Stories* and trying to blow bubbles with her gum, rolling and arranging it over her tongue and puffing flatulent, abortive splats. "Hello, Frieda Mae," Elliott said. "You holding down the fort all by yourself?"

"Oh, Mama's back yonder behind the meatcase somewhere," she said. Without moving, still staring into the magazine, she shifted her gum into her jaw and raised her voice and said, "Mama, they're out there teasing Johnny Boy again!"

"Well, that's Johnny Boy's lookout," said a voice in the back, and then they saw her, coming out of the storeroom, lugging a case of canned goods. She was a huge woman, a larger and older version of Frieda Mae, and her face ran with sweat as she maneuvered the box toward its proper shelf and lowered it to the floor with a thud. She stood up, gasping for breath and wiping her face with the stained butcher's apron she wore. "Whatchall need, Elliott?"

"Mama sent a list," he said, handing it to her. "Put in a big can of grapefruit juice, too, and a couple pairs of work gloves."

"Swear," she said, scanning the list, "we're jist about out of spuds. Emmett's gone to Lubbock for a load of chicken feed and some fresh produce, but he ain't back yet." It was common knowledge that Emmett Box made business trips to Lubbock twice a week in his jitney Diamond T truck, bought whiskey from a bootlegger in the flats, and slept with a whore at the Knapp Hotel. When the trip fell on a Saturday, he never returned earlier than the following Tuesday.

Elliott followed Mrs. Box back to the meatcase and ate a cold wiener while she sliced the salt pork and wrapped it. At the counter, Grady was talking to Frieda Mae, who said nothing and pretended to ignore him. But Elliott saw that she had put down the magazine and was filing her nails, and she began to giggle now and then at one of Grady's particularly elaborate gestures. "I sweeearr! if you're not the silliest old thang," she said, giggling.

"He working for yall?" Mrs. Box said.

"I guess so," Elliott said. "Dad picked him up somewhere and brought him home today."

"Well, I tell you right now," she said, "I ain't going to charge nothing to him. We've done lost enough on these transhunts. He can put whatever he wants on yall's ticket, but I ain't going to charge nothing to him."

"He doesn't look like much of a risk, I'll admit," Elliott said, grinning.

"No, it ain't that. I'm not one for holding nobody's looks against 'em. He cain't hep it if he's cripple. I reckon if it wudn't for his back he'd be right handsome, all that wavy black hair and all . . . but poor thing cain't hep the way his back is. No; it's jist that we've lost all we're going to on these transhunts, and I ain't charging no more to none of 'em, unless it's on somebody's ticket I know. I'll charge to my regular Mescans, them that comes up ever year, and I'll charge to anybody's hand that'll sign their tickets. But we've done lost enough on these transhunts jist drifting through, say they're working for so-and-so, charge up a big bill, work maybe a day or so, and then take off like a turpentine cat."

She gathered up the other things on the list and took them to the counter. "Listen now," she said decisively, as if much worry and deliberation had gone into the matter. "I am just not going to put in any of them old spongy taters, they ain't fit to eat. You tell your mama we was out, which we nearly are, and I'll send her some good ones in a day or so if I catch somebody going down that way. Or you might try at the café . . . they buy by the bulk on some things and once in a while Bud'll sell you a pound or two, if that hussy of his ain't got her back up about something." She tried to squeeze past Frieda Mae to get to the box where they kept the credit tickets. "Well, move!" she snapped at the girl. "Jist set there like a big bump on a log." Frieda Mae wandered off around the store and finally found her way back to a row of shelves near the pop cooler where Grady sat. She stood there flicking a feather duster listlessly from time to time while he resumed their conversation with comic gestures and furtive whispers behind Mrs. Box.

Outside, Johnny Boy had climbed the gas pump and was listening to Chinless Bill telling a story about a one-legged whore in Waxahachie. Less Pirtle saw him and said, "Get off there, you little fart. You're too young for such things."

"Kiss my ass," the boy said. When Elliott and Grady came out, he climbed down off the pump and went over to Elliott. "What you got in the sack?" he said. "Gimme some of what you got in the sack."

One of the men said, "Better watch old Flossie there."

"I ain't Flossie," the boy yelled, kicking the gas pump.

"She'll throw you and blow you if you don't watch her," Leroy Teed said.

"You shut up," the boy said. "You bastard. I'll tell my daddy on you and he'll make you get off this porch."

"You better watch your mouth, Flossie," said the Teed boy in the Navy shirt. His voice was flat and harsh, and the air of easy banter stopped for a moment.

"Is your name Flossie?" Elliott said lightly to the boy.

"That's old Flo," one of the men said. "Ain't she sweet, now? Look at them rosy cheeks and that fat little ass. Kiss me, Flossie."

"You old bastard," the boy said, running at the man with fists clenched.

"Take it easy, Greasy," the man said, averting his head to miss a weak thrust from the boy. "You're cruisin for a bruisin."

"Hey, Flossie," Less Pirtle said, "I heard if you jackoff it'll make a hair grow in your hand."

The boy glared at him defiantly, and without thinking brought up his hand to look. The men roared, and the boy snickered reluctantly, knowing he was trapped but at the same time trying to establish his smooth but grimy palm as proof of innocence.

"Say, Flossie," Chinless Bill said, "you drive your mule up to lope him, or you jist wait till he comes up?" They laughed again, and Johnny Boy screamed obscenities.

88   Grady followed Elliott down off the high porch and

out across an open plot of ground to a corrugated-tin building some twenty yards beyond Box's store. Faded letters on the side indicated that the building had once housed a blacksmith shop and garage. A newer but cruder sign jutting out from the false front read "BUD & SHIRLEYS CAFE."

"What're you going that way for," Grady said. "The gin is back yonder, idn't it?"

"In a minute," Elliott said. "Be right with you."

"I'll wait out here," Grady said, settling himself against a porch rail and taking out his harmonica. Through the front windows of the café, he saw a man playing a pinball machine in the corner. The man was pudgy and balding, and he wore a dirty apron rolled up around his waist. He pushed and tugged at the pinball machine, sweat glistening on his pink face.

Elliott sat down at the counter. "Evening, Bud," he said, but the man did not look up or acknowledge his greeting. For several minutes, while Elliott fidgeted with a sugar jar, he went on shoving and pounding and tipping up the front of the machine to slow down the balls. When they were all gone, he cursed, slapped a slug into the coin slide, then yelled "Fluffy! Goddammit!" still without looking up and started the next game.

Somewhere in the back, above the bump and click and thump of the pinball machine, a child cried, and eventually a woman appeared from the kitchen, fastening back a strand of her cinnamon hair with a bobby pin. "Why, hello, honey," she said to Elliott. There was tension in her face, behind her eyes, but she smiled at him. "Haven't seen you in a while. How you doing?"

"Okay," he said.

"How's your mama and them?"

"All right I guess. Uh, Fluffy, you got any potatoes?"

"Potatoes? Sure. Fried, mashed, baked—what you want to go with them?"

"I mean just raw potatoes. Mrs. Box is all out, see, and I thought maybe you'd let me have a couple of pounds or so."

"Well . . . I don't know." She glanced quickly across at Bud. "Could we sell Elliott some spuds?" The only answer was a string of curses directed at the pinball machine, which had tilted. She said, "I guess it'll be all right. If I can find a sack. How come you're not out chasing gals, don't you know it's Saturday night?"

Elliott grinned, looking down awkwardly. "Shoot. What girls are there around here to chase."

"Well now. How about Gail Coursey? Or one of the Teed girls? Or that cute little gal of Huffakers'? I bet you've got a dozen hearts fluttering after you all the time."

"Aw, they're all just kids, still in high school. Or else got six guys hanging around already."

"So what? You'd only be one more, wouldn't you? Seven's a lucky number."

"TIME TO CLOSE UP!" It was Bud. He yanked the plug on the pinball machine, gave it a final kick, and started around the café turning off lights.

"Guess I'd better get on my way," Elliott said.

"Here." She handed him a lard can filled with potatoes. "I couldn't find a sack. And we don't have any scales, so I just guessed. It ought to be at least two or three pounds."

"How much I owe you?"

"Just take them," she said, lowering her voice.

90   "No, I want to—"

"CLOSING TIME!"

"Go on, honey." She glanced nervously toward Bud. "You can pay me later. I'll get it back, don't you worry." She smiled.

On the way past Box's store to the seedhouse where they'd hidden the liquor, Grady said, "Bygod, from afar 'tis beauty truly blent . . . and where is any author in the cosmos teaches such beauty as a fair damsel's eye. How come you didn't invite me in there to bask in the rays of pulchritude?"

"Fluffy? Yeah. She's a really nice person. I sure feel sorry for her."

"How come?"

"Well . . . that guy she's married to, for one thing."

"I'll be goddam," Grady said. He stopped and looked back. "Beauty and the Beast. Who'd have thought it. Well, that goes to show, you can't ever tell about us freaks." He walked on, then stopped and turned back again to look at the café. It was dark except for a single bare bulb over the sign. "I'll bet his name is Shirley, and she's Bud."

Elliott snickered. "She's Shirley all right. But everybody calls her Fluffy. I don't know why."

"Wouldn't be too hard to guess."

"Nobody around here can figure out why she married him. From what I hear, he met her when he was off working at the bomber plant in Fort Worth during the war. Some people say she married him for money, say he promised her a bunch of stuff and every time she threatens to leave, he buys her a car or something and then can't make the payments on it and the finance company takes it back. Might be something to that—his folks used to be pretty well off, owned a piece of land with a good well or two on it, but him and his old man drank and gambled most of it away. I don't know. You hear all kinds of rumors. I don't believe much of it. She's always real nice to me."

"Well, if it was me in your place I sure wouldn't complain about that," Grady said.

"You're taking it all wrong. Heck, she's a lot older than me, and besides, she's married and got two kids."

"Yes," Grady said, with a heavy sigh, "I see you have much to learn."

They pushed open the sliding doors of the seedhouse and groped their way inside, fumbling around in search of the liquor jars.

"Darker'n a witch's tit," Grady said, with mock indignation. "Vous criez, Tout est bien, d'une voix lamentable."

"What's that mean?" Elliott said. "Hurry up and open that jar, I've about lost my high."

"Hell, how do I know?" Grady said, grunting, twisting off the lid of the Mason jar. "But it sounds good, don't it?" He repeated the phrase.

"Too es byen," Elliott echoed. "That means 'All is good.' Or maybe 'All is well.' Yeah, I think that's what it means. Sort of like Mexican. Muey way-no."

Grady had the lid off and was taking a hurried sip from the jar. He swallowed it, groaning, and almost choked. "God, that's terrible," he said, handing the jar to Elliott. "Wish I had a barrel of it."

"Where'd you learn French?" Elliott said.

"Ah, parley-voo franscase. When me and Sergeant York was on the Western Front in nineteen-and-eighteen, no-man's-land bygod, saving the world for democracy—and I'm here to tell you it was rough, killing Huns all day and romancin the beautiful mamzells all night, and oh, they was long and lovely and hot and hungry, nest pass? And me and old Sergeant York used to—"

Elliott was following him avidly until he realized that Grady could have been no more than nine or ten years old in 1918. "Aw, come on," he said. "You don't even know French. "That's just something you memorized."

Grady turned to face him. "You are assaulting the honor and integrity of a gentleman, sir," he said coldly, and there was an uneasy silence of several seconds before Elliott knew he was joking, and then Grady laughed.

Elliott said, "I tried to learn some French when I was overseas." He remembered the widow of the French officer who said —Je suis seule ce soir avec mes rêves, but he didn't know then what it meant. He met her in Casablanca. In the Select Bar. She sipped crème de menthe and told him of her husband who had been killed in Tunisia and later she took him to her room. She was once pretty but she was growing old. He tried, but it was all very strange and he was still weak from the hospital, and finally she had to do it herself. Then she said —Ah, darling, it is all right. Il faut gémir quand nous faisons l'amour. She sat by the window. —Je suis seule ce soir avec mes rêves. He had not thought about her since. "I shacked up one time with this French girl in Casa. Really good-looking, you know, really built and everything, about eighteen or nineteen . . ." Immediately he was disgusted with himself for lying. He took another drink and handed the jar to Grady. "But she knew English pretty well—"

"Puts me in mind of a girl named Fay," Grady said. "Bindery gal for a book publisher where I was a while, one time in Pennsylvania. My, how she loved to get her loving."

"That where you learned French?"

"Fay was a great big old Irish gal. No, it wasn't no language she taught me."

"Let's open up that grapefruit juice," Elliott said. "I can't take this stuff straight."

Grady carried the can of grapefruit juice to the door, where there was a faint haze of light from the pole across the ginyard. He squatted down and punctured the can with a makeup rule. "We don't have anything to mix it in yet," he said. "The jar's still too full. Unless maybe you're thinking of pouring some of it out."

"No, I wouldn't want to do that."

"Well, just chase it for a while, straight from the can," Grady said. "Squaring the circle is a question of approximation involving irrationals, and besides, maybe there'll come some joyous queen to bear us the twisted gold meadcup, some ring-adorned maiden, as the Old Jedge used to say. . . ." He rolled the doors together, muttering to himself, and went back to the corner where they had put the groceries and the guitar and the other jar of liquor. "I don't suppose you ever knew the Old Jedge, did you?" he said, looking at Elliott through the darkness that was beginning to lift now as their eyes became accustomed to it.

"Who?"

"Jedge Piroute. Matthew Arnold Piroute, Esquire."

"Runs the paper in Lamar?"

"*Ran* it. They buried him a couple of weeks ago. So I'm told. Six months to the day after he sold out to some big-time boys from the city."

"Seems like I heard something about it. Sort of an onery old cuss, always raising cain, stirring things up, wasn't he? I remember my grandad used to read the paper and get so mad he could hardly talk. I never did understand it much, but Grandad was always saying that one of these days somebody would run that old pirooter out of town. That's what he called him: that old pi-rooter."

"Yep. That's the Jedge."

"Didn't somebody sue him one time, and then they had a big fistfight on the courthouse lawn during the trial? I barely remember it. . . ."

"Could have been any one of a hundred times." Grady chuckled. "The Old Jedge was a veritable plague visited upon this land, and the people had a Joblike time endur-ing him. Yessir, he drank his whiskey in the open and spat on the sidewalk, and he hated their gods and made fun of their politics and he even set hisself up to instruct them on the finer points of human behavior, down to and including reproduction. They might have tolerated all that, but he also coveted their worldly goods, little enough of which he ever got. *That* was something they could never forgive him. He wanted to be a prophet, and rich at the same time."

Elliott was confused. He could not understand why his grandfather would not have sympathized with, or at least happily tolerated, such a man as Grady described. Maybe it was because his grandfather had been an old man and had not himself understood. Or maybe Grady was just shooting the breeze again. Making it all up. But he sounded serious. Maybe it's because I'm about half drunk, Elliott thought. He took another sip from the jar, swigged some grapefruit juice, and let himself slip back into a mound of cottonseed at the base of the big pile that reached almost to the ceiling twenty or thirty feet above him. He decided once and for all that he liked

Jedge Piroute. "Souns like a man after m' own heart," he said, happily exaggerating the thickness in his voice.

"He taught me the printing trade," Grady said. "That wily old bastard." Elliott thought he sounded almost wistful. No, reflective. Hell, Grady couldn't sound reflective. Just quiet. And faraway. Elliott settled into the cottonseed, listening drowsily.

"I was just a kid," Grady said. "Run away from home, counting cross ties for the first time. Old Jedge hired me to feed his collie dogs and hoe weeds off a vacant lot he owned, where the *Messenger* shop is now. He was printing in a little old hole-in-the-wall over on Main Street in those days, had him a·old fourpage Babcock and a old Model 14 Linotype and about three fonts of busted type. Finally traded somebody out of a dinkly little old four-column casting box, and put me to work on that, casting boilerplate and killing type, pouring pigs for that old Model 14."

Elliott said, without much interest, "Where was your home, where you ran away from?"

"Montague County. Little place called Sunset, north of Fort Worth. Except I was living with one of my sisters in Wichita when I run away. It's a long story. My old daddy died . . . he was a funny, mean little old feller; there was a story that he'd been in trouble with the law a long time ago when he was a young man, said he'd squealed on the gang for robbing trains and got off with a pardon, had to change his name and leave wherever it was he was from, and settled there on a piece of wornout bottom land there in Montague County. But I don't know if a word of it's true. Anyway, he'd been married once before and had a family, before him and my mama got hitched. I never knew my mama. She died having me, and the rest of the kids were all grown up and married off by then. Runt of the litter, that's what my daddy always called me. But he was a good old man, when he wasn't on a tear, and he taught me how to drink whiskey and when to cuss, and he said to me, Grady, nearly everbody's got some kind of a hump on their back. Grady-cum-lady, he'd say. Old hunchback Grady." He paused to sip from the jar and then gave it back to Elliott. "Well, he died when I was about fourteen, and they took me to live with one of the married gals in town. But I didn't get along too good with them. I was used to living out there with my daddy in the country, and so I just took off one day on the Fort Worth highway and never did go back."

"We lived in Fort Worth one time. . . ."

"Turned out to be a long way around to the West Coast. Got to Amarillo, grabbed the wrong rattler and went south instead of west. Yep—south to these goddam windy West Texas plains. Crapped out in a boxcar and next thing I knew there was the Old Jedge goosing me with his cane and yelling ever dirty word you ever thought about. Turned out I'd made my bed on his consignment of newsprint." He laughed. "Lordy how that man could cuss. I tell you, it was a pure art with him, and a lovely thing to behold, once you got used to it. 'Gawwwd dahhm ut,' he'd say, like that, like a yankee . . . and he could give it ever shade of meaning from you-know-what to pretty-please. I was used to some rough treatment, but that old man could scald your hide off with about six good words. He had me scared to death the whole time I worked for him. Which wasn't too long."

"From what you said, I thought you'd been working for him all this time," Elliott said.

"Pretty close to twenty-five years now . . . but that's   97 just off and on. Never long at a time. I'm a tramp, son. Feet built too close to the road. No, first time I worked for the Old Jedge lasted about two months, and thanks to him, since then I've seen about ever place worth seeing on this side of the water." Grady laughed. "I let one of his collie dogs get loose, and then on top of that, the same week he was trying to teach me the type case and I set a typo that didn't nobody catch on the proofs. It had come up one of those big old spring dusters, must of blowed sand for two weeks straight, see. The Old Jedge wrote a story about it, and he come up with one of those screwball, old-timey three-decker headlines nobody but him could write. I won't forget that one, long as I live. Supposed to say, 'Mayor Calls on Citizens to Pass over Main Street to Keep It from Blowing Away.' But I set it from a scrambled case, and it come out 'Piss' instead of 'Pass.' "

Elliott choked on a long sip from the liquor jar. He handed it away, coughing, giggling, tears running down his face.

"You'd have thought I'd raped the preacher's daughter," Grady said. "The old man his self had yelled out stuff worse than that fifty times a day, in hearing distance of half the town, but he took on like a bobtail filly in flytime over that typo. Said I'd defamed the denizens of the grandest city on God's earth and deliberately wrecked his business, broke his pore old heart, left him high and dry to get the paper out all by his self. Charged me with everthing but stealing the subscription list. Run a story on the front page next week, said I was just a bent-up little pissant and anybody that seen me ought to step on me. I guess if he'd had a wife or daughter there's no telling what I'd been up for. 'Course it was all lies except the part about leaving him to do all the work—*that's* what was bothering him. No, he didn't have to fire me that time; I figured he might kill me if he caught me. California looked mighty good, and I sure wasn't sad about leaving these dusty plains. A couple of years later, me and a old Wobbly was passing through on our way to slug-up on a new daily up in Ohio. We needed to make a day for grub, so I figured what the hell, I'd look in on the Old Jedge. Met me at the door with a apron and a line gauge. Never said a word. Just poured me a swig of Beam, pulled his eyeshade down, and went back to cussing and sticking type."

"How long you stay that time?" Elliott said.

"I dunno. Not long. The Old Jedge had a habit of firing everbody about twice a year, just on principle. Godamighty, what a tantrum he could throw! One time when he'd blew up and tied the can on the whole crew, we was all standing around waiting to get our pay, and a machine tramp comes in fresh off the road, looking for a day's work. Now here's the Old Jedge with the whole week's paper to get out his self, and I knew he was damned anxious not to turn away no help. But he'd die before he'd let on. So he tells the dude he's not hiring. Well, the dude proceeds to set his self down at the machine and whips out a dirty old silk handkerchief, spreads it on the keyboard, and pecks out a clean galley of type in about two seconds, blind. That was too much even for the Jedge. He says to the tramp, 'What do you work for?' and the tramp, seeing the situation, says, 'A dollar a hour.' That was back in times when lots of people was working for a dollar a day and glad to get it. Oh my god. The Jedge cussed and he fumed and he stomped around, went outside and yelled at a kid going by, kicked a dog, threw 99 down his eyeshade, finally come back in and told the guy he was hired. Then he come over to pay us off, and he said, 'Hell, I was going to offer him at least a dollar and a half.'"

Elliott got up, laughing, and went over to the corner to urinate.

"Yessir, childern," Grady went on, "the Old Jedge was wheelin and dealin back in those days, promoting everbody right out of their shoes, running a front page full of rumors and lies and come-ons for the chamber of commerce plus all the blood and gore he came across or dreamed up, laughing his self sick at the way they gobbled it up and then cussed him for doing it, running the old *Messenger* ninety percent ads inside and the rest boilerplate, and on top of that he was hooking 'em right and left in the job shop and shuffling mortgaged machinery on the side, hiring and firing and cussing and praying for all he was worth." He chuckled and then was silent for a while, and then he said, "It took about all he could make to pay the lawyer for libel suits and buy whiskey and keep his old Packard running. When they bought him out, I reckon he got nearly enough out of the old *Messenger* to bury his self with. Where's that jar of juice? It's my birthday bygod, and I'm ready to celebrate."

LET ME BE YOUR SALTY DOG. They went to work in earnest on the liquor, feeling easy and happy. But even after several gulps, Sedberry's potion was still almost too strong to drink. It dropped sharp and bitter to the bottom of their stomachs and sent up a gassy aftertaste like ammonia that hung in the backs of their throats and rose through their nostrils and made their eyes wet and filmy. But they had begun to relish the discomfort; if nothing else, it gave proof of time and place. "I drink, therefore I am," Grady said. He climbed to the top of the high center pile of cottonseed and settled himself. Elliott started after him but the seed shifted and he went sprawling back to one of the smaller mounds. His laugh was cut short by a rustling sound outside, and he froze, shushing Grady in a whisper. Then one of the doors was eased open on its creaky rollers.

"Elliott?" said a heavy whisper. "Yall in there?"

"My god, scare me to death," Elliott said. "'S Frieda Mae."

"No," Grady said. "Free t'me. Two-bits to you."

"What you doing out here, Frieda Mae? Your mama'll throw a fit."

"Oh, she don't care. I brought yall some paper cups. What yall got in the jar?"

"The lady has come to share with us the nectar of the gods," Grady said, handing down the liquor to Elliott. "Don't show off your bad manners; get up and pour this fair damsel a draught of our choicest vintage that hath been cooled a long age in the deep delve-ed earth." Frieda Mae giggled.

Elliott floundered through the cottonseed to take the paper cups from Frieda Mae and then find the grapefruit juice. "Cocktails for three, coming up," he said. Even in the doorway the light was too dim for him to know exactly what he was doing, but without spilling any he managed to slosh some of the liquor into three cups, fill them with grapefruit juice, and slog back toward the pile of seed in the center. He handed two of the cups to the dark outline of Frieda Mae, who had seated herself primly on a mound about halfway up the big pile, and Grady slid down beside her to take his drink, almost causing an avalanche. "Heck," Frieda Mae said, after taking a sip, "I cain't taste nothing but the fruit juice."

"Bygod, bartender," Grady said, "when I order a drank, you bygod better leave the bottle, or I'm just liable to throw down on yew and blow yore head clean off." Elliott handed him the jar. Grady held it up in the dim light of the doorway as if examining the label. "Château Sedberry," he said. "Hmmm. Day before yesterday. That was a good year." Elliott, laughing and gasping for breath, fell down in a sprawl.

102   Grady resumed his exaggerated drawl. "Yessir, bar-

tender, I want yew to know," he said, "that yore a-messing with a man that's knowed from here to Waco for his steady aim and his darin resourcefulness and the lightnin draw of his trusty smokin sixshooters." Then he mimicked the voice of a child: "Hey, Paw, who *wuz* that 'ere masked man that give me this yere silver ca'tridge?" Frieda Mae giggled and poured from the jar.

"How's it taste now?" Elliott said.

"Better. But ugh! I cain't stand that grapefruit juice. Couldn't yall find something else to put in it? Here, gimme some more," she said to Grady, "to kill the grapefruit taste."

"Why don't you just sip it straight?" he said, and she did.

"My god, Frieda Mae," Elliott said. "You're a regular tosspot. I didn't know you had it in you."

"She hasn't, yet," Grady said.

"Yall are nasty," Frieda Mae said, giggling.

"Nobody's perfect," Grady said. He tried to put his arm around her and she pulled him across her lap and pushed him down the pile of seed. He clambered back up and caught her by the thigh and they began to wrestle, grunting and giggling and rolling around. They stopped and had another drink and then started all over. Frieda Mae climbed to the top of the big pile and waited for Grady to reach her, then she grabbed him by the shoulders and tossed him down the back slope and jumped after him, laughing so hard she began to hic. Elliott lay at the foot of the mound near the door and listened to them struggle. There was a lull, and then Grady's head appeared over the crest. He peered down into the darkness at Elliott. "Hey," he whispered. "Want dibs on first?"

"Iss your party."

"Yeah, but you're footing the bills."

"Happy birthday," Elliott said, giggling. "I might get lost in a wrinkle."

"Okay. Don't say I didn't invite you. It's your own fault. . . ." Grady disappeared into the darkness.

Yup, he thought. Iss m' own fault. One a my cultural faults. He laughed aloud. Can't stan' pigs. Sorry, iss jus a fault a mine. Cul-chu-ral fault. Good thing I'm drunk. Might take her on if it wudn't for that. Be like trying to put a wet noodle in a tiger's ass. He giggled to himself, listening to Frieda Mae's grunts and passionate protests and feeble denials, the mandatory ritual of country girls who steadfastly preserve their virginity through countless penetrations, copulations, orgasms.

Articles of clothing rained down from time to time, and Elliott was drifting away in the silence when Frieda Mae screamed "What are you doing!" in a voice neither passionate nor inquisitive. "What are you trying to do to me down there!" she yelled, and suddenly she appeared, huge and naked, on the crest of the cottonseed pile, screaming at the top of her voice. "Dirty queer!" she yelled. "I know what you are, you dirty prevert! You old ugly crippled prevert!" She bounded down the side of the pile in long strides, trying to find and pick up her clothes as she went, and she slipped and came rolling down in a flurry of flying clothes and cottonseed, crashed into Elliott, jumped up hopping on one leg trying to get her underwear on, tugged back the door, and ran off yelling insults, aspersions, threats.

Grady huffed over the pile, shirttail flapping, and sat down to put on his shoes. "Pervert," he said. "Godamighty."

104

"I didn't even know she knew the word," Elliott said.

Grady said, "Damn you, Grady Haker. Leaning too much on technique." He looked up at Elliott. "Heard once a famous man said it ain't the size, it's the technique. Don't believe nothing you hear and only half of what you see."

Elliott handed him the jar and he drank the liquor straight off, without any grapefruit juice. "Makes good mouthwash, at least," he said. "Hell, I supposed everybody savored the pleasures of standing at rack and manger before the meal. Been traveling in high society too long, I guess. Forgot about these country girls."

Elliott said, "I hope you won't pay any mind to what she said."

"Which insult?" Grady said. "About bein queer, or about bein cripple?" He laughed and took another drink.

"She's jus a dumb pig."

"I suppose . . ."

When Grady was more or less dressed, they struggled out the door, lugging the sack of groceries and the liquor jars and Grady's guitar, which he dragged along by the neck.

"Reckon she'll make trouble?" Grady asked.

"Dunno. If we can get across the ginyard in one piece, probably be all right. Don't feel much like making no tactical maneuvers."

"Anybody shoots, you light out. No use gettin yourself killed on my account."

Elliott laughed. "Crazy sombitch," he said. "I think you really mean it."

"Jus prop me up agin the wall and load up my trusty old hogleg and leave me one ca'tridge for my ownself. I'll hold 'em off till you can make good your escape. Thass a   105 order now, hear? Jus tell 'em back home I died a better man than I lived. O 'tis a far, far better thing that I do than that which I have ever done heretofore . . . whereas . . . the aforementioned . . ."

"She better not make trouble," Elliott said with drunken indignation. "After she guzzled down half our liquor and got herself felt up by the man with the greatest technique in the whole world. Not to mention size."

"No . . . let's don't talk about size," Grady said.

When they were almost to the gin office, the lights at the store went out. "Take cover," Elliott said, fearlessly falling into the spirit. "Ole Lady Box may have the cavalry out after our hides." They made a ragged, staggering dash to the office and hid in the shadows under the tin awning that covered the wagon scales. Elliott peeked around the corner. "We're safe," he said. "She's jus closin up for the night. Hand me that other jar." He could hear the men on the porch, laughing and talking in the dark. Then they began to leave, going off in various directions, and he saw shapes that he could identify as Leroy Teed and his brother and Dud and one of the other men coming along the road into the light from the gin pole. Johnny Boy followed them, splattering through mud puddles, although they tried to run him back from time to time with muttered threats and curses.

"Damn, I'll be glad when these goddam roads clears up, so's I can get back to town," said the Teed boy in the Navy shirt. One of the men called him "T. J." and Elliott placed him now in his mind.

"T. J.'s done got citi-fied on us," one of the men said. "All that high life in Lamar."

"Hell yes," T. J. said. "Yawl just green 'cause you ain't

got a big-paying job at the Chevrolet house like some people I know, and a fancy hotel room. . . ."

"Little bud," Leroy said, "if it's so dang fancy, how come you're out here ever weekend sponging off the folks? . . ."

"Up yours," T. J. said. "I'll have you know I come out here to hep Daddy fix that old truck. Him and Momma don't care for me comin out here—"

"Then how come you ain't fixed it?"

Someone said, "Heck, ain't nothing you can do in town you can't do right here, T. J."

"Shit I can't," T. J. said. "Go to the picture show, shoot some snooker, go out to the Y-Nott and play the new pinballs, they already got one of them fancy kind out there, got these little old flipper kind of things you hit the balls with. . . ."

"Bet you can't do this in town," Dud said, going up to the light pole and unbuttoning his pants, dancing around to get the tight jeans open. "Bet you can't piss on a street lamp in the middle of town."

When they came around the gin office, Elliott called out. "Hey, Leroy," he said, holding up the fresh jar. "You-all care to have one for the road?"

"Sonofagun," Leroy said happily, "yall been out here all this time? That real stuff, or something you got off a bootlegger?"

"C'mon and have a nip. More poison here'n we can carry home."

"What you got," Box's boy said, running up to the scales. "Yall got some whiskey, ain't you. I'm gonna tell my daddy, yall got some whiskey out here. You better give me a drink or I'll tell."

107

"You'll sprout wings and fly, you little shit," T. J. said. "Get the hell out of here."

"You can't make me, you dirty son of a bitch bastard," the boy said.

"Whew. Tastes like that well water down on the Wardlow place," Leroy said, coughing back tears. "I don't believe I've ever drank anything that foul before."

"Wait till a feel hits you. Taste wone matter, that happens. We got any that grapefruit juice leff, Grady?"

Grady rummaged around in the sack of groceries and found the grapefruit juice. Some of it had leaked out, and there were wads of cottonseed stuck to the can. Grady handed it to Elliott and sat down on the steps of the gin office and began fumbling around with the guitar, making jumbled, strident noises on the strings and cursing happily under his breath. Leroy sat down beside him. "I don't believe I know you," he said. "I'm Leroy Teed." They shook hands. "This is my little bud T. J., and this here is Dudley Thomas, and that old boy over there is Haskell Glenn."

"This my frin Grady," Elliott said. He was trying to mix drinks for everyone in paper cups, but he had to stop while introductions went around. "Grady," he said drunkenly and emphatically, "is the smartes man in the whooole world. With m' frin Grady it ain't the size that counts, iss the technique. Ain't that right?"

"You play much on that guitar?" Leroy said to Grady.

"Some. But I can't seem to get the sonofabitch in tune."

"Maybe that's because you're holding it backwards."

Grady was bent over the tuning screws, twisting them at random. He looked up. "You cagey rascal, you're drunker than I am," he said.

"Well, you are holding it wrong. Supposed to hold it around thataway."

Grady jumped to his feet, waving the guitar. "Goddammit, Grady, you addlepated idiot," he yelled. He sat down and began unwinding the headers and pulling off the strings. Leroy looked at Elliott with a puzzled frown, and Elliott shrugged.

"I believe that old boy's left-handed," Dud said. "He's got to string her upside down."

Elliott poured grapefruit juice into the liquor jar. He held the jar up, the way Grady had done in the seedhouse, as if to inspect the label. "Ahhh," he said. "Thass a good year, day before yesterday."

"Hey, quit muttering and pour us a drink, how about?" Dud said.

"Reckon it'll taste like salty dog?" Haskell said.

"Need gin for that," Elliott said. "This ain't no ordinary salty dog. . . ."

"That's a special breed," Grady said. "That there's a super-turbulent trisumptuous saline canine."

Elliott giggled, spilling some of the liquor. "Yeah," he said. "This here is Mistah Sed's Super-Turblent, Tri-whatever-you-said, Saline Canine." It took all of his breath to get it out.

T. J. said, "You talk awful fancy, don't you." He did not smile, and his voice was hard and cold. No one spoke. Elliott tried to think of something light to pass it off, but his mind was too fuzzy and the man's tone so old and familiar to him that it made him weary and angry and sick all at once, and he simply grinned and poured out the drinks and went over and sat down against one of the poles that supported the shed over the scales.   109

Leroy sipped gingerly from the paper cup. "That ain't salty dog," he said, "but it'll do till some comes along." He threw back his head and began to sing. *Got some taters fit to peel,* he sang, *need a mama good to feel.* Grady finished restringing the guitar and he joined in, picking up the fast breakdown beat and thumbing out runs with a country hammer-on. *I got you money in thirty-two, you let a Dallas daddy make a fool of you, honey let me be your salty dog.* They went through several verses, stomping around on the scales in a hollow thumping clatter.

"Hey, goddammit. Yawl gonna wake up somebody," T. J. said. He and Dud and Haskell were sitting on their heels up against the side of the gin office. Haskell said, "Hey, Dud, lemme see another one of them Eight-Page Bibles."

"I ain't got no more," Dud said. "Don't you ever get tired a reading fuck books?"

"Here," T. J. said. He fished out his billfold and took out a flattened wad of grease-stained papers, frayed and splitting along the creases where they'd been folded. He fanned them out in his hand. "What you want—Popeye, Betty Grable, or Winnie Winkle?"

"Lemme see Popeye. I don't think I seen that one."

T. J. flipped it to him. "Don't let us catch you slipping off in the dark," he said. "Them things'll sap your log if you don't watch out."

"Then how come you're always carrying a batch?"

"Same reason I carry this." He held his billfold up in the light so they could see the ring-shaped bulge in the middle of it. "Always be prepared. Boy Scout's motto." He went over and refilled his cup and came back.

110   Box's boy said, "Gimme a drink of what yall got."

"Flossie, a sniff of this and a Tootsie Roll would lay your ass out clean."

"Aw, come on. Gimme a sip."

"Ain't it about your bedtime, Flossie?"

"Come here and give me a goodnight kiss, Flo."

"Don't call me that, you bastard," Johnny Boy said.

"Don't you call me no bastard. Flo, honey, you're a real sweetheart, you know that? Look at them sweet dimples, T. J."

"She's a sweet piece all right," T. J. said. "Come here, Flossie, and play me a tune on the old bone phone."

"You ol' shitass."

"I told you, don't call me no shitass."

Haskell said, "Yall hear that'n about this old boy that drove up to a gas station hunting for the crapper—?"

"Gotta go, you gotta go," Dud said thickly.

"Let him tell the story," T. J. said.

"Well, he'd done taken a big dose a salts, see, and man, his bowels was really in a uproar, so he guns up to this gas station, see, and he jumps out and he says to the old boy running the place, Where's the john? It's one a them kinda junky old places, see, and the old boy says, Well all there is, is a old one-holer out yonder in back. So this old boy he takes off like a streak outta hell around the corner, man, he is really digging out."

"I awready heard it," T. J. said.

"Aw, go on and tell it," Dud said.

"Well, he ain't hardly outta sight when the old boy running the place remembers about this real low clothes-line they got stretched back there, where the old lady's put out her wash, and he goes around there to tell him to watch out for it, and all of a sudden he hears the gol-damndest noise and commotion, bam, pow, kaabuweey! 111

And all the yellin and hollerin and cussin, the goddam-mest uproar you ever heard. So he run on around there, and he seen the old boy a-laying there on the ground, all tangled up in that clothesline, and man, he is spread out and skinned up and bloody, and I mean a mess, he has done shit, and what I mean, it is all over him, covered up in shit and blood and ripped-up clothes, and he's just a-laying there spitting out teeth and a-puffing and a-moan-ing. So the old gas station boy, he says, Goldang, buddy, I'm plum sorry I forgot to tell you about that dang wash-line. And the old boy just looks up at him, kinda through one eye, sort of sheepish, through all that shit and stuff, and he says, Aw shoot, thass awright—I wouldn't never a made it anyhow."

"I know what you said," Box's boy yelled. "I'm gonna tell my daddy."

"I'm gonna kill your ass," T. J. said, "and tell God you died."

Dud worked a crumpled pack of cigarettes out of his shirt pocket. He held it out to the others, still scissored between his fingers. "Have a Hubert Terrapin," he said.

"What you want to smoke them damn Tareytons for, Dud?" T. J. said. "Shit, that's what they sweep up off the floor after they make cigarettes." Dud grinned and looked up at Elliott, who was pouring more drink in his cup. Johnny Boy ran between them and grabbed first at the jar, which Elliott swung away from him smoothly without spilling any, and then at the cigarettes, which the boy managed to wrest from Dud and hang onto. He ran off, laughing and screaming. Dud jumped up and gave chase. "You little fart knocker," he said, clomping away, long-legged, into the dark. "Bring back here my Hubert Terrapins."

Grady was bumping out a rocking blues on the guitar, using a makeup rule to fret the strings. "Hot damn," Leroy said, "he's pretty good on that old thing."

"Sounds like nigger music to me," T. J. said. "I heard only coons and queers could play that junk."

"Listen long enough, you'll hear anything," Elliott said.

"Yall settle down," Leroy said. "I wanta hear him."

"That old box sure ain't much," T. J. said. "Sounds warped to me."

"Well, blame not my lute," Grady said, bobbing his head from side to side with the beat. "I'm kind of rusty, been a while since I done any of this. Besides, my friend, 'tis the small rift within this here throbbin core that hides a sadness soft. . . ."

T. J. stood up shakily against the side of the building. "You're one of them fancy talkers, too, ain't you." Grady ignored him.

"Set down," Leroy said, "before I lay one on you."

Elliott passed the liquor jar to Leroy. "Hey, Grady," he said, "you wanna hear some real guitar playin, this your man."

"Heck, I ain't no better'n he is," Leroy said awkwardly.

"Shit no," T. J. said. "You never learnt but three chords. I could do better'n you 'fore I learned to blow my nose."

"You shit and fall back in it, too, little bud," Leroy said. "You still ain't learned to blow your nose, somebody always having to do it for you."

Dud had caught Johnny Boy out in the road. They could hear him grunting and the boy squealing like a cornered shoat. "Come here, yall," Dud shouted. "Hep me take his pants off."

"Let's fix that little bastard," T. J. said. He and Haskell got up and went off towards the sounds of struggle. Leroy said, "We got to get on towards home anyhow. Sure appreciate the drank. Yall have to come over to the house one of these days, and we'll play some together." Elliott and Grady followed him off toward the road.

They watched in the half light from the gin as T. J. and Haskell and Dud scuffled with the boy, down on the wet road that was now muddy only in scattered places. The dry earth had soaked up most of the afternoon rain and the passing of tractors and travelers on foot had packed the roadway into a grainy damp surface.

Box's boy screamed, pleading, "Come on now, yall, you better quit. You let me go now dammit, or I'll tell my daddy on you." They were working furiously over him, undoing his belt and tugging the pants down over his flailing legs. He threshed violently, and in the wild frenzy of his surging to wrest beyond them, he landed a hard, wet shoe full in T. J.'s face, stunning him for an instant and leaving crusts of mud over his face, clinging in his hair and eyebrows.

"Goddam you little bastard!" T. J. shrieked. He pummeled the boy, who lay now exhausted and sobbing. Then T. J. dragged him to his feet, heaving and straining, driven in a fury. "I'll fix your ass good."

The boy pulled up his pants and managed to roll out of T. J.'s grasp and break away, running on up the road away from the store because that was the only route open to him and he kept trying to double back but T. J. was behind him in a broken crouching gallop, darting back and forth with his arms spread wide. Finally he caught the boy again. "Hey, Dud," he called out, breathing heavily. "See if they ain't some binder twine out yonder by the gin cistern."

114

Dud brought him the roll of cord, and by then Elliott and Grady and Leroy had reached the place where he was holding the boy in front of the church. A full moon was rising, and they could see the boy's face shiny with tears. Elliott said, "Let him go. He's had enough."

"Hell he has," T. J. said. "I'm gonna fix your ass," he said to the boy. "I'm gonna tie you up with the dead people and maybe that'll teach you to leave guys alone."

The boy screamed and fought against him, but T. J. slapped him with the heel of his hand and held him around the neck like a bulldogged calf. Then he dragged him across the churchyard and into the cemetery and began to lash him to a tall, thin tombstone that they could hardly see in the moonlight. Grady said thickly, "We make the grave a bed . . . nor time nor death is ever gonna part us more, 'tis but a night, a long, moonless night . . ."

"Snakeshit," Haskell said dreamily. "Between yore thighs where yore beauty lies . . ."

"Ain't Shakespeare," Grady said indignantly. "Iss . . . Edgar A. Guest. Yeah. Edgar, Ansel, Aching, Asshole, Guest. Make the grave our bed and then we are gone. . . ." He limped on along the road with the sack of groceries and the guitar.

Elliott climbed over the graveyard fence and wandered through the markers striking matches, trying to find his grandfather's grave. He thought of the time after he got out of the hospital, when the Major got him R-and-R leave back to Casablanca and he hitchhiked up the North African coast from Casa to Saint Jean-de-Fedhala, to the American cemetery. He had looked a long time, and finally he found it. Rich's name and grade and the date of his death were neatly stenciled on the white cross-span

RICHARDS, LEONARD E.

T/3 AUS   KIA 25 MAY 44

and tacked below in mechanical confirmation was a bent and dented dogtag, held by a brad through the notch they always said was there so they could wedge the dog-tag in your mouth when you were killed. He'd always known it was just gory scuttlebutt. But maybe they put the other one in your mouth. No. The other one was to be nailed on the casket. Or maybe they only found one of Rich's dogtags. Anyway, they did not have to worry about putting one in his mouth. He had stood at Rich's grave a long time. I couldn't ever really feel it was Rich down there, he thought. Just pieces of him, anyway, and how could they really know it was him. It didn't matter. But he had thought about that a lot, that somehow in the midst of all that confusion and fear with the Nebel-werfers dropping in on them and the machine guns, the Germans opening up with everything they had in one last desperate attempt, that somehow in the midst of all that, somebody had put together enough pieces of a human body to put a name on it and put it in a bag and get it all the way down the peninsula and across the Mediter-ranean and all the way back to Saint Jean-de-Fedhala through everything else that was happening, how long and difficult it had all been, how automatic and routine. Old Rich never did get to see the city of Romulus and Remus after all.

Elliott could not find his grandfather's grave, and fin-ally he gave up and started back to the road just as a light came on in the parsonage behind the church.

"Let's go, T. J.," Dud said. "You're waking up the whole

country." But T. J. went on furiously winding the twine around the boy, binding him to the tombstone. Then Elliott saw Grady put down the groceries and the guitar and crawl through the fence. He picked his way slowly out through the graves, careful not to step on any of them, and went past T. J. and began to cut the boy loose. "That's enough," he said quietly.

"What the goddam hell!" T. J. erupted.

"I said that's enough." He stood on the pedestal of the tombstone and faced T. J., and his voice was calm and hard. It surprised Elliott because it did not sound like Grady.

T. J. stood there glaring at him in the moonlight. He spat. Then he said, "Well, shit, I don't like hittin no cripple."

Grady said, "Yeah, I know. You only hit kids. And probably drunks and women. That's your speed."

"By god . . . you just better be glad it ain't your fancy-talking buddy over there. He ever bucks me, I'll stomp a hole in him. You just better be glad I don't believe in hittin cripples."

"That's as good an excuse as any," Grady said.

"Come on, T. J.," Leroy said, starting up the road with Dud and Haskell. "Before I have to get in there and clean your plow."

"You and who else," T. J. said. "You and whose army." But he tucked in his shirt and started to follow them, backing off and angling out across the cemetery. "You ever mess with me again, hunchback," he said, "you'll get a lot worse."

Elliott and Grady went up the road to Sedberry's where they had tied Old Phoebe Lou. Elliott handed Grady the sack of groceries and helped him get up on the mare's broad back, and then he took the reins and led her out into the road, cradling the last jar of moonshine with the same arm that held the reins.

"You know that old boy?" Grady said.

"Mmm. Used to, I guess, when we were kids. He's a couple years younger than me. He must be the one they said quit school and ran off and joined the Navy. That's while I was gone. There's a whole slew of Teeds. I know Leroy and some of the older ones better. I guess he's probably the worst one of the batch."

"He'll be all right," Grady said. "He just shits a little close to the house, that's all."

Elliott led Old Phoeb down the road, until they began to encounter muddy draws and deep water-filled ruts where the rain had been heavier. Then he led the horse up to a corner post at a crossroad and mounted, first taking a heavy drink from the jar and handing it up to Grady, who drank and threw the lid out into the darkness and held on to the edge of the sorrel's rump while Elliott squeezed himself up in front. Elliott gave the mare her head and she sauntered out across a maize field, stopping now and then to graze on the ripening grain. Elliott and Grady passed the liquor jar back and forth and settled themselves into the slow rolling gait of the old horse. The clouds were clearing away and the moon had risen high ahead of them. The level prairie tipped away toward the caprock, so that each time they went over a rise they could see a long shallow basin of land before them, dotted here and there with the shadow of a windmill, a clump of scraggly trees around a farmhouse, the distant ridge of mesquites that marked the ranch bound-
118   ary.

Grady sang jumbled and incoherent verses of songs Elliott did not know, and he tried to play the guitar but there was no room between them to strum and he couldn't turn sideways because of his back. He took out his harmonica and blew a few bars but that also was too difficult, holding the instrument with one hand and the guitar and sack of groceries with the other. He slapped out the spittle in the palm of his hand and put the harmonica back in his shirt pocket.

—Platitudes, platitudes, he muttered.

—Wassat?

—Man doth not live by wine alone. Way my mind's running. Love. Truth. Plain. Faith, hope, charity. The greatest of these. Platitudes.

—Platitudes and plongitudes, Elliott said. —Forty-eight south platitude, one hundred twenty-five west plongitude.

—Reckon where that'd put us.

—Back in the saddle. Somewhere in the horse platitudes.

—Cheated, didn't you? Looked at the map, didn't you? I call that puttin the chart before the horse.

—You crazy bastard. Crazy smartmouth bastard. Always got a come-back.

—Don't tell me you're another of these mean drinkers, Grady said. —Gonna jump on me for smartin off.

—No, Elliott said. —Me, I'm a happy drinker.

He was. He drank to be happy, to relieve the depression and boredom, and he was happy now. But there was a sadness in it, too, a kind of pain that in itself made him easy, more at peace than he'd been for a long time. He felt the sweep of the land, and the coolness of it, and the familiar sweet odor the land could have when it was wet   119 and fertile, and for the first time since he was a boy he felt that he had come home, that he belonged here, that it would be all right now. The sadness was for his mother and father and for the land itself, and for his grandfather, sharecropped and tenanted and rented off across three states, chased and ruined by boll weevils and erosion and land speculators until, an old man even in his middle years, he had come up the caprock to this treeless plain and started again, this time for good: he bought and held on, and made it home. But the same wandering route, the same erratic search, had to be repeated and endured by his sons and heirs; yet this was the home place and they came back. Coming back was part of it.

He had groped there drunk out of his mind looking for the dust and bones of his grandfather without even thinking of all this, and there was sadness in that. But coming home made it all right. It seemed now to have something to do with Grady. He had never known anyone like Grady before, even in the service; he had bought bootleg booze from Sedberry and romped with girls in seedbins and listened to the guitars and it had never been the same way. Grady was from the outside, beyond, yet he, too, belonged here. Grady knew.

—Someday I am gonna write a book. Book about all the folly of man. Gonna call it

—"Folly Wolly Doodle All Day"

—and the idea of it will be that

—if you just

—doodle

—all day . . .

Time was so real in his head that he could taste it, skulled flickering projections of places he'd been but could not remember or had only imagined, worlds of fantasy where everything was old and expensive and eternal, deep mahogany and burnished leather and buildings patinaed in time, mountains and rolling green hills and a girl with russet hair who loved only him, somewhere, when at last he had done the great things he was destined to do, had become the man his past denied him: Lieutenant Rowan carrying the message to García, Bride and Phillips at their posts until the last sending out CQD and SOS from the sinking *Titanic,* Red Grange scoring four touchdowns in twelve minutes against Michigan, Lindbergh flying the Atlantic, Lou Gehrig batting .379. Ticker-tape parades up Broadway. Smooth, mellow voices on the radio. Applause. Movie stars and handsome authors of famous books dressed in dark shirts and tweeds, smiling as they boarded trains and planes and ships. Heroes of Peace, Stories of Achievement. Ideals That Inspire. Win One for the Gipper. Don't Die on Third. Get In Line, or Get Out. Stand on Your Own Footing

against the reality of square old cars, dried cow chips across the pasture, sandstorms, the frozen yellowed city of Fort Worth sweltering in the ancient lost and forgotten league-and-labor of a nation broken, for the time, in a sunny graybrown haze, like an old picture, the halted towers of the city and clattering black jitneys and dusty deserted streets, the house above the river, vanished

the musty farmhouse, Mama crying, dirty lace curtains, girl cousins in feedsack drawers, thick flowered wallpaper held with wideheaded tacks, fighting on the school yard, bloody, crying, choking down dry slobbers, big boys telling dirty jokes beating up teachers riding horses down the hall sandstorms W. Lee O'Daniel PASS THE BISCUITS 121

PAPPY rootbeer at the drugstore in Lubbock movies Tom Mix

the army

not a threat, that's a promise.

A promise: people dying.

The nightwatchman in Lamar shot down with his own cheap Smith & Wesson by the town drunk in a ridiculous tussle in an alley next to the Rose Theater where Bob Steele was saving the rancher's daughter, the old man's boots in the street and streaks of blood on a '31 Chevy where he'd fallen. The war. A hungry Arab killed by a nervous guard one night near Casablanca, then the enemy, *Gott mit uns*, prisoners shot under one pretense or another, and after that occasional unrecovered bodies lying blackened beside the gutted tanks Swastikas half covered in the hot moving sand Black Crosses as the outfit marched along toward Oran, marching along the broken, pitted asphalt strips, platoon leaders calling out *rHoad guards phOST*, then tiredly, *road guards in,* fading away in the sounds of shuffling boots. G.I.'s getting killed: the first one by a strafing Me. 109 along the road into Algiers, and on the beach at Paestum south of Salerno, thirty men from his company died, and he saw many of them as they went down or simply vanished. The CO was killed a few yards away that night they tried to cross the Rapido, and Carr and Modony up ahead of him on some mountain toward Cassino and all up the peninsula he'd seen them die. Funny how he remembered their names. At one time there were only five men left in his squad, he and Rich and the old guy from Colorado and the two Mexicans, but then the replacements came in, and some of them were killed and other new ones came. And then Rich. Old Rich was the last. A Nebelwerfer got Rich.

Rich in front of it like a flock of geese, and the cold bloody pieces and the circle of light rising into the lilac pendant, smell of lavender, Grandma's beautiful heaven-smelling shrubs, buckets of moss, the lilac tree but golden-rimmed with hazy grime of gusting sand bent in the blowing whining dirt, dry coughing gritty

and now the lilac cordate purple valentine, ribbon streaming streaming THIS DECORATION MAY BE RETURNED TO THE PHILADELPHIA QUARTERMASTER DEPOT TO BE EN-GRAVED tossed to him indifferently from a large pile by the medical records clerk checking his 201 file at Embarkation FOR MILITARY MERIT on the back and a space for the name "wounds suffered under fire in the performance of duty" the gold cameo of Washington first in war in peace in the hearts of his countrymen in the purple hearts of his countrymen in bands of red and stars of red against blinding white from the circled shield and green leaves lilac When the Deep Purple Falls in fresh clear showers settling the dust wet and brown-smelling beneath the cover in colors carefully within the lines deep and crisp Over Sleepy Garden Walls until the last man falls. Last man down. Gets his ass shot off. That's not a threat, that's a promise, trooper. Move out, trooper. Stand tall, trooper. Take cover, trooper. Die trooper.

Trooper. After all these years: trooper. Custer and the dying troop. All the way back to that. A time of brevets and banners and skirmish lines. And still that sense of time, as if he'd been there, too, the thin gaunt faces and stringy mustaches, quality in the eyes of the officers and hard hungriness in the men, the long lines of mounts and the men of the troop, harsh and grained, strung across the dusty scrub hills, Custer and Keogh and Hodgson and Sturgis and Crittenden and Benteen and Reno, those

123

crazy names for which history had had to be written. Benteen. And Reno. Reno of the skirmisher's line. Into the valley of death. Reno of the skirmisher's line and the Rhee scout's bloody brains, of "retreat" and "fall back with faces to the enemy," and retreat again, and the rout to the bluffs, Reno of cowardice and courts of inquiry and alcohol and madness. Where did you go after that, Major Reno? Across the river and into the trees, up the bluffs. Up yours. To Fort Rice and Standing Rock Agency and courts of inquiry and oblivion, alcohol and madness. It all came to him, each figure and outline and shade, the years and the places, in a furious, frozen procession, and he lingered upon it painfully, sweetly, as if in a fever.

—You sort of got a thing about old Reno, huh.

—I guess I do. *At the gallop: Ho!*

Old Phoeb stopped to munch on a maize head.

Grady was a wounded trooper and they were trying to find their way through Sioux territory to the Steamer *Far West* with news of the massacre. And provisions for the fort. He began to whistle "Garry Owen," off key, and Grady picked it up, singing

> "Let Bacchus' sons be not dismayed
> But join with me each drunken blade,
> Come booze with me and lend your aid
> To help me with the chorus"

and Elliott sang the only chorus he knew

> "In the Fighting Seventh's the place for me,
> It's the cream of all the cavalry,
> No other regiment ever can claim
> Its pride, honor and undying fame"

—Shhh, Grady said. —Don't want no dog soldiers to hear us.

—Yeah. Gotta hold it down. For the honor of the regiment.

—For the honor of the regiment, and pride, and undying fame.

—Specially undying fame.

Elliott was beginning to feel a faint nausea from all the liquor and from the slow rocking motion of the horse. Old Phoeb came to the bar ditch near where they'd crossed coming out. The water had gone down, leaving hardly a thin trickle in the muddy, weedy bottom. The old sorrel stopped, and Elliott sank down on her neck, wishing he could vomit and trying not to.

Old Phoeb put her head down, docilely, and he swung under her chin, clinging desperately and trying to right himself, and then she raised her head and he flopped off into the ditch on his back and folded up on top of himself in the bottom.

—Hey, old buddy. Where'd you go? Grady whispered loudly, feeling up the horse's broad back.

Stunned and winded, Elliott tried to turn over in the ditch, grunting and floundering through the thick weeds.

Very carefully, Grady took a sip from the jar, now almost empty, and placed it before him on Old Phoeb's back. Then he felt in his shirt pocket and took out a big kitchen match and struck it with his thumbnail. There was a brief, frozen moment when Elliott saw the light burst open and Grady holding it before him, searching, like the gnarled scout at trail's end, and then Old Phoeb skittered and fished to the side and Elliott saw Grady's legs up and flailing as he went backward off her glossy rump in the dying flame and the fruit jar flipped off and burst on a layer of caliche that had eroded out in the bottom of the ditch. Elliott tried to climb up the side of the embankment, but he kept slipping back. When he finally crawled to the top and peeked over, he was almost face to face with Grady, stretched out on his stomach with a potato in one hand and the remains of the guitar in the other. "Grady?" he said. "Hey, fella?"

There was a long silence, and Elliott couldn't move. Then Grady opened one eye and groaned. "It's okay," he whispered tightly. "Shoot, I wouldn't of made it anyway," he said, and rolled down into the ditch on top of Elliott and they lay there a long time laughing and gasping and finally went to sleep.

BUNNY SNOWSHOES. Grady sat high atop the cotton wagon in the faint autumn breeze. —Yessir, last night I even got in bed with my hat on. How is it, they cry, that such a dark and evil plight is come to be rendered forth, and lo the answer is given: Old Grady is touched. Light in the upper story. Unhinged. Pied. And after all these years. That must be it. All the years, Grady. That she cried and waved. O yes. Well, all I know is, I ain't never been in one place this long before, except maybe a couple of jails. Big-time fascists. Scissorbills. Peckerwoods. He snapped his suspenders, hawked and spat over the side of the wagon. —Well, nemo mortalium omnibus horis sapit. A nation that was not called by name. A people that provoketh me to anger continually to my face, that makes sacrifice in gardens, that bygod burns incense upon altars of dust, oh I am sought of them that asked not for me, I am found of them that sought me not

—Well, Grady.

—That the worst you've ever done?

He squinted, watching the workers in the rows of cotton scattered across the field around him, crouching, stooping, some on their knees, others standing to rest, the long sacks stretched out behind them like huge puffy gray worms. —I ought to have hit the road six weeks ago. Here I am, getting to be a regular straight-out old scissorbill. Farmer Brown. Worse than that. A flunkey. Yes, bygod. A flunkey for the money interests, exploitin oppressed peoples that live in squalor and pain. Woe unto them that decree unrighteous decrees and write grievousness which they have prescribed. Tried to tell that to the old man this morning. All he done was nod his head and say, I reckon so, and go right on setting me up to strawboss this outfit. Says you just get up there and keep the weights and watch everthing till we get back. Tried to tell Salazar. Look, you're the boss of this bunch, I said. Here they are breaking their backs at slave labor, couple a dollars a hundred, having to live in a tent and a dinky little old two-room shack, ain't you going to stand up to that? And all Salazar done was laugh, like he always does, the crazy Mescan. And Mr. Randall

The weight book is over yonder on a string by the wagon tongue. Just watch and see to it that they strip them stalks pretty clean, and don't let 'em scatter it too much when they empty out their sacks. Maybe you better do the emptying. That wagon's pretty full, but it'll hold what they pull this evening. Elliott ought to be in from the gin with a empty one before dark. We'll be back by supper, I reckon.

—Heck, I told you, I don't want to have nothing to do with running this outfit. I'm just one of the hired hands, my ownself.

128

You can pull some of your own if you want to, but I'd rather you just set here and keep an eye on the rest of them. I'll make it up to you on your wages. Anyway, looks to me like you'd rather get rid of that sack. Pulling bolls is hard work.

—Hell, you don't have to tell me that. It's slavery, that's what it is, and when the working class unites and raises up one a these days, there's going to be hell to pay and no pitch hot for these capitalist masterlords. Ain't that right, Salazar?

Salazar laughed. *We're just work for him. His the boss-man.*

—Yeah, you're a boss-man, too. That's the trouble. Should have told him that.

When Grady thought of Joe Salazar laughing, he had to laugh, too. Salazar was very fat and brown and smooth, and he laughed in hard little gasps that shook him all over. Grady sang —Madrid que bien resistes, Madrid you wondrous city, para la Nochebuena, seran ahorcados, mamita mía, mamita mía

—Red yeller green, stop wait go. Assholes and elbows. Well, it ain't funny. Poor bastards. The only reality of anything is the possibility of its

in a time-space continuum

sure it is, my friends, and why the hell should I go around trying to show the fly how to get out of the fly bottle when maybe he likes it there. In a time-space

crock

maybe he don't even know it is

And don't care. And wouldn't care if he did know.

Grady twirled a boll of cotton under his nose, absently sniffing at it as if it were a flower. Lint and dust from the boll made him sneeze, and he cursed, leaning over the   129 side of the wagon to snort the mucus from his nose and wipe it away with the back of his hand in a clean swift snap. He looked up. "Well, I'm a sonofabitch," he said aloud. —Look at that crazy Mescan. Just look at him. Down there pissing on that cotton and then sticking it back in the bottom of his sack. Thinks I don't see him. Oh, you worthless pepperbellies. Sneaky dang rascals, I swear. Not worth a snowball in hell.

His gaze swept the field in a slow arc. —Excepting of course sweet little ole Miss Christina right yonder. Howdy-do sweetheart. You little ole hot tamale. Heh. Won't even look up here at me. Chihuahua. Who'd ever think it, under them old overalls and baggy shirt and sunbonnet. Just lean and mean and hungry as a snake. Real honest-to-goodness pepperbelly there. Heh. I swear, it feels like dippin your old thing in a vat full of hot honey and vinegar. Hecho en Méyhico. And there's ole Big María. Wonder what her problem is. She don't smile much, like she ought to. Always hard to get in a gal's pants that don't smile. Well, you just stick around awhile, honey, and one a these days old Grady will tell you a funny.

He probed in the cotton beneath him and took out a huge leatherbound edition of *Paradise Lost* and began to read *all his thoughts of mischief, gratulating, thus excites: thoughts, whither have ye led me, with what sweet compulsion thus transported to forget what hither brought us, hate, not love, nor hope of paradise for hell, hope here to taste of pleasure* . . .

After a time he put the book aside. —I swear. If it ain't old Mama Flores, down yonder on the far end stuffing her sack full a green bolls. And got all them kids helping her. Little shits. I see you, old Mamacita, you growlyfaced old wooleybooger you. Goddam. Why can't they just pull the cotton. But nope. Too busy figuring out ways to cheat a man.

—well

—it's hard work

—Hardest work I know. Down on your knees in front of a dinky little old sprout, pulling off stuff you can't even eat or drink.

He felt the wagon creak. A voice below him said, "Hey, Gradyhaker, where's the thing, for these scale . . . por favor. . . ."

"Right here in my hand," Grady said. "I'll take care a that."

"What you call it, pea?"

"I'll pee on you, hombre, in about two shakes of a mare's tail." The man laughed. Finally Grady got up and waded in the cotton over to the sideboards and climbed down, dangling the short leg. "Pedro-Francisco-Hayseus-Christos-Valdéz," he said. "You guys don't give a man a minute's peace, Frank."

"The sack I done hung him up for you," Frank said. "You ought to be happy for that. E-smile. Big laugh. Funny joke. You e-some guy, Gradyhaker."

"If I was anybody at all," Grady said, "I wouldn't be hanging around here, rassling cotton sacks and riding herd on a bunch of hombres like you. How many rocks you got in that sack?"

Frank laughed. "Hey, why Joe Salazar ain't do this no more? His always do these scale, last time before."

Grady grunted, tugging on the rope to get the beam of the scale down so he could hook the pea on it.

"His always haul the wagons, write in the book. You know?"

"Maybe he got to keeping weights too much with his pencil," Grady said. "I reckon he'll get his job back soon enough. Can't be any too soon to suit me. He's just gone off somewhere with the man to look at another patch for you-all to pull. Frank, you got sixty-nine pounds here. Seventy-two on the scale, and knock off three for the sack."

"Chingado. His got to be at least ciento. Lemme see."

"There she is. You been whistling too much hot-cha at them señoritas. Probably got your tea to boiling and wandered across on a row that's been pulled over."

"Son-of-the-beach. Joe, his not going to like him."

"It ain't only Salazar you got to worry about. Mr. Randall wants to get this patch pulled over before bad weather sets in." He climbed back up on the wagon and Frank threw him the loop of the sack. He pulled it up and began shaking out the cotton, holding his head back to avoid the flurry of dust and dried leaves that swirled around him. "There's lots of cotton there, you just have to get out and hustle. Quit singing mañana to them señoritas."

"How you know," Frank said, grinning.

"Which one a them lovely things you been taking down in the short rows, hey?"

"Qué? . . ."

"Pinchee," Grady said. "You savvy pinchee?"

"Ahh, pinchee," Frank said happily.

"How about ole Big María? You ever had any of that?"

Frank grinned again, embarrassed not for himself but for Grady. "If I pull much bolls these year," he said, "make lots of dinero, I'm marry with Lupe Salazar. Joe's uncle, hey?"

132

"Niece. Joe's *her* uncle. So that means you don't mess with Big María, right?"

"His not a good thing." He nodded toward the workers in the field. "Some of our guys, they get mad easy." He looked at Grady without smiling. "Sometimes his okay, the girl she's ah . . ." He shrugged. "Sometimes not so good, make trouble, big fight. You know?"

—I know, Grady thought. —I know the rules, and I know the exceptions. Little ole Miss Christina is an exception, and Big María ain't. I believe I prefer the exceptions to the rules. Like the Old Jedge. He sure enough was an exception, all right. And that big dumb kid, he's probably one, too. But if he's one, so is coming in off the road and settling down for all this time and letting him and his old man turn a guy into a damn plowhand. And a Simon Legree to boot. Maybe the whole time and place is an exception. He waded over through the cotton and drew up the weight book. —I'll have to think awhile about that one.

He opened the weight book, and at the end of the row of figures beside the name F. Valdéz he wrote 97. He looked up for a minute or so, lost in thought, then erased it and wrote 93. When he closed the book, it slid over the side and dangled at the end of its string. —Weighing with a pencil, the sum and logic of mathematics in its pure-state language the Old Jedge once said. Too much water under the bridge, childern. And not a drop to drink. Salty dog. Goes halfway around the world to fight a war, and then comes back home to this. Reckon what the Jedge would made of him. Think he'd of learned something. Maybe he did. I swear I don't believe I ever ran across another one just like him. Not in no place like this, that's

133

for sure. And the place is what does it. At least if the place is like this one, things changing too fast and too slow at the same time. Anywhere else he'd be selling shoes and voting Blackleg Republican. Throwing biscuits ever Wednesday at the Lions Club. Which is probably

no

problem is, and hier stossen wir auf die grosse Frage he's got hisself a real big itch, if he can ever find where to scratch. Or what

preaching? Yeah he wants to preach all right, but not no sermon ever wrote for a church

selling insurance

probably ads or advice or performing noble deeds among the rich and respectable at the very least teaching school. He'd like that, dressed up in a J. C. Penney coat and tie, spreading The Word out of books. But it wouldn't ever work. He's blind in one eye and got Superman X-Ray Vision in the other one, he wouldn't know whether to yell sawww or giddap. O how you going to keep 'em down on the farm.

after they've seen

but what's he ever seen. Two church socials and a county fair. Twenty years or so of West Texas sandstorms, ten-cent cotton, and a Harley Sadler show. The war. Ought not to forget that. But so's a lot of 'em. They don't have a itch like that. Or maybe they do. Maybe there's a lot of 'em these days.

"Hey, Gradyhaker," Frank said. "This wagon, his full. We don't pull no more now, buenos tardes, hey?"

"I'll bunny's tired you. Get your tokus back on that row," Grady said. "We still got two good hours of day-light, and there's a empty wagon on the way. Ought to be

here a long time and waiting before you get that sack
filled up again."

"How? Joe Salazar, his gone with the man?—"

"Elliott's going to bring it."

"The young one?"

"That's right."

Frank took off his heavy straw hat and scratched his
thick black hair vigorously with both hands. "Sí. His a
funny guy, you know?"

"Funny?"

"You know. Not ha-ha. He never talk—not like you,
Gradyhaker, laugh all the time, tell jokes, no? What's the
matter his ah that way?"

"Hell, I don't know. Maybe he ain't getting enough
pinchee."

"You are crazy, Gradyhaker. Poco loco."

"Thus spake he," Grady said, and he began to raise his
voice, booming it out as Frank went off down the turnrow: "And a great black cloud of grief come upon the
noble son and yea with both hands he taken up there the
dark dust and scattered it over his comely face and de-
filed it and on his fragrant doublet black ashes fell, and
bygod he lay in the dust . . . lay there mighty and might-
ily fallen, and the handmaidens cried aloud in the grief
of their hearts, oh lordy those gloomy companions of a
wild and disturbed imagination, the melancholy madness
of poetry without inspiration, faith without hope . . ."

Frank looked back, shaking his head and laughing.
"Poco loco," he said. "*Muy* loco."

". . . men without women, trouble without cease—" He
had to stop and think. "Childbirth without fear . . . oh
mygod, the whole damned human race bereft of honor   135

and dignity and nickel beer. . . ." He dug out the book and went back to reading Milton.

After an hour or so, the women began to filter toward the wagon to weigh their final loads of the day, because they had the children's sacks to check and evening meals to prepare. Shortly the men were straggling in, too, singly and in small groups. Grady bantered with them all, feigning annoyance, making the men hang their own sacks on the scale, protesting that their weights were excessive and fraudulent, but finally recording for each one an arbitrary figure that was invariably greater, if only by a pound or two, than that registered by the scale. The Mexicans made a thin and scattered procession down the turnrow in the direction of the house, toward the pickers' shack and sidewalled Army tent where they were quartered, children darting and scuffling, the women chattering quietly, all of them lumpy and misshapen with the empty cotton sacks twisted over their backs and shoulders like huge bandoliers.

Last to be weighed and emptied were the big fourteen-foot sacks of the best pickers, lean quiet men who stayed late and set their daily goal at a thousand pounds and often made it. Above their banter Grady heard a tractor in the distance, coming up fast. It was Elliott, towing the empty wagon. He slowed to ease across the ditch where the turnrow intersected the road, then came chugging down the turnrow in road-gear past the line of Mexicans, spreading a wake of dust over them. None of them moved from the trail or seemed bothered by the dust; they were amused at the spectacle of Elliott grimly clinging to the steering wheel of the speeding tractor as it bucked and jarred across the furrowed corrugations along the ends of the rows. An unusually rough jolt bounced him up off the steel-sprung seat, which dipped and then slapped him hard on the butt as he came down, so that he could retain his air of command only by standing up and easing back on the throttle as if he'd been planning it that way all along. He slowed to a stop, left the motor running, and went over to Grady, who had the day's last sack on the scale, trying to keep it from dragging the ground while he read the weight.

Grady said, "Well, Far-darter, it's about time you showed up. I believe we've packed about ever boll on this one she's going to take."

"Hey, guy," said the owner of the sack, nodding at the scale. "Cuánto, hey? His the best these time, no?"

"Probably full of rocks," Grady said. "If you've pulled eight hundred today, I'll besame your culo." He turned to Elliott. "Goddammit, go turn that thing off. Man can't hear hisself think."

Elliott looked at him sharply, then walked away. "Look who's running things," he muttered. "Go turn it off yourself."

"What?" Grady yelled above the chugging of the tractor.

"I'd just have to crank it up again," Elliott said. "We've got to get that one loose and this one hooked up."

"Then go on over there and throttle it down some. I can't stand that damn popping noise. Okay, José, here's ninety-three, knock off say five for the sack. That makes, let's see . . . nine hundred and twelve. Pretty fair for one day, I reckon, if half of it wasn't green bolls or rock."

"Chingao," José said happily. "Mañana. Mañana, I'm ah pull whole bales. Hey, muchachos? Hey?" The men   137 laughed, shaking their heads, punching his arm. "Hokay, cabrón," he said to one of them. "You see. You all ah see. Right, Gradyhaker?"

Grady shrugged. "You better load up on free-holies tonight then. And lay off the pinchee." He winked and the men laughed.

"Hasta mañana, Gradyhaker," they said. "Buenos noches."

"Yeah, bunny snowshoes to you, too."

"Where's Salazar?" Elliott called out from the tractor. He came over carrying an armload of books that he had taken from the empty wagon.

"How come everbody's so worried over that lardass hombre all of a sudden? Him and your daddy went over to your uncle's, I reckon, to see if his cotton ain't about ready to pull."

"I was just asking," Elliott said. He put the books down on the ground beside Grady. Several of them were stained with heavy grease and badly mutilated, shredded as if by some gigantic saw. "Guys at the gin said they wish to hell you'd do your reading in the crapper or someplace, instead of the cotton trailer," Elliott said.

"I'll be damned," Grady said. He picked up one of the torn books, carefully holding it between thumb and forefinger, as if it might disintegrate at any moment. "I been wondering where this one was."

"It's not much good for anything but scrap paper now," Elliott said, spreading the pile with his foot. "Some of them got through the suction, clear into the stands, and from what old Barney Reid said, the night crew had to shut everything down two or three times to get the pieces out."

"Well, it dudn't matter a whole lot," Grady said. "I

never could make much out of this one anyway." He held up a tattered page. "Listen to this. Let's see. Can't find where the sentence starts. Maybe it's cut off. But just listen to this:

> '. . . relief wherever you be let your wind go free who knows if that pork chop I took with my cup of tea was quite good with the heat I couldn't smell anything off it Im sure that queer-looking man in the porkbutchers is a great rogue I hope that lamp is not smoking fill my nose up with smuts better than having him leaving the gas on all night I couldn't rest easy in my bed in Gibraltar . . .'

"Yeah," Elliott said. "I think that's the one I tried to read. Stayed with it nearly all the way through. Sure was hard. But I liked some of it."

"Why?"

"I don't know. I guess it was the words, or something. I got the notion there must be lots of . . . oh, great ideas in it."

"Sure," Grady said. "Listen, here's another place:

> 'All songs on that theme. Yet more Bloom stretched his string. Cruel it seems. Let people get fond of each other: lure them on. Then tear asunder. Death. Explos. Knock on the head. Outtohelloutof-that. Human life. Dignam.Ugh, that rat's tail wriggling! Five bob I gave. Corpus paradisum. Corncrake croaker: belly like a poisoned pup. Gone. They sing. Forgotten. I too. And one day she with. Leave her: get tired. Suffer then. Snivel.

139

Big Spanishy eyes goggling at nothing. Her wavy-avyeavyheavyyeavyyevyevy hair un comb: 'd . . .'

He read it fast and monotonously, with exaggeration. "Yessir," he said. "Lots of big ideas in that." He laughed. "I can just see the old boy on the machine that got ahold of that one—"

"Machine?"

"Linotype. The old boy that set it. Some old bottle slogger that barely made it out of the eighth grade, got hisself in the union setting grocery ads and never done nothing else but maybe cookbooks and Nancy Drew. Enough to make a man take the pledge. Still, he'd be the one to do it, all right. Follow copy right out the window. Anybody that thought about it would wind up a basket case. Let your mind roll on, that's the only way. Ain't no wonder they think ever guy that writes a book or draws a picture is crazy. He is."

"There must be something to it," Elliott said. "They printed it."

"You got everthing all sorted out, ain't you."

Elliott sat down by one of the wagon tires and leaned back against it, bouncing his head gently against the rubber sidewall and staring off into the evening sky. "I wish I did," he said. "I wish I was like some of these people, philosophers, I guess it is, and these college professors and scientists and all these famous people, seems like they all know, like having a bunch of pigeonholes where everything is all figured and divided out. And when you run up against trouble or some big question about life and God and what's right and wrong and how to act or get along with people and make something of yourself, why you just go look in the right pigeonhole and there it

140

is." He shifted uneasily. "Maybe you'll laugh . . . but I'm all the time trying to make up lists of things—you know, different headings for the way I feel and what I think." He sighed. "But doesn't ever seem to get me anyplace."

"Shoot a mile," Grady said. "If you're just looking for some kind of a system, for a bunch of categories, ain't no need bothering with philosophy or none of them other things. It's all been done. Lots of places. Matter of fact, here's one right here." He picked up *Roget's Thesaurus*, one of the few books in the pile still more or less intact. "Nobody else has ever done a better job, or a worse one, when it comes to making up the pigeonholes." He scanned down a page at the front. "Existence, existence abstract, existence concrete, existence formal . . . intrinsicality . . . relation, relation absolute, relation continuous . . . right down through matter, volition, right on down to the very last word: institutions. More things, Horatio, than dreamed up by your philosophy. And looky here," he said, with some surprise at the discovery. "It even finishes off with a nice round number. One thousand, for the word 'temple.' I never noticed that before. What was it the Jedge used to say? Don't trust round numbers? Maybe it was old Dr. Sam Johnson that said that."

"But those are just words," Elliott said. "I'm talking about—"

"Yeah, but people don't know the difference. To nearly everybody, the words are the things theirselves, and when they've got the word all nice and figured out and wrote down and quoted and put in its place and tacked onto something or somebody, why they've got the whole problem solved right there. Nemo mortalium sapit horis something or other."

141

"I don't know if I understand that or not," Elliott said, without much interest.

"I sure as hell don't," Grady said. "But that's the way it is. I'll tell you this: you go ahead and get your lists all set up and fix your pigeonholes and everything. Then pretty soon, maybe the very next thing, you're going to think or feel something and then, my friend, you try to find one of your neat little squares to fit it in. You ain't going to be able to do it, that's what . . . 'less maybe you cheat a little on old Sol. I don't care what it is, whether it's some gal's pants you want to get into, or what God is, or something about politics you read in the newspaper, or even two and two makes four, it won't always work."

Elliott thought about it. "But if you've *really* got all the pigeonholes? . . ."

"You can't, for one thing. But let's say you do. Say you start out with all these"—he held up the book—"and you add a new one ever time it comes along and you keep 'em all nice and arranged and toted up. And finally you get 'em all. Even then it won't work."

"Why not?"

"I've found you a argument," Grady said, "I'm not obliged to find you a understanding. Hell, I don't know. Maybe *because* I don't know, that's the reason. Some people would say it's because you won't ever get all the categories, all the little squares, all the words, that they just keep going on and changing theirselves up and confounding and scattering abroad, from thence upon the face of all the earth, yea, upon a plain in the land of Shinar. . . ." He chuckled. "Well, anyway, I don't know about that. Maybe you can get 'em. But even when you do, there's still something else working against you. It's the crossfire. Time and memory, bygod, space coeval, the predications of past present and future contained inherent compelled at once and forever in the pure instant, the perfect eternity, the sole and absolute being immediately separate and conjoined, for no two leaves of grass in nature differ only numerically but in points of extension and motion on a continuum that cannot be divided and bygod, everthing changes and everthing is always the same."

Elliott looked at him from the corner of his eye. Finally he said firmly, "That doesn't make any sense. 'Everything changes and everything's the same.' That's like saying this is a cotton field but it's not a cotton field, or saying you're Grady and somebody else, too."

"Ah, there might be a chance for you yet," Grady said. "Well, you think about it some. But don't think about it too much. Too much thinking softens your brain, the Old Jedge used to say. Or maybe it was your nuts. Anyway, you gather quite a bit of wool as it is. Maybe something's already got softened up."

"I'm doing all right," Elliott said. "At both ends. Don't you lose any sleep about it."

"All I know is, most of the time you're surlier than a sowhog, don't pass the time of day without getting your face all out of line. Me and one of the muchachos just been talking about what a sour apple you are. He says maybe you ain't getting enough pinchee."

"I'm doing all right," Elliott said. "I haven't felt this good in a long time. Since I got out of the Army."

"That so?"

"Fall's about the only good time of year in West Texas. Hot in the summer, cold and windy in the winter, sand   143 blows all spring. But smell that fall air. Gin smoke, cottonseed, sugar-cured hams . . . I can't describe it, but it sure makes a guy feel good."

"Well now, we're lovers of the beautiful but with no loss of manliness," Grady said. "First thing I know, you'll be turning poet on me." He climbed up onto the wagon. "Better see if you can't tromp some of this down before we try to move it, or you'll lose half a bale on the way to the gin." He looked down at Elliott, who was still staring off into space. "Hey, if you're feeling so full of mirth and joy all of a sudden, I wish you wouldn't keep standing around with that hang-dog look on your face. I'd swear, you and the melancholy Dane—"

Elliott turned quickly. "There's nothing the matter with me."

"You sure don't show it." Grady scratched his chin. "How does it go, now? Something about heavily with his disposition, and the good earth. Yeah: 'This goodly frame the earth is but a sterile promontory, and bygod the most fair and excellent canopy, this noble o'erhanging firmament.' And now this here is the good one. Listen: 'This majestical roof fretted with golden fire seemeth nought but a foul and pestilent congregation of vapors. But what a piece of work' . . . and so on. 'This majestical roof fretted with golden fire.' I like that."

"All right, dammit," Elliott said. "Joy and mirth." He turned and jogged off toward the idling tractor, jumped onto the seat, and gunned it forward, trailing the empty wagon in a large arc out across the field and then turning and bouncing back at full speed toward Grady on the loaded trailer that was now silhouetted in the red ball of sun floating above the shadowed rim of land. Grady leaned forward on the sideboards, watching as Elliott swung back toward him glaring through the spokes of the steering wheel as if they were gunsights. Grady squinted, faintly puzzled, grinning, waiting to hear the motor throttled back. But the popping and roaring increased, and when the tractor and wagon were thirty feet away and closing fast, bearing down, bouncing, throwing dust, Grady jumped, arms flailing and legs churning as he hit the ground and rolled away through the powdery furrows and then leaped to his feet cursing at the top of his voice and peering into the cloud of drifting dirt that covered the tractor and wagons.

"You goddam crazy sonsabitching idiot!" he yelled, but it was lost in the roar of the tractor, now standing unclutched and braked at open throttle, angled alongside the loaded wagon. Elliott jumped down over the bull-wheel, laughing. "Where's all your joy and mirth," he said. "And all that poetry and stuff you get such a kick out of."

"Turn that goddam thing off," Grady barked, and when Elliott ignored him, he stepped upon the drawbar and pulled the throttle back, then went around and opened the fuel-line petcock. Slowly the popping of the motor lapsed into silence. "I swear, sometimes I don't think you've got a lick of sense," Grady said. "What the hell made you do a stupid thing like that?"

"You ought to have seen me behind the wheel of a jeep," Elliott said. He was bent over, trying to work the pin out of the wagon tongue and disconnect it from the tractor. The empty wagon had skidded alongside the loaded one and come to rest scarcely two feet away. "You aren't hurt, are you?"

"Oh no," Grady said. "Just a few ribs here and there, and a brain concussion. Not to mention the muscles of my 145 bowels, which are stretched clean out of sight. How in the name of goodly-greaved Achilles did you manage to do this?" He walked around and around the tractor and wagons, shaking his head.

"Know-how, that's all. You just have to know when to hit the clutch and then lock down on one back wheel. She spun in here pretty as you please."

"Know-how, hell. Pure luck is what it was. And that's something you ought not to mess with. Run out on you one a these days. Me, I'm already wearing dead man's shoes. Like somebody said, luck's a chance but trouble's sure. I've about done all the bluffing I care to." He stood on the drawbar to hold it down while Elliott jiggled the wagon tongue and worked the pin loose.

"Look at all that stuff, Grady," Elliott said, nodding up at the wagon. "Like money in the bank. Been a long time since there's been a crop like this. At least it's the first good one I've had a piece of."

"That why you come up with all this piss-and-vinegar, all of a sudden?"

"It helps. You know, I've been thinking. When this crop is all out, I'm going to get me a car, and then just load up someday and take off. Mama and Dad sure will fuss about it, I guess. But I'll stay and help put up the land. Then I'll take off. I think I've got to do it."

"Which way?"

"Heck, I don't know. California maybe. Just someplace away from here. You could come with me, if you wanted to. Far as you'd want to go."

Grady nodded, chuckling. "Well, I don't know about it," he said. "Here you are wanting to hit the road, and it looks like I've just now sort of found me a home."

146   "I think you're the one that's getting soft in the head,"

Elliott said. "Hey, what kind of car do you think I can get with three or four hundred dollars?"

"Piece of junk, probably. 'Less you're lucky."

"Sure would like to have a new one. A Chevy maybe, with a good Fisher body. Not like these danged rattletrap Fords that every country hick drives. But you have to get on the list for a new one, and probably have to wait six or eight months. I don't have that much time."

"If you're getting all so rich, why don't you and your old man start paying these hands a decent wage—"

"There you go again. Far as I know, everybody pays the same. Two dollars a hundred."

"You ever try bending over all day, dragging a cotton sack around on your butt, for two dollars a hundred? Bygod, if there was a union for these people, you danged scissorbills would get in line in a hurry. And another thing: what about that chicken coop they're living in?"

"That's not a chicken coop, Grady. It's a shack. A cottonpicker's shack. My grandma and grandaddy lived in it the first two or three years after they came to the plains. It was all they had. And when they finally built the house, they built it just like the shack, except for having a shedroom. Besides, this bunch of Mexicans has been coming up here from the Valley every fall since I can remember, and they've always lived in that shack and I've never heard anybody complain. Some of them are living in a tent this fall because they brought more hands along, but it's their tent and I imagine they've lived in it all over the country. Idaho digging spuds, beets in Colorado, pulling cotton down here . . ."

"That ain't a reason," Grady said. "Exploiting is still exploiting. . . ."

"What you've got in mind is plumbing and electricity   147

and thick carpets, I guess. We could use some of that, too. While you're at it, I wish you'd campaign a little for us, too."

Grady went off around the wagon, mumbling.

Elliott cranked the tractor. "Come on," he yelled. "Help me get this load hooked up. We might as well pull it to the house."

"Ain't we going to carry it on to the gin?"

"Not me," Elliott said. "That's Salazar's job."

"No telling when they'll get back. We might as well do it."

"I'm tired. You haven't done a thing but lay up on that cotton all day—"

"Tired, hell," Grady said. "You don't know what tired is. I'll have you know I helped your mama wash all morning, must of carried forty gallons of water from that cistern, and I been out here in the heat since before ten o'clock, lugging cotton sacks and keeping after these vile and nefarious Mescans, while you ain't done nothing but hang around over at 'Lysium all day, setting on your butt at the café probably, playing taffy-toes with that fry cook's wife. Say, I heard there was a tent show setting up over there. You see anything of it?"

"Yeah. On the lot across from Box's store."

"What is it? Tent rep? Or carnival, or what?"

"Picture show." He pulled a yellow handbill from his pocket and unfolded it. It was printed in corrupt Spanish and extravagant English. "Tonight is Tim McCoy in *Badland Riders*. And a serial with Bob Steele and Big Boy Williams. Looks like it's about airplanes and stuff."

"*The Black Squadron*," Grady said. "Saw that ten, fifteen years ago. But it's a good one. Let's take that cotton over there and go to the show."

"I told you, I'm tired."

"Hell, I'm tired, too, right down to my bones . . . and the ones that ain't tired are all busted up from that fool stunt you pulled. But a bath and some of your mama's fried chicken and cornbread ought to just about fix up everthing that ails me. What you say?"

"I don't know. I'll think about it."

"We might even work up a little rondy-voo with a couple of señoritas. Or play some more games with ole Free T'Me."

"I forgot to tell you. She ask me about you this afternoon."

"She did, huh?"

"Matter of fact, so did her mama, now that I think of it. 'My, I haven't seen Mr. Haker at the store in a month of Sundays, he's not sick or anything I hope,' she says, very sweetly. What've you been up to, that she calls you Mr. Haker?"

"Maybe that's not all she calls me," Grady said, grinning.

"I don't believe that. My god, Grady, she's old enough to be your mother."

"And mean enough to be my daddy," Grady said.

KOME FIND YOUR OPPORTUNITY.

ohhh yes my frins, don't shake your heads don't turn away don't say Brother Claude Watkins has taken leave of his senses oh no you heared me right for it says just as plain as day right there in Revelations oh yes get your Good Books before you my frins and read it taking heed: for all nations have drunk of the wine of the wrath of her fornication REPENT else I will come verily unto thee quickly and will fight against them with the sword of my mouth, there it is frins, Revelations two-and-sixteen

but of course Napoleon's action had, you see, produced results far beyond his intentions. Oh yes, indeed. Great Britain was quite indifferent to the rights of the Greeks and Latins over the Holy Places, and I must say, equally suspicious of Russia and France. Consequently in January 1853 the emperor took steps to

send your love offerings to me, the Reverend Dale
Weeks, care of this station

piangi, il tuo dolore più del l'ira
born to lose   and now I'm losing yewwwwww
rrr fifty-thousand-watt clear channel station in the
heart of

ANTI-CHRIST the coming world dictator, yes my fellow
Americans, wild beasts of prophecy expose this gigantic
deceptive fraud. Sixty-five million Catholics and Protes-
tants of America led astray by the greatest religious HOAX
OF ALL TIMES, who is guilty? My fellow Americans,
prophecy points the finger at Mr. X

is Jolly Johnny's Platter Patter Parade coming to you
all night

says plainly my frins, And if any man shall take away
from the words of the book of prophecy, God shall take
away his part out of the book of life and out of the holy
city below

a blewww moon over my shoulder and an ooolllddd
love still in my

national anthem, ending today's

He tuned back to Jolly Johnny and stayed with him for
a time, although Jolly Johnny told corny jokes and there
were too many commercials. The records were good: "I'm
Always Chasing Rainbows," and Frankie Carle doing
"Without You," and "Atlanta G.A." by the Andrews Sisters. But there was too much static and other stations
kept drifting in. Elliott, on his stomach, reached out for
the dial, fumbling, found it, and tuned back across until
he hit a solid, heavy signal, a smooth, mellow announcer's
voice saying *—and greetings from the Deep South, as the*
Roosevelt Hotel presents Leon Kelner and his orchestra
from the beautiful Blue Room of the Roosevelt Hotel in
romantic old New Orleans, the Paris of the Americas. . . .   151

The music was heavy and vibrant and luxurious, and above it came the soft pleasant sounds of light conversation, chimes of tableware, the occasional seductive laughter of a girl.

The only light in the shedroom was the radio dial's tiny yellow glow. Elliott reached toward it and turned the volume down, so that the sound would not disturb his mother and father in the front bedroom. With one hand, he tried to pull the radio closer to his bed, to compensate for the lowered volume. A cheap, plastic-cased postwar model, the radio itself was not heavy, but it was more or less anchored in place by its power supply, a disparate array of battery cells on the floor beneath it. Elliott muttered a curse and raised the volume slightly, begrudging the compromise of his privacy, finally settling his irritation upon the circumstances that there was no electricity to operate the radio, that like everything else in the house, like everything in his life, it was makeshift, out of joint, impermanent, and yet ultimately fixed and immobile.

Wonder what ever happened to that old Wincharger Grandad used to have, he thought. Now *that* was something a lot better than all these darned batteries. The wind generator, which was solely for the purpose of operating his grandfather's massive eleven-tube Philco superheterodyne radio, had stood for years on a tower beside the smokehouse. (He now vaguely recalled having seen some remnants of the tower in a patch of weeds that were encroaching on that side of the yard, where no one ever went these days.) He remembered the Wincharger's long thin blades turning slowly and evenly, *whick-whick-whick*, in the grating endless wind, his grandfather always beside the radio late into the vacant nights, staring solemnly ahead, never speaking or even moving except to ferret out the spitcan from beneath his chair to deposit a glob of tobacco juice. The old man loved the gospel programs, not so much for their raucous preachers as for the hymns and the hillbilly records played between incessant spiels for patent medicines, Protestant icons, and all imaginable and marketable heavens upon earth. Elliott endured them because he loved the old man (although he did not know it) and because his mother would relent at bedtime when he pleaded to stay up with his grandfather. But if the old man dozed in his chair, as he often did, Elliott would turn the knob in search of other reports of the known universe, found eventually in the high and fluid hissing crackle of dance bands and mellifluous announcers who spoke without drawls, sophisticated ladies and All-American boys and average families whose greatest tragedies were cluttered closets and harmlessly eccentric neighbors, throbbing dramas played out against the exotic noises of elegant penthouses, nightclubs, spacious bungalows, moving trains, never-never lands of Centerville and Metropolis, fragments, abstractions, modulations of amplitude, dimensions merely of sound, the only undistorted voices which had come to him in his narrow tope, in his voluntary but unreasoned exile, and they were truly, veritably wind-borne and by air and time alone absolved, had dimmed away of quite natural and proper course in the inexorable years beyond his childhood, indeed, had been finally and infinitely surpassed by the iron and concrete fantasies of war.

Now even war memories were less immediate, and the lush velvet music revived old illusions, old raptures. He tracked an image for the sound: swirl of colors, darkly vibrant; muted shadows, deep carpets, silver trays, im-   153 maculately tailored men exuding charm and ease from the sanctity of tuxedos and dinner jackets, glamorous young women with wide smiling mouths and tiny points of light in their eyes, the faceless resplendent orchestra, the debonair young man who was saying —*a medley of favorites, featuring the bittersweet saxophone of Milton Howard . . . as first we hear . . . "I'll Walk Alone."* . . .

He waited for sleep but it never came. He often reached the brink, but something held him back, and the best he ever achieved was a kind of carefully controlled yet insentient trance, in which everything seeped together and fused into the flowing strata beneath him, colors and music and laughter: he was the handsome man with the dynamic voice, covered in splendor and adulation, rich, famous, forever inviolable.

Then, long before dawn, he knew again that he wasn't. He opened his eyes, raised his head, and settled it back against the scrolled iron headboard. The radio had subsided into a faint hum, an occasional crack of static. He turned it off and threw back the bedsheet that had tangled about his legs and waist. "But I will be," he said. I will. Now. If I put it off. It has to be now. I don't know how. If I only knew. But I will. I will.

He got up, still in the heaviness of half-sleep but moving quickly in the cool blue light of the early September morning, shaved, and dressed in a white shirt, green tie, and the blue wool suit he had worn only once, to high school graduation three years before. From the decrepit old chifforobe that was his closet, he took another shirt and his only sport coat, a two-tone affair with wide lapels and plaid panels inset across the shoulders. He went out on the back porch and put on his brown low-quarter Army shoes (which he had not worn since coming home), and then pulled the old Ford up to the gas barrel behind the barn and filled the tank. Before he drove off, he slipped back into the house and left a note on the kitchen table:

> Forgot to tell you, I had to go to town. Have to fix up something about my G.I. Bill papers, probably be back early but don't wait supper.

Elysium was dark and quiet except for a light here and there in kitchen windows and the white floodlights across the ginyard. Box's store had not opened yet, but the café was lit up and two cars were parked in front. On impulse, when he'd almost passed by, Elliott braked and wheeled in beside the building.

The six or seven customers were mostly ginhands, scraggly members of the night crew wolfing down breakfast or men on the day shift who'd stopped by to have their thermos jugs filled with coffee.

Fluffy was down at the far end of the counter, talking to a solitary coffee drinker in a rumpled dirty suit and snap-brimmed hat. Elliott had seen him once or twice around the café. According to rumor, he rented a farm up north of Lamar but spent most of his time gambling. Emmett Box, with a knowing shrug, had said Yeah, he's one a them professionals, which caused some interest, because not many people around Elysium knew a real, sure-enough professional gambler. There were also rumors about him and Fluffy; according to one, she had run away with him once but came back when she discovered she was pregnant with Bud's child, which some said was really the gambler's anyway. Elliott considered all the stories wishful thinking born of spite and frustration on the part of Fluffy's admirers, a legion which included almost every male above the age of ten who hung around the café. His only reaction now was to wonder why the gambler was up so early. Must have just come from some all-night poker game, he mused. Or maybe shooting craps over at County Line.

Fluffy was laughing. She winked at Elliott, indicating that she would be over to serve him shortly. "Just a cup of coffee," he called back.

When she brought it, she said, "Good morning, sunshine. You're sure up and at 'em today. And goodness, all dressed up to the nines." She wiped a spoon on her apron and put it beside his saucer. "You really do look nice in your suit. What're you up to anyway? Running off to get married or something?"

"Oh," he said nervously, sipping his coffee, "just going to town."

"My goodness, don't look so glum about it. Wish I was going to town." She put her elbows on the counter and leaned forward, so that her breasts extended above it, stretching her white blouse tight across the points and pulling it open at the throat so that he could see the deep cleft. But he would not let himself look a second time. He thought she had the prettiest face he'd ever seen.

"Where's your partner in crime today?" she said.

"Grady?"

"You and him are about like Mutt and Jeff these days."

"I guess he's working. Or will be when it gets light enough. We're trying to get out the last few bales on the home place." He was talking to himself as much as to her. "I really ought to be helping. But . . . something I have to see about in town." The coffee was bitter and he felt a distant wave of nausea. He reached for the sugar jar.

156   "All by yourself?" she said.

"All by myself."

"Well, if you'd talk pretty enough to me, I might go with you."

He grinned, feeling the blush creep up his neck. "Sure you would," he said.

"Yeah, I know," she said wistfully, looking around her and making a face. "Somebody gotta run the joint. Wait a minute, I think I hear the baby crying." She turned and went back through the kitchen. Elliott heard her arguing with Bud, and then another door beyond the kitchen slammed. In a few minutes she came back carrying the baby, silenced now by a bottle, and laid it in a basket on the counter. "More coffee?" she said.

"No," he said. "I've got to be going."

"Well, have a good time. Write if you get work."

Get work. If she only knew. The coffee had brought him fully awake, and for the first time the reality of what was ahead spread itself before him, came down on him like a net. He suffered a moment's panic in its seizure, the sense of being drawn up in it, choked, held back, but just as suddenly the lines gave and went slack and he walked on out to the car and got himself moving, against the anxiety, in the same instinctive way that had come to him early and been nurtured through adolescence and finally out of necessity perfected and refined in the Army: don't think about it. Think about something else. And if you can't do that, don't think at all. Blank out. White. Open. Nothing.

By the time he got to Lamar, the sun was up. There were a few people on the street and some of the stores were beginning to open. As he passed the Chevrolet agency, a man who was rolling up the big paneled door of the garage raised his hand listlessly in the customary greeting and Elliott as he went by acknowledged it, realizing several blocks later that the man was probably T. J. Teed. He wondered if T. J. had recognized him, if the wave had been intentional or merely the usual instinctive gesture.

Waiting for the light to change at the intersection of Main Street and the highway toward Lubbock, he felt the tightness rising again in his stomach. Boy, it would sure feel good to just turn around and go home, he thought. I'd have to mess around Lamar for a while till after lunch, to make it look good. Then get on back in time to help Grady with some of the chores and maybe make a haul to the gin. But even as he thought about giving up, he knew he wouldn't. He had to go on. And he'd better get started, because saying he was going to "town" wouldn't necessarily mean Lubbock to them; getting there and back was a long day's drive and he had a lot to do, even if he had no way of knowing how to go about it.

Ideally, he would have known the exact location of the office, just how long it would take to get there from home, where to park so that the old car couldn't be seen by anyone inside, which door to enter, who to ask for. And most important of all, what to say and how to act. Of course there were ways to find out some of those things. He'd even thought of making a dry run. But that would take too long, postpone everything all over, and there was also the chance that the trial would be so immediately difficult and awesome that he would give up. He could have asked Grady, who was probably the only one around who might know and would tell him. But finally it was something he had to do himself. There was too much to lose if you had to ask somebody. The best he could do was to get an early start, take along some extra clothes in case he spilled something or had to fix a flat, and above all, keep his mind busy, circling, in a silent whiteness, away from all the unknown things that lay ahead.

That's how he made the trip: arguing with himself about the identity of T. J. Teed and why people always waved at you whether you knew them or not and which town his father would think he was going to and why Fluffy was married to Bud and what Grady would say about having to do the work without him and what a jour printer was and who invented the atomic bomb and how much a new car cost and what kind of machine made the stove bolts that his father had used to fasten a block of plywood over a hole in the corner of the windshield of the old Ford.

He wished the car had a radio. But what good would it do, he thought. Just shake me up more. Probably nothing on this time of day but soap operas. Maybe Hop Halsey and the Drugstore Cowboys. Won't be none of that hillbilly crap for me. Not if I can help it. More like Hub o' the Plains Serenade Time or Jim Worth's 1340 Platter Party that always opens up slow and easy with something by Wayne King or Jan Garber or some smooth orchestra like that. Wonder what I'll use for a theme. What was the one old Rich always liked so much. Artie Shaw, I think. "Keepin' Myself for You." Or maybe it was "Grabtown Grapple." Then the damn name. That, too. Awkward. And hick-sounding. Wild Bill Elliott. Too long anyway. Have to change it, that's for sure. What. Ran? Ran Randall. Ran Dall. Ron. Randy. Randy Randall. Randy Randall, the Radio Voice of the Great South Plains. Randy   159

Randall's Club o' the Kilocycles. Rhythm with Randall. Requestfully Yours, Randy Randall. Randy Randall with Today's News.

He passed a huge black billboard with gigantic silver letters: FIVE MILES TO THE HUB OF THE PLAINS LUBBOCK TEXAS POP. 51,000 (EST.) AND GROWING EVERY MINUTE A GREAT BIG TEXAS WELCOME TO THE HOME OF THE LUBBOCK HUBBERS THE TEXAS TECH RED RAIDERS AND THE FINEST FOLKS AND FRIENDLIEST MERCHANTS IN THE WHOLE WORLD. A mile or so beyond the sign, he realized that he was sweating. It was mid-morning now, and with the heat of summer not yet broken, the air inside the car grew stifling, even with all the windows open. Elliott pulled off the highway. Keeping the old car idling out of fear that it might not start again, he wiggled out of his coat and wiped his face with a handkerchief. Sure not going to make any big impression if this keeps up, he thought. Good thing I brought another shirt. Ought to have brought two or three. If I had that many. He waited for a truck to pass, squinted at the sun, and eased off, listening to the tires crunch and pop across the graveled right-of-way and onto the pavement heading north again toward the Hub City.

The simplest thing would have been to stop at a gas station and ask, or look up the address in a telephone book, but instead he found himself driving around aimlessly with the rather faint and vacant hope that he would eventually come to it. He tried to stay away from the downtown area, where there were stoplights at every corner and multiple lanes of traffic. Boy, this place sure has grown up during the war, he thought. Didn't use to be much bigger than Lamar. I never did like big towns.

Except maybe Cowtown. He was driving slowly through parts of the city which reminded him of those few years when they had lived in Fort Worth, when he was small. Quiet tree-lined streets and green yards, sidewalks with kids rollerskating and big clean cars here and there in the driveways. The house they had rented in Fort Worth was not as nice as these, but it had a bathroom and electricity and a high front porch. The porch had railings that he could straddle to make a pony, and in the summer there was a cool place under the steps which he pretended was a cave. He played with some kids who lived down the street. There was a girl who lived in the next block, and they played in her basement. It was warm there in the basement when it rained, and they covered themselves with blankets. Once when they hid under the blankets, she took off her panties and he looked at her. He wanted to look, but it bothered him and made him hurt in his stomach, the way it did whenever he hit his funnybone or rode a swing too high. Her mother came down and saw them under the blankets and made him go home. I can hardly remember it, he thought. If only we'd stayed there. Maybe I would like big towns.

He passed along a wide avenue on the west edge of town, small hamburger joints and laundries, a book store, a movie house, a row of shops with fake Tudor fronts, service stations. All this on the east side of the street and across from it, scattered on open expanses of sparse ill-kept grass, were large angular buildings of yellow-brown brick with vaulted arcades and dull red roofs of curved tiles, vaguely resembling a Spanish villa except that the buildings were more like forts than haciendas, and there were random lapses in the architectural integrity: clusters of surplus Army barracks here and there, a massive   161 gray-green statue of Will Rogers astride his fiery steed Soapsuds, a few cube-like buildings of glass and brighter but unmatched brick devoid of all cultural ornamentation or identity.

I guess that's the college, Elliott thought. He recalled having seen it in the past, on one of the family's infrequent trips to Lubbock before the war. It had seemed much smaller and insignificant then. Several of the buildings were surrounded by cars swarmed over by young men and women with their arms full of boxes and books and lamps and hangered clothing that they were carrying into the buildings, laughing, shouting greetings, indulging in mock scuffles. Elliott caught it all in a quick glimpse; he was trapped in the wrong lane of traffic and had to make a quick turn onto a one-way street that was leading him back into the center of town. Wonder how it is to be like that, he mused, thinking of the kids he'd seen. They seemed much younger than him, yet he realized that they weren't. Some of them probably even vets, he thought. I ought to look into that. They say the government will pay your way, or part of it. I remember now, the Major was telling me something about it, what did he say? It had to do with the G.I.'s Bill of Rights. But I bet the stuff they teach is tough.

Drifting, he'd gotten into trouble again. He was hemmed in by traffic on both sides, and the bustle and rush of downtown was straight ahead. He tried to maneuver toward an outside lane, but the old Ford flooded and sputtered whenever he accelerated. At a stoplight the motor died, and he endured several anxious minutes, afraid it had vapor-locked, listening to the starter grind away weakly before it caught just as the light turned green. The car lurched into the intersection and in an

instinctive glance toward the traffic to his right, he unexpectedly caught a flashing glimpse of his destination.
It scarcely registered until he was in the middle of the
next block, going away. So that's where it is, he thought,
feeling a certain relief that was immediately tempered by
the troubling sense that the whiteness had been lost,
given up, that he could no longer hide in his carefully
acquired nullity.

Edging slowly around the courthouse square, he
squinted nervously at the tower clock. It showed a few
minutes past eleven. The air was hot and almost motionless; he felt sweat in his hairline and behind his ears.
When he shifted forward on the breadboard seat, his
shirt clung to the tattered cushion behind him. Maybe
I ought to just park someplace and get something to eat
first. Sure. Why, heck, it's too close to dinnertime, probably wouldn't be anybody there.

But then, I don't know.

If I just knew. Even what the routine is. Nothing ever
seems to work out simple, the way they do it in movies or
books. If you could only go in and say something like,
I saw your ad in the paper and I wish to apply. Like those
sample letters we had in school, to practice on. Indented
form, inside address, salutation, Dear Sirs: I am in search
of a position as blank and would like very much to be
considered as an applicant for such a position with you,
as the standing of the Blank Company is such as to make
me very desirous of connecting myself with you if possible. I am blank years of age, strong and eager to work,
and although I have never done blank work, I am confident that I could learn quickly. My teacher, Miss Blank,
has given her kind permission to use her name as refer-
ence. I am of good appearance and strictly correct habits.

I shall be glad to accept any suitable position within your gift without regard to the present amount of salary, being perfectly willing to allow future advancement to be determined by my ability. Very truly yours. Sincerely yours. Requestfully yours, Randy Randall.

But there hasn't been any ad. At least not one that I know of. Well, shoot, someday I'll look back on all this and laugh. It's a big day. And everything is going to be all right. I know it is. He drove on for several blocks and circled around, looking for a parking place. He found one on a side street off East Broadway. It was the part of town he knew best: second-hand shops, lunch counters, warehouses, hardware stores. He rolled up the car windows and locked the door on the driver's side, knowing it was a futile gesture because the other door had no lock and could be opened with a pair of pliers or by simply twisting and snapping the baling wire that held it shut. Let's just hope nobody needs a shirt and sport coat that bad, he thought, wondering momentarily if he shouldn't change into a fresh shirt so that if one were stolen it would be the sweaty, rumpled one. But he couldn't change on the street and the door was already locked, so he went on, straightening his tie and fanning his coat to circulate air into it, trying to catch his reflection in the store windows as he passed by.

At the corner was a familiar hamburger joint, Shorty's Silver Spoon Café, where he and his father always had lunch when they came to Lubbock. He was tempted briefly by the smell of frying grease and onions and pies. But his resolution held. Business before pleasure. When it's all fixed up, then I'll come back by here and celebrate. Can't go throwing money around until you know where the next dollar is coming from. It struck him then, with sadness and amusement, how much that sounded like something his grandfather would have said. He set off at a brisk pace.

More than a block away from his destination he spotted it, because of the sign. The sign stretched across the entire front of the building just above eye level, with the huge blue letters KFYO outlined in pulsing orange neon. On each side was a panel, one of which read "1340 Kc. on Your Dial," the other "CBS Affiliate for the South Plains," and below everything ran the legend: "Kome Find Your Opportunity."

He stopped to read the sign again, carefully. So that's what it stands for, he thought. I never knew that. It's an omen. I don't believe in omens, but that's what it is. I've come to find my opportunity, and here it is.

Despite the tightness in his bowels, he found confidence to walk on down the street, going past once to look inside. But the window blinds were drawn against the noon sun, and although the door was glass, he could see nothing through it except hazy colors, unidentifiable parts of furniture, decorations that seemed suspended in the depths of a muddy lake. He walked on several doors beyond, trying to be casual and inconspicuous, slowed, then snapped his fingers as if he'd forgotten something, as pretense for wheeling and going back. He passed the door again, glimpsed only a blurred movement in the dim interior, strolled on, damning his foolishness, sure that he had been watched and was now being laughed at. He cursed under his breath, straightened, inhaled deeply, turned and went inside, conscious only of the door closing slowly behind him, its cylinder making a whispering hiss as it drew shut.

He'd expected to find the office filled with secretaries, 165 announcers, performers, important people busy running the place. But there was no one in sight. A desk and vacant chair near the door, potted plants, clutter of paper and magazines. Nothing else but sound, the low steady drone of electric voices from invisible speakers

your friendly Mark Halsey Drug Stores where

on the corner, right on the price, and right on your way

song stylings of Miss Joan Edwards who muses melodiously upon a dreamy Latin theme as we hear

Elliott, clearing his throat nervously, fixed an expectant smile on his face. When no one appeared after several minutes, he edged cautiously around the corner and peered toward a large window through which he could see a man, his back to Elliott, seated at a desk covered with stacks of phonograph records and surrounded by turntables, filing cabinets, and a bank of dials and lights and meters. Elliott stared intently, mesmerized by the instruments, the whirling drums of lathed steel and green velvet on which were turning the shiny black discs, the long beam tracking over them, lifting and floating as if in rhythm with the meter needles bouncing in sudden arcs across mystic numbered scales that made visual the pitch and throb of sound, mechanical and immediate and absolute.

The man at the desk wore headphones, one over an ear and the other raised jauntily to the temple, and it gradually occurred to Elliott that it was his voice, deep and crisp, coming from the speakers

by the makers of fine products for home and industry

sure to listen

this station weekdays at nine

now

Calumet, the double-action baking powder

Friday's edition of Swingtime

latest release

Pickens Sisters, Jane, Helen, and Patty, who tell us

The music began again, and the man took off the headphones and stood up. Instinctively, Elliott stepped back out of sight. He heard a door open and footsteps approaching. The man appeared, reading from a sheaf of papers in his hand. He was unshaven and ugly: heavy jowls, narrow eyes, blotched sallow skin. Elliott wondered how it could be the same man he had heard. The man went on across the room without looking up and into another office and reappeared with a cup of coffee and a larger stack of papers. Then he saw Elliott.

"Umm," the man said, swallowing coffee. "You need something?"

"Ah . . ." Elliott said. "I was, oh, wondering . . . ah I'd like to see about a position."

" 'Position'? What kind of 'position'?"

"Well . . . I don't exactly know. . . ."

The man sniffed. "You don't, huh?"

"Well . . ."

"Secretary's on her lunch hour." He sipped from the cup and went on toward the studio. "I couldn't tell you anything myself. Besides, I'm working the board. You'd have to talk to Worthington anyway."

"Is he around?"

"Around?" The man grinned. "I don't know. I'll see in a minute, maybe." He disappeared around the corner.

Elliott leaned against a desk. Maybe the worst part is over, he thought. At least I'm sticking with it. But as time passed, he could feel the cramp rising again in his stomach, harder this time. He swallowed repeatedly in an effort to control it, but nothing happened. He began 167 to worry about his sweat-stained shirt and the odor, about a scuff on the toe of one shoe, about his hair sticking up in back. He licked both palms and tried to smooth it down, wishing there was a mirror. No one came. He noticed a grease spot on one knee of his suit. That darned filthy old car, he thought. Must have rubbed off from the gearshift or something. Still no one came. Once he heard footsteps and jerked away from the desk, fighting a wave of saliva welling up. The footsteps faded away. Still no one came. Then he saw the small muscles on the back of his hand moving, fluttering. "No," he said. No trembling. I won't show it. He waited again and still no one came and he whirled and pushed through the door as fast and quietly as possible and walked away, feeling the sun and the heat thrown back by the walls and windows of the buildings and the streets, black and bubbly under the sharp noon glare. He walked as fast as he could without running until he reached the next block and then slowed but went on directly to the car and got in and sat down, breathing heavily.

Stupid, he thought. A grown man. He pounded the steering wheel in frustration but the wheel was soft and springy and his blow went glancing off lamely. Stupid. He felt like crying, but the tears would not come. It was bottled up in him. Getting it out was like trying to blow into a hard wind. Fear, he thought. No, I'm not a coward. Maybe I am, but it wasn't ever like that. Even in the war. I never ran. Scared. Everybody's scared. Stupid moves, sure. Dumb. But I never ran.

He wanted to sit there for a long time, quietly, finding the white hollow ease, but the heat in the car was unbearable, even when he rolled down the windows and opened the hood vent. He got out, locked the car again, and

168

wandered down the street. At Shorty's Silver Spoon again, he realized that he had not eaten all day, discovered with some surprise that his mouth was so dry and feverish that when he tried to clear his throat he almost choked. He went inside and ordered a hamburger and a glass of iced tea, immediately gulping down the glass of tepid water the waitress set before him. The café was filled with an assortment of mechanics and clerks and farmers, shabby men in gray shirts. The waitress joked with them in a tired, automatic way. "Yeah, well maybe that's what you told Jake and Wanda," she said to one who was paying his check at the cash register, "but you sure wasn't fixing no irrigation motor when I seen you. Might have been somebody's pump, but it sure wasn't no motor. What was you going to irrigate, anyways?"

The man laughed. "Thought you'd of been working that night."

"You know what thinking done, don't you," she said, winking to the other men along the counter, some of whom laughed at what was apparently a private joke.

When his order came, Elliott drank the tea but the hamburger nauseated him and after nibbling at it he paid his check and wandered outside again, along the street through clusters of people, withered old country folk shopping for bargains at Levine's, coveys of Mexicans, fat mamas surrounded by dark, silent children with big eyes, flocks of pubescent señoritas in flouncy floral dresses, small and frail and giggling, teenage boys haunting the pawnshops and shine parlors and dime stores that emitted smells of stale popcorn, leather polish, and aftershave moist and cool in the doorways as he went along. The crowds thinned away and he was passing the big department stores and banks along Broadway and the Hilton 169

Hotel and Hemphill-Wells and then down side streets again, circling, lost in the sun lights and colors and sounds, seeking the cool shade where the windows were without reflection, clear and crystal deep into oblivion: signs to read, objects to desire, cheap and curious notions, a dull gray façade offering mottled proclamations, hue and cry, stark black ciphers blocked about by muddled halftones REDS RIP U.S. ROLE IN GREECE Molotov in Claim We're Interfering TEXAN SLAIN BODY FOUND IN CAR O.P.A. Sets Hog Ceiling Prices CUBS BOW TO LEADERS AS DODGERS WIN See Photos and Story Section C FELLER'S 1946 HOPES FADING FROM VIEW as he passed it several times and then found himself there again, looking up at the old iron sign reading SOUTH PLAINS DAILY CASCADE-COURIER, staring into the bleakness beyond the building's dirty green windows. BANK ROBBERY FOILED. Million-Dollar Fire Levels Cotton Mill. KILLER GIVEN LIFE IN PRISON Reporter's Testimony Seals Case. By Elliott Randall, Staff Writer. Exclusive by Elliott Randall. Read Elliott Randall in the *Cascade-Courier*. He went inside and stood at a high metal counter piled with newspapers. "I'd like to see somebody about a job," he said.

A girl's head appeared from behind one of the piles. She smiled. "Mechanical, business, or editorial?"

None of these seemed quite right. Finally he said, "Editorial, I guess," deciding by process of elimination, certain that he didn't want either of the first two but wondering if "editorial" meant that he might be hired to write those dull articles about politics and the high rate of death on the highways.

"That's Mr. Ceefs," the girl said. "Upstairs."

He went up a narrow stairway into a large open room filled with rows of desks, most of which were cluttered but unoccupied. In the rear of the room two men were arguing, and nearby a prim grayhaired lady pecked erratically on an old typewriter. At the top of the stairwell was a telephone exchange board and another girl, much like the one downstairs, who stared up at him vacantly through the web of wires and plugs.

"I'm looking for Mr. . . . . Steves?"

"Oh. That must be *Ceefs*," she said. "He's talking on the phone right now, but you can go on in in a minute." She pointed across the room toward a small office partitioned off in one corner. Through the open door Elliott could see a small roundfaced figure that reminded him of pictures of Calvin Coolidge, perhaps because of the hat he wore, an old-fashioned fedora with a wide satin edge on the brim. The hat bobbed up and down as its wearer shouted vigorously into the phone, wheeling in his chair from time to time and waving his arm in wild oration.

Elliott walked slowly across the room, marking time until he saw the man put the phone down and turn to a typewriter beside him. At the doorway Elliott rapped on the sill.

"Open," said the man without looking up.

"Mr. Ceefs?"

The man went on typing. Then, still not looking up, he said, "Goddammit, it's open."

Elliott stepped inside the office and stood there rigidly, trying to clear away the tightness in his throat without coughing or making any noise, wondering whether to interrupt the man's typing or wait for him to stop. Nervously he scanned the office. With the door opened back, the sign on its window was reversed. ƨℲƎƎƆ ᴎOTƨᴎIW .ᴚ To pass the time, Elliott reconstructed it. Then the title below it. E, d, i, t—"Editor & Publisher."

At last Winston Ceefs said, "Well?"

"I'm . . . I'm wondering if maybe you had a job. . . ."

"You are, huh." Ceefs rolled the yellow-brown paper out of his typewriter and turned toward Elliott, still not looking at him, scanning the sheet of paper, pausing to scribble corrections on it with a large black pencil. Elliott smiled anxiously. The smile drained away with the passage of time. When Ceefs finished reading, he shuffled the sheet of paper together with several others and placed them at one side, exactly square with the corner of the desk, the top of which was bare except for the typewriter, the telephone, the neat stack of pages, and a wooden statue of a bowlegged cowboy with buckteeth and an idiot's grin. A plaque at the base of the statue read I AIN'T MAD AT NOBODY.

"Clean desk, clean mind," Ceefs said. "Now. You're looking for a job." He closed his eyes and tapped the side of his nose with the copy pencil. "You sure, now, that you're not looking for a position?"

"Sir?" Elliott knew that he was under attack but not exactly why. Mercifully, before there was time for him to speak again, Ceefs went on. "Dialectics," he said. "I've been around this world long enough, you can bet that. Young people never listen. But I'm not such a monster. No. Problem is, everybody wants a position these days. Nobody wants a job. Nobody wants to work."

"Well, I want to work, sir."

"Doing what?"

"Well . . . anything. Whatever you've got."

"Maybe you want to be a star reporter." He pronounced "star" slowly and emphatically: *stawrrrr*, opening his eyes in mock wonder, grinning intensely. "Somebody in a fancy overcoat that goes around solving crimes and yelling, 'Rip up the front page, hold the presses.' "

"Sir, all I want—"

"Look here, you one of these university boys, are you?"

The faint sarcasm in Ceef's voice was puzzling. Elliott had considered lying about having gone to college. His lack of such status was clearly a handicap in getting a job; far more than that, it was a grievous error on the part of both himself and the universe. Yet Ceef's attitude gave Elliott courage to admit the truth. "No."

"Not one of these journalism stew-dents?"

"Nossir."

"That's something, at least. But now just what is it that makes you think you want to be a newspaperman? What kind of experience you had in this line?" Before Elliott could answer, Ceefs leaned around the desk and shouted out the door for a copy boy. Eventually one appeared, a gangling lad who hesitated a minute too long at the door. "Goddammit, Rutherford, get your ass in gear," Ceefs said, handing him the pages of copy. "Tell Curly I want all that in ten-point and I'll write him a head when I get the proofs. Which you damn well better get in here the minute they come up." When he turned back to Elliott, he looked as if he'd never seen him before. Elliott knew the exact place at which the interview had been interrupted, but it was obvious that Ceefs did not. "They'll think about that, all right," he said, looking through the open door vacantly. "Winnie Ceefs tells the truth, and it hits 'em where they hurt. It's all in your dialectic, you know that?" Elliott nodded. Ceefs narrowed his eyes. "You tell me about yourself now," he said.

"Well, in the service—" He was off stride. He hadn't   173 planned it that way, starting off in midair, trying to find his feet.

"Come on now, boy. You're not no vet."

"Yessir. I've got over three years' service." He raised his shoulder slightly to emphasize the discharge emblem in his lapel.

"Didn't notice your Ruptured Duck there," Ceefs said. " 'Course these days anybody can buy one of those. You must have been drafted with your didies on."

"I was seventeen when I went in, right after high school."

"Which makes you—?"

"I'll be twenty-one next month."

"Navy? Air Corps? What'd they have you doing, flying paper kites and shooting Japs with a nigger-shooter and a pile of spit wads?" Ceefs laughed, as if the image he'd conjured was not only hilarious but vastly original.

"Nossir, I was in the infantry. Most of the time. Then after I got . . . oh, wounded, they assigned me to a military history outfit. That's where I got some experience typing and writing, you know, stuff about what battles certain outfits were in, unit histories, things like that, and I helped the PIO some—"

"That so? Where you wounded?"

"At Anzio. But not in the landing, actually it was quite a while after that—"

"I mean, what kind of wound?"

"It wasn't anything serious. I'm okay now."

"Got the Purple Heart, did you?" Ceefs seemed impressed that he'd been wounded but was obviously relieved that the damage was healed.

"And so you're looking for a newspaper job."

"Yessir, I'd be willing to try about anything you'd offer

me. I promise you, I learn fast." It was coming now, the way he had rehearsed it. "And I believe a fellow owes more than just his time to the man that pays him his salary, there has got to be that commitment to—"

"I've been over there, you know," Ceefs interrupted suddenly.

"Oh?" Elliott said, showing far more interest than he felt. Here it comes, he thought. War stories. But that's okay. Keep him on my side.

"Oh yes, I was a little too old for this one, couldn't get in uniform," Ceefs went on, smiling now, into the distance beyond Elliott. "Not that I didn't try, understand, but these old gray hairs and"—he rubbed his back ominously —"they said somebody's got to stay and do the part here, your free press performs a mighty important duty in wartime. But the very minute you could get civilians in there, I said sure, send me in there, let me do my part. President's orders, you know that?"

Elliott shifted forward in his chair trying to show that he not only understood but was highly impressed.

"Yes sir, President Truman himself. I've got the letter right here somewhere." He began to fumble around in a desk drawer. "Several of us news people. Some pretty big names in this business, I'll tell you that. Ted Dealey of the Dallas *News*, for one. And one or two bigshots off some papers back East. One from Baltimore or someplace like that. Pretty tall company for a small-town boy like Winnie Ceefs. Of course this town is not going to stay small, nossir, we're building a great agricultural and industrial empire. . . ."

"You were a war correspondent?"

"No, oh no, not that exactly. A special fact-finding mission, it was called. Get in there and see the conditions first hand. Flew us over in special Army planes, how about that? Now, this mostly had to do with the bombed-out cities of Europe, you see. Civilian governments, refugee plans, things like that. But I'll tell you, V-E Day hadn't been over hardly anytime at all when we went in there, and there were some pretty close calls, I'll tell you that. Still plenty of snipeshooters and guerrillas and Nazi ragtags running around. But we went right in there, and proud to do it. President's orders." He paused in his search for the letter and sat frowning down at the open drawer. "Where the hell is that letter. Not that I'm any big Truman man. No sir, these price controls are absolutely ruining business, and here the war's been over more than a year. You wouldn't believe the newsprint situation, on account of all this government intervention and red tape and sticking its nose in every fellow's business, and no two ways about it, your friend Harry S. is soft on these communists, that's the real danger. . . ."

Elliott waited, lost but reverent, as if in a catacomb. Guy sure has to know a lot to be a newspaperman, he thought. Hope I can catch on quick enough.

"It's all your dialectic, boy. That's the whole trouble right there. You understand what a dialect is?"

Elliott dredged earnestly for an answer. "Well . . . it's a . . . sort of . . ."

Ceefs held the floor. "Everybody has got the wrong dialectic, that's the problem." Elliott took slight comfort from the vague realization that his ignorance had been passed over. "Now, not none of this intellectual cow hockey," Ceefs was saying. "Just your plain old everyday dialectic. Take these commies over in Europe now—and don't think for a minute it's got to be the Russians, though we ought to have went in there and whipped them while we had the chance just like Patton always said. Damned best general we ever had, you know that? I met one of his fellow officers over there, told me a great deal about the man. He was one that had the right dialectic, don't kid yourself. Well, now, these Reds have got their eye set on world domination, don't you forget it, and it's all a matter of your right dialectic. Oh, it's coming, it's coming . . . right here in this country. Don't say it can't happen here. They've been at it a long time, clear back to when Roosevelt let in all the Jews, a lot of godless atheists and one-worlders with this Yew-nited Nations, holding away the dialectic on the man on the street and god knows what all behind our backs all these years, we didn't see it then with all that smoke screen about the New Deal and getting over the Depression and then having to beat back the Axis foe. A man has got to run his own business and see to his family and help keep the community running, I always say that, but by-damn it's a time coming when you've got to choose up sides and decide if you're a patriot and a Christian, and I'm here to see that this newspaper runs it that way, as long as I draw a breath. I don't mind saying it—I don't care what they say. That's the tradition of the freedom of the press in this country, and when they take that away then we'll know, you'll find out all about your dialectic when *that* happens. The blood of patriots has got to water the old liberty tree now and then. Thomas Jefferson said that. And Christ said either ye are for me or ye art against me. That's how it's got to be." He paused, blinked, looked at Elliott. "You understand what I'm saying, now don't you, son?"

Elliott nodded.

"Well now. I've been sort of babbling on here. But   177

these are things you young fellows have got to be think-ing about."

"That's certainly right," Elliott said. "Yessir."

"Well now. You're a bright young fella, and so you're looking for a job."

"Yessir, I sure am."

"Hmm. Well now, one thing, you ought to watch your appearance. Of course we can't all dress like a spiffy dude, I remember a time when things got a bit down at the heel myself. But a fellow can't ever be too careful of his appearance. First impression, that means a lot. Why, you come in here like a calf in a sandstorm, creep-ing around like you was looking for something to steal. One of my ad salesmen did that, I'd tie a can to his tail right away. Like saying, 'You don't want to buy an ad today, do you?' Why, that's no way to get the job done. You got to get right in there with your head up high, big confident smile on your face, good firm handshake, give 'em your name right off. I don't even know your name. . . ." Elliott moved instantly to correct the error, but Ceefs gave him no chance, wheeling around in his chair to gaze out the window. "Got to sell yourself first off, I even tell that to the guys in the pressroom, keep those shoes shined and that hair cut, yes sir."

"That's right," Elliott said, getting back in step.

"Okay. Let's see now, what are you good at?"

"Just about everything," Elliott said. "You give me a chance, and I can show you. I learn fast. . . ."

"Know anything about printing?"

"Nossir, but I could learn." He thought of Grady. He was not sure he wanted to be a printer, but it might be a way to start. Grady would teach him.

178   "Think you could write news stories? Farm news,

Lions Club, weather reports, it's not all glamorous and exciting. . . ."

"Yessir, I've had some experience like that, like I said, in the Army. And before that I used to write up stuff for the school paper at home, it was just a ditto sheet we made up but—"

"What school is that? Here in town?"

"Down close to Lamar. A little place out south of there called Elysium. But they don't have school out there any more. . . ." He lapsed into silence, flustered by the irrelevance of his last remark.

"You made good grades, did you?"

"Pretty good."

Ceefs dug wax from his ear and looked at it. "Know anything about cameras?"

"Well, a little. I helped some Signal Corps guys a few times. I could get on to it quick enough if somebody showed me how. . . ."

"I like farm boys," Ceefs said. "Show me a farm boy and I'll show you somebody that knows his stuff. Common sense, that's what it is. Backbone. Knows how to use his hands. City punks. Don't know the meaning of hard work. Always stirring up trouble. I've got their number, don't think I don't. Knock some heads together. Well. Let's see." He got up and left the office. Elliott could hear him talking loudly in another part of the building.

I think you did it, Elliott said to himself. He put his head back and breathed out heavily. Yessir, I think you did. He's out there fixing it up. Wonder what I'll get. Probably jack-of-all-trades for a while, from the way he talked. Not much money, probably. But we'll show 'em. Zoooom. Boy, won't old Grady be surprised. I might even get him a job here, too, after I've got all set up. And   179

Fluffy, won't she be proud of me. And there might be one or two others sit up and take notice, too. One or two young ladies I know of that think they're so high and mighty. Wait till all of 'em hear!

When Winston Ceefs came back, he sat down at the typewriter, rolled a sheet of paper into it, stared at it silently, yawned, finally turned to Elliott. "Well, I'll tell you."

"Yessir."

"I don't have any jobs just now. I hate that, you being a vet and all. I like to help our boys. But I've already put on about all I need. You come back and see me some other time."

Elliott felt his chest tighten, involuntarily. He stared at Ceefs. When he tried to speak, his voice almost broke. Ceefs turned back to the typewriter.

"I'd really appreciate anything . . . anything you can do," Elliott said earnestly, lamely.

"Some other time maybe. Now I've got a lot of things to do." He began to type.

Later Elliott remembered going slowly back across the empty newsroom and down the stairs but everything after that was lost, until he came to himself behind the wheel of the old car on the highway headed toward home, guiding it rigidly, bolt upright, holding the speed at a steady pace well below the legal limit. The cramp in his bowels drained away, leaving him limp and mindless, taking big slow sips of air and breathing out heavily as if reviving from a long throbbing run. When he began to tremble, he pulled off the highway near an irrigation well, got out and splashed water from the spillway over his face and chest. The water was stagnant, having stood in the spillway since the late-summer crop waterings, but it cooled him and stopped the trembling. He walked back to the car and got his clean shirt and went behind the pump shed to change. I wanted it too bad, he thought. You never get anything if you want it too much. I should have known that. He dried his face and hair with his soiled shirt and stuffed it under the front seat of the car as he pulled back onto the highway. Well, I came close anyway. Miss may be good as a mile, but at least I learned something. He was sure right about one thing, a guy's got to have the right kind of appearance, handle himself right, know what to say. But you've got to get that early. Reckon how I'll ever make up for lost time. Polish. That's what they call it. Culture, position. Dear Sir: I wish to apply for a position with your firm for which I feel very qualified since I am a highly polished, cultured, and refined young man just returned from three years serving my country, having been awarded the Congressional Medal of Honor, Silver Star, and twelve Purple Hearts, sixteen unit citations, forty-three campaign ribbons, one hundred and eleven Good Conduct Medals, and a Sharpshooter's Badge, all due to my upbringing and my fine education at Hometown Central High School where I got all A's and was voted Most Likely to Succeed. Sure I was.

All I ever got was what Rich gave me. And the Major. Military histories and cheap novels. Custer and old Reno. *Napoleon's Campaigns in Italy*. *The Keys of the Kingdom*. *The Sun Is My Undoing*, by somebody named Marguerite Steen. Good old Marguerite. Marguerite and the Major. Good intentions and bad advice. Some hope, maybe. I guess you can't knock that. But whatever it was, it   181 was too little and too late. I wonder what he meant about all that dialectic stuff. Maybe old Grady will know.

It was sundown when he got home. The heavy yellow light from the vanishing sun was like fire on the windows of the house, on the trees and sides of the scattered out-buildings, hard and dull on his face. At first he mistook the sun's reflection on the windows for lamplight inside, but then he could see that the house was dark and still. He parked the car in the bare, hardpacked area they called a front yard and went around to the kitchen door. There he saw that shape of his father, dark and faceless with the light behind him, coming up from the cow lot with a milk pail in each hand.

"See you made it," his father said, going past him into the house. Elliott could hear him puttering with the cream separator, arranging the pans and spouts, mumbling.

"I said, get your business all fixed up?"

"Yes."

"Taken you all day, did it?"

"Yes."

"Fellow have to get hisself all fancied up in a dress suit and tie to talk with those government fellows?"

Elliott took off his coat and sat against the rim of the cistern.

"Yeah, you can just set there and rest," his father said. "I've done all the chores. Except you better go gather up the eggs for your mama. She's not feeling too good, got the sick headache or something. In yonder on the bed already, I reckon. I'll scramble us up something for sup-

per." He came to the door and handed Elliott an egg

bucket. "You didn't think to stop off at the gin on your way in, did you?"

Elliott stood up. "Hands need an empty trailer already? Heck no, I didn't even think about that. I'm sorry, darn it."

"Well, no need to worry now. Me and Grady saw to it before he left. Anyway, they ain't got that other wagon full yet. I'm going to have to get on to them in the morning. . . ."

"Left? Where'd he go?" Elliott said.

"Over to Teeds', I reckon. Leroy come by and said a bunch of them was getting together at their house to play some music, wanted Grady to come. So Salazar carried him to the gin when he took that last bale, and I reckon he hitched a ride with somebody from there. Said for you to come over when you got in, if you wanted to."

"I thought maybe he'd left for good."

"He will be, one of these days. Myself, I'm surprised he's stayed this long. Told me last week some guy offered him a printer's job in town. But said he didn't like the conditions somehow. No matter. He'll be taking off one of these days. Sure is a good hand, though, when you can keep him working and not talking. I'll hate to lose him."

Elliott took his coat into the house and went out to the chicken coop, stepping carefully to avoid the little piles of brown-and-white droppings. He gathered the eggs from the nests mechanically, conscious only of trying to breathe in the caustic reek of manure and feathers and soured chaff that covered the dirt floor. "Schicken shit and schocolate pie," he said, pondering the childish phrase from so long ago, the faded memory of delight and secret defiance in saying the forbidden word, the sad 183 innocent impossible attempt to hide in twisted sounds and associations.

He took the eggs back to the house and lit the lamp on the kitchen table and set out plates while his father fried sausage and heated a pan of biscuits left from breakfast. Before he sat down, Elliott went to the front bedroom where his mother lay in darkness with a damp cloth across her face. "You want anything to eat, Mama?" he said.

"Oh no," she said weakly. "You-all go ahead. If I get to feeling better, I'll fix myself some cereal or something."

He and his father ate in silence. When they had finished, Elliott went back to the shedroom and took off his Army dress shoes and stretched out on the bed.

"Ain't you going over yonder?" his father called from the kitchen.

"No."

"Well, I reckon Grady can hook hisself a ride home. If he's coming. But now if you want to, you go ahead and take the car. . . ."

"No. It's all right."

"Well, I think I'll go on to bed. We've still got cotton to get out, and the weather's going to change one of these days before you know it. There'll be an old blue norther blowing down on us any day now."

"REACH ME A ROSE, HONEY, AND POUR ME A LAST DROP INTO THAT THERE CRYSTAL GLASS." The night was deep and timeless and he did not sleep, although the lines and arcs of light behind his eyes softened and spread and sometimes almost vanished until he brought himself back to them, and when at last a car came, far into the darkness, he thought for a time that it was only inside him, until he knew then that the lights were on the walls, turning and wheeling and flowing across the shedroom as the car clattered in a circle beside the house and then stopped, the beams of its yellow headlamps dimming and rising with the erratic revving of the motor. There were voices and the clanging *whump* of a car door being shut. As the vehicle chugged away, he turned on his stomach and put his head against the screen of the open window beside his bed, listening to the limping, irregular footsteps of the figure he could not see as it passed the window, going toward the cellar.

"Grady?" he said in a loud whisper.

"It sure as hell ain't the Simple Cobbler of Agawam," Grady said. "Where are you, boy. Darker'n the back side of hell . . ."

"Wait a minute," Elliott said, "till I put my boots on." When he got to the cellar door, Grady was holding it open, peering down into the darkness.

"You're so brighteyed and bushytailed, you can lead the way down there and strike a light."

When they had felt their way down inside and gotten the lamp lit, Grady machine-rolled himself a cigarette and sat back on the bed, admiring his handicraft for several minutes before he held a match to it. "So round, and firm, and fully packed," he said. "Free and easy on the draw. Lordy, lordy, you're speaking of the woman I love." He squinted wearily through the smoke at Elliott. "Son, I'm telling you, old Grady is about wore to a nub. You ought to have been with us tonight. It was a good time had by all." Elliott stared moodily at the floor. "Well, what you want to talk about?"

"Nothing really, I guess."

"Nothing? Hellfire then; get your tokus out of here and let a man get some shuteye. I've done a hard day's work. And some night work, too." Neither of them moved. "Where was you today, anyhow?"

"I had to go to town."

"And left me to do all the work. Take you all day to go to town and back?"

"I went to Lubbock."

"Oh, the big city. What you doing tomcatting around up there, don't you know you're liable to get your taffy pulled? Why, Lubbock, Texas, is a veritable din of inequity, full of ice-cream parlors and painted ladies and 186 all sorts of sin just laying in wait for innocent country boys. I even hear they got sidewalks up there, and one or two streetlights. . . ."

"You're not doing very good."

"Well, I'm tired," Grady said. "Tard, tard." He took off his shoes. "I'd swear you wasn't waiting up to kiss me goodnight, but if you're just going to set and look at the floor, I'd as soon you do it in the dark if you don't mind, so I can get some sleep. Your daddy'll probably have both of us up and jumping through ourselves before it's good light. . . ."

"That's one thing for sure," Elliott said. He heaved a deep sigh.

"All right, let's have it," Grady said. "This hump on my back is really just all the troubles of the world. I might as well have yours, too."

Elliott sighed again, and when it became apparent that he was not going to speak, Grady went on, slowly, carefully, "You know, I think the trouble is, you take everthing too serious," he said gently, avoiding Elliott's eyes. "You ought to take things a little easier, and get out and have a good time once in a while. How come you didn't come on over to Teeds' place tonight? Me and Leroy left word with your daddy. . . ."

"I didn't feel like it."

"See, that's what I mean. How come you didn't feel like it? You act like there's some big secret ceremony or something that a guy's got to go through just to have hisself a little fun. Well, you ought to have been there anyway. We had a good time. Nothing fancy, just set around and plunked on the jitter boxes mostly, had us a little nip now and then out at the barn. Seems like the old man is pretty much like all these other scissorbills, all high and righteous when it comes to the fruit of the vine, 187 but none of that seems to have taken much hold with them boys of his, long as they can slip around a little and he don't find it out. Anyway, there was a pretty good bunch there, some fiddler from up around Lamar and a couple of old boys from somewhere that Leroy knew. Fiddler's a great big old fat boy named Mac something or other. Mac Baker. You know him? Must weigh close to four hundred pounds. And can't talk plain. Know who I'm talking about?"

Elliott nodded vaguely.

"He kept trying to tell Leroy and them something about petroleum menustrating over the highways." Grady laughed. "Come to find out, he was talking about the State Highway Patrols. What he meant was 'administrating.' But he sure can play that fiddle. Hotter'n a depot stove."

Elliott remained silent, and Grady leaned over in his face. "And how come you didn't tell me about them sisters of Leroy's? They let on like they're prim and proper, full of that two-bit Baptist hogwash of the old man's, but you never can tell about that kind. Wildest gal I ever knew was a preacher's daughter. One of them gals of Teed's is enough to make a man leave home, sure enough."

"Which one?" Elliott said glumly.

"Why, I don't know their names. They don't go round introducing theirselves to ever tramp printer that comes along with a hard on. But looks to me like a feller like you, why he ought to be right in there a-grabbin and a-chompin. . . ."

"What kind of a chance does a guy like me have with those girls," Elliott said. "No money, no fancy car . . ."

"Why, I do believe you're one of these romantics," Grady said. "Knight in shining armor, big white horse, soft music, hearts and flowers, heartbreakin sunsets, and they lived happily ever after. Shoot, you've seen too many picture shows. Guy don't need none of that for what I'm talking about."

"I don't remember any of those Teed girls being such hot stuff. One of them was in my class at school and she was about as skinny and ratty as I ever saw. Dumb, too."

"What's brains got to do with it? Most people's brain is between their legs anyway. Yessir, I believe you're not only a romantic, you're a blamed aristocrat to boot. All I can say is, if that's the one I saw, she ain't skinny now. And you missed yourself a dang good time by moping around here all night."

"You see T. J.?"

"Old Badmouth hisself. Yep, he was there with bells on. Come out from town just special for the occasion. Old boy plays a pretty good guitar, though, when he wants to. Says he's going to get hisself up a string band, play for dances and stuff. He sort of wants me to play with 'em . . . or Leroy does. Like to killed old T. J. to have to ask me."

"You going to do it?"

"Hellfire, I'm a printer. Or was. Not no musician. I've already gone and let you and your daddy almost make a hayseed out of me. Nossir, when we get this crop out for you folks, I'm hitting the road. It's already got to be too much like home around here, and that's the only reason I've stayed this long. Oh, I guess I might play with 'em some, long as it's just parties and country dances and that sort of thing. But old T. J., he's got big ideas. Thinks he can get him a radio show and make records and be on the Grand Ole Opry in no time flat. He'll do good to make traveling money, at least for a long time." He paused.   189

"I don't know, though . . . he might make it. He's just onery enough and bullheaded enough, and he likes to do those crazy, half-assed songs like 'Pistol-Packing Mama' and 'Don't Fence Me In' that everbody thinks is so great these days. But that ain't my kind of music."

"I don't understand it," Elliott said. "How you can even think of putting up with him."

"Why, he ain't nothing new to me," Grady said. "His kind are coming and going all the time. Besides, I'm getting tired of taking sides. Older you get the more you come to find out that a man's got enough to do just riding his own horse. Anyway, that ain't no reason for you to let old T. J. get under your skin the way you do. Custom hath made it in him a property of easiness, bygod, singin at gravesides."

"But he's worthless," Elliott said. "He's stupid and mean and crooked as the day's long. . . ."

"Since when did you get to be such a jewel of great price," Grady said. He leaned back and put his head against the wall and closed his eyes.

After a long silence, Elliott said, "Grady, you ever hear of some guy named Walter Prescott Webb?"

"Webb?"

"Somebody told me one time he wrote a book about the plains—"

Grady went over to his guitarcase and brought back a large red volume, thumbing through to find the title page. "I imagine it's the same old boy that done this one here on the Rangers. Seems like that name rang a bell. I don't know of any other book he wrote. What you want to know about it?"

190   Elliott was silent again. Then, still staring blankly at

the floor, he said, "You were talking about the get-together over at Teeds'. I went to a party once . . ."

"Hooray for you," Grady said, settling himself back on the bed again. "I bet you've seen a school play, too, and maybe even one or two hog killings."

"No, I mean a *real* party . . . like you see in the movies. Big fancy house, servants, ladies in long dresses . . ."

Grady opened his eyes slightly and looked at Elliott warily. "Whereabouts was all this?"

"California. San Francisco."

"Lordy, for a country boy, you get around. When was you out there, during the war?"

"Yeah. Right after V-E Day . . ."

"I can't feature you at no fancy dress ball."

"Well, I knew this Major overseas—"

"A major? I thought you was just a buck-ass private in the rear ranks. How come you hobnobbin with majors?"

"I was a *corporal*," Elliott corrected quickly. "I even made buck sergeant before I got out. Three stripes." Grady accepted the reprimand with a gesture of mock awe, rolling his eyes.

"When I was in the hospital, the Major used to come to see this nurse. That's where I got to know him, because of Lieutenant Luba. We called her Lieutenant Susy. Ell-Tee Susy. She was real nice, and the Major was sort of like an uncle to her and some of the other nurses. He used to bring them cigarettes and Scotch and nylons, and sometimes he brought me books. And when she was busy, the Major and I just sat around and talked. He was a college teacher before the war, see, and—"

"I thought you was going to tell me about this party   191 you went to. What's all this got to do with Walter Prescott Webb?"

"I'm coming to that. The party was at the Major's house, see. But before that, at Bagnoli—"

"Wait a minute now. You keep backing up on me."

"That was in Italy. Army hospital there, close to Naples. Lieutenant Susy found out that they were going to send me back to Casablanca, to the . . . well, she called it the nutward. The Walnut-Astoria, because the colonel in charge of it was named Astor or something." He kneaded his cheek with a knuckle. "Anyway, I was all right, see, and this Walnut-Astoria was supposed to be a really bad place. So Lieutenant Susy and the Major got me released from the hospital at Bagnoli and somehow got me assigned to the Major's outfit. He was with the AMGOT in Naples—"

"The AM-which?"

"AMGOT. American Military Government. He was in charge of the military history section. Which was mostly just me and him. We had an office in a big old house close to the ocean that had belonged to some queen or princess or whatever they have in Italy, and we didn't have anything much to do but sit around and drink coffee and shoot the bull. It was one heck of a lot better than being in a line company . . . or some hospital. All I had to do was sort of keep the place straightened up and sometimes I looked up stuff for the Major in books and files. And I drove him around, out to the hospital to see Lieutenant Susy and up to Rome and all over, even back to Anzio once, and we'd go around to check on the terrain, find out where the front lines had been at certain times, and then the Major would talk to G.I.'s so he could make up records on their units and stuff like that. Any-

192

way, we got to know each other pretty well. He wasn't very gung-ho or anything like that, and he told me all about his family back in San Francisco, showed me his daughter's picture—she was about my age, I guess, and real pretty—and he'd talk about art and politics and history and a lot of things that were real interesting, but I didn't understand all of it. You asleep?"

"Mmph," Grady grunted, his eyes closed. "Listening."

"Shoot, if you don't want to hear about it," Elliott said, standing up.

"No, no. Set down. I'm listening. Get on to the party."

"Well, the Major was always going on about me coming out there to see them after the war, and how I ought to go to college out there and stuff like that. I told you he was a history professor. I guess that's what it was. At the University of California or whatever they have out there. But it looked like the war never would be over. After V-E, we kept sitting around Naples not doing anything, and so one day the Major just got up and went over to PBS Headquarters to see some guy he knew in Personnel, and he came back with orders for us back to the States, and on top of that, thirty days' leave. I don't know how he did it. He was always wangling deals like that. You wouldn't have thought it of him, but he was a real smooth operator."

"Okay," Grady said, with a sigh. "Now we finally got you back home."

"Yeah. I thought about going on out there to California with him. It would have worked out real well, since I was supposed to report to Fort Ord when my leave was up. He even invited me. But I didn't go. Instead, I came home on furlough. Seems like every time I get away I always come back." He realized that Grady was looking at him now, and he was embarrassed by the shared gaze, the faint, almost undetectable rhythm of Grady's unspoken acknowledgment.

"I stayed here a couple of weeks," he said lightly, breaking out of the mood. "Long as I could. Then I went on out and reported in. At the time, it looked like they were going to ship me to the Pacific. That never happened, but in the meanwhile I still had some leave time coming, so I decided to go up to Frisco and dazzle the Major and his rich wife and his hotsy-totsy daughter."

"Dazzle 'em?"

"Yeah. I was what's known as a Combat Veteran, chestful of fruit salad, a Purple Heart, been all around the world. It made me feel pretty dang cocky, I guess . . . and I didn't know shit from Shinola. Seems my head is always about six months to a year catching up with the rest of me. . . ." He went on muttering, gazing at the floor again, ponderously, but it was mostly habit. Despite the vague note of self-pity in his tone, he found pleasure in calling back the sharp vision of that day, his mind's picture of himself, fresh and healed and free, the immense exhilaration of it, really and absolutely free, for the first (and, as it now seemed, only) time in his life, carefully outfitted in the set of tailored gabardines that were regulation but not issue and bought at the PX especially for this event, the expertly fitted smooth tan uniform which except for insignia was exactly like that worn by officers, on which he'd had sewn the most frayed faded shoulder patch and chevrons and ribbons he could find to give it the proper aging, so that with his overseas cap set at an appropriately rakish angle, he could carry himself forth stoically, almost wearily, into the air that was brisk and

pungent from the sea over great jagged cliffs, green and

white and heavy brown below the wooded mountains where sprawling estates flashed by the speeding bus coming up from Monterey, an occasional high mansion spinning slowly past in the distance, finally the fabled city of slanted streets and smiling girls on Grant Avenue and the backdrop of misty hills across the Bay and ships steaming beneath the Golden Gate, cable cars up Hyde Street to Russian Hill, to the Major's house. From the street it had reminded him of a villa in the mountains north of Paestum that had been the regimental CP for a time after Salerno. There was a white wall in front of it, and beyond that the shadows of many trees, deep green in the dying light of sunset. He had walked past it twice, to make sure it was the right one and try to think of what he'd say as an excuse for showing up unannounced, wishing he'd had the courage to telephone before coming.

"I was about half disappointed there wasn't a butler," he said to Grady. "It was really something out of a movie. A kind of courtyard in front with statues and stuff and big marble stairs on each side that went up in opposite directions and then turned and came together at the front door. I was about ready to hightail it if somebody had said boo. But I'd come that far, so I went on up and knocked. Waited a long time, because you were supposed to use this big fancy brass knocker that I thought was just some kind of ornament. I kept banging on the doorframe and finally this scary-looking Chinese woman opened the door. I guess she was Chinese. She had puffy eyes and a little mouth, looked like something out of *The Drums of Fu Manchu*, and I had a lot of trouble understanding her. Finally got it through that I was looking for Major Campbell. She let me come in and took me off to some little room where the lights were real dim, 195 and I could hear fancy music and a lot o talking going on and I caught a glimpse through some big doors down the hall where all these people were standing around in fancy dress clothes and holding glasses—"

He demonstrated with an imaginary goblet, satirically overextending his little finger. "Boy, I figured I was really in hot water then, and I started thinking about some way to get out before the Chinese woman came back. But then I said to myself, Heck this is what you've been wanting, isn't it? So I hung on, and pretty soon this other woman came in. She almost caught me prowling—"

"Prowling?" Grady said.

"I was looking at all the pictures and stuff, picking up these little statues, they were all over the place. You never saw so much stuff before. And these pictures were *real* pictures. You know: very old and you could actually see on some of them where the painter had touched his brush. There was one I remember that looked like the Three Musketeers. A bunch of guys with pointed beards and ruffly shirts and those big old floppy hats with feathers in them and high boots clear up to their knees. I bet it was a hundred years old or more. And it was real. It wasn't printed or anything like that. Another one was a picture of some bottles and glasses with fruit and stuff in them, and you could *see* that glass. I mean it was clear like real glass, but you could see it. How do you suppose a guy could ever do that? You ever see any pictures like that?"

"Yeah. I reckon."

"Sometimes you see something like that on the front of the *Saturday Evening Post*," Elliott said. "But it's not nearly as good. Are you listening?"

"Son, I'm not only listening, I'm plumb spellbound. Hurry just a mite, won't you."

"Well, anyway it turns out that this other lady is the Major's wife. The Major, he's not even there. They'd shipped him right on overseas again, to the Philippines or someplace. So me and the Major's wife, we're both in hot water. I'm scared to death I'll knock something over or say something out of line, and she's trying to place me in her mind—because I told her I'd served with the Major and she's supposed to know me but doesn't and she can't even remember my name and keeps calling me Sergeant Randolph. Finally this great big guy busts in from somewhere waving an empty glass and yelling a lot—"

"Why's he yelling?"

"He's just yelling. Stuff like 'Hail the conquering hero' and singing 'Over There' and carrying on in general. And he comes right over to me and gives me a big hug and starts rubbing his cheeks on me like he's kissing me, like those French guys do. Boy, I was about to keel over, till I realized he was about half drunk. His name was Ronald. Ronald . . . Webber, or Webster, something like that. It doesn't matter."

"No, it dudn't matter," Grady agreed wearily.

"She kept calling him Ronnie. Ronnie this and Ronnie that . . . and you know, I've thought a lot about it since then, and I've about decided that he was her boy friend. I'd sure hate to think that about the Major, but they were awful friendly that whole night, hugging and feeling around on each other. And far as I know, they weren't related. . . ."

"Happens in the best of families," Grady said. "Get on with your story. I swear you've got more quick switches   197 and sidetracks than the Illinoise Central. It don't take *me* that long to tell a story, and I'm about the world's worst."

"Anyway, this Ronnie guy was mad because he couldn't find any more liquor, and the Major's wife kept telling him to drink punch

—it's Grandfather's recipe don't you see, she said to a group of people who had joined them in the hall. —He was in the ah restaurant business you know and when the Earthquake came his business such a lovely place near the Montgomery Block where there is now this most exquisite little Italian travel agency

—let us go, noble warrior, Ronald Webster said. —Let us go in quest, brave knight, of some magic potion to drive away the bad fairies. And the good fairies, too, hey?

—and his ah business was almost demolished in the Earthquake although it escaped the fire all his lovely wines and liqueurs smashed you see and the story is that Grandfather simply poured the lot of them together in a big cask in order to save what he could from breakage and in that way he discovered this simply marvelous punch which according to all reports he served to the rescue people and even to the Salvation Army ladies for you see it really isn't at all very alcoholic one of the really cherished family traditions I have clippings from the newspapers which I must have framed Ronnie dear do behave yourself

—Sergeant, wouldn't you agree that non-alcoholic punch is an affront to nature? Hey, Sergeant. Where's your shield? You're supposed to come home from the wars either on it or carrying it. Or didn't your mother tell you

—I guess there's lots of things my mother didn't tell me

—Did she by any chance tell you where the Scotch is?

—Des malheurs de chaque être un bonheur général,

said a tall lovely girl with auburn hair. —Bot if a pearsong iss, how do you say, pissed off

—Ronnie please I'm telling Dr. Edmonds' wife about the punch yes stories from the old *Examiner* and the *Chronicle* telling about Grandfather and his punch and how much it has meant to San Francisco's history and heritage

"But this Ronnie guy gets her in a big hug, with me just standing there, and finally she told him to look in the kitchen and he grabs me and takes off rattling a bunch of silly stuff about the nectar of Mars and noble warriors coming back on your shield. He kept muttering about a phone number. 'Pope's phone number.' That's it. Said that over and over. You know what it means?"

"Means he drinks fair-to-middling Scotch and talks stupid," Grady said.

"He finally found some, and we had a drink of it. Tasted like kerosene to me but I was ready for anything. Only I hadn't had anything to eat all day and boy it hit me like a ton of bricks. We went on back and he took me into this big room where all the people were. You should have seen it. All these guys in fancy dress suits and tuxedos and ladies wearing long dresses with all kinds of flowers and ribbons. I'd probably been scared out of my wits if that drink hadn't fixed me up so I was ready for anything. The Major's wife tried to head old Ronnie off but he kept dragging me around like a puppy dog introducing all these people. I couldn't understand half their names or remember the ones I did. And all these guys were called 'doctor.' Doctor This and Doctor That. Heck, for a long time I thought they were all . . . well, you know, *doctor* doctors, like the kind you go to when you're sick. But after a while I caught on that they were mostly teachers. How come they call teachers 'doctor'? Is that some sort of formality or what?"

"The sheepskin," Grady said. "Philosophiae Doctorius."

"Oh. Well, I didn't understand half of what they were talking about. Good thing I'd had that drink. I just stood there acting like old Cary Grant or somebody"—he crooked an arm rakishly and braced his back to demonstrate—"with a big silly grin on my face and nodded at everything that went on.

Someone else in the group said to the tall girl —But of course you forget that Leibniz also asserted that the realm of essence exists only in constant conceptualism by

—real nylons, can you imagine!

An old man with a gray goatee stood at a wall of books, reading aloud to no one from a small green volume: —He's a bootlegger, said the young ladies, moving somewhere between his cocktails and his flowers. One time he killed a man who had found out that he was nephew to von Hindenburg and second cousin to the devil. Reach me a rose, honey

—The unrealized American potential for productive pluralism and meaningful marginality reinforced by identity diffusion, said a short young lady with pimples.

—in welche Sie Ihre sogenannte Persönlichkeit haben zerfallen lassen. Ohne Figuren kann ich ja nicht spielen.

—Hugh had her down and was spreading

—Really? I once had an uncle named Hugh

—Are you enjoying your visit, Captain?

—Yes, ma'am, I sure am. But I'm just a sergeant.

—Goodness, is that higher than a captain?

—however requisite to the demands of war and strife, it has darkened the very heart of our beloved city, said a small man with sad eyes and a thin mustache. —We've but a leaden door at our Golden Gate, and a tomb of night hides the splendor of this once-gleaming Orb of the Occident

—Dear dear man. Yes isn't that grand. "Leaden door at the Golden Gate." And you simply must put those very lines in your next volume. Oh yes, Grandfather had this entire plan in mind you see when the site was chosen and through those very windows one once could see at night the city's most dazzling panorama of the entire Bay area, with the cars flashing on the bridges and the ship lights and the signs, the neon lights of the city. Oh how grand it will be when, when . . . The Lights Come On Again, All Over the World

From those near enough to overhear, there was a round of polite applause, muffled by the heavy draperies.

—Boy, to me Frisco is still really pretty, even with the blackout

—oh please I do wish you wouldn't say "Frisco," Sergeant Randolph. It sounds so much like something things are fried in . . . or what gangsters say when they search one another you know

"Get on to the part about Walter Prescott Webb," Grady said. "Or else."

"Okay, there was this guy, who found out I was from Texas. That was after the Major's daughter came in, she'd been out with some Navy officer—"

"Oh god," Grady said. "Get on out of here. We've got all day tomorrow and maybe even a month of Sundays for you to go through all this."

"Just let me tell you about this one guy," Elliott insisted. "Somehow he got the idea that I'd gone to the University of Texas—"

"How'd that happen?"

201

"Well . . . I don't know."

"You tell him you had? Or just let him think it?"

"Anyway, he started talking about some book by this Webb fellow." He looked up at Grady. "You know, when he mentioned the name, all I could think was that he was talking about one of those Webbs that used to live up yonder by Three-Mile

—intrigued by a particular point he makes regarding a unique socio-cultural phenomenon which he describes as the "cultural fault." He observes, don't you see, that the geographical conditions play a vastly important role in the cultural development of people and institutions. Not a profoundly original position these days I suppose but specifically and most importantly Webb has applied this thesis to the plains area, showing how the backwardness of the region is a result of abortive metamorphoses imposed upon individuals in the mass migration from lush forest and mountain areas to the essentially flat treeless plain. This he describes as the "cultural fault" using the term "fault" in its primarily geological sense of course yet with obvious implications with regard to

"He seemed to think I ought to know all about this fellow Webb and his ideas. I guess because he thought I'd gone to the University," Elliott said. "I couldn't make heads or tails out of it, but I'd had another drink or two and for some crazy reason, that business about cultural fault got stuck in my head and I went around all over the place saying it to everybody."

"That's all? That's the story?"

"Yeah. I just thought you might know what he was talking about."

"And that's all? Jesus H. Christ," Grady said. "On a crutch. You been keeping me awake for that?" He rolled

202

over to the edge of the bed, sat up, and began to undress. He watched Elliott expectantly for several minutes, waiting for him to leave, but Elliott did not move. So he went on taking his clothes off. When he was stripped to his shorts, he sat back down on the bed and rolled another cigarette. "You live a careful life, don't you," he said.

When Elliott did not answer, he shrugged and went on in a lighter tone. "Well, at least I guess you must have got your money's worth out of this daughter of the Major's."

Elliott said, "Huh! You think she'd pay any attention to me? I was full of those fancy notions about how the Major would have told her all about me and she would be . . ."

"Be what?"

"Well . . . all hot to trot. But she came waltzing in with this Navy lieutenant—" He had recognized her immediately from the snapshots the Major had showed him. He knew the face very well. Once he had tried to sketch it from the photographs, but he'd always had trouble drawing girls. He could never get the nose right, and her delicate chin and wide beautiful mouth eluded him. At last he gave up and put her in shadows and made the sketch look very arty with graded washes and elaborate brush marks. The Major had praised it and sent it home. Or said that he had.

—the most divine place for dinner on this lovely cliff in Marin atmosphere absolutely fabulous cuisine Wilson knew the maître d'

—dear dear Wilson. Lindy, you really must take Wilson over and show him off to the Frederick Wheelings. They've been dying to meet him. Yes. Oh dear. This is ah Sergeant oh yes Randolph

—Randall

—Yes. I'm afraid I've forgotten your first name may I introduce Naval Lieutenant Wilson Manner and my daughter Lindy. Sergeant Randolph served with your father, Lindy.

—Please to meet you I'm sure. The Major has spoke very often of Lindy

—My name is Linda

—Dear dear yes. She was born the day after Lindbergh landed in Paris you see her father named her Lucky Lindy

—Alias the Lindy Hop, said Naval Lieutenant Wilson Manner.

—Father is such a square.

—Oh no. Heck, Lindbergh was always one of my heroes, too. I mean, that was a very exciting era in our history

—He should have named her the Lone Eagle

—Oh, you. You think you're so clever, Wilson. Do you know Mother what this idiot did as we were driving out to San Rafael? We were driving along, and a silly cat ran across the street in front of the car. The cat was already across the street and everything, and this big goof just literally jumped on the brake like a wild man oh the tires squealing and the car practically skidding all over the highway. I was absolutely terrified. I simply could not imagine what, and so after we finally got stopped and Wilson the silly fool calmly backs the car very slowly and very properly, all the way back to where the cat ran across. Then he said, as if absolutely nothing had happened, he said, 'I tawt I taw a puddy-tat.' Isn't that just the wildest thing you've ever heard? Say ta-ta to everyone for us Mother we've promised to meet some people at the Mark

—The genuine Ronald Webster Eight-to-One Kickapoo Cocktail, said Ronald Webster.

—What's eight-to-one? The odds on survival?

—Beauty is momentary in the mind, recited the old gentleman with the gray goatee. —The fitful tracing of a portal

—Lissen, Elliott said, to no one in particular. —Here's to the Wayward Girl with Lips That Curl

—Yes?

—lips that curl . . . over her cultural fault

—I beg your pardon?

—Where's everbody going. Lemme tell you what we got in Texas, we got this cultural fault

—so nice meeting you Sergeant Randolph, and do be careful overseas

—cultural fault . . . from not having no Kickapoo Cocktails. Lemme tell you, see, I was reading this about these old guys someplace in the olden days a book the Major gimme, they used to, in their tribal meetings or councils or whatever it was, they used to talk about everthing first, and then they'd get drunk and hold another meeting. Or maybe it was the other way around. Anyhoo the liquor loosened 'em up so they could think good and they could come up with just any kind of idea about what to do. Shows you the power of alcohol

—I'm sure you'll find that it was ancient Egyptians. That is of course if one can believe Herodotus. The process was to drink first, debating affairs of state while under the influence, and then when in a state of complete sobriety reconsider and apply proper restraint to such   205 imaginative and prescient proposals as might have been set forth. One concludes that while alcohol obviously frees the tongue it is hardly beneficial to the mind

—Hey where's everybody going. Night's so young and you are so be-yuty-ful

—Poe says it was the Goths. "Sober that they might not be deficient in formality, drunk lest they should be destitute of vigor."

—Everyone knows what a fraud Poe was

—I do hope you understand, Sergeant. Dear dear, we'd love to have you join us, but we've tickets only for our group you see

—Tickets?

—I supposed Ronnie told you. We're attending the symphony you see. A benefit for our boys at the front. Even in wartime, culture and the arts are to be maintained perhaps the need is even greater in times of strife I *am* sorry that you can't join us but . . . the tickets you know perhaps some other time if you're in San Francisco ever again

—I'll be here all right. I like this place a whole lot, all these hills and everything. Yes, ma'am, I sure do like hills. No cultural fault where they got hills. You heard about the cultural fault in Texas? Have to tell you about that one a these days

After that he was out in the purple night, alone, passing the pale streetlights painted black on the seaward side, going through the turns down Lombard Street thinking, This crazy street is drunker than I am, laughing. There seemed to be a huge military band blaring somewhere behind him, playing a recessional. He knew there was no such band, but its presence was very real to him in his alcoholic haze, and he kept mock-solemn ca-

206

dence with its steady, mournful beat, going along skipping to pick up the step and trying to quicken the count so that he could get someplace before he fell down. Approaching a silent intersection, he called out "Road guards, POST!" and marched in place until the ghostly sentinels could take their position. Then he trudged on across the street and wearily called back the guards, beginning to tire of the game. Coming back from the front. Home from a war. Hell, you can't win 'em all. Win some, lose some, a few get rained out. Rained out, washed out, flooded. Bombed, strafed, shot off at the ankles. *I tawt I taw a puddy-tat.* Why can't I ever think of funny things like that to say? Maybe I will someday.

Grady said, "Goddammit, I forgot to pee, and now I've got my shoes off." He slipped his bare feet into his high-topped brogans without tying them and limped up the cellar stairs with the shoe tongues flapping and the laces making little clicking sounds as he shuffled into the darkness. Elliott followed him and they went away from the house and urinated.

"You know," Elliott said, "I couldn't remember whether to salute that stupid Navy lieutenant or not. The Navy's got all those crazy regulations about not saluting while uncovered. Or at least the Marines do. I saluted a Marine captain one time in Naples and the smart-aleck didn't return it. Refused to return it, the bastard. He saw me a mile away and he just strutted by with his head in the air."

"Yessir," Grady said. "You live a mighty careful life."

THE FITFUL TRACING OF A PORTAL. The first hard norther came blowing down one Saturday in early November. The land turned gray and slab-like, almost the color of the winter sky, and all across it in flat square plats were the black spikes of stripped cotton stalks, laced with scraps of wispy lint that had eluded the pickers. Winds gusted along the ground, sending colorless dirt in spreading arcs, whipping at the flimsy buildings in sudden and erratic thrusts that rattled windows and howled across the tin chimneys of kerosene stoves, making the dampers dance and pop.

The main body of Mexican field hands had left and gone back to their homes in the Rio Grande Valley, leaving only the more ambitious or desperate families to do scrap picking. With harvest work slackening, it had been decided (by mutual but unspoken agreement) that Grady and Elliott were to have the day off, Elliott having at last surrendered, however reluctantly, to Grady's grandilo-quent railings against all-work-and-no-play. Their original plan had included the use of the Ford to drive into Lamar, but Mr. Randall without any sort of direct refusal made it clear that he did not intend to give up his only means of transportation to and from the weekend spit-and-whittle sessions at Elysium. Business to tend to, he muttered vaguely, and I got to be around in case them hands need a empty wagon. But I'll carry you-all over to 'Lysium when I go to the gin, and you can hitch you a ride with somebody into town.

After the morning chores they washed up and dressed for the occasion, Grady in a pair of new khakis, Elliott in fresh Levi's and a white Western-style shirt his mother had given him for his birthday. By the time they had hitched a wagon loaded with cotton to the car and towed it to the gin, most of the Saturday butter-and-egg traffic to Lamar had already passed through, and so they settled down to wait for a stray or straggler. Grady wandered off toward Box's store, leaving Elliott sitting with his father and seven or eight other men around the big heater in the gin office.

The men swapped stories and carved on the crude benches while they waited for their loads to be suctioned from the wagons into the rumbling gin stands. From time to time loaded wagons bumped up onto the wooden weight platform in front of the office, and each time Barney Reid, the gin manager, would spit and curse and heave his great bulk from its comfortable position near the stove and go up front to read the scale and then open the door and yell at the new arrival until the wagon was pulled on through the weight shed and into the long serpentine line that led across the yard to the suction canopy.

Elliott got up and wandered off into a corner, where he

sat against the wall and took out of his jacket a paper-back copy of *Major Barbara* that Grady had given him. He was struggling with Euripides on money and gun-powder in Act II when T. J. Teed brushed past Barney at the door and stomped back to the stove. "Hey, any of yawl seen Leroy?" he demanded.

There was a collective impulse to laugh when they looked up and saw how he was dressed: a huge and ob-viously new black felt hat with a flat-blocked crown and six-inch brim rolled straight along the sides, bright green satin shirt with scalloped red insets at the shoulders and multi-colored embroidery on the front, natty gabardine stockman's pants tucked into a pair of cheap Acme cow-boy boots decorated with yellow butterflies spread across the toes. But any open attempt at humor was stifled by T. J.'s sense of himself, by his strident manner, his brisk-ness and zeal. So they simply looked at each other with knowing grins and a few stage coughs.

"Box said he was out here," T. J. said impatiently. "Yawl seen him?"

One of the men said, "I think him and Wilmer Callo-way is out at the bagging shed. I seen them headed that way while ago."

"What the hell's he doing out there?"

"I dunno. Day crew's been having some trouble with the press. Maybe him and Wilmer's helping 'em. Maybe they're just out there shooting the shit."

T. J. went back to the front and looked out across the yard toward the gin. Behind his back, Chinless Bill Story said softly to no one in particular but grinning and drop-ping an eyelid, "Looks like Christmas come early this year."

210   "Yeah," Less Pirtle whispered loudly, "but I thought

Christmas trees suppose to have balls on 'em. Reckon that one's got balls?"

T. J. wheeled, but both men were busy looking at the ceiling. The others ducked their heads or hid their grins with big hammy hands. T. J. watched them with narrowed eyes for a minute or two, then walked back through them to a window at the rear. "All right," he said, "just take a look across yonder and tell me what you think of *that*." When no one moved, his voice became urgent and testy. "Come on, goddammit, and cut out making them goony faces at one another."

Tom Lightner hacked deep in his throat, clearing away the phlegm and tobacco juice. "They was just hoorawing you, T. J.," he said. But T. J. insisted, and one or two of them got up and went to the window. Their exclamations and T. J.'s smug swagger brought others to look, and finally even Elliott went over to a side window that gave a view in the same direction. What they saw, parked beside the gas pump at Box's store, was a huge and ancient bus-like contraption painted bright green, decorated with blue and yellow guitars and the legend T. J. TEED & HIS WEST TEXAS RAMBLING RHYTHM-MASTERS in six-inch red letters that ran the length of the side. Some of the letters were made to resemble notes and behind them ran the five floating lines of a musical staff. In the vehicle sat a woman Elliott had never seen and two men that he recognized as Dudley Thomas and Mac Baker, the huge fiddler from Lamar.

"Hey, that's some wagon you got there," one of the men said. "Your name on it, and all."

"Now let's see you laugh," T. J. said.

Some of them went outside to get a better look, and T. J. followed, spitting at the stove as he went by. Leroy 211 appeared from behind the gin and came out to join the group. T. J. said, "Damn it all, bud, where you been? I looked all over for you, even went out to Daddy's place. . . ."

"Looks like you got us a real bus there," Leroy said. "What is it, anyway? Looks like an old Franklin chassis."

"That, my friend," said T. J. grandly, "is a nineteen-and-thirty-one Packard Eight with a special-built panel body."

"Cemetery hearse, ain't it?" one of the men said.

"Hell no," T. J. said. "What if it is. It ain't painted black or nothing like that, is it. And I'll tell you this, that baby runs like lightning, smooth as a baby's butt. One-owner car, and I've got the man that'll vouch for it."

Barney Reid laughed and swore. "All I can say is, there's a gap of daylight between ever piece of it . . . and looks to me like ever piece is moving. In a different direction."

"Kiss off," T. J. said. "I ought to know a good deal when I see one. I been overhauling 'em long enough. And believe me, I got that baby tuned up like a horny tomcat."

"Still looks like a hearse to me," Chinless Bill said.

"It's a hearse all right, little bud," Leroy said. "But you sure got her fancied up."

"Come here," T. J. said, with a pull of his head, indicating that he wanted to talk to Leroy alone. The other men began to straggle back inside. "Listen, I got a dance job tonight all fixed up, over at County Line—"

"County Line?" Leroy said. "Dang, that's sixty, seventy mile or more."

212   "Why, hell yes. What you think this is, some little old

punk high school outfit? I done quit my job at the Chevrolet house, put ever thing I got into this."

"Quit your job? How you gonna pay your bills? And keep up that hotel room? Daddy hears about you quitting your job, he'll yank your butt back home and put you on a cultivator."

"He ain't gonna hear about it, 'less somebody like you tells him. Not till I'm famous. Then he can hear all about it he wants to. You just let me worry about that. Listen, what we need right now is some gas money, something to operate on till we get paid for the dance."

"Who all you got coming?"

"Mac's with me in the car, and Arliss Jones and another old boy from town is supposed to meet us over there. But I promised the guy six men—"

"Who else is that in the car. Ain't that Dud?"

"Yeah, but Dud can't play with hisself, let alone a piece of music. He's just going along for the ride."

"Well, what'd you need?"

"Eight, ten bucks ought to do it, till we get paid."

"No, I mean who to play? You ain't hitting *me* for no loan, I'll tell you that right now."

"Hell, I need anybody I can get my hands on. A good lead guitar, which is you, and—"

"How you know I'm going?"

"You're going all right. Don't give me none of that." He turned away from the wind and spat. "Where's that hunchback buddy of yours, anyway?"

"Last time I seen him he was out at the store."

"What's he doing out there?"

"Heck, I don't know. Hustling Frieda Mae, I guess. Or maybe her mama. He's a real switch hitter."

213

"You think maybe we could interest him in going along?"

"Maybe. If the price was right."

"I'll make it worth his while. Right now we owe Box for a tank of gas. That baby's been setting on empty for ten miles, and Box won't even come out to the pump till we show him the folding stuff."

"Not *us*, little bud. You. Won't he put it on a ticket?"

"Hell no. The sonofabitch. And me a vet and all. That's the kind of bastard guys like me went off and won the war to protect. I told him we had a dance, and the bastard can see plain as day he ain't fooling with some hick outfit any more. . . ." He gazed at the hearse, taking it all in, and the hard wrinkles in his scowl went away.

"Well, don't you get any ideas about filling up and driving off without paying him," Leroy said as they walked toward the store. "Daddy'd skin your ass and mine, too." As they approached the hearse, a gust of wind hit them and Leroy hunched down into the collar of his coat, peering through the dust. "Hey, who's that besides Dud and Mac? That looks like Vaudine Honeycutt. You fooling around with that? Don't you know Honey'll put a slug in you where it'll do the most good, one a these days?"

"It's a friendly arrangement," T. J. said. "Honey keeps the law and order, and I take care of his wife. Long as he's wearing that deputy's badge and got a big old car with a whip aerial on it, he's happy."

"Yeah, but a badge ain't all he's wearing. Don't forget about that .38 po-leece special."

"Shit. Honey couldn't hit a bull in the ass with a bass fiddle and you know it. Anyhow, he's my friend. My good buddy."

214

Vaudine was calling to them from the hearse. "Come on, for crying out loud," she said. "I thought we was going to County Line."

"Honeybunch," T. J. said, sticking his head in the car window, "you sure you haven't got a buck or two on you?"

"You kidding? Even if I did, you wouldn't get it."

"Come on, bud," T. J. said. "Let's see if we can find your hunchback friend."

Elliott watched them from the corner of the gin office. Then, chilled by the wind, he went back inside. He tried to read again, but he couldn't concentrate. He paced, slowly, behind the circle of men around the stove, and finally he went to the door. "I'm gonna see if anything's happening at the café," he said to his father, who looked up at him silently for an instant before he nodded and turned back to the conversation.

The café was crowded but he found a stool at the counter. Unexpectedly, he also found Grady, hunched over the soft-drink cooler behind a pie rack, pouring the last drop from a gin bottle into a Grapette and munching from a cardboard tube of Prize Peanuts. "Man's got to keep his strength up," Grady said.

"You seen Leroy and T. J.?" Elliott said. "I think they're looking for you."

"Well, I don't guess they've found me. What's their trouble?"

"Far as I could understand, T. J. wants you to play a job with them."

"Yeah, I spotted that circus chariot he's got parked out front of Box's. Old T. J. is a real artist, you know that? I admire a man with taste, however corrupted it may be."

Fluffy dashed by with four or five glasses of water cupped in her hands and slid one down in front of Elliott. "Hi, honey," she said in a strained voice. "I'll be with you in a minute."

"Just a coke when you get time," Elliott called after her. "What's wrong with Fluffy?" he said to Grady. "Her and Bud at it again?"

"I reckon. I just got here, my ownself. She give him hell while ago, and he's been throwing dishes around back there, I heard that. I reckon he's juiced up again."

"Where you been? Over at the store?"

"You could say that."

"How's Free-To-Me?"

"I don't know about her, but her mama's doing nicely." He grinned. "Now."

"Good lord, Grady," Elliott said, glancing around to see if anyone was listening, lowering his voice. "You can't go around . . . why . . . it's . . ."

"It's what?"

"Well, for one thing it's . . . well, it's a reflection on Mama and Dad. . . ."

Grady sighed, shaking his head slowly as if in disbelief. "Reckon you'll ever grow up?" he said. He swigged the last of the gin and Grapette. "Now look, you don't worry yourself about my social life. I only work at your place. You-all don't own me. Anyway, I don't reckon anybody is going to kiss and tell."

"All the same, you ought not to—"

"Yessir, I think I am gonna have to look up that old boy that said he needed a job printer. Job printing is about the next thing to ratting, but you dang scissorbills
216 just keep crowding a man."

Leroy and T. J. came in, talking heatedly. "Hey, Grady," Leroy said, coming over. "Want to play for a dance?"

"Whereabouts?" Grady said.

"Place called County Line," T. J. said. "It ain't far. Over in the next wet county. 'Bout fifty miles or so."

Grady thought about it, munching peanuts. "Might as well," he said at last. "I'm going to be sick anyway." The crowd had thinned out, and Leroy and T. J. sat down at a table.

"Well, well," Fluffy said, pinning a wisp of hair back out of her eyes. "If it ain't the Rover Boys. Yall want something, or you just taking up space?"

"Fluffy," T. J. said, "come go to a dance with us. You seen my new car?"

"Boy howdy," she said. "For about two cents I would." She glanced toward the kitchen, disgustedly. "I ought to just pick up and go. But some other time, I guess. Where's the dance?"

"County Line. Come see my new car." T. J. led her to the window.

Grady said, "Elliott, you want to go?"

Elliott glanced at T. J. and then at Leroy. "Okay by me," Leroy said, "if he don't care. Hey, little bud," he called out, "we got room for him, too?"

T. J. came back from the window. "I don't know," he said, taking a hard look at Elliott, then turning back to Leroy. "Maybe none of us gonna go. Little short on gas money at the moment. That's only temporary of course, till we get paid for playing the dance." He spotted the copy of *Major Barbara* in Elliott's pocket. "What you reading there, Brains?"

Elliott showed him the book. On the cover was a voluptuous blonde, gaudily lithographed in a tight blouse and skirt cut in the vague semblance of a military costume. She stood with outstretched arms toward a crowd of men in the foreground. Beneath the title was advertised, "Shaw's Classic Drama of 'Blood and Fire'!"

"Any pussy in it?" T. J. said. Elliott shrugged.

"And old Pyrrhus says, If I should overcome the Romans in just one more fight," Grady muttered, "bygod, I were undone."

"Now listen here," T. J. said. "Don't start that shit—" He made a show of rising from his chair but Leroy caught his shoulder and he sat back. Leroy said to Grady, "You're good friends with Miz Box, how about going over and sweet-talking a little. . . ."

"Nope," Grady said. "You're right about one thing. Me and her is friends. And I don't hustle my friends." He smiled. "You're my friend, and I ain't ever hustled you, have I?"

"Look," Elliott said, trying not to be too anxious. "I could probably rake up a few bucks. . . ."

"Yeah?" T. J. said. "Come on then. Let's get at it."

"You sure it's okay if I go?"

"Sure, sure. Why not?"

"Well, I thought . . ."

"Listen," T. J. said, sitting down beside him at the counter, "maybe I talk a lot, shoot off my mouth, drink a little too much sometimes, but I don't mean nothing by it. I don't bear no grudges, if that's what's worrying you. I'm just an old country boy like everbody else, maybe I don't talk as fancy as some people, use big words, and put on a show, but we're all friends, ain't that right? How much you got on you?"

218

Elliott looked at Grady. "Heck, we're not really dressed up to go to a dance."

"Ah, them blue jeans look okay. Least you ain't wearing overalls or something like that. I think maybe I got a necktie in the car you can have. Come on and let's get that gas."

"I'll have to write a check. How much . . ."

"Oh, fifteen"—he shot a quick glance at Elliott—"twenty ought to do it, have a little to spare case we run into trouble on the road. Make it twenty-five if you got it, I'll see you get her back right away." He turned to Fluffy. "You better come with us."

She wrinkled her nose in futility and mopped at the counter with a soggy gray rag. "That sure is a nice car. Yall have to give me a ride in it sometime."

"No time like the present."

Elliott wrote out a check for twenty-five dollars on his father's account at the bank in Lamar, and Fluffy cashed it for him, rifling around under the counter to find enough one-dollar bills and change to meet the amount. When he realized that she was using most of her register money to cover the check, he offered to take it to Box's store, but Fluffy insisted, squeezing his hand and winking as she gave him the money. "Don't spend it all in one place," she said lamely. T. J. lifted the bills and coins from Elliott's open palm.

Elliott looked at Fluffy. "I don't guess you . . . you and Bud could . . . maybe close up and come with us."

"Oh lord no, honey," she said. "Much as I'd like to. He's on another tear, already got so bad I had to take the kids over to his mama's a while ago." There was a loud crash in the kitchen, pots and pans clattering, the breaking of a few dishes, the thump of something heavy and soft hitting a wall. Fluffy slapped down her counter rag in disgust and sauntered back through the swinging door, rolling her eyes toward the ceiling as she disappeared.

T. J. stalked off to Box's store to pay for the gas, yelling orders to the others to fill the tank, check the oil, and air the tires. All the while, Dud and Vaudine and the fiddle player sat in the hearse staring into the distance and politely ignoring Elliott, Grady, and Leroy as they carried out T. J.'s instructions. Box came to the window once to see how much gas they'd taken and then followed T. J. out of the store and told him to get his ass in gear and move the hearse before it scared off all his regular customers. "Prophet without honor," Grady said, chuckling.

They piled in, trying to find comfortable positions in the huge vehicle, which despite its size had no seats except the front one, occupied by T. J. and Vaudine. Behind it had been constructed a makeshift wooden bench, hardly wide enough for two people, but Elliott crowded in on it beside Leroy and Dud. Further back, in the cavernous hull of the hearse sat Mac, crosslegged on the bare floor of the chassis like some massive, saggy-jowled idol in a ten-gallon hat amid a jumble of musical instruments, wornout tires, tools, and greasy rags. Grady crawled back with him and found sitting room beside a wheel well. "Goddammit, be careful," T. J. said. "Don't get on that case there. That's my new Vol-U-Tone amplifier."

"Amplifier?" Leroy said.

"Damn right. Hook up to that thing, they can hear them old guitar wires a-humming all over the country. Cost me seven bucks down and two-fifty a month at Monkey Ward, so take it easy back there."

220   They idled past the café and were about to turn onto

the road when Fluffy came out on the café porch. She was untying her apron and struggling to put on a coat. "Hold it," Grady said, peering out the back window. "She's waving at us." When she ran up, he swung open the back panel and she said, "Yall still want to take me riding in your buggy?"

"Sure," T. J. said. "Hop in."

"Wait a minute now," Leroy said. "What's Bud got to say about this?"

"Oh, that fathead," she said. "He's done and drank himself into a coma, and I'll tell you, I'm fed up to here, that's all. I just ran everybody out and locked up and left the sot there on the floor to sleep it off. Fell right in the red beans, that's what he did, and it's good enough for him."

Vaudine said sympathetically, "Why, I swear."

"Let's don't set here all day jawing," someone said.

"Get in," T. J. said.

Leroy hesitated again. "If Bud don't happen to like it . . ."

"The lady knows her business," Grady said, extending his hand to pull her inside. Elliott wished that he had spoken up for her first, and he especially regretted having struggled with Dud and Leroy for a seat on the bench instead of crawling into the back, where now Grady was whispering with Fluffy and helping her get settled beside him on one of the old tires. The light happy feeling he had had drained away for a time, until he convinced himself with furtive glances backward that she was paying no more attention to Grady than to anyone else.

They stopped briefly at Old Man Teed's place so that Leroy could change into a clean shirt. He came out smelling of Rose Hairoil and wearing a big cowboy hat almost 221 as flamboyant as T. J.'s. As they roared off again, T. J. said, "Leroy, couldn't you find no other hat for your buddy back there?"

"Nope," Leroy said. "But he's welcome to mine if it'll fit."

"Goddam, if this ain't going to be a ragtag bunch," T. J. said. "First money we get paid, I'm seeing to it that yawl get your butts down to the J. C. Penney's and get some good-looking outfits. If you're going to be in my band, you're going to have to look like something."

Leroy's hat was almost a size too large for Grady, but he took it and clamped it on his head, deliberately pushed down so far that the brim folded his ears forward. "Oh forth from his dark and lonely hiding place," he chanted over their laughter, "sailing on obscene wings athwart the moon drops his blue fringed lid and hooting at the sun cries out, Where is it at, where is it at?"

On the way through Lamar they stopped in the flats to buy a fifth of Old Crow from a bootlegger. Elliott took advantage of the stop to crawl around Mac into the rear beside Grady and Fluffy. But the long trip was uneventful. They made two more stops along the way for gas and oil, and each time T. J. patted the car proudly and said, "Passes anything on the road but a gas pump," handing more of Elliott's money to the attendant and playing host with the bottle of Old Crow. Most of the route was over rough country roads, and the roar and clatter of the Packard limited conversation to sporadic grunts, cries of exaggerated terror from backseat drivers, requests for the bottle, and T. J.'s rambling, maniacal curses as he spun out of turns and sped through flocks of screaming, fluttering chickens.

WHERE IN DREAMS I LIVE.

It was growing dark when they reached the secluded crossroads beer joint and dancehall known in neighboring dry precincts as County Line and officially designated Troy's Kotton Klub by a red neon sign flashing and humming in the cold autumn dusk. Several cars were parked on three sides of the blank-walled, windowless building, a low angular affair of cinder block and rickety wooden frame cobbled together in random pattern on the edge of an open pasture.

The crowd was drifting inside, settling at tables and booths scattered around the dance floor. T. J. found the owner supervising the sale of beer from ice-packed wooden chests that lined an alcove along one side of the entrance. "Howdy there, Mr. Troy," he said. "Seen anything of my other boys?"

Troy chewed on a dead cigar. "They're setting up over yonder," he said without looking up, thumbing toward a platform in the shadows beyond the milling crowd. He spoke with heavy sarcasm. "If it's all the same to you, I'd just as soon you hotshots get started. This damn crowd ain't much as it is, and they're not too happy about paying a cover charge just to play the jukebox."

"Better believe it," T. J. said. He started off, then turned back. "Yeah, before I forget," he said. "It's five apiece for the boys and ten for me." He watched Troy. "And fifteen for expenses."

"Don't give me that shit," Troy said. "I hired you for thirty dollars flat, and that's it."

T. J. shrugged. "You get what you pay for."

"What's that mean?"

"Oh, might mean anything. We're good, and you know it. And the people know it. You said yourself they're tired of playing the nickelodeon. Be too bad if something was to happen, some of us got sick, after you advertising live music and charging 'em cover. . . ."

Troy squinted at him. "Listen. Get this. I ain't paying you no fifteen dollars for no expenses."

"Okay, okay. But look, I brought some friends along, how about coming up with a bottle for us. For them, I mean. You can do that, can't you?"

"You know I can't sell whiskey," Troy said. "Last thing I need is trouble with the Liquor Control boys."

"Come on now," T. J. said with a lazy wink. "Nobody's talking about you *selling* any whiskey. I know, and you know, how things are. Get me a bottle. Just so everything stays smooth and easy. I'm happy, you're happy, business is good, we're all friends here."

"You sonofabitch," Troy said. But he went off into an-

other part of the building and came back with a fifth of

Haven Hill in a paper sack and handed it to T. J. Then he counted out three ten-dollar bills from his wallet. "I don't usually pay till the job is done," he said, but I want your ass out of here the minute that last number is over."

Vaudine had maneuvered Elliott and Fluffy to a table near the dance floor. Dud wandered off to buy setups and while he was gone T. J. brought over the new bottle and gave it to Vaudine. "Keep your eye on that," he said. "Don't let nobody swipe it, and see if yawl can't stay out of it till the other is gone. Me and the boys might like a drink now and then, you know."

The band led off with "Ida Red," fiddles flying and Leroy singing, "Ida Red, Ida Red, I'm plumb fool about Ida Red." The lights dimmed, except for two cold white floodlamps that illuminated the band platform, and the crowd filled the dance floor in seconds, swinging and whirling and shouting "Whoo-eee" and "Take it away, Leon."

Elliott had had several quick hot gulps of Old Crow on the way, but now he switched to beer on principle, the principle being that he paid his own way and was not drinking T. J.'s liquor. He recalled then that it was his money T. J. had used to buy it. Although that complicated things a bit, by the time he got to his third beer it had ceased to matter. The beer made him happy and relaxed. Yet he suffered assault from other directions, from a thousand sad and boneless phantoms, ghosts without eyes, shadows that cast no form or identity save a nettled ache that spread and ebbed. One of the things that he suffered from was Fluffy, sitting across from him smiling and tapping the table in time with the music. It might have been that he was in love with her—desperately, terribly, long-

225

ingly in love with her—but he knew quite clearly and absolutely that he could not be in love with another man's wife, a woman not only married but older and, above all, a mother. Even if he could convince himself that he was in love with her, he didn't know what to do about it. So he sat morosely chipping with a thumbnail at the label on his beer bottle while the music rose and throbbed around him in the dark whirling rush of bodies and voices. First Vaudine and then Fluffy tried to get him to dance, but he offered various excuses. Finally, after several more beers, he allowed himself to be led to the floor by Fluffy, who insisted that she could teach him the Spanish Two-Step.

"You got to screwch up close like this," she said, setting her pelvis forward against him, "so you can feel my body and my legs moving. That's the way you lead. Here, hold me up tight now." Flustered by the sudden intimacy of her flesh, lost in the turmoil of alcohol and swaying bodies, he drifted and stumbled and yet somehow remained rigid, throbbing, mute, mindless, his senses functioning only at the points of contact with her, the stiff ridged cups of her brassière, her thighs, the plane of her stomach, the soft firm mound floating and rubbing at his groin. She kept him at it through "Silver Dew on the Bluegrass" and two waltzes, but when the Rhythm-Masters struck up "Put Your Little Foot," she gave in and half led, half carried him back to the table. By that time everybody was switching partners and Fluffy had her choice of the stags and stalkers. She was promptly whirled away by the biggest of the lot, a tall cowboy with knotted jaws and pearl buttons on his skintight rodeo shirt. Elliott had another beer and tried to build up courage to ask Vaudine to dance, but Dud beat him to it. They went off listlessly to the strains of "Cotton-Eyed Joe" and left him to guard the whiskey bottles.

Time lost its logic and continuity. There were long endless moments, vast deserts of eternity, when he saw and felt in his mind all that ever had been and would come to be and then hours had elapsed (and for all he knew, days and years, too) when he stirred to discover himself talking to strangers, laughing, sharing drinks, trying to say something to T. J. and Vaudine when they came over for a drink, being ignored, yelling at Grady when he waltzed by with a plump redhead, another beer, then whiskey, drinking it straight from the bottle, suddenly realizing how very drunk he was, so drunk that he would pass out if he kept still and then, mindful of his duty to his friends, he gathered up the remaining whiskey bottle in the paper sack and stumbled off, clutching the sack in both hands as if it were some kind of divining rod or handle that would guide his course, weaving and rolling and tilting yet always holding his feet beneath him very carefully, circling slowly and timelessly on the infinite perimeter ofthe floor among the tables peering through the smoke and shadows into happy faces, loving people, waving and moving and gliding with the music ever constant sweet and sad and thick *for I'll be all smiles tonight*

and even those who know me
    will think my heart is light, though my heart will break tomorrow
I'll be all smiles tonight
        I'll
    be all smiles tonight, love, I'll
    be all smiles
        tonight

—Where you goin there, buddy. You carryin a heavy load, right?

-Howdy. How yew. Mighty pretty lady there. Mighty pretty.

—M' one true love. Budon tell m' wife. Hee hee.

—Have a drink, frin.

I'll deck my brow with roses

—so she turns and says to the old boy, Smells like a shingle off a shithouse to me.

—Ain't he the filthiest thang. I swear to mercy, Bojet, if you don't stop that filthy talk

—Lemme tell you-all about this here cul-tur-al fault we got

—Hooo. Sho is drunk out tonight, ain't it

An inflated condom floated past, a circle of white rising up out of the black to him for one fearful frozen instant before someone burst it with a lighted cigarette.

To the tune of "Steel Guitar Rag" someone sang, —Comeanticklemyballs, comeanticklemy balls but leave my prick alone

—Ready on the left, ready on the right, ready on the firin line

—Ain't you sharing your liquor, good-looking? a pretty girl said.

—Hava beer, Elliott said. —Have wun m' beers. Gotta pocket full. But 'is here bottle property m' buddies. Property m' frins. Gotta see nobody screws m' frins.

The band was playing "There's a Star-Spangled Banner Waving Somewhere." —I just love that, a girl said.

—Don't you just love that. I get all prickly feeling inside.

—Goddam it, Laquita, the war's over.

228   —I know that. Don't you think I know that.

—Let's me and you fuck.

Elliott passed by the band platform. Leroy was sitting on the rear of it, drinking a beer. —Man, man, he said. —Looks like you're on your way.

—Who you? You wun m' frins?

—One a the best.

—Then I sposè sokay you hava shota this

—I can use it, Leroy said, taking a swig. —Man, we ain't getting no rest at all. They got us playing in shifts.

Dimly, shielding his eyes from the glare of the flood-lights, Elliott could see three figures in action on the plat-form. Big Mac was the only one he recognized. —Whur's all m' frins? he said to Leroy.

—Dunno. I seen 'em dancing with Fluffy a while ago. T. J.'s probably off playing twinky-toes with Vaudine, if her old man ain't got here yet. But Grady ought to be back pretty soon. We're having to take turns playing, tried to stop for a break and them idiots like to tore the place down.

Elliott wandered off into the men's room and edged his way carefully along the wall past a huddled group of crapshooters. He urinated long and pleasurably into the tin trough, fumbled the finish, and wet the length of his inseam. "Issa fault of . . . the cultural fault," he said, laughing into the mottled faded mirror on the towel rack.

—Eighter from Decatur, said one of the crapshooters. —Big Eight coming out of chute number one. Snake-Eyes in the circle, Craps you're on deck, and Domino, start saddling up.

—Five. Everthing's fives. World got five sides. The hard way.

—Everthing's the hard way. Shoot, slim, you're covered.   229

—Talk to 'em, sonny boy. They listen to you.

—All you gotta do is hold your mouth right. You ain't holding your mouth right

At the door he met Dud coming in. —Hey, where you been with our bottle, Dud said.

—Nope, Elliott said. —This m' frins'. Sorry. Savin this for m' frins. Fellas give it to me, said pertek it. I'm perteking it.

—What the hell, that sure looks like our bottle to me.

—Sorry. Ain't the one. This m' frins'. He wheeled and disappeared into the shadows behind the band platform, leaving Dud with a vacant, puzzled look on his face.

T. J. was arguing with Leroy and Grady. —Read 'em and weep, he said. —I'm the one calling the shots around here.

—Heck, Leroy said —I don't like to play all this Hollywood junk.

—That's what they want and that's what we're giving 'em.

Grady shrugged and blew a long shimmering wail on his harmonica.

—And put up that goddam french harp, T. J. said. —None of that hick stuff in this band. Do "Fiddle Boogie-Woogie," "Smoke Gets in Your Eyes," and "Mexicali Rose," then you can hit 'em with a little of that cornpone.

—How about "Smoke on the Water"?

—Yeah, that's good as any. Lots of vets out there, they'll eat up that shit. I'll be back for the next set and I don't want to hear none of that old-timey crap while I'm gone, you hear. He stepped off the front of the platform and disappeared through the crowd.

They were strumming stray chords and checking to see if the instruments were tuned together. Grady took a plastic cigarette case out of his shirt pocket and cut an oval guitar pick from the side of it with his maize knife. The cigarette case was riddled with holes and he had to look it over carefully to find a piece big enough. Elliott lurched away, unnoticed, stumbling around the tables on the opposite side of the room.

—What you got to do is, you got to start in real young eating hot peppers. If you start real young eating hot peppers, you won't never lose your hair

—That's a crock

—How many bald-headed Mescans you ever seen?

Off in a corner two men were fighting in slow motion, very carefully and precisely, punching each other fiercely at close range to avoid attracting attention that would get them thrown out in the cold to finish their quarrel. Elliott watched them for a time, then moved on.

—*The moon was high and so was we,* somebody sang.

—Open up the spaghetti, Dad, we're coming to a fork in the road

—Don't tell me about no goddam Japs, I was on Iwo

—Lissen, jarhead

Someone in the band yelled —Shoot low, Sheriff, I think she's riding a Shetland

There'll be smoke on the water on the land and the sea
    when our army and our navy
overtake the en-emyyyyy

—Hey, Grady, a woman screamed. —You're good.

—I know it, childern, Grady said.

—If I ever get my hands on that sonofabitch. Who'd ever thought he'd have guts enough to steal my bottle

—Oh my god. Honey just walked in the door. Heading this way. I didn't figure he'd make it till after midnight, if he come at all

—Don't have a hissy fit. We got all our clothes on. How many times I have to tell you, Honey's my friend

—And he's my husband, I guess I ought to know

—Easy now, just don't get your tea to boiling

—Oh my god, you got lipstick all over your collar

—He ain't going to be looking at no collar. You just give him a big old smile and a good feel when he gets over here

Elliott wandered by.

T. J. jumped up. —Now where the name of Jesus H. Christ do you think you're going with my bottle

—Iss m' frins'. Jes perteking it for m' frins.

—Gimme that goddam bottle. He grabbed it, but Elliott held on, wrenched back and forth like a rubber bone in the jaws of an angry feist. Then T. J. tripped him and he went down in a lump, losing control of the bottle, scrambling to avoid the tables and chairs behind him. The scuffle, unnoticed in the general hubbub, ended.

—Why howdy, Honey, how you doing. We'd just about give you out of coming.

—Oh, you ought to of knowed I'd be here sooner or later. Yawl having a good time?

—Sweet baby, you must of got off early

—Yeah, nothing much happening in town. I come on down with one of the boys from the Liquor Control. Honeycutt stood over their table, gazing slowly around the room, one thumb hooked in his Sam Browne belt, big gray Stetson pulled down over his steely, narrowed eyes. —Anything going on around here?

—Come on and dance with me, Honey, Vaudine said.

—Same old thing, everybody having one hell of a good time, T. J. said. —And that's because they got the best damn dance band in the country, right?

232

—Yeah, if you're good for anything, T. J., it's plunking on a git-fiddle.

—You want to dance, Honey? Vaudine said.

—Seen any funny stuff going on? Honey said.

—Shit, buddy, I been too busy keeping the music going. I just now got off to come over here and see how your old lady's doing. Hell, set down, take a load off the floor.

Honey laughed. —Reckon I will. Man's got to ease up sometime. You're never off duty, y'know, when you're wearing one of these tin stars. He flicked his big Stetson back with a weary forefinger and put his elbows on the table. Vaudine scooted her chair up beside him and ran her arm through his.

—Think you could stand a little nip, old buddy?

—How about that. You know how to treat your friends, all right. Well. Providing it's all legal and everything, I don't see why not. Just a little one.

—Why, ain't we got a Law setting right here? T. J. said, bringing up the bottle in the paper sack from under the table. —Couldn't nothing be more legal than that.

Honey punched him lightly on the shoulder. —You sonofagun. Be a cold day in August when you get caught with your pants down. Holding his hat over the bottle, he took a long swig, blew hard, and reached for a water glass.

—Good stuff.

—Like a busted drum, T. J. said.

—Huh?

—Can't beat it.

Honey sat back and slapped the table with his palm. —Always got a comeback, ain't you, he said, laughing.

—Have another, T. J. said.

—No, I said just one.

—Come on.

—Well, I'll tell you, that one there sure made me feel like a new man.

—Then don't you reckon the new man ought to have a drink?

Honeycutt roared and reached for the bottle.

Elliott rolled slowly from under the table a few feet away where he had lain all the while in a drunkenly lucid daze since the scuffle with T. J., staring straight up at the bottom of the table and conscious of every sound and movement around him, conscious most of all of his condition and the softly whirling shuffle in his mind, yet unable to move, numb to any touch, trapped in himself, in furor and peace, in blank fear and a lovely, soothing blackness, then suddenly and inexplicably driven away from it and on his feet again, stumbling past the beer coolers toward the door.

Outside, he sobered a bit in the chilly night air, but not enough to plot his course, to comprehend what he was doing, why he was there, except to keep moving, keep looking for something he could not understand and would not know when he found it. He wandered slowly through the rows of parked cars, bumping into giggling couples passing to and from necking sessions, fights, forays to replenish their liquor supplies.

—It was him all right, someone said. —I'd know his ashes in a whirlwind.

—than a welldigger's ass in Amarillo, might ought to drene my radiator tonight

—Signs. Omens.

234   —Don't believe in 'em, any more than planting peas

according to the moon. Still, signs are a kind of comfort sometimes

—Now stop that, said a girl's voice in one of the cars.

—Haven't you never read the Ten Commandments

—No, but I seen the movie

—I'd of whipped his ass good, too, if I hadn't hit my eye on that chair. Yessir, that's what I says. I says, Eat me daddy like a peanut pattie, and he says, What, and I says, You heard me, Mescan. Motherfucker tore three buttons off my shirt, that good cowboy shirt Mama give me for graduation. Taken ten stitches in my eye, just because I hit that damn chair. I'd of whipped his ass if that hadn't happened. Finally I says, Hell Mescan, I can't see, and maybe you think he wasn't glad of it. Wayne and them was there, they seen it and they said I had him whipped when it happened. Yeah, he started it and I finished it, by god. Eat me daddy like a peanut pattie, that's what I told him.

Elliott came to T. J.'s gaudy Packard hearse, parked at one side some distance from the building. The motor was idling, and he stood for several minutes puzzling drunkenly over the wisps of gray vapor that fluttered around the exhaust. He fumbled for the rear door and swung it open.

There was a harsh curse from inside. —Shut that goddam door! Get the hell out of here! Someone scrambled back in the darkness toward the driver's seat.

Then he saw Fluffy. She sat up, into the flickering red light of the neon sign. She was naked to the waist, and she was trying to cover her breasts with her coat. The cursing voice was behind her, getting wilder and louder. Fluffy said softly to Elliott —It's all right, honey. You go on now, and shut the door.

He stumbled back inside the dance hall. The heat and heavy air closed down on him. He made repeated attempts to find his way to the table where he had begun the night's circular journey but always he was foiled by the crowd and, finally, by his own exhaustion.

—That big guy over there, Honeycutt said. —In the gray suit. Liquor Control. Me and him's like that. He held up crossed fingers.

—Boy howdy, Vaudine said. —They sure grow 'em big down in Austin.

—Yawl got something working, Honey?

—Nah. He's just keeping his eyes open. You got to keep your eyes open in this business. Looks like a pretty average night though.

—Tell you what, T. J. said, twirling the whiskey bottle slowly on its rim.

—Yeah?

—I know, and you know, that this here is legal hootch, right?

—Sure.

—But before you and your buddy leave, yawl might want to take a look in that room over yonder behind the cash register.

—Troy? Honeycutt said, eyes narrowing.

—I got to get on back to the band. You'll keep that under your hat now, right? Till after we're through?

Honey gave him a long, nodding wink and reached for the whiskey bottle.

The band was playing "San Antonio Rose." *Deep with-innnn my heart lies a melody, a song of old San Antone.* Reeling backward to avoid bumping into a fat blonde wearing a snood, Elliott struck one of the rough wooden

columns that supported the ceiling. Sharp pain flashed in
his ear and then drained away, but it was enough to
bring tears. The wetness in his eyes blurred what little
light was left; blinded and weary and tormented beyond
bearing, he felt the great circle of light rising and he
spun away, flailing toward an open passageway *wherein
in dreams I live with a*

    memory
  beneath the stars   all   alone
in an empty corner where he raised his arms and screamed
at the top of his voice but no sound came and he pitched
back on the wall and slid down sobbing wildly with the
refrain going into its high sudden change of key *moon in
all your splendor*

    knows only my heart
      bring back my rose my rose
lips so sweet and tender

        *like petals falling apart, sing once again of my
dreams I live*

Grady found him there, with faint marbled stains on
his face where dust from the floor had settled in the drying tears. The lights had been turned on and the place
was empty except for a few stragglers. Grady got him on
his feet and tried to support him. Together they made it
to the door. Then Elliott broke away and reeled off toward the hearse. He sat down on the rear bumper trying
not to vomit.

The West Texas Rambling Rhythm-Masters were gathered around T. J. at the front of the car. T. J. pulled a roll
of dollar bills from his shirt pocket and began to count
them out on the hood in piles of three.

"Hold on," Arliss Jones said. "You said we'd get five."   237

"That sonofabitch Troy," T. J. said. "That's the kind of sonofabitch we went off to war for, boys. Can you imagine the ingratitude of that bastard. . . ."

"What're you talking about?"

"Well, he pulled a fast one on us. Don't worry, I'm getting hurt along with everybody else."

"Well, sir, let's just take ourselves back in there and have a little chat with the gentleman."

T. J. held up his hand. "Easy now," he said. "That's exactly what you don't want. First place, it wouldn't do no good. I've already had my say with him. Second place, he could make it tough for us other places. We're just getting started and we can't stand no trouble. You guys know that. We've been had, that's all. Nothing to do but take it and be happy for small favors."

Grumbling, cursing under their breath, they picked up the money. "If this is the way it's going to be," one of them said, "you can count me out from here on in."

"Now listen," T. J. said. "We got us the makings of a good band here, and I want you all to know I appreciate everything you boys are doing. I'm gonna make this up to you. I'm gonna take care of everything. I didn't want to say nothing about it before, but I've got it all fixed up for us to play on the new radio station at Lamar ever week, starting next month. How's that sound?"

"What's the pay?"

"Well, I'll tell you. It's gratis for a while. They're just getting the station started. But don't you see what it means? Pure hundred-percent publicity, and that's the only way we'll get dances and stage shows and all kinds of stuff. Why, pretty soon old Troy is going to be begging us to come back, and we'll be naming the price. Tell you

238   what, I'll guarantee ever one of you six bucks apiece the

very next dance job we get, which if I have my way about it is going to be pee-dee-que. And that's just the beginning. Give me a couple of weeks and I'll have us lined up for a job every Saturday night. That's if you agree to play on the radio. Now, you gonna stick or not?"

There were mumbled sounds of assent. "What about Grady?" Arliss said. "Is he going to stay?" Elliott had passed out again, and Grady was trying to get him stretched out in the back of the hearse, moving instrument cases and junk to make a place for him to lie down.

"He'll stay, if I ask him to," T. J. said. "Now come on. Let's get out of here before I decide to go back and take a poke at that cheap sonofabitch Troy."

PAYING OFF. T. J. and Vaudine were arguing. "Then you can just let me out at the courthouse," she said. "There's a old hard bench in the County Clerk's office I can sleep on till Honey gets back."

"Sugarbunch, I can't help it," he said. "I got to see that the boys get home. . . . " He took one hand off the wheel and put it under her dress, running his fingers along the inside of her thigh. With a great show of indignation, she rapped him on the wrist, pushed his hand away, and with a toss of her head flounced over against the window.

The rear end of the hearse was packed with swaying bodies. Still very drunk but brought awake by the pulsing nausea that filled his body, Elliott squinted and tried to raise his head. A man he did not know was sitting on his arm. The man made no effort to move, and Elliott realized that he was asleep. Big Mac had taken up his cross-legged buddha's position in the center, staring over the driver's seat impassively focused into the darkness beyond the flickering headlights. Leroy was in the corner necking with a telephone operator from Lamar who'd attached herself to him at the dance. Grady sat opposite Elliott on an old tire, dozing.

"Where's Fluffy?" Elliott whispered hoarsely. His mouth felt as if it had been glued shut.

Grady opened one eye. "So you ain't defunct after all," he said. "Here we are, giving you a grand and awesome funeral, carrying you off to the boneyard in this opulent automobile, and you, ungrateful fraud that you are, have the audacity to rise up from the dead." Elliott put his head on the floor again and let the vibrations lull him back to sleep.

Much later, the vibrations stopped and he woke up. Doors opened and slammed. People were getting out at the back. Through the front windows he saw that the hearse was parked on the deserted courthouse square in Lamar. Mist was falling, and it made hazy domes around the silvery street lamps, like smoke sifting through moonlight.

He stirred. His hand had closed on a wad of paper. He held it up to the light and saw that it was one of the lurid pornographic pamphlets that T. J. called Eight-Page Bibles. It appeared to have been drawn by several artists with widely varying styles. The printing was shoddy and blurred, and he could hardly make out the title, which was, he finally decided, Tillie the Toiler. For no particular reason, he stuffed it in his shirt pocket.

Grady stuck his head in the back door. "Hey there, fleet-footed Achilles," he said. "You need to wee-wee, or anything?"

Grunting, Elliott eased himself up slowly and got out,   241 crawling over Leroy and the telephone operator. Blood pounded in his neck and he gagged on the sour taste in his stomach. He stumbled along behind Grady, Dud, and Mac up the sidewalk toward the courthouse. It was silent and dark except for one or two lights in the basement. At the stairs they met T. J. coming out. "Yawl going to the john, you can forget it," he said. "Everthing's shut up. 'Less you want to go on down to the end and use the sheriff's and get locked up for disturbing the peace and being drunk in a public place. What a bunch of clowns."

"Dod damn," Mac said. "I dodda doe. *Bad*, I dodda doe." He clutched his crotch and sagged his knees together.

Grady nodded his head toward the side of the building. "Hell," he said, "plenty of bushes right around yonder." He led the way. They climbed over the low railing of castiron pipe and scattered into a clump of scraggly hedge shrubs and evergreens. Big Mac let go in a thundering rush and sounded a great sigh that echoed into the street.

When Elliott had finished, he leaned against the base of a bronze statue. It was the figure of a man, draped in a riding cloak and clothes of the last century. The figure struck a stern, heroic pose, head held high, one foot set forward and raised slightly on a low mound. Elliott stared sickly up at the statue, trying to stop the throbbing inside him, eager for the cool mist falling on his face.

Dud wandered up, buttoning his pants. "Hey, who is that?" he said, indicating the statue. "I seen that thing all my life but I never knew who it was."

Elliott shook his head weakly. Grady, on the other side of him, struck a match with his thumbnail and bent over the inscription. He read it aloud:

I love the bright lone star that gems
The banner of the brave:
I love the light that guideth men
To freedom or the grave.

MIRABEAU BUONAPARTE LAMAR
1798–1859
Second President of the Republic of Texas

T. J. joined them. "What I say is, piss on Mirabeau
Buonaparte Lamar," and he did, sending Elliott darting
away from the pedestal. Dud laughed and followed T. J.'s
lead, but having already relieved himself in the bushes,
his contribution was meager and short-lived. Mac tried
again, too, and Arliss Jones arrived with a fresh supply,
augmented by a bottle of beer which he drank as he
urinated, jokingly complaining about being the middle-
man. They jumped and staggered and ran around the
statue, grabbing at each other's flies, scuffling, grunting,
panting.

Elliott wandered off to the hearse and crawled inside.
Leroy and his girl were in the front seat, giggling and
talking in low tones. She took out a compact, patted and
fluffed her hair, and began to put on fresh lipstick. The
mist was turning to light rain. Grady and the others came
back to the car, to Elliott's great relief.

T. J. tossed a keychain to Leroy. "Here go," he said.
"Just see that you get my wagon back sometime tomorrow."

"Not me," Leroy said, getting out. "I got a date."

"Well, what if I have, too?"

"Sorry. It's your buggy. Get these boys home in good
shape, now, and tuck 'em in. Reckon you'll sleep out at
the house?"

243

"Aw, come on, bud. I'm beat. You have to go out there anyway, to get home."

"Don't worry about me. If you do stay at the house, tell Daddy I'll be home sometime tomorrow." He winked at the girl. "By suppertime."

"Aw, come on. I'll flip you for it."

"Not with that two-headed dime of yours, you won't." Leroy and his girl strolled away down the street.

"Shit," T. J. said, with a look of disgust toward the hearse. "If this ain't one hell of a mess." He handed the keys to Arliss. "Okay, you're the one to get off first, that means you get first turn at the wheel. Take good care of her, hear, and don't wake me up till we get to your house." He stretched out on the bench behind the driver's seat, took off his boots, and pulled his hat down over his eyes.

In the back Grady struck up "Let Me Ride in Your Little Red Wagon" on his harmonica, but the music was soon lost in the whine and rattle of the Packard. Elliott fell into a deep sleep, and when he began to filter back to consciousness, long afterward, he lay dazed in pain for several miles, absorbing vibrations from the car, motionless, eyes held shut, feeling the hearse speeding and slowing, whining in low gear, slipping to the side and then spurting forward; and gradually he realized that they were on muddy roads. He sat up and peered through the windshield. Ahead of them in the east were faint gray lines of dawn in a cold, cloudless sky. He shut his eyes and sprawled back against a guitarcase in reflex from the sick heavy thudding in his temples.

Mac was driving. His bulk covered the greater part of the front seat. Too large to squeeze behind the wheel, he 244 was planted squarely in the middle, steering with his left hand. T. J. lay asleep on the bench; apparently he had not moved. Elliott and Grady were alone in the back.

There was a thumping clatter beneath the car, as if something were being dragged. It increased in volume until, some fifty feet down the way, they came to a smooth halt in the middle of the road, rear wheels whining and the motor in a constant, steady roar. For several seconds no one moved. Then T. J., from under his hat, said, "High center. Goddam the luck." He leaned forward over the seat. "Dammit Mac, get out and pull us off. I'll steer."

"Dod damn, T. J.," Mac said. "What you fank I am, a dod-damn mule?" But he got out, went around to the back, fished out a rope, tied it to the front bumper, and with the feeble assistance of Grady and Elliott, dragged the huge vehicle twenty feet or so down the road until the chassis was free of the high mound between the ruts.

Elliott had done little more than lean against one of the fenders, but even that effort exhausted him and made his head pound so furiously that he could hardly keep his feet long enough to flop back inside and lie down. Grady uncapped a hot beer and offered it to him, but the mere thought of it made him retch. Trying to ease the fluttering agony in his head and stomach, he huddled up and drifted off again into a merciful stupor, rousing occasionally when the motion of the vehicle changed abruptly in its various turns and slides and momentary stops.

When he awoke, feeling only slightly better, Mac was gone and T. J. was driving. The sun had not yet risen but white light filled half the sky, and Elliott, spotting familiar landmarks, realized that they had passed Elysium and were only three or four miles from home. Apparently the rains had been heavier here; the going was slower   245 and more treacherous, and T. J. fought the wheel with the fury of a frustrated banty rooster, whipping the gearshift about, tromping the gas pedal, cursing the universe. He zoomed over a long rising stretch where the water had drained away and left a reasonably solid roadbed, then failed to slow in time for the abruptly falling slope on the soggy downhill side. The car swerved, jumped the ruts, and skidded off toward the ditch.

"Oh you goddam motherfucking worthless goddam shiteating . . ." T. J. ranted, pounding on the steering wheel and dashboard. Elliott and Grady watched silently as he revved the motor to find traction, trying to back and fill, but the spinning rear wheels buried down in place and sizzled, filling the hearse with the sharp oily odor of burning rubber. "Get your asses out and push!" T. J. yelled at them. "I wouldn't be in this goddam mess if it wasn't for you cocksuckers. . . ."

"Ask me pretty," Grady said. T. J. snarled. They got out, stepping gingerly in the muck, and pushed and tugged for a quarter of an hour without budging the vehicle.

"Give it up as a bad job," Grady said to T. J. "Pile out and we'll walk on down to Randalls'. Get some rest and then come back with a tractor when it's good light—"

"Fuck you," T. J. said, rolling up the window and locking the door. "I've had all of you two I want for one night."

"It's only a mile or so," Elliott said.

"Then get the shit out of here and leave me alone," T. J. yelled from inside. He climbed over the seat into the back. "If I want anything from either one a you, I'll rattle your cage."

"Hey," Elliott said, suddenly remembering the check. "What about my money?" He rapped on the window.

T. J. raised his head. "You do that one more time and I'll get out and stomp the holy shit out of you." He fumbled under the seat and brought up a revolver, waving it erratically. "You'll get your goddam money, you prissy asshole. You'll get it all right, when I'm goddam good and ready to give it to you. Now if you and that birdbrain hunchback don't get the fuck out of here, I'll give you both something you ain't asked for."

"Come on," Grady said, wearily. "It ain't worth it."

From the slope where they started walking, the house was visible off across the fields to their right. But to Elliott the distance seemed endless. Every step sent a wave of pain up through his stomach and chest, racking and spilling at the base of his skull with each beat of his heart. The road they were on ran parallel to the house rather than directly to it, and there was no course except to walk to the crossroad and then turn toward home. Angling across the fields would have saved them half a mile, but water stood in long silvery pinstripes between the soggy mounds of the cotton furrows, and the turn-rows were wet black sloughs.

Even staggering along, Elliott was ahead of Grady most of the way, and the distance between them lengthened when he began to run, weakly, flailingly, the last fifty yards or so, driven by a thirst for water so physically painful that it blocked out everything else—Grady, the throb in his head, the fatigue, the near collapse of his nervous system. He craved a long sweet drink from the cistern, but he reached the windmill first and dropped to his knees and twisted his head up under the spigot to fill 247 himself with great heaving gulps. The water was bitter and flaky with minerals, but it soothed his fevered throat and brought ease.

He was sitting there against the pipe, head back, eyes closed, feeling the soft slush of the sucker-rod pumping slowly in the well when Grady limped up under the tower and sat down beside him. Grady rested until he could breathe easily, then took a drink from the faucet, spat, and began to rub his face and neck with a damp bandanna. "Whoo-ee," he said. "Well, the gourd has got bitter leaves . . . but fain would I yield me up to my sorrows. *Fain*, bygod." Elliott did not move. It was daylight now, but high thin clouds were moving in to cover the sun, and there was wetness everywhere, seeping and dripping from black wood, lying in shallow ashen pools, muffling the land, drenching it in a chilled, infinite vapor.

"Cherish not rancor in yore heart," Grady said lightly. "Howbeit that the gods devised all these here evils in this wise, that he who knows neither sound heart nor bygod the multitude of men's reproachings will ever reap the lovely fruit. . . ." He gave up when he saw that Elliott would not answer or even look at him. He stood up and turned aside and blew his nose. "I'll see to it he pays you your money," he said.

"It's not the money!"

"Well. What then?"

Elliott chewed his lip. "The whole damned mess. Running around the country like a bunch of gypsies, or some wild tribe of white trash, raising hell till all hours. And that stupid idiot—!"

"Lo, such godawful wrath and indignation, a fire kindled in thine anger—"

248   "Don't start that crazy stuff, dammit!" Elliott yelled.

"You're as bad as any of them. Maybe worse. Let me tell you one thing, I'm fed up with it."

"That so?"

"Yeah, that's so."

"And just what is it that has offended your royal highness?"

"Plenty, I'll tell you that. Strutting around here like you own the place instead of just a hired hand, telling everybody what to do. And talking all that crazy nonsense, acting like you were some kind of high and mighty college professor or one of those high-class intellectuals, like you know everything in the whole world. Just because you've traveled around a few places and can play a guitar and use big words, just because you've read a lot of books, that doesn't make you a . . . a"—he floundered, then came up with it—"a Einsteen."

Grady chuckled. "No," he said, "it sure don't. That all that's bothering you?"

"No, it's not!" He was blinking back tears. "I saw you tonight—"

"I imagine you did. Several times."

"I saw you!"

"I don't know what you're getting at—"

"With . . . Fluffy."

"Yeah? And what was me and Miss Fluffy-tail up to?"

"You filthy . . ." He sputtered to a stop. "You ought to *know* better—"

"Well, I don't know everything. You done said that, yourself. Now where was it you seen me and Fluffy?"

"In the back end of T. J.'s car, that's where."

Grady nodded slowly. "I see," he said. "Old Galahad. Well, it wasn't me. Not that I wouldn't give it a whirl."

"You're lying."

Grady looked at him squarely. "Think about it real careful, son, before you call old Grady a liar." Then he grinned. "But if I'm lying, how come sweet Fluffy-tail run off in the middle of the night with a toolpusher from Hobbs, New Mexico?"

"I don't believe it."

"And I don't care if you don't believe it. That's what happened."

Elliott struggled to his feet. "Damn you," he said, stumbling off toward the house wiping the water and mud from his face.

"Wait, son. I want to—"

"Leave me alone. I've had enough of you."

Grady limped along behind until he came to the cellar, where he stopped and raised the door. "Better get your head up," he called out. "If I know your old man, he'll have us on a long pull and a dead lift before long." Elliott went inside and slammed the door. Without taking his clothes off, he slumped across the bed. When the pounding in his head had eased, he fell asleep.

He slept until past noon, knowing that because the cotton crop was almost harvested and the rain had come, there would be little work to do that day. His father made one or two half-hearted attempts to rouse him at mid-morning but Elliott pleaded that he was sick, suggesting an attack of flu or the return of some exotic wartime malady. His father knew the truth, or strongly suspected it, and Elliott knew that he knew, but there were no words between them about it. When he finally got up, it was because his father was banging around behind the house, clanging oil cans together and rattling wrenches and making a constant clatter that irritated his conscience as much as his head. Standing at the kitchen waterbucket with his shirttail hanging out, he shrugged off his mother's offers to fix him food, taking instead aspirin and great dripping dippers of rainwater. His thirst quenched momentarily, he tugged on his boots and went out back where his father was working.

"What can I do?" he said listlessly.

"I've done most of it," his father said. "Rigging up busters for the maize ground and them long rows over on the north side that's already been stripped. But there's hi-gear bundles to be seen about, and it's going to dry out in a day or two and we'll need that stalkcutter ready to go."

"What's Grady doing? He go after that other wagon at the gin?"

"Grady's gone. You'll have to do your own work for a change." Mr. Randall walked around the tractor and crouched beneath it, disappearing in a maze of metal rods and springs and plows.

"What do you mean, gone?" Elliott said.

"What I said. Gone."

"What? When?"

Elliott's father stood up. "Right after breakfast. Gathered up his stuff, most of it, and I went with him up yonder to the draw and helped old T. J. Teed push his circus truck out of the ditch. Then Grady took off with him, back to Lamar I reckon. You boys must of really had a night of it."

"What did he say?"

"Grady? Not much of anything. And him and T. J. sure wasn't carrying on any long conversations. You-all have some trouble between you?"

"What was he going to do? You think he was leaving for good?"

"I imagine. When a man gets his stuff and takes his pay and hits the road, that's usually a pretty good sign, ain't it? He's been ragging me for a month or so about having him a job in Lamar anytime he wanted it. That could of just been talk. But I got the notion he meant it. Anyway, he's a born drifter, and if he don't hit the road one day, he will the next."

"Didn't he say why he was leaving? Didn't he leave a note or anything?"

"No, he didn't leave no note. He was just quitting his job, not killing himself." Mr. Randall had crawled under the tractor again with a handful of wrenches. "He didn't say why he was leaving. And wasn't no need for me to ask. Wasn't no law against him going. But come to think of it, he did leave some stuff for you. Said he had more than he could carry. It's all down yonder in the cellar I reckon, in a box or something."

Elliott started off toward the cellar. "Can't you see about that later?" his father called after him. When he did not stop, Mr. Randall said, "Don't spend all afternoon messing around down there. I want to get them hi-gear bundles shocked sometime this year."

Even with the cellar door thrown back behind him, there was not enough light for him to see clearly. He bumped around, stumbled against the quilt box, groping through familiar cartons of canned goods and old clothes and magazines until his eyes adjusted to the gray light and he saw the box, in the middle of the old bed Grady had slept in. In the box were books, ten or fifteen yellowed paperbacks, Grady's tattered thesaurus, a high school textbook on the history of early European civilization, a German-English dictionary from which the cover had been torn. Elliott took the books out hurriedly, pawing down into the bottom of the box, where he found a rusty maize knife and a set of guitar strings. He spread it all out on the bed and stared at it, bewildered. There must be something, he thought. There has to be something. Or is it just junk? Just the leavings? Is that what it means? It has to mean something.

He turned back to the books, flipping through them, holding them up by their covers and shaking them. All he found was a makeup rule that had apparently been used as a bookmark. Slowly, one item at a time, he placed everything back into the box and put it under the bed.

JOURNEYMEN. Back in the summer Grady and Elliott had patched together an open-air showerbath behind the smokehouse, using a posthole digger to plant tall cedar poles for the main supports, bracing them with two-by-fours along the top, then filling in the gaps with scrap timber and burlap bagging. At the west end, high against the eave of the smokehouse, Grady fashioned a five-gallon can with a spigot that could be opened and closed by pulling on a length of jack chain. Early each morning before they went to the field, Grady filled the can with water, making several laborious, sloshing trips from the well and climbing awkwardly up the side of the bath-house to deposit the contents of his pail. Occasionally Elliott performed the chore, but for the most part it was a job that Grady had undertaken on his own, a private ritual that he performed not without a show of anguish and oppression, muttering and cursing under his breath and frequently erupting in wild unintelligible bombast, yet always protecting his right to be abused, taking that as indemnity, that and the secret but immense satisfaction of knowing that the shower can would be there, filled to the brim, warming all day under the searing August sun. They bathed after supper, first turn going to Grady one night and to Elliott the next. Mr. Randall had scoffed at the contraption but then reconsidered and tried it. After that he gave up his nightly bout with the teakettle and laundry tub, and they had to flip a coin to determine the order of hygienics because the shower can held scarcely enough even for two, and the last man invariably had to rinse from a cold bucket brought up fresh from the well. There were days when they all suffered. Elliott's mother had also scorned the showerbath, convinced they would "catch their death in the night air, gallivanting out there naked like little children," but she, too, had second thoughts as the efficacy of the shower became established and certain refinements were added— a corrugated-tin door on leather hinges, a piece of plywood flooring, a spray head on the spigot. The piece of plywood was so scanty that it hardly eliminated the problem of muddy feet—the bather still had to stand on the bare ground to dry himself—and despite the new spray fixture, the water continued to dribble down much as it had before, because there was not enough gravity or pressure to make the sprinkler sprinkle. But with increasing frequency the men as they came from the field at sundown would glimpse Elliott's mother refilling the can from atop a shaky step-ladder, and once or twice they caught her scurrying from the shower in her faded flannel robe. When they reached the house, she would   255 ignore their muttered complaints about the condition of the water can or offer the puzzled suggestion that it had perhaps sprung a leak.

With the coming of fall, ali that had passed. Grady and Elliott kept the shower more or less in operation as late as October, but though the days then were still warm enough to heat the can, the land no longer held its heat when the sun went down and bathing outside in the dusk became increasingly difficult.

Now sleet and snow had fallen a few times, dry powdery ice that scattered thinly across the countryside and disappeared in a day or two; and with the winter winds gusting, the old showerbath stood as little more than an odd and useless relic of another time, its tin door sagging, the burlap blown loose and flapping. For reasons that only Elliott could know, it was one of the places he haunted, after Grady had gone.

He roamed about the farm, poking in deserted outbuildings, stumbling over the freshly listed cotton land, cut deep to hold it against the spring sandstorms, to catch whatever rain might come. He wandered through the orchard with its scrabby little trees that bore sour cherries and withered apples, through the tattered grape arbors, rotting down now and covered with drifted sand from previous duststorms. And he came to the bathhouse.

Along the top at one end, a two-by-four still held the corner pole firmly anchored to the smokehouse. He could climb up there and sit, close to the smokehouse eave where there was some protection from the bleak north wind. The floor and timbers of the bathhouse had never really dried, although the mud at the bottom had hardened and packed. From it came a moist, sour odor, heavily opposed by the lingering scent of Lifebuoy soap.

Elliott would sit there for an hour or two and then climb down, invariably tearing loose another plank or ripping off a strip of burlap as he went away. At other times he went to the well and crouched inside its open tower against the wellpipe. Once, after a trivial argument with his mother, he went there in the midst of a rustling winter sandstorm and sat all afternoon on the edge of the concrete stock tank, listening to the creak and clang of the windmill tugging at its brake. The blowing dust raged and tore against him, but he braced himself on the rim of the water trough and sat there until sundown, when the wind began to settle.

The cellar was another of his retreats, and he took to it with increasing frequency. Grady's bed was still there, and with it the good Aladdin lamp, the only one they owned which burned white and clear and gave enough light to read by. Elliott spent his time in the cellar rereading the books Grady had left, along with others that he came upon from time to time, and he began to sleep there occasionally, reading until he dozed off and later awakening to find himself fully clothed and the lamp burned dry.

For the most part his parents took his silent, moody behavior in stride. But it eventually began to wear on them, especially after he moved his clothes and the radio and other sparse belongings from the shedroom into the cellar. His father made occasional attempts to keep him at work with odd jobs around the farm, but there was really nothing of importance to be done until the spring rains came and a new crop could be started, and even Mr. Randall began to spend more and more time over at Box's store, swapping stories and playing dominoes with his cronies. Elliott's mother nagged him about what she   257 called his "strange ways of doing" and found excuses to send him to town on errands. He ignored her or passed the chore on to his father; now and then he submitted by driving the old Ford to some small town away from Lamar, to O'Donnell or Tahoka and once even as far as Lamesa, where he went to a movie, sat through it mindlessly, stopped for a hamburger steak at a truckstop, and came home with nothing more than the vague relief of having performed some distant social and familial duty.

Rumor filtered back that Grady had been seen in Lamar on several occasions, that he was working at either the newspaper or a printing shop there. From what he heard, Elliott assumed that Grady was also still playing, at least sporadically, with T. J.'s band. He allowed several weeks to drift by, and then, closing himself up in the cellar on Saturday afternoons, he began to tune in their weekly broadcast from the new station in Lamar.

There would be commercials, delivered by an announcer with a high-pitched drawling voice hawking specials at Smiley's Food Store & Hardware or urging listeners to "try a vegetable laxative—try Nature's Remedy, and remember: NR tonight, tomorrow all right," followed by station identification

KMIR, a frinly voice from a frinly town Lamar Texas six-eighty on yore radio dial

and finally the introduction, drowned out by the booming whang of an electric steel guitar that led into the rousing theme sung breathlessly by the entire group

Gather round listen in, here we are once again   we come to you without a   care   We hope our playing and singing, good cheer to you is bringing

a voice, probably T. J.'s, calling out (because the line could not be sung to the same rhythm)

*T. J. TEED AND HIS WEST TEXAS RAMBLING
RHYTHM-MASTERS ARE ON THE AIR!*

an instrumental bridge, up high and furious, then fading
back and in over it a third voice, obviously practiced and
less nervous but filled with the same wrought-up fervor,
working hard for deep smoothness and round vowels and
hard endings with the proper blend of home-folks warmth

—Yessir, howdy friends and neighbors, how's your
mama-and-all-them out yonder listening in? Doing real
fine, I know, and yessir they're surely going to enjoy another *big* Saturday evenin session with T. J. Teed and
all his West Texas Rambling Rhythm-Masters. Yessir it's
time for music EVERYbody enjoys, music by the Rambling Rhythm-Boys

And as the music ground to a halt

—now here's *your* friend and mine, old T. J. himself, all
set to tell us about the first number they've got lined up
for us this afternoon. Step right up here and tell us about
it, T. J.

—Thankyew, Jonathan, T. J. said jauntily. —Johnny
Moss there, friends and neighbors, doing a real fine job
of getting our show on the air for you. To start things off,
we've got a favorite instrumental tune for you, our version of a really really great swingtime tune, yessir we're
gonna get in the mood with . . . "In the Mood"

Their rustic rendition of big-band swing was at once
lush and halting, redeemed largely by whoever was
seconding the steel guitar and by the fiddling of Big Mac
Baker, whose style in rare moments bore uncanny re-
semblance to that of Joe Venuti (a matter of pure co-
incidence, since Venuti's mere existence was to Mac as
distant and unknown as Mars or opera pumps). The
band's next number, at the request of "A Weekly Lis-   259

tener," was Leroy's plaintive version of an obscure Jimmie Rodgers tune

oh you Mississippi river
with your water so deep and wide
my thoughts of you keep rising   just like the evening tide

and every program followed the same pendulous pattern, drawing from a grab-bag repertoire that might shift instantly from the latest Hit Parade pop tune to an old Roy Acuff standard, from traditional breakdowns and marches like "Soldier's Joy" and "Under the Double Eagle" to "A String of Pearls" and back again to Tin-Pan-Alley renditions of "Swanee River," "Home on the Range," and "The Old Gray Mare." The band's complement was equally hybrid—it was a floating aggregation that nominally offered itself as a string band but frequently included a piano or drums or both. Once Elliott was shaken by the off-key squeaking of some reed instrument that seemingly appeared from nowhere to attempt a chorus of "Summit Ridge Drive," à la Artie Shaw. Sometimes it was obvious that the broadcasts were carried out by only T. J. and some stray mandolin or banjo player. But regardless of the size or condition of the group, T. J. kept up a running chatter throughout each number ("Play it sweet now, boys," "Ah yes, Big Mac on the fiddle," "Take your gloves off and use both hands," "Don't pick it, it'll bleed"), identifying from time to time whatever real or imagined instrumentalist was taking the lead. Several weeks passed before Elliott caught Grady's name and knew for certain that he was there. The song was "Monon Blues," and Grady's lazy, thumping style confirmed his identity. But T. J. cut it short to announce

—Time for one more little tune this afternoon folks,
260   done for you by old Leroy, who's going to sing for us one

of his very own tunes, a little song he wrote hisself, little thing called "Kinda Wondering." But before we ast Leroy to step up to the mike I want to remind all you good folks out there that yours truly T. J. Teed and his West Texas Rambling Rhythm-Masters is going to be playing tonight at a great big dance right here in Lamar down at the V.F.W. Hall, we want to see all you folks out there tonight, and then on Monday night we'll be over at the high school auditorium in Jal New Mexico for a great big show there for all the wonderful people at Jal, and don't forget the big New Year's Eve dance next Tuesday night at Smokey's Club in Post Texas, out on the Fort Worth highway there, where me and all the boys will be on hand to say howdy to nineteen-and-forty-seven. And of course we'll be right back here next week at the very same time, so send us your cards and letters, tell us your requests, let us know how you like the show

Leroy closed the program with his soft, crooning country ballad, done in the style of Ernest Tubb

Tonight I set here kinda wondering
    wondering if I've done   right or wrong . . .
The lyric was rough and hackneyed in spots *and all of these things, that happiness should bring, they have surely caused an ooolllld love to drownnnn* but Elliott found himself drawn into it, a distinct chill brought to his arms and to the base of his skull as he lay stretched on the bed, head propped against the iron railing, legs crossed at the ankles, scissoring his feet absently, staring into the darkness of the cellar, feeling the blood rise in his chest like bubbles pulsing and building, in throbbing contrast to the slow, gentle song *wondering if I've done right or wrong,* pondering on past its close into an expanding whiteness that grew at him from the dusty cel-   261

lar, until aroused and shaken back by the booming, rollicking theme

whatever the weather
you'll find us together
playing our songs with flair
so if it isn't too hard   why don't you drop us a card
WHEN T. J. TEED AND HIS WEST TEXAS RAM-
BLING RHYTHM-MASTERS ARE ON THE AIR!

By the time the music had faded and the nasal-voiced announcer was saying ". . . in tune with KMIR Lamar Texas Gateway to the Great South Plains," Elliott was on his feet, changing into a fresh shirt, and giving his boots a quick swipe with a corner of the chenille bedspread. He gassed up the Ford and drove to Lamar as fast as the car could make it, but when he reached the radio station —a small box-like building several miles out of town on the Lubbock highway—it was deserted except for a lone engineer-announcer who stirred lazily in response to Elliott's gestures through the control-room window, finally deigned to come out, and laconically supplied the information that, yes, the crippled fellow had been there with the band, but they had all scattered when the program was over, and he had no idea where Grady might be found. "Think maybe he works off and on at Lamar Printing & Office Supply," he said. "You might go by there and ask somebody."

Elliott drove back into town, circled the square, and found a parking place a block from the printing shop. Although it was the week between Christmas and New Year's, the usual Saturday afternoon throng of farm families filled the sidewalk, their number and mood 262 strengthened by a balmy lapse in the cold blustery weather that had prevailed since November. Elliott, pushing through the crowd, caught a glimpse of Grady disappearing around the corner of the block ahead. He ran to catch him, calling his name, and when he turned the corner, Grady was waiting there, looking back. "Howdy, rowdy," Grady said. "Ain't you kind of lost?"

"I'd like to talk to you," Elliott said.

"Well, come on up to my place. I thought I'd go and take me a little nap for a while. Me and T. J. and the boys are playing a little dance tonight, and I got to have my beauty rest." They strolled on together down the side street, self-consciously. "What you been up to these days?"

"Nothing much. I thought you might be working this afternoon."

"At the job shop? Well, sometimes I do, but things are pretty slow today. Usually are on Saturdays. It's butter-and-egg day, and the scissorbills are all busy stocking up on beans and lard and telling each other lies. Not much call for letterheads and business cards and sale posters."

"I heard you on the radio."

Grady chuckled. "That's something, ain't it? I never heard such a commotion in my whole life. I don't know how I ever got roped into it."

"It's not all that bad," Elliott offered.

"Well, sometimes we do okay. Sort of depends on who shows up. Problem is, T. J. can't hardly ever get the same bunch together to rehearse, and we sort of play whatever comes along in somebody's head. But the people seem to like it, and I'll say this, old T. J. is always in there hustling. He thinks he's about to get us lined up with some sponsors. I'll believe it when I see it, but he's doing pretty good with dances and shows and stuff around the country. I don't make 'em all, just sort of set in whenever I feel like it and there's a empty spot for me."

They turned down an alley and came to a wooden stairway that extended up to the second story along the rear of a dilapidated frame building. "I got a room up here," Grady said, leading the way. "How's your mama and dad doing?"

"Pretty good, I guess," Elliott said. "The crop turned out good. Now if we can get rain for another one."

Grady grinned. "Don't ever end, does it? Well, if you wasn't worrying, you'd worry because you didn't have anything to worry about. You buy yourself that new car yet?"

"No."

"I thought maybe you'd done rigged yourself up and taken off on us. Hadn't seen you around."

"I've been thinking about it a lot. But Mom and Dad are getting up in years, and I'm about the only one there is to look after them. I don't know what to do, really."

"Well, I expect it will all work out," Grady said.

Grady's living accommodations had changed from the cellar he had inhabited on the farm. The small shabby room was neat and uncluttered, the quarters of a practiced bachelor, and it held the familiar old musty smell of fettered tenement air. In it were only the most essential furnishings: a bed, a table, two straight wooden chairs, a lamp, all old and scarred and wobbly. Partially hidden by a curtain in one corner was an ancient wooden icebox and on top of the icebox a hotplate, several pans, and some canned goods. "I can't offer you much but a warm beer," Grady said, taking two from the icebox.

"Hard to buy ice around here in the winter, and even

when they make some down at the plant, I can't remember to bring up a piece."

Elliott spotted Grady's open guitarcase on the floor beside the bed, overflowing as always with books and laundry and strange, unidentifiable objects. Near it, propped against the wall, stood a guitar Elliott had not seen before. "See you got a new box," he said.

"Yeah. A little Martin," Grady said. "I made a pretty fair deal on it from one of the boys that picked it up somewhere. I was always having to play on Leroy's, or borrow one from somebody else. I hate to own the danged things, they're so much trouble to carry around and I'm always losing 'em. But you get to be a man of means, and invariably you start acquiring property. You remember that cheap little box I bought off of Sed?"

Elliott sipped his beer. It seemed that they had used up all the bits and scraps and evasions, and now that Grady had unintentionally called up that night of their first meeting, the distance back to it drew silence down on both of them.

Several minutes passed before Elliott said quietly, "Grady, I'm sorry about what happened—" but Grady moved to avoid him, clearing his throat noisily and scraping his chair back as he rose and went to the icebox for two more beers, although neither of them had finished their first one.

"How's old Frieda Mae these days? And her mama? Business as usual, I reckon."

"Just tell me this," Elliott said. "I just can't understand why T. J. . . . . why you . . ."

"You mean how come he carried me back to town with him? Heck, me and old T. J. is about two of a kind, you   265 ought to know that by now. I don't guess he was any too happy about doing it, but he'd had a chance to sleep off some of his temper by then. And of course me and your daddy did get him out of that ditch. I don't know; if your daddy hadn't been there, he might of even taken a shot at me. But as it was—" He shrugged.

"But you're always talking about exploitation. If there was ever a case of somebody using other people, it's guys like T. J."

Grady said, "Son, let me tell you about this old boy I was reading about the other day. Named Pyrrho. Pyrrho of Elis. One of these old Greeks, see. Now he'd kicked around a lot, been a soldier, seen a lot of country, done a lot of thinking, especially for an old boy back in those days. What he thought up was this: he decided that about the only way a man can get through this old world with his head in one piece is to not pay any attention to anybody else's rules, on either side of the room. He said there ain't nothing at all that you can know for plumb sure, so you have to just stand back and let the other sides fight it out for theirselves, long as they don't bother you none."

"But what if they do?"

"Well, then he said go along with 'em. Because they just might be right, and even if they're not, you ain't got no way of knowing. Anyway, old Pyrrho says there's not a single idea man ever had that's worth getting hurt over."

"I don't know what this has to do with T. J.," Elliott said. "It sounds like an easy way out to me. I don't see how anything would ever get done if everybody thought that way."

266   "Well, it's a lazy man's rule, all right. But when you

get to be my age you sort of get tired of all this yelling and kicking. You find out it comes easy but goes down hard, and you start to prize the hard things that look easy. How to drive a nail, swing a hoe or a shovel, how to climb a tree and kick the coon out, light a fire with one match in a windstorm. . . ."

Elliott waited for him to go on, but Grady only looked up at him and grinned. On the table behind him were the cigarette maker and a pyramid of freshly rolled cigarettes. Grady took one and lit it. "Same old cheery self, ain't you," he said, squinting through the smoke. "How's your beer?"

Elliott sloshed it. "Got plenty," he said. "Tell me some more about this Pyrrho guy—"

" 'Oh, the jour printer with gray head and gaunt jaws works at his case,' " Grady recited.

"I never did find out what that means," Elliott said. " 'Jour printer.' "

Someone on the landing outside called Grady's name. The door opened and Leroy stuck his head in. He glanced at Elliott, nodded, then said, "Hey, Grady, I need a little help."

"Yeah?"

"It's T. J. The crazy idiot's down in niggertown, drinking and raising cain. I was over at the Rexall Drug and Honeycutt came in and said he'd heard about it from some jig that runs a place down there, said he thought we ought to go get him before there's trouble."

"Well, ain't that Honeycutt's job?"

"I suppose so. But he thinks it would be better if some of us went. He don't want to have to arrest T. J. and make him mad. And to tell the truth, I think he's about half scared of what they might do to a Law down there." 267

"Where's the sheriff? And the city cops. Can't they handle it?"

"I don't know. They're all off somewhere. Besides, it ain't that big a deal. Honey just thinks we ought to go down there and get him. I can't find none of the other boys, and I don't think one man ought to try it by himself."

"Not even when it's your own brother? Can't you handle him?"

"No, not even when it's my own brother. Hell, you know how T. J. is. And I'm like Honey, I don't like to be messing around down there alone when there might be trouble. Thing is, two or three of us could go in there and get him and I don't think there'd be any problem, long as we keep together and mind our own business and don't get some gun-happy Law mixed up in it." He looked at Elliott.

"You know there's no love lost between me and T. J.," Elliott said. "But I'll go with you if you think it'll do any good."

"I reckon you're right, Leroy," Grady said. "Let me get my coat. You got any idea which place he's at?"

"Honey didn't know for sure. He's probably making them all. But there ain't that many. We ought not to have much trouble locating him if he's raising all the stir I expect he is. And he's driving the band's bus. We ought to be able to locate that easy enough."

In Randall's old car they drove out to the flats on the eastern edge of town and stopped at the first joint they came to. It was an ancient frame residence that had been redecorated long ago with a red front, now faded, the roof outlined in strings of yellow lights, and around the door a variety of tin signs advertising Mead's Fine Bread,

Garrett's Snuff, Royal Crown Cola, and Delaware Punch. The place was quiet, so Elliott waited behind the wheel while Leroy and Grady went in to inquire about T. J. Instead of returning to the car when they came out, Leroy called to Elliott, "Park it here and come on. He's at Stain's Place. Just down the road a piece, on the next corner."

Elliott joined them and they went on down the street in the falling winter light, trudging through drifts of sand and shallow ruts, past vacant lots and an occasional darkened shack. The street, little more than a wide rutted lane, was lined by dirt embankments several feet high created by the cutting away long ago of shallow ditches on each side and by the piling up of drifted sand in the weeds on open plats. As they went along, Grady took out his harmonica and blew "Camptown Races" and a medley of jigs and shuffles.

"Boy, if that ain't off key and out of place, I never heard it," Leroy said.

"Don't you know that old business about soothing the breast of the savage beast?" Grady grinned, slapping the instrument in the palm of his hand to clear the spittle. As they aproached the corner, his music faded in the amplified thump and wail of rhythm-and-blues emanating from the low, elongated barracks that housed Stain's Place. The building was surrounded on three sides by farm trucks and jitney vehicles.

Grady led the way through the clusters of dark faces that flocked about the entrance laughing and calling to each other, figures that fell silent and watched warily as the three strangers approached and pressed their way cautiously inside. Grady and Leroy exchanged tense, expectant glances as some of the blacks turned to watch them sullenly. Elliott immediately spotted T. J. whirling a Mexican girl wildly across the dance floor, shouting and sloshing beer from a quart bottle that he held by the neck, swinging it, slowing frequently to take a long draw. When the song ended, he slapped the girl on the bottom and followed her over to a row of tables where other Mexicans sat, an uneasy minority in the roomful of blacks. Grady, trailed by Leroy and Elliott, edged carefully around to the booth where T. J. and the girl sat with several of her friends, whose reactions to T. J.'s antics ranged from passing indulgence to silent hostility. A young Mexican with a thin mustache stood a few feet away, alternately baiting and teasing him. "Hey, borracho," he said. "How come you wear e-stupid cowboy shirt, hey? How come you e-sing like ah gorl, hey, hombre?"

T. J. ignored him. "Wah-hoo," he yelled, grabbing at a girl across the table. "Oh, Mother, come after me, the hogs is got me." When he saw Grady approaching, he waved his big hat. "Well, well. Looky who's here. Yawl come to join the party?"

"Looks like a hot time in the old town," Grady said.

"Hell, don't just stand there, set your bony ass down." He motioned for others at the table to move closer together to make room. The benches were already crowded but Grady and Leroy found a few inches on each edge where they could crouch precariously, maintaining a balance by placing their legs at right angles and stretching one arm along the back of the seat. T. J. glanced up at Elliott, seeming to see him for the first time. "Goddam, look who's tagged along. If it ain't old Brains hisself." Elliott grinned uneasily. "Dammit," T. J. said. "Git yourself a chair or something and set down, I never could

270

stand nobody looking over my shoulder while I'm drinking." Elliott edged away, looking for a chair, and T. J. raised himself from his seat and yelled across the room. "Stain!" he shouted. "STAIN, goddammit!"

At one end of the room was a crude packing-box counter that served as a makeshift box-office, bar, and pickup stand for plates of food that were passed out through a small window in the wall at the rear. From behind the counter appeared a huge black man wearing a dirty pin-stripe suit and pointed shoes that shone like liquid tar. There was a ridged line, a scar, from the corner of his mouth to the top of one ear. He came a few steps away from the counter and stopped and looked at T. J. without speaking.

"Hey, boy," T. J. yelled. "Brang some more beer out here for my frins."

"We done all out of beer," Stain said. He started back.

"What?" T. J. yelled. "What the goddam hell! I want some beer out here, boy, and I want it *now*." He banged the table, muttering and cursing. "You black mother-fucker," he said under his breath, but loud enough for those around him to hear. The jukebox was playing again and couples filled the dance floor, but in that part of the room no one spoke.

Stain stopped and turned. "I told you," he said evenly. "We done out."

T. J. looked away, grinding his jaws. He picked up his bottle again and sloshed it, as if to test the contents. "What the hell," he said sarcastically. "I guess there's still enough here to go around for my frins, when it's got to where a white man can't even buy beer in a dump like this." He laughed harshly and pushed the bottle toward 271 one of the Mexicans. "Go on, hombre, have a swig." The man looked at him momentarily, then sipped quickly from the bottle, nodding his head agreeably.

Leroy said, "Hey, little bud, don't you think we ought to be getting on? We supposed to be at the V.F.W. Hall about an hour from now."

"Shit, we'll make it," T. J. said. "I've got time to get my ashes hauled, ain't I?" He laughed and reached out to pinch a black girl passing by.

"Betta watch that, big boy," she said sharply. "You be paying for something you ain't got none of."

T. J. laughed again and hugged the girl next to him. "How 'bout it, seen-yor-ita," he said. "I got a big old car outside with a bed in back and everything."

She pulled away from him, feigning annoyance. "I don't know what you mean, anyway. You go e-screw those black one, hey?"

"Aw, come on, sweet thang. I'll do right by you. I might even put you on the radio, how 'bout that?"

"What you mean?" she said, pouting but cutting her eyes back at him.

"Hell, you're about to get fixed up with a famous man, didn't you know that? Why, I play on the radio ever week and got my own band and play for dances and all kind of shows, gonna start making jukebox records pretty soon."

"I don't hear nothing of that." She tossed her head, but moved against him slightly.

"You ain't talking to no poormouth white trash, I'll tell you that," T. J. said. "I pay my own way." He pulled a roll of bills from his shirt pocket and the girl locked her gaze on it. "Yesiree, I'm ready to put my money where my mouth is. Where my dong is." He roared at his own joke. "What you say, hot tamale? Four dollars."

The girl sneered. Eventually she said, "Ten."

"Make it five."

"Ten."

"For a quick roll in the back of my fancy bus? You're drunker than I am, honey pot, if you think I'll go that high."

"Eight dollar. That's all."

"Honey, you sure yore name ain't Gonzáles-Stein? I think *yore* people must of been camel riders. Mediterranean Irishmen."

"You borracho," she said. "Big talk, no money."

One of the men at the table said, "Why don't you just go e-someplace else, hey? We don't need these kind of e-stuff."

T. J. bristled but before he could reply Grady said to him, "I believe we ought to go on and get that dance started, reckon?"

T. J. leaned across the table and pointed his finger at Grady. "Hunchback, I don't care if you can play good guitar, I don't care if you play the best damn guitar in the whole world. If you don't keep your nose out of my business, I'm gonna stomp a mudhole in you and then I'm gonna stomp it dry, you hear that? So keep your mouth shut, see. I'm gonna start breaking some heads around here, goddammit, man can't even buy a beer and here's all these niggers getting it from someplace." He looked around him and spat, then turned to the Mexican girl and resumed negotiations, oblivious to the fact that several of the men at adjoining tables were huddling together in whispered conference, watching him solemnly.   273

Grady motioned for Elliott to follow him. They went around a corner behind the booths to the men's room. The door was open and several men were inside, relieving themselves into a clogged commode, into the wash basin, on the floor, which was an inch deep in liquid and debris, urine, water, and beer, cigarette butts, paper towels, wads of tissue. Grady and Elliott waited outside until the men had left and then went in, trying to hold their breath against the stench and stepping gingerly to avoid as much of the muck as possible. Grady closed the door and locked it, and while Elliott urinated he went to the only other opening, a small window set high in the wall. He pushed and tugged at it but it would not open.

"What're you doing?" Elliott said.

"Looking for a way out," Grady said. "Case it comes to that."

"You think it's *that* serious?"

"Yeah, I think it's that serious. There's at least three muchachos out there just waiting for a chance to get a shiv in old T. J., and the black boys ain't any happier about him than the Mescans are. On top of that, the niggers are looking for any old excuse to jump on the pepperbellies, and we're right in the middle." He found an empty pop bottle on the window ledge, took it by the neck, and swung it through the air a few times to test the leverage. Then he put it in his armpit, under his jacket.

"What're you going to do?" Elliott said.

"Not a lot we can do except go back there and try to get him out quick as we can, one way or another. Just hang on tight and play it by ear."

Stain met them outside in the hall. "There gone to be trouble," he said. "If you-all don't go ahead on and take him out of this place. I believe if I was you-all I'd take

274

my friend and get on back to where you belong. I done got enough trouble with them Mescan folk out there."

"There ain't nothing we'd rather do," Grady said. "How about you giving us a little help?"

"You don't want me in it," Stain said. "When I steps in, it's gone be for good. You be taking him home in a basket, little bitty pieces."

"No," Grady said. "All you need to do is have one of your gals help us get him outside. Rub up on him a little bit, let him think he's hot on the trail. Once she gets him outside, we'll handle it."

"What if he don't see it that way? Them gals carrying blades, too, don't you know, and they'll cut somebody faster than me. And I tell you this, ain't a one of them that wants none of *his* jelly-roll, no matter how hard up she get. He think he's mean, and he is. But he ain't even seen mean till he's tangle with Thelma or Lucille or one of them."

"She won't have to worry about no trouble," Grady said. "Just get him out to where there won't be no scuffle in all this crowd. Tell her there's five dollars in it for her and she don't even have to turn no trick."

"I collects the cash around here," Stain said.

Grady handed him the money. "Reckon how much of that she'll ever see."

"She see all she need." He went off to make the arrangements. Soon a tall, lanky Negro girl appeared at T. J.'s table with a quart of beer. A loud verbal exchange erupted between her and the Mexican girl, but several other blacks hovered into the area in a casual show of force until the Negro girl had clearly gained the upper hand. The señorita flounced away and T. J. moved over to an adjoining table with the black girl, pawing her 275 and feeding her glasses of beer from the bottle she'd brought. At last he stood up, reeling, and took her by the arm and led her off toward the door.

Grady and the others scurried outside to catch them as they reached the Packard hearse. "Hey, bud," Leroy said lightly, "you all set to go play that dance?"

"Fucka dance," T. J. said. His face had gone slack from all the beer, and he was fumbling to open the car door, holding the girl with one hand and feeling for the handle with the other and trying to locate his keys at the same time. Leroy stepped in between him and the girl and took his arm so that the girl could slip free. She giggled. "Kiss my black ass, little old skeeter peter," she said, vanishing into the darkness.

T. J. whirled around, trying to focus his eyes. "Whadda goddam hell!" he roared, starting forward, but Elliott and Grady blocked him off and Leroy pinned him against the car. Realizing now that he had been tricked, he began to sober, seething furiously and cursing at the top of his voice. He pushed Leroy back and took a wild swing at Grady, who stepped aside and stood back with Elliott, watching T. J. flounder in the dust, stumbling and grunting in a fierce desperate and futile effort to catch one of them until at last he collapsed against a fender of the Packard, heaving and panting, hair down over his eyes, sweat rolling down his neck and staining his lavishly fringed red-and-yellow cowboy shirt.

"Oh you dirty sonsabitches," he gasped. "You dirty shiteating bastards. Call you my frins, and jus look what you done. This any way to treat a vet? Hell no. Guy that's taken care of you and looked out for you? Hell no. Fine fucking bunch a frins you are."

"We just trying to keep you out of trouble, little bud," Leroy said. "Just looking out for your own good."

"Shit you are!" T. J. said. He began to shout curses again, but Leroy cut him off. He stepped up and put his face close to T. J.'s. "That's enough now," he barked, and when T. J. started again, Leroy slapped him hard with his open palm, spinning him down against the hood of the car. His face registered total surprise, eyes widening and his lips faintly trembling. Leroy said, "A man can put up with only so much. You're entitled to your fun but now it's time you shaped up. And you better do it, or I'm going to clean your plow so hard you'll think you been hit by ten pounds of shit in a five-pound bucket. You hear me?"

T. J. sniffed, rubbing his face where Leroy had struck him. He stood up and began to brush the dirt from his shirt. Grady said, "Elliott's car is down yonder a ways. Come on and we'll give you a ride."

"I ain't going nowhere with yawl," T. J. said. His eyes were moist with beery tears. "Anybody that would treat a guy like yawl do."

"We got a dance to play," Leroy said. "We're already late."

"I'll get to the goddam dance, don't you worry none," T. J. said. He went around to the driver's side of the hearse, tucking in his shirt. "All I can say is, you guys damn well better be there your ownselfs, and you damn well better play just the way I say."

"You sure you feel like driving?" Elliott said. "We'll be glad to give you a lift."

"Listen, smartmouth, I don't need you to look after me. By god, I've warned *you* enough, next time I'm gonna 277 break your fucking neck. If I ever see you again, your ass is grass. You're probably the one that started all this anyway, you and your prissy high-hat ways."

"Let's go," Leroy said, starting off toward Elliott's car. "He's a grown man, he can find his own way."

They were down the dusty road and passing into the shadows beyond Stain's Place when they heard T. J. start the Packard, its motor sputtering and choking and flooding, then revving into a roar as he gunned out and sped off toward them. A few yards away, bearing down, he turned on the headlights, and they moved over in single file along the ditch to let him pass. As he sped by, he darted the car toward them, honking the horn and yelling, then whipped back at the last minute. They could hear him laughing and whooping clear to the end of the street, where instead of going on toward town he turned and sped off around the block again. They watched his lights flashing between the scattered buildings as he spun at the corners and raced down the straightaways.

"What's that crazy fool up to now," Leroy muttered. "Better keep your eye on him." He was behind them again, spinning around the corner at Stain's Place on two wheels, skidding out of the turn and coming up on them at full speed. "Don't act like you're paying him any mind," Leroy said. "He's only showing off." This time they divided, Grady and Elliott on one side as Leroy absently moved to the other. Elliott walked along the edge of the ditch with Grady limping behind a few feet and further down the slope, playing "Wayfaring Stranger" on his harmonica. The roar of the Packard rose to a screaming wail, and Elliott looked back just in time to see it bearing directly down upon him. He dodged toward the ditch and then, unaccountably, dived back across the road. At

278

that instant Grady dropped his harmonica and stopped to pick it up. The right front fender of the speeding hearse hit him low in the back and as T. J. fought for control of the careening vehicle Grady bounced up across the hood and hung there for a split instant and then hurled off on the opposite side, bouncing and skidding as he hit the ground and flailing into the dust. The Packard went on into the ditch and up the embankment, stalling as it scraped a utility pole and came to a halt.

When Elliott reached Grady, he was lying on his back, sprawled against the slope of the ditch. The lower part of his body was twisted at an odd angle and his legs, although they did not move, looked limp and doll-like. He stared at Elliott vacantly and then his eyes moved away and he looked past him into the darkness, shock waving up into his eyes. Blood was beginning to run from his nose and from the scratches on his face where he'd skidded.

"Oh god!" Elliott said. He looked up and saw Leroy scrambling toward him. "Oh god, Leroy! Somebody! Get a doctor!" Leroy turned and ran toward Stain's Place. Dark figures gathered on the road, coming out cautiously from the joints and houses.

Grady moaned and tried to move his head. Elliott knelt beside him. "Oh god, Grady, I'm sorry," he cried. "Can you hear me, Grady? Listen to me. . . ."

Grady grinned blankly. "Where's the slipboard, boys," he said. "I'm going on slide days." He coughed. "Lordy, lordy, this ole lobster shift gets old."

"Listen to me," Elliott said. "You'll be all right, just hold on. He was after me, that's all. You'll be all right, Grady. Can you hear me?"

"Red yeller green," Grady said. "Cried and waved her   279

wooden leg." He focused again on Elliott. "Come down here, son," he said, reaching up. "Want to tell you something." Elliott bent over him. "Journeyman," Grady said.

"What? What about 'journeyman'?"

"That's what it means," he said, softly and directly, and he died.

Elliott stared down at him, blood pounding in his ears. "No," he said, over and over, rocking, nudging Grady, shaking him gently. But the eyes were gray and blank, the mouth fixed into its fleering, haunted grin. A car approached and lights descended upon them, harsh painful balls of white rolling and spinning and turning, flashing out from their centers, voices rising and falling, Elliott numbed, shrieking in his head, weaving on his knees, until Leroy came back. Then he stood up, above the lights, and took off his jacket and covered Grady.

The incident was investigated an hour or so later by Deputy Floyd Honeycutt, and after several weeks had passed, during which cautious but persistent inquiries were made by a number of people whose motives differed widely—Elliott's father and Leroy and even Old Man Teed on one or two occasions—it was concluded by duly elected officials of the town and county that Grady's death had been the result of "an unavoidable accident," and their opinion was eventually legalized by the issuance of a death certificate to that effect, the county coroner's signature being affixed to it by a part-time secretary in the sheriff's office, the coroner himself, proprietor of the town's chief drugstore, suffering his usual incapacitation from long-standing addiction to certain opium derivatives dispensed by his place of business.

280   However, in view of the testimony of several witnesses,

including that of his own brother, it was deemed neces-
sary that T. J. Teed be formally charged with the mis-
demeanor of Driving While Intoxicated, with the resul-
tant fine of one hundred dollars and a sentence of three
days in the county jail. The pecuniary portion of his debt
to society was paid with money advanced by his lawyer
(the major portion of whose own income derived not
from his salary as county attorney but from a franchise
for pinball and condom-dispensing machines in the
dancehalls and honky-tonks where T. J. and his band
played), and, with a tip of the wink to Honeycutt, T. J.
fulfilled the terms of his penal servitude by entering the
jail late one Saturday a few minutes before midnight,
sleeping off a hangover through Sunday, and issuing forth
again at approximately 12:30 A.M. Monday (jaunty but
somewhat ruffled that the night jailer had inadvertently
dozed off and so prolonged his confinement almost half
an hour beyond the required time), having thus not only
satisfied the conditions of the legal codes of the State of
Texas but further enhanced as well his reputation among
the varied troop of fans and camp followers who looked
to him as a flowering example of at least one local boy
who knew how to make good, and was making it. Without missing a lick, as they liked to say.

The details of all this reached Elliott in bits and pieces,
through rumor and gossip and a vague, abbreviated account on the back page of the *Mirabeau County Messenger*. He believed everything, or at least he accepted it. But
in a strange, other way, he believed nothing, for none of
it was understandable. It mattered, and yet it did not
matter, for it was the way things should not be but had
always been. He drew upon his old instinctive defense,
found it rising up in him cool and white and full of ease,   281

nourished it, fell silent, passed his days and nights in careful deliberate attention to minute and mindless performance of detail, bodily functions, the barest minimum of life process.

He and his father had arranged for Grady's funeral. Elliott had pondered bringing him back to Elysium, but burial in Lamar Memorial Cemetery would save the expense of hiring a hearse for the trip, and so after a brief graveside service attended by the Randalls, Leroy Teed, and Big Mac Baker and presided over by a thin, scruffy minister of unknown origin or belief supplied by the funeral home, Grady's body was laid into the ground of the city cemetery in a remote, almost deserted corner reserved for paupers, foreigners, members of religions other than Protestant, stillborn children, and nameless drifters careless and thoughtless enough to die in the vicinity.

Elliott sent his parents home to Elysium with Leroy and drove the Ford into town, to Grady's room on the alley behind Lamar Printing & Office Supply. He collected the guitarcase of books and a few other relics, depositing the odds and ends of Grady's clothing and remnants of junk in a garbage can on the alley as he left.

He had planned it that way, not only in order to gather up Grady's belongings but so that he could go to the grave again, alone, on his way out of town.

The gravediggers hired by the funeral home had just finished filling the grave as he returned. They were leaving, two old men and a young one, shovels shouldered, trudging along the sandy lane that led to the backside of the cemetery. They waved to Elliott as he passed.

He stopped the car in the shade of a Chinese elm at
the edge of the older section of the cemetery and walked

down the lane to Grady's grave. It was bare except for a single spray of flowers that Elliott's mother had ordered and a small metal frame stuck in the ground at the head of the grave. It held the white paper marker, protected by a sheet of clear plastic, with the printed heading HERE LIES and a line beneath on which the name had been inked in. *Grady O. Haker July 6, 1908–Dec. 28, 1946.* Below, in flowery script, "Rest in Peace."

That won't do, Elliott thought. I'll have to see about a marble stone of some kind. With some sort of inscription he'd like. I wonder what that would be. With Grady, there's no telling. I'll look through his books, and maybe I'll find something.

He had expected it to be easy, coming by one last time, and it was. But as he stood there, longer than he had intended, he felt himself inexorably caught up by the emptiness and confusion and mystery of it all, and he looked to the sky, trying to calm himself and hold it down, as one swallows against nausea and fear. I never got to tell him, he thought. How would I have said it anyway. I didn't know. And I still don't. He looked down at the grave. What sense is there to it, Grady? Doesn't it have to make sense? If it doesn't, why are we trying so hard, when all it does is hurt? I'm tired of hurting, Grady. It wasn't even you he was after, he was trying to hit me. Maybe he should have.

Elliott gave over and began to sob helplessly, not out of sorrow or out of suffering even but only from the total and eternal immanence of his existence and all anguish, from its having been and forever being, and out of an old and dormant self-pity that he himself recognized and now indulged, head down, arms useless at his sides,

wracked with soundless grief *that it should have been oh*
me it should have been me he was after me I've got to
tell you oh god I'm sorry, you've got to know that
　　I know you're sorry, how's
　　　　　　the rest of your family
　　yes he'd say that wouldn't he
　　just like T. J. except
and god that I should have that now, stricken with that
　　　with him
　　it was me he was trying to get he'll
　　be okay, just shits a little close to the house that's all
oh grady
　　grady don't die no
　　no might as well, going to be sick anyway wearing
dead man's shoes don't pay to be gung-ho, break a man
trying going broke everthing that's any good breaks up
going broke having these
　　　broken dreams empty words i know still live
in my heart all alone i
　　didn't ever get to tell you you've got to know
　　　and that moonlit night by the
alamo　　and rose
my rose of san antone o mooninall your splendor
　　knows only my heart
　　knows only
　　that everthing changes and everthing is always the
same that all knowledge is uncertain and vain yet fain
would i yield me to my sorrows
　　no me grady　　why?
piss 'steada pass, working on a long pull and a dead
lift　　why? works at his case the jour printer gray head
and gaunt jaws shits too close to the house journeyman
284　　shit i

never would have made it anyway
why grady   why   tell me why

He went back to the car by a different route, ambling
through the tombstones, reading occasional inscriptions,
calculating life-spans of the deceased, absently holding
some vague notion that he might come upon the grave of
the man Grady had called Jedge. He did not know exactly why he would do that, except that he might discover the distance in space, and relationship in death, of
one man to another. But he did not encounter the grave,
nor did he look for it. Driving home, he pondered briefly
his experiences among graves, first Rich's in the midst of
the rigid white angles of Saint Jean-de-Fedhala, searching for his grandfather's in the churchyard at Elysium,
now Grady's and, in spirit at least, that of Matthew Arnold Piroute. He had the fleeting wish that they could
all be together side by side in the same place, yet in trying to discover why he should want such a thing, he
could find no reason, discover no connection between
them that would provide rational explanation for such an
impulse, and he laughed suddenly, almost losing control
of the rattling old Ford as it bounced down the road toward home.

From the time that he learned of Grady's death and its
aftermath, Elliott's father had been increasingly disturbed and outspoken over the way T. J. had, as he put
it, "got clean away without a scratch." " 'Course I wasn't
there," he said to Elliott, "but from the way it's told, that
old boy flat committed a murder. And got off scot free. If
I was a betting man, I'd bet there was some money
changed hands in that deal, wouldn't you?"

Elliott would not talk about it. He spent more and   285

more time in the cellar, occasionally taking food there and spending days and nights hunched over books in the hot light of the kerosene lamp, nibbling a cold biscuit, rarely sleeping, going outside only to relieve himself and draw fresh drinking water from the cistern. Out of their concern, his mother and father tried to keep the cellar door open, pleading his need for fresh air, but he fastened a piece of rope to the inside of the door and tied it down. Then they had to find excuses to come into the cellar. "Need a jar of them black-eye peas for dinner," his mother would call out, and he would take it up the stairs, loosen the rope slightly so that he could raise the door only enough to pass the jar out to her. Whenever his father managed to gain entrance on some pretext or another, he would say awkwardly, "Just want to see how you're doing." He no longer tried to enlist Elliott's help for work around the farm; it was clear to him that his son's behavior was somehow tied to Grady's death, and he tried to talk about it, in his invariably circuitous manner. "See where T. J. Teed's been down to Dallas to make a Victrola record," he would say. "Hear he might even be on the radio up at Lubbock, too." He waited for a reply that did not come. "Yessir, I guess he's really getting around these days. I don't understand it. Sure don't seem right." Still Elliott did not speak. "Sure looks to me like somebody could of done something," his father said.

"What?" Elliott said.

"Well, I don't know. But a good lawyer would, I reckon. We ought to have looked into that at the time, if we'd only known. Maybe it's not too late."

"What could a lawyer do?"

"I don't know. But he's got all them law books and rulings and stuff, he ought to be able to find something.

Heck, as many books as you read, I'd think you'd of come across it by now. I'll tell you this, if old Grady was alive, *he'd* know. Or know where to find out."

Elliott laughed bitterly. "Don't you see that if Grady was alive, there wouldn't be any need to know?" He looked away, across the flickering lamp. "I wonder if that's the way. How things change and still stay the same."

"Well, now you're talking beyond me," Mr. Randall said, getting up and leaving him staring into the white ball of light.

The next day Elliott drove to Lubbock, found the only bookstore that he knew to be in existence within four hundred miles, and bought every book on jurisprudence in stock—three, to be exact. In addition, he placed orders for a four-volume set of *Commentaries on the Laws of England* (he'd heard Grady talk of Blackstone, as if the name itself were the title of a book) and two dozen other legalistic titles selected at random from a list shown him by the flustered clerk. That done, he roamed through the modest stock of books on hand, pulling out volumes of all types, sizes, and subjects. The bill was over seven hundred dollars, which he paid in cash from the money he had been saving for his new car, and it took the clerk, with Elliott's assistance, almost half an hour to load all the books into the old Ford. Home again, he had them all down inside the cellar within ten minutes, pouring over the pages fiercely, ravenously, as a man makes love to a prostitute.

"THE UNREALIZED AMERICAN POTENTIAL," HE READS, "FOR CULTURAL RESYNTHESIS AND REVITALIZATION THROUGH ROLE ANALYSIS AND COMMITMENT PATTERNS." He blinks, pinches the bridge of his nose, reads on aloud, squinting, "In terms of societal self-direction along progressive lines, differential association suggests itself as a hypothetical variable. . . ."

He scans several pages, to a paragraph that begins —*Resignation as a central principle is manifest in psychosocial crises of all cultures and ages. It was Marcus Aurelius who admonished, "Say to your child as you kiss him in the morning, 'Perhaps tomorrow you will die.'" Neuroses, it is implied, are the price humanity pays for cultural development and*

On the back of an envelope he scribbles *Marcus Aurelius,* pushes the book into a pile beside the quilt box, reaches for another.

A March duststorm howls above him. Sand filters down from the ventilator shaft and from cracks in the door, 288 making little mounds on the cellar steps. He listens, watches the sand motes drift down, abruptly shifts his gaze into the hot white fiber filament of the lamp. It has become something of a habit, this staring into the ball of light. His eyes grow accustomed to it, and where once was only the painful blinding whiteness there now emerges substance, at first faint and rudimentary, vague outlines, figures, details. Through the tiny mesh of the domed filament, fired into brilliance by pressure in the belly of the lamp, he sees the piles of books, scattered and angular, mountains of lore, vast sagas, hieroglyphic oases, names, dates, facts, answers:

—*The highest recorded wind-speed is 231 m.p.h., recorded April 24, 1934, at Mt. Washington, New Hampshire. Wind-speeds as high as 680 m.p.h. have been calculated from tornado damage. The windiest place in the world is Commonwealth Bay, George V Coast, Antarctica, where gales reach 200 m.p.h.*

He finds nothing about sandstorms in West Texas. He seizes a book from another stack, reads

—*The theoretical knowledge of right and law in principle, as distinguished from positive laws and empirical cases, belongs to the pure science of right. The science of right thus designates the philosophical and systematic knowledge of*

A footnote at the bottom of the page catches his eye, and he copies it out on another scrap of paper. *LEX TALIONIS: the law of revenge and retribution.* The paper has been crumpled into a ball, and he has to spread it out and straighten the folds in order to make the notation. On the back he finds, in his own cramped, ugly script, *der ewigen Wiederkunft.* He cannot remember having written it, and he turns in frustration to another pile of books, fumbling through them in search of a vol-   289

ume which may solve the mystery. Moving the books, he
flips through them, fixes on random pages, circled words,
marginal notes, impenetrable lines

*—his order, it was here we formed the skirmish line and
here the Indians made their first charge*

*—as a ladder by which one surmounts the statements
themselves, then he sees the world rightly, said Wittgen-
stein. Whereof one cannot speak, thereof one must be silent*

*—for my knowledge of wayward, forward men and
women is that they lead wicked, miserable lives and die
wretched deaths. Their ways are hard, their days are som-
brous and sad; their nights starless and sleepless, their
hope for time and eternity has faded away*

At last he sights the book he has been seeking. *Langen-
scheidt's Deutsch-Englisches Wörterbuch.* The cover is
gone, and on the title page someone (Grady?) has scribbled in thick black pencil lines, *"Hier sitze ich und warte,
alte zerbrochene Tafeln um mich und auch neue halb
beschriebene Tafeln."* He thumbs through the book,
glancing down at the wrinkled piece of paper before him,
cannot find "ewigen." The nearest entry is *ewig* ADV. eternal, perpetual. He flips to the back of the book. *wieder*
ADV. again, once more . . . *~kunft* return. "The eternal
return again?" Something like that. Must be. The perpetual returning. He puzzles over the phrase, repeating
it again and again until the words are empty babble.

He opens another book and at the very beginning reads
*—The most fundamental of the group of ideas of which we
are to review the history appears first in Plato; and nearly
all that follows might therefore serve as an illustration of a
celebrated remark of Professor Whitehead's, that "the saf-
est general characterization of the European philosophical
tradition is that it consists in a series of footnotes to Plato"*

yeah I reckon so, but if that's right that's what's wrong with it old Grady always said it, just a big-time fascist

He reads —*But typically, there are two conflicting major strains in Plato and in the Platonic tradition*

sure, the grief of knowledge, son, and the swelling of ever mashed finger is

that evertime

you get one fact established you learn at one and the same time its opposite and not

only that but all the pieces of gray matter in between The reward of sin is death.

yeah but let me tell you about this old boy named Boethius, says that what he learned from philosophy is that to hate the wicked were against reason

There are more things in heaven and earth than philosophy. You said that, yourself.

yeah but then again there's something in this more than natural if only philosophy could find it out. He said that, too. Call me what instrument you will you can fret me but you can't play me

—*who was shot through the breast as the skirmish-line made its change of front; but now bullets were flying among the horses, several of which were hit, the command being surrounded by overwhelming numbers and still no support had come. His ammunition was running low, and already the reserve in the saddle bags and pockets had been drawn upon. A quick survey of the situation convinced Reno that he must get out, he must do so quickly or remain there forever. He gave the order to get to the horses*

Fall back, facing the enemy. Mount. Dismount. Mount.

but in the confusion many failed to hear or understand it. A little clearing of about ten acres had been found in the center of the timber which had evidently been the camping- 291 *ground of a Sioux medicine-man; it was, perhaps, the place where the tepees of Sitting Bull himself had stood. In this clearing Reno formed his troop, the men leading in their mounts and standing to horse*

—*he sat his charger, trying desperately to plan his next move*

gave the command "Mount." As he did so, a large party of Sioux broke through the timber and fired into the troops point-blank. At Reno's side fell the Rhee scout Bloody Knife, shot through the head, his brains splashing into Reno's face and splattering his uniform

struck between the eyes spattering blood and brains over face of

—*Logic,* he reads from another book—*at least as understood by the Academics, ultimately fails by virtue of the inherent requirement whereby every major premise demands a minor one, a phenomenon which inexorably begins to move The Idea away from its Essence, initiating an irreversible process resulting finally in destruction of The Idea*

He tosses the book aside in disgust, takes one from another pile, reads aloud

—Couldst thou make men to live eternally,
  Or, being dead, raise them to life again,
  Then this profession were to be esteem'd.
  Physic, farewell. —Where is Justinian?

                              [READS.]

  Si una eademque res legatur duobus, alter rem,
    alter valorem rei &c
  A pretty case of paltry legacies!

                              [READS.]

  Exhaereditare filium non potest pater nisis—
  Such is the subject of the Institute
  And universal body of the law.

When all is done, divinity is best;
Jerome's Bible, Faustus, view it well.

[READS.]

Stipendium peccati mors est. Ha! *Stipendium*
&c.

That's hard.

He laboriously deciphers the frustrating italics. —If the same thing bequeath to two people, one retains, the other a palisade made from stakes . . .? —Not able to disinherit a son the father except— *Stipendium* n. tax tribute, soldier's pay, military service, campaign; wages, reward. Peccati. *peccatum* n. mistake, fault, sin.—The . . . soldier's pay . . . no; wages . . . reward . . . the reward of sin is death.

He fumbles for something to mark the page, absently discovers in the rubbish on the table the pornographic cartoon he found in T. J.'s car. He sets it as a marker, against the spine, and closes the book.

The reward of sin is death.

—*That's what you get. I hate owning the danged things. If you play a guitar it's going to get out of tune. But then, if you don't, it'll still get out of tune anyway he said they's good uns and they's bad uns but they ain't many like you that got both and knows what to do with it, my old daddy see, said now just set yourself awhile in that there chair with the binder-twine bottom while I pick on this old box Grady-cum-lady I can hear him now*

I can hear him now. *Stipendium peccati mors est.* Revenge his foul and most unnatural murther

and so

out upon the plain of

cultural fault, for one sees

—*the reconciliation of the law with itself; by the annul-*   293 *ment of the crime, the law is restored and its authority is thereby actualized*

Melibeus answerde agayn, and seyde,

"I graunte wel that I have erred; but there as thou has toold me herebiforn that he nys nat to blame that chaungeth his conseillours in certein caas and for certeine juste causes, I am al redy to chaunge my conseillours right as thow wolt devyse. The proverbe seith that 'for to do synne is mannyssh, but certes for to persevere long in synne is werk of the devel.' "

longstanding as in the claim of the Prior and Convent of Durham Cathedral; in 1283 began the dispute over administration of the spiritualities of the diocese, a dispute which erupted again in 1672, 1890, and 1920. It was not, in fact, until 1939

He picks up a small gray volume with pages that are yellowed and flaking at the corners. The book is filled with words in strange archaic character.

— Ælfwine þā cwæð, hē on ellen spræc; nū mæg cunnian hwā cēne sȳ

nū mīn ealdor ligeð forhēawen æt hilde; mē is þæt hearma mæst; he wæs ægðer mīn mæg and mīn hlāford

Much of this has been translated in the margins, whether by Grady's hand or by someone else's he cannot decide. *Now that my lord lies dead, cut down in battle— to me that is most grievous. Now who is bold may prove it; I will make manifest my nobility to all.*

He sits back, gazing into the lamp. He fumbles for a pencil, finds one, its point worn blunt, uses Grady's maize knife to shape a new one, crudely. From some dark corner he extracts a Velvetone Linen-Finish Writing Tablet. Many pages at the front are covered with notations in

his feverish scrawl

4 Aug 1943 Letter from Mother today, says it is hot and dry at home. As I have no other letters to write, I will attempt to put down some of my thoughts in regard to the Army. We have been working very hard the past few weeks

one of my buddys named Leonard Richards of Chicago, Illin. and I got a three day pass and went up Pikes Peak over the weekend

regards to Camp Carson, it is a pretty rough place to be at, a guy in my Outfit says they explored all over the country to find the worst place and thats where they put the army camps. But you can see the mountains from here they sure are pretty and cool looking. According to rumor they are fixing to send us Overseas but I can't say where because its supposed to be a Military Secret

danger of accepting something as law just because somebody wrote it, as in "Longfellow once said xyz"

DO YOU KNOW YOU EXIST?

ABSOLUTE TRUTHS: ??

Rich says I'm the kind that reads jokes on restroom walls and watches the last runner in a race, whatever kind that is

23 August 1943 So Long to Camp Patrick Henry Va, we're off and running. Boy they sure do pack these Liberty ships, I was sick the first two days out but have got to where I can stand it now

Richs argument about a Prime-Mover—who created God? if he just always existed why couldn't everything else just always exist

5 or 6 January '44 Like they say in the south of france boy this is a bunch of happy horshit you all or maybe its in Southern Rodesia they say that, all I know is I am about fed up

295

this ungodly occupation and preoccupation with protecting our country God Bless America land that I love stand beside her and guide her, boy I sure used to like to hear Kate smith sing that song

12 Ap 1944. Its like high school when we all stood up and said I pledge allegiance to our flag and to the country for which it stands one nation indivisible and all that rot because it was just rot because not one guy there ever thought anything about it it was just something that we got out of classes for and most guys griped about it because why in hell did they have to stand up and put their hand on their shirt pocket and say a bunch of gibberish like fourth grade kids

there was lots of good for fourth grade kids then America america I remember that part about purple mountain majesties and from sea to shining sea America has all changed a lot or is it me thats changed

talk with Major: if man has right to think for himself, thus he has right not to think for himself. ??? Look up Daycart (sp?) (maybe D'cart)

He scans the pages hastily, alternately moved and embarrassed by the naïve intensity, his callow ineptitude, often simply puzzled by cryptic entries:

—*I have wondered at the low gray sky wondering if it is the same as twenty years ago*

—*MOST SECRET EQUALS BRITISH SECRET*

—*More evidence that man invents, shapes, alters to produce whatever god he needs and will go to any length to justify it*

Where is the evidence? he wonders. I wish I had written that down, too.

—"*How immaterial are all materials! What things real are*

there, but imponderable thoughts?" Melville, Moby Dick.
These lines are in the Major's handwriting, scribbled
along the edge of a page. He has never understood it (or
why the Major wrote it there), but now he rips a sheet of
blank paper from the back of the tablet, hurriedly copies
the words, reads them over again, gazes into the light,
puts the page aside, atop a jumble of other scraps, passes
on to more recent entries.

—*Plato was right, so was Locke, so was Kant, so is*
(the last name is undecipherable). —*The golden mountain does exist.*

—*I do not understand life or what it is about, and the
more I seem to learn (now reading Rousseau, Montesque,
pre-French Revolution) about great ideas, etc., the less I
understand and the more baffled I become. Life seems at
its best to be some sort of cruel joke without any purpose
or meaning*

"Gets worse instead of better," he mutters aloud. "Ye
gods: 'life or what it is about.'" With the pencil he
crosses out what he has just read, slashing repeatedly to
obliterate it entirely. Abruptly an association, an echo,
sounds in his head—Arnold? Croce? Emerson? Conrad?—
and he turns to a pile of books, thumbing through them
anxiously until he finds the marked passage.

—To seek for meaning in human experience is a major
function of every responsible intellect.

"Prince Teodor Józef Konrad Korzeniowski," he mutters vaguely, wearily, throwing the book into a corner.
He turns to the last entry in the tablet.

—*The world has a way of eluding me. I am Almost. Big
things in a small way, large waves on little ponds, a million near-misses, do only*

He reads no further. This, too, he strikes out, pressing the pencil so hard that it tears the paper. He pushes aside the tablet, topples a stack of books, one of which flips open before him, reversed, its pages fluttering on the spine. He turns it to him.

—Walt you contain enough, why don't you let it out then.

"Yes," he says. "Yes!" *It is time to explain myself—let us stand up.* Yes, but how? He copies the lines into the tablet, taking care to enclose them in quotation marks. *I am possess'd! Embody all presences outlaw'd or suffering.*

—*What is the sound of one hand clapping? We know the sound of a door opening. What is the sound of an open door?*

—*And yet,* he writes carefully —*the reward of sin is death.* He finds the book and opens it to the page marked by Tillie the Toiler's comic transgressions against body and soul, art and flesh. On the page he finds the phrase and copies it out. *Stipendium peccati mors est.* For to do sin is mannish, but to persevere long in sin is work of the devil. To do sin is mannish. Grady said that, even. Lots of guys need to have their wisdom teeth loosened up now and then

yeah but you wasn't listening I also said

just because sometimes there idn't anything else you can do I don't

      believe in hurting people I believe in love but
I don't all the time know what that means   even old Grady didn't know what it meant but there's times son when you've got to make a stand

      yes it is time for us to stand up   form a skirmish line   time for change   has changed books jet airplanes electricity plastic mouthwash civilization is the price humanity pays for neuroses

was a time when a man was a man bygod he didn't have to dillydally around worrying over things trying to figure it out reading a bunch of shit that don't make sense went out and horsewhipped the scoundrel that

or just plain strapped on his hogleg and called him out

sat his charger in the clearing   of these dirty ignorant bastards no respect for anything

good but a dollar just look at what they did to

Fluffy I don't care

if you believe it or not that's what happened   and they did it to you too so I guess you'd be talking out of the other side of your mouth but I never said anything different shit it was bound to happen sooner or later it just happened

sooner

but he did it can't you see that?   oh that dirty worthless bastard if anybody ever needed killing he does yeah the Old Jedge used to say it

reflected great credit upon our fair community because there is so damn many people that needs

still

at the bottom of you

community of feeling with these people der ewigen Wiederkunft a smug self-deceiving remark that force settles nothing That there should absolutely be nothing at all is utterly impossible in this retreat or "charge," as he termed it in his report to the bluffs boys shot through the head brains splashing into his face and spattering his uniform and disconcerted oh

he nys nat to blame that chaungeth his conseillours in   299

certein caas how would he understand that never read a
book in his life whereof one cannot speak and such is the
Institute and universal body of the law his study fits a
mercenary drudge who aims at nothing but external white
trash worthless of humanity

How do you figure it?

Look at Grady. All he knew. Played that old guitar, the
way you knew what it was, what it all said, you didn't
have to talk about it but

T. J. can do the same thing can't he
and Grady went right along, what's the difference? There's
a difference in there if I could just figure it out, had just
the faintest Idea away from its Essence of purple nipple-
tipped mountain majesties from sea to shining sea nights
starless and sleepless soldier with three stripes hope for
time and eternity well you can fret me but you can't play
me to seek for meaning thereof one must be silent

He has given up all effort to write it down in the tablet
and sits limply staring into the light. After a time he stops
the jumble in his head, echoes dying away, silence again
in the whiteness. He bends over the table again and
writes —*I can't shake it. The past is all there is.*

All I know is that I do not know what may be contained in the next second of time and point of space. The
past is all there is. A time when men knew. My leader lies
slain in battle and that to me is most grievous. It will not
be said of me that I sought my homeland while my lord
lies here, cut down in battle. They knew it then, call them
savages if you will, they knew there is within them a
force and strength that is its own answer, because it has
to be. Not because it is right, or final, but only because it
exists. Has always. Was. Is. The bold may prove it; I will
make manifest my nobility to all. He knew that he must

get out, and that is what he did, leading the charge. The sepulcher of the murderer is the assassin's sepulcher. Their ways are hard. Stipendium peccati mors est, that's hard. Lex talionis, that's hard.

But nobody ever told you it would be easy.

I am al redy to chaunge my conseillours right as thow wolt devyse. But which counselor? Ah, your ownself. That's hard, too, ain't it?

But easeful, Grady, easeful. I feel it. Easy but getting hard. Toiling. Tillie the Toiler. Fluffy. Ah yes. Fluffy easy. Toil. He laughs, and his open mouth settles into a grimace of throbbing blood, sweet flowing pain, ecstasy of her body, smooth muscle, soft dripping lips, brown nipple mounds belly hair cunt. Yes, Hard, getting hard. I feel it. What is the sound of one person making love? Everyone knows the sound of two people making love; what is the sound of one?

It roars in his head, rills his body, driving and pounding, until the light explodes and he lies back, panting, exhausted, released. It has come, he says, feeling the strength rising up from between the sockets of his hips where for so long there has been only an empty sodden ache. Time to stand up. I will make manifest my nobility to all. Stipendium peccati mors est.

He cleans himself. Other appetites return. He is ravenously hungry. He turns out the lamp and comes up from the cellar in the cool dusty moonlight. He urinates, discovering with surprise that the pleasure of release is an almost unbearable ecstasy, and he prolongs it. The house is dark and silent. He slips into the kitchen and takes food from the icebox and cabinets, bowls and cans and boxes, and carries it out to the cistern, where he draws up the oak bucket full of cold rainwater, with tiny slivers and 301 fuzz from the bucket and bits of tree root and scum churning as the bucket comes to the surface. He tips the bucket and drinks greedily, slopping water down his shirt. Then he eats, devouring the food swiftly yet consciously savoring the tastes, cold salmon and cornbread and black-eye peas and greasy bacon left from breakfast, hard biscuits and homemade jellies and sweet Bermuda onion and canned peaches and grapefruit juice and a slab of pound cake.

"Lex talionis," he says. "For these be the days of vengeance, that all things which are written may be fulfilled."

INTO THE CLEARING. He did not have to make a plan of any sort, but there was much preparation to be done, and he went about it slowly and carefully and deliberately in the days and weeks that followed. It was late spring and rain had not yet come; there was no separation of color across the flat plains. The sunlight filtered weakly through heavy hazes of suspended dust that blended sky and earth into a matte of ashen brown.

Bit by bit, piece by piece, he assembled his equipment: a pre-war NCO's campaign hat, a field pack complete with cartridge belt, canteen pouch, and bayonet scabbard purchased from an Army-Navy Store in Lamar, a pair of Willie Lusk's stovepipe cowboy boots that were made to order and cost him seventy-five dollars, frayed canvas gauntlets to which he affixed a fringe of leather. He worked a week with a fencing crew over in the Double U Ranch and instead of cash wages he argued the foreman out of a pair of spurs and an old worn saddle

303

that had not been used in many years. He spent much time repairing the saddle, patching the tattered pommel, adding a new surcingle and thongs and straps and softening it all with repeated applications of saddle soap. Rolled up in the saddlebags he found an equally ancient pair of stiff, curled chaps, which he also cleaned and repaired. He took his expensively tailored gabardine dress blouse from the old trunk in the cellar, pressed it with flatirons, carefully reaffixed to it all his ribbons and decorations, and sewed on new sergeant's chevrons. He shined his brass insignia and scrubbed down the field pack, handling it all, the flaps and buckles and webbing with old familiarity, finding a strange inexplicable delight in performing what had once been nothing more than a dull and meaningless routine. To the boots he applied neatsfoot oil; they were made for work rather than show yet infinitely splendid in the utility of their narrowed toes and cattleman's high slanting heels and sixteen-inch tops that reached to the knee. When all this was done, he turned to the weapons, which he had saved for last.

Grady's old Army Colt was rusted and stiff, and after a couple of snaps, the cylinder locked. He discovered broken bullets wedged in two of the chambers. The ejector rod was stuck with rust but he managed to clear the damaged cartridges with a small stick. Then he broke the weapon down to parts and frame and carefully cleaned and oiled it. When it was reassembled, he fired six rounds, slowly, in order to feel its balance and recoil. When that was done, he knew the weapon as well as he ever would, and he knew that it would function for him. He made a holster for it from scraps of leather left from the piece he had bought to mend the saddle.

There was not much to be done to his grandfather's old

12-gauge Winchester Model 21. He sawed off the barrels a few inches above the forestock and then cleaned it carefully. He did not need to fire it.

He longed momentarily for an M-1 Garand. It would be heavy and difficult to handle, but he knew the weapon better than any other and had always promised himself that although he had no use for guns, he would buy an M-1 if any were ever sold as surplus after the war. What the hell for? Rich had said. It's lousy for shooting anything except people. It's probably the best combat weapon ever made, but almost any other rifle you can name is better for targets or game. Still, he wanted one. He knew some guys who, although they agreed with Rich, managed to get hold of an extra Garand and break it down and smuggle it home. He had not done that. He wished that he had. But he could manage with what he had.

By Friday of the last week in April everything was ready.

The sand blew the next day. It began at sunup with a clear wind pulling at the ground in ragged gusts, and by mid-morning the sky was filled with yellow-brown dust that shut out the sun and held the prairie suspended in a cavern of howling grit. He heard the wind rising and pounding, and, hating the sound, he huddled in bed in half sleep until almost noon.

He dressed quickly: the freshly pressed gabardine blouse with its rows of multi-colored ribbons, a pair of faded Levi's (he had debated about the pants, had finally simply eliminated everything else and settled for that which was most accessible, comfortable and functional), the boots, which he pulled on slowly and proudly, stomping down into the heels and standing to admire the burnished high tops, then covering them with the legs of the Levi's, which were so long that they broke across the instep and he had to shove them back up to buckle on the spurs.

Around his neck he tied a flowing black silk scarf, added at the last moment only because he had discovered it accidentally in one of the boxes in the cellar. Then the hat, tilted down across his brow and the brim arched up ever so slightly fore and aft, secured by the leather strap at the back of his head.

In the howling wind, he carried the saddle up out of the cellar and left it astride the tongue of the stock trailer on his way to the lot where he had penned Old Phoeb the night before. He led the horse out, let her stand at ground hitch while he hooked the trailer to the Ford, then coaxed her up into the trailer and closed the rear gate. He put the saddle and halter in the back seat of the car and went back to the cellar to wait.

A few minutes before three o'clock, he turned on the radio so that the tubes and circuits could warm up. The radio came to life just as the theme was getting underway

gather round listen in for here we are once again
we come to you
without a care

and he waited until he heard —Howdy frins and neighbors this is your ole buddy T. J. Teed a-pickin and strummin and hummin and singin, along with all the West Texas Rambling

He turned off the radio, put on the fringed gloves, and picked up the cartridge belt, fastening it across his chest like a bandolier. In two of the clip pockets he had distributed, loose, a box of .41-caliber centerfire cartridges; the rest of the pockets were stuffed with shotgun shells.

To the gunbelt were attached the canteen, freshly filled, the empty bayonet scabbard, and the holstered pistol. He strapped it on and adjusted the holster on his hip so that, with his arm resting at his side, the butt of the pistol rode approximately midway between his elbow and wrist. Then he tied down the holster with a leather thong around his leg. Taking the pistol out with his right hand, he held it loosely by the handle and flicked open the cylinder gate. He chambered five bullets, closed the gate and checked the cylinder to see that the hammer, at safety-cock, would rest on the empty chamber. He did not load the shotgun but simply took it by the barrels and carried it along to the car at what would have been "trail-arms" if the weapon had been long enough to be, properly speaking, trailed.

He had wanted to ride the horse all the way but he knew that she could not make the trip in time, if at all. So he drove to the outskirts of Lamar and parked in the graveled drive of what had once been a filling station, its former function marked by little more than the gutted and rusty remains of two old handpumps still standing in the drive. The roof of the attendant's shack had rotted away, all its windows were gone, and spiny mounds of rustling thistles were building against the western wall, piled there by the biting, sand-filled wind.

Elliott backed Old Phoebe Lou out of the trailer and saddled her. He had planned merely to drape the chaps across the pommel instead of wearing them. But he recalled how the old horse had been spooked and lamed as a colt by the cotton sack hung from the saddle horn, and that gave him proper excuse to don the chaps. He struggled into the field pack, which he had filled according to training with clean socks and canned rations and 307 (to square up the pack and hold its shape) Grady's bulky old copy of *Paradise Lost*. It disturbed him that the saddle was too small for Old Phoeb's back, but its tree and seat were flexible enough to flatten and spread, and the sorrel did not seem to mind, although it made the stirrups too short even at their fullest extension and he had to mount with his knees bent forward at an uncomfortable angle. In the saddle he paused only to load the shotgun and hang it on the saddle horn with a leather thong tied to the weapon's stock just behind the triggers. Then he pulled Old Phoeb's head toward town and prodded her into motion, taking care not to rake her with the spurs.

He had not counted on the buffeting of wind and sand, which at times seemed almost to stop the old horse in her tracks. He worried that he might be too late, but as they plodded on across town the horse seemed to sense his urgency, became somehow aware of her own role, and strode to meet it. Because of the sand there were few people on the streets, and those who were paid little attention to the strange procession. A man grinned and waved, and he returned the wave. Some small boys shouted to him, but he could not understand them because of the wind.

By the time they crossed through town and were well on their way to the radio station, he had had to make certain adjustments. He reversed the headstrap on the campaign hat and buckled it under his chin to keep the hat from blowing away, and he took his feet out of the stirrups and let them dangle to ease the cramps in his legs. The straps of the field pack cut into his shoulders. He wiggled out of it and held it in his lap, against the pommel. He drew up the neckerchief around his mouth and nose in a vain effort to breath easier in the gusting, blinding sand. The horse nickered and snorted, and he leaned forward to rub her face and ruffle her mane.

Despite it all they reached their destination on time, perhaps even five or ten minutes early, according to his watch. The brightly painted Packard hearse was parked alongside several other vehicles in the crude dirt parking lot roughed out beside the station building.

He dismounted at the head of the lane that dipped away from the highway out to the station, then led the horse to the place where the lane widened into the parking area. There he stopped, some thirty feet from the cars. He took off his gloves, loosened the saddle cinch, and walked around the horse, patting her flanks and withers, moving up to rub her face and muzzle. He waited.

A loudspeaker hung over the entrance to the station, and had he been closer, he could have heard what was being broadcast. Some of it drifted to him now and then through the shifting and whirling of the wind, the almost unidentifiable strains of "Near You," a fiddling hillbilly breakdown, Leroy singing one of his favorite Ernest Tubb songs

on my way to Italy
from the gulf of Mexico   riding on a tanker
feeling mighty low
my good gal's behind me, no loving for so long
I'm going back to Texas
for that's where I belong

then the theme, largely drowned out by the wind. But he needed only a few notes to recognize it. "Yes, Phoebe Lou," he said to the horse and stepped away from her, cradling the shotgun across his forearm.

Then they were coming out of the entrance, fighting the door in the wind, clutching instrument cases, strug-   309 gling against each other for position. He heard T. J. behind, driving them, shouting above the wind. "Load 'em up!" T. J. yelled. "Let's go, let's go."

They had not seen him. He did not move, except to release the safety on the shotgun. "Teed!" he called out, into the wind. Then they looked across at him. They went on, scrambling around the back of the hearse, trying to get the instruments loaded, holding on to their big floppy Western hats, but they looked at him quizzically and he could hear them muttering about him. One of them called out something, but he could not understand it, and he paid no attention.

The wind dropped momentarily. "TEED!" he yelled again, and although Leroy was there, too, they all seemed to sense that he was addressing T. J., who now stood apart from them, still in the door of the radio station.

"Goddam, boys," T. J. said. "Would you look at that now. Here comes Red Ryder. Hey, Red Ryder, where's Little Beaver?"

"Step out, Teed, and defend yourself," he said.

"What?"

"I said, I'm calling you out. Get your gun, or just move out into the open. Either way, you're a dead man."

T. J. laughed nervously. "You're crazy," he said. "Hey, boys, just listen to that crazy birdbrain. What kind of game you playing anyway, Birdbrain?" The men around the hearse laughed.

He raised the shotgun and fired both barrels into the wall behind them. For a moment they stood frozen with surprise, then scattered for cover, cursing and yelling.

T. J. ducked behind a nearby car and crouched at the hood. "What the shit you want, Randall?" he said. "You're gonna get somebody hurt with that scattergun."

310

He put the shotgun down on the ground. "I want you," he said. "And I don't intend to use any scattergun. Arm yourself and come out."

"Hell, man, take it easy," T. J. said. "Cool off now. What's got you so riled up anyway?"

He drew the pistol, released the hammer on the empty chamber, then cocked it again on a live cartridge and fired past T. J.'s head.

"Goddammit," T. J. screamed. "I'm unarmed, can't you see that. You wouldn't shoot somebody in cold blood would you." T. J. went on talking, wildly, and at the same time edged along the car toward the hearse. Then he darted out to the door opposite the driver's side, leaned in across the seat, and reached under it fumbling and came up with his gun. He raised his head quickly and glanced through the windshield at Elliott, who had not moved. T. J. ducked, then popped up again with his weapon raised to fire.

Elliott aimed at arm's length and shot into the windshield. T. J. howled and flopped over the seat into the rear compartment. With the windshield shattered, it was impossible for Elliott to know whether he had hit his mark. He cocked the pistol again and eased around toward the back of the hearse.

"Come out," he called. There was no answer, then suddenly a rapid succession of shots from inside opened holes in the rear door and went spinning off wildly. Elliott advanced. "Come out, Teed," he said again.

T. J.'s face, cut from the shattered glass of the windshield, appeared murkily in the back window. "Goddammit, I'm out of shells," he yelled. "Give a man a chance."

"You're a dead man," Elliott said.

"Hey, boys, come help me," T. J. screamed. "Call the

law. This bastard's out of his mind. You got to help me stop him or he'll kill me." But no one moved. Elliott reached out and opened the rear door of the hearse. T. J., who had turned to look through the front windows in search of possible aid or escape, wheeled and fired wild. He stared at Elliott, eyes wide, breathing hard. Elliott raised the pistol and shot him. T. J. pitched backward into the jumble of instrument cases, and when he had stopped quivering, Elliott reached in and grasped one of his ankles and dragged him out on the ground. He shot him once more, in the chest, holstered the pistol, then stepped back and kicked him in the face.

He walked back to where he had left the shotgun, listening to the wind and the clink of his spurs. It was only then that he saw the horse. She had been struck in the neck by a stray bullet, and she lay now on her side, pawing the air and trying to lift her head, blood spilling down her poll and chest.

He took off the saddle and rope halter, patting her head and easing it to the ground. "Yes," he said. "I know. This, too. Now."

He stood up and chambered another cartridge. "You wouldn't want me to be cheated, would you?" The old horse whinnied and lay still. "I didn't think you would," he said. "Tom Mix always had to do it this way, didn't he?" He stepped back and shot her.

He opened the cylinder gate and ejected the five spent shells, then reloaded, filling all six chambers this time. He broke open the breach of the shotgun and reloaded it. The wind raged and tore at him, and above it he heard the faraway wail of a siren. He took a deep breath and straightened his hat and started off down the lane to
312   meet it.